The Unexpected Son

Also by Shobhan Bantwal

THE SARI SHOP WIDOW

THE FORBIDDEN DAUGHTER

THE DOWRY BRIDE

Published by Kensington Publishing Corp.

The Unexpected Son

SHOBHAN BANTWAL

KENSINGTON BOOKS
www.kensingtonbooks.com

KENSINGTON BOOKS are published by

Kensington Publishing Corp.
119 West 40th Street
New York, NY 10018

All Kensington titles, imprints, and distributed lines are available at special quantity discounts for bulk purchases for sales promotion, premiums, fund-raising, educational, or institutional use.

Special book excerpts or customized printings can also be created to fit specific needs. For details, write or phone the office of the Kensington Special Sales Manager: Kensington Publishing Corp., 119 West 40th Street, New York, NY 10018. Attn. Special Sales Department. Phone: 1-800-221-2647.

Kensington and the K logo Reg. U.S. Pat. & TM Off.

ISBN-13: 978-0-7582-3203-8
ISBN-10: 0-7582-3203-9

First Kensington Trade Paperback Printing: August 2010
10 9 8 7 6 5 4 3 2 1

Printed in the United States of America

Acknowledgments

As always, I offer my initial prayer of thanks to Lord Ganesh, the remover of obstacles.

My heartfelt appreciation goes to my warm and supportive editor, Audrey LaFehr, who has placed her faith in me again and again. Special thanks to Martin Biro and Maureen Cuddy, consummate professionals who make my writing career a pleasure.

The friendly and dedicated editorial, production, public relations, and marketing folks at Kensington Publishing richly deserve my gratitude and praise for a job well done. I look forward to working with you on my future projects.

To my agents, Stephanie Lehmann and Elaine Koster, I thank you for your invaluable help and guidance at every step. I would not be here without you.

I am greatly indebted to four talented doctors, Shilpa Hattangadi, Anil Kagal, Ajit Divgi, and C. J. Lyons, for patiently answering my medical questions. Any inaccuracies and/or mistakes that may appear in this book are entirely due to my own lack of understanding and not these very committed and helpful medical professionals.

The Writers' Exchange at Barnes & Noble in Princeton, New Jersey, and the Writers' Group at the Plainsboro Public Library deserve my thanks for their insightful comments and suggestions. I offer a grateful hug to my many other friends, who are my cheerleading group.

And last but not least, to my super-supportive family, especially my husband, Prakash: I am deeply grateful to have you in my life and for putting up with my idiosyncrasies—and for loving me in spite of them.

Prologue

There was something odd about it, despite its plain and inconsequential appearance. Vinita gazed at the mystery envelope for a long moment, weighed it in the palm of her hand. Her instincts were prickling. It went beyond mere feminine intuition.

She didn't receive any letters from her family in India anymore. Cheap long-distance telephone rates and e-mail had put an end to that somewhat antiquated form of communication.

The smudged postal seal on the envelope read *Mumbai*—one of India's largest and most populous cities—a place Vinita was very familiar with. The envelope had that typical "India" look—multiple postage stamps in various colors and sizes; thin brown paper; and the sealing flap placed over the vertical edge, unlike the American-style horizontal edge. But it didn't look like the occasional wedding invitation or the quarterly statements from the bank where she and her husband maintained a small account in rupees.

There was no return address, but it was sent to her attention—neatly hand printed. She slit it open with her finger and eased out the contents—a single sheet of white, ruled paper. Her hands shook a little. She wasn't sure if it was anticipation or anxiety. Or both.

The message was brief—a few lines penned in blue ink. She scanned it quickly, trying to ignore the tingle crawling up her spine like the cautious progress of a venomous spider. The subject matter was bizarre. The writer's name was missing. The trembling in her hands edged up a notch.

Only minutes ago, it had looked like any ordinary Saturday morning—a day to recoup after five hectic days of poring over spreadsheets, memos, and databases till her eyeballs ached and her back turned stiff as cardboard.

This morning, lying in bed, through drowsy eyes she'd watched the first shimmering rays of sunlight poke their fingers through the window blinds. The sound of the wind whistling through the pale green spring foliage was a sign of a brisk but sunny April day.

May, her favorite month, was right around the corner. The dogwoods and azaleas in the neighborhood, weighed down by fat, succulent buds, attested to that. Spring was always such a buoyant season, so full of promise. It had brought a contented smile to her lips.

Reminding herself that it was time to emerge from the warm cocoon of the down comforter, she'd sat up in bed, stretched like a slothful kitten, and leaned back against the headboard. She'd managed to grab more than two extra hours of sleep. Her reward for waking early on weekdays.

Her husband was on a business trip to Detroit, and wasn't due to return until the following week, so she had the weekend to herself. She'd planned to indulge herself by brewing a cup of scalding *masala chai*—strong tea delicately laced with her own blend of five spices—instead of the usual coffee-on-the-run she drank on weekdays at the office. Then she was going to eat lunch at the taco place and do some shopping at the mall.

Working late the previous evening had prevented her from looking at the mail right away. Exhausted, she'd tossed the stack of correspondence on the nightstand, eaten a quick meal of leftovers, and gone straight to bed.

Now, as she sat on the bed in her aqua print pajamas and checked the mail before getting dressed, she wondered if the weekend of self-indulgence she'd been looking forward to was already beginning to wilt and curl at the edges. The tacos and the shopping spree no longer appealed.

Who could have sent her the odd message? An old friend? An acquaintance? She blew her disheveled bangs out of her eyes to read it again, more carefully this time. Perhaps there were clues she had missed the first time.

> My dear Mrs. Patil,
> I am writing to tell you about your son. He is suffering from myeloid leukemia. Many years ago, I made a promise that I would never reveal anything about him, but this is a serious matter. A bone marrow transplant is his last hope. My conscience will not allow me to let a young man die without having a chance to try every possible treatment.
> Your brother may be able to give you all the details.
> I leave the matter in your hands.
> Best Regards & Blessings,
> A well-wisher

Setting the letter aside for a moment, Vinita rose from the bed. The cool air in the room seeped right through the soft flannel of her pajamas, giving her goose bumps. Her bare toes curled the moment they touched the cold wood floor. Shivering, she padded over to the window and threw open the blinds. Crossing her arms, she tucked her freezing hands under her armpits.

The daffodils growing in the front yard were a blaze of heartwarming yellow. The blue and white hyacinths provided a lovely contrast to them. Her bulb plantings from last fall had been worth the effort.

Her neighbor, Doris, was pushing a wheelbarrow filled with seedlings from the garage to the area beneath her bow window. Vinita couldn't help smiling at the sight of her neighbor's industrious little body hobbling as fast as it could to keep up with her agile mind. At seventy-two, Doris was a bundle of energy, despite her arthritis. She put women half her age to shame. Her neat clusters of flowers and rows of lush vegetables were a delight.

Looking on the sun-drenched landscape and Doris's short, gray curls lifting in the chilly wind as she parked her wheelbarrow and pulled on her gardening gloves, Vinita stood in silent contemplation.

Who was this nameless letter writer? And why had he or she chosen to remain anonymous? Something about the message was disturbing.

How could someone spring something like this on a total stranger? Whose son were they talking about, anyway? Was it possible the letter was mailed to her erroneously? But what if it wasn't a mistake and she was indeed the intended recipient?

Was this someone's idea of a sick joke? But then, why would they spend over forty rupees to mail something all the way to the U.S. as a mere prank? Everything about the letter spelled serious intent. This was no hoax. And yet it made no sense.

The author appeared to be educated. The writing was clear and precise. And the old-fashioned salutation and blessings at the end meant the person was older than Vinita. The writer couldn't be a practical joker.

Of course this was a gaffe, she reflected. It had to be. She had no son. Her only child was Arya—her bright and impetuous twenty-three-year-old daughter.

Turning away from the window, Vinita picked up the perplexing letter once again and tapped it against her palm. Should she trash it and let it go? Or perhaps she should wait until her husband returned home and discuss it with him?

On second thought, that would be a terrible idea. She couldn't afford to bring up anything that even remotely involved her past. Not now. Not ever.

Maybe she could talk it over with Arya? Bad idea again. Her daughter would be the last person to understand any of this, especially Vinita's past.

The past! Something dark and vague flickered in her brain. Could it be . . . ? *Don't let your imagination run away from you,* she reprimanded herself. And waited for her heartbeat to settle into its natural rhythm.

Whom could she turn to for help in solving this puzzle? She

began pacing the length of the room, hugging herself to stave off the mild shivers racing up and down her body. But it helped very little.

This was ridiculous. Ordinarily she wasn't an excitable sort. But here she was, turning into a nervous puddle over a simple letter.

She pulled her husband's plaid robe from where it hung over the bedpost and slipped into it. It smelled like him—soap and his brand of deodorant—the comforting scent she loved and breathed in each day. She could have used a calming hug from him right about now, feel his hand smooth her hair.

Twenty-five years of marriage and she still missed him dreadfully when he was away from home. Had he remembered to take his blood pressure medication? Had he remembered to pack enough underwear to last him the entire trip?

Pulling the robe tighter around herself, she stopped and read the letter a third time. It did mention her older brother, Vishal—her only sibling. And that was another mystery. How and why did the writer assume her brother knew anything? Besides, the letter was mailed from Mumbai, while Vishal lived in Palgaum, a town in southwestern India, where she and Vishal were born and raised.

Was it possible her brother knew something about this? Maybe he could shed some light on the mysterious message and its equally enigmatic writer, the well-wisher.

She glanced at the bedside clock. It would be early evening in Palgaum. Picking up the phone, she took a couple of deep breaths and dialed her brother's number.

Two sharp rings and he answered, sounding pleasantly surprised to hear her voice. "Vini! How come you're calling on a Saturday?" She usually called on weeknights because weekends were too unpredictable, packed with social commitments and household chores.

"Because what I have to say couldn't wait," she replied, sounding curt even to her own ears.

"Is something wrong?" he asked, wariness making his voice sound like a low rumble.

"I don't know yet."

As he started to respond, Vinita cut him off. "I just got this really strange letter from someone in India."

"What letter?"

"It mentions something about a son . . . my son—"

"What?"

"—and that he has leukemia . . ." She trailed off. She didn't know how to explain it all. The whole thing sounded preposterous.

There was a long silence before her brother spoke again.

"Good God!" Vishal's voice was a stunned whisper.

Part 1

Chapter 1

Palgaum, India—1976

The applause lasted a few seconds before fading. For Vinita it was an evening to remember. She'd rehearsed for this one occasion, the grand annual college gala, for many long weeks. And all that preparation had been worth it, if only to hear the pleasant sound of hundreds of hands clapping in unison.

She took her final bow before the appreciative audience with humble grace, her hands joined in a *namaskar*. Remain humble when accepting praise, was what her *nritya guru*, her dance teacher, emphasized to his students. To be able to dance skillfully was a gift, a privilege. It was not to be used for satisfying one's ego. Humility. Always.

The instant the heavy, faded curtains closed on the stage, she exhaled a quick, hard breath. Then she ran backstage, her *ghoongroo*, the traditional dancing bells tied around her ankles, making a racket. She waded through the folks standing in the wings, waiting for their cue calls. She heard the emcee's voice on the microphone, announcing the next item on the program.

While she made a beeline for the women's dressing room— her long braid, intertwined with jasmine strings, swinging like a pendulum—she realized she was wheezing audibly. It was a demanding routine she'd just completed.

Sweat ran down her face and arms. Voices swirled around her, spoken in whispers so as not to reach the microphones on stage. Now that the much-awaited yet much-dreaded performance was over, everything that had happened became a blur—the blinding footlights; the quick surge of anxiety as the curtains parted and the hush settled over the sea of faces in the audience; the melody of the South Indian dance music; and minutes later, the final, frantic rhythm of her recital's finale synchronizing with the crescendo of the instruments.

It was all so familiar, the galloping heartbeat and the urge to take cover and run. And yet every presentation was a fresh new experience to be savored—if it was executed perfectly, that is. And today it was.

The evening's program was packed, with a lineup of music, skits, dances, stand-up comedy, and even a juggling act. She was glad her recital was placed toward the beginning, so she didn't have to pace in the wings, cracking her knuckles, waiting her turn.

"Very nice, Miss Shelke," someone murmured as she brushed past them.

"Good performance, Vinita," said another.

"Thanks," she panted absently, not bothering to look at their faces. Instead she kept striding toward the dressing room. She had to get out of her elaborate costume and join her friends in the makeshift open-air theater to catch the rest of the evening's entertainment.

The dressing room was blissfully quiet. There was only one other girl, getting ready for her performance in a play. They smiled at each other.

"How did your dance go?" the girl asked. She was carefully gathering up the pleats on her sari.

"Very well, thanks," said Vinita, and proceeded toward the bathroom. "It's a huge audience—bigger than last year. Good luck with your play."

At the sink, Vinita scrubbed and rinsed off the greasy makeup. The cold water felt marvelous against her heated skin.

She dried her face and studied her image in the mirror. Her performance was a success. The audience's reaction had assured her of that. The young, noisy crowd of students at Shivraj College wasn't shy about booing and heckling a less-than-acceptable performer. They'd sat in silence while she'd gone through the intricate footwork and facial expressions of a *varnam*—a complex, classical Bharat Natyam dance composition that told a story of love and longing. In the end had come the gratifying ovation.

She emerged from the bathroom to find the other occupant of the dressing room gone. Ridding herself of the elaborate rhinestone jewelry and form-fitting silk costume traditional to the dance form, she changed into a cinnamon-colored *salwar-kameez* outfit: knee-length tunic worn over drawstring pants and topped with a long piece of gauzy fabric called the *chunni*.

Then she unfastened the ankle bells. In a couple of minutes she had her hair neatened and a touch of face powder dabbed on.

Haphazardly she stuffed her things into her shoulder bag and thrust her feet into sandals. She didn't want to miss any part of the evening's excitement. This was the entertainment highlight of the year for both students and faculty.

Rushing out the door onto the cool, dimly lit porch that wrapped around the ancient, ivy-covered stone building, she bumped into something hard. Or someone.

"Ouch!" Her breath caught in her throat. Her bag slid off her shoulder and fell to the floor. The bells inside tinkled.

She stumbled backward. Whoever he was, he looked tall and threateningly large in the shadows cast by the sturdy stone columns. And he was strong. Her elbow was smarting from the collision.

"Miss Shelke!" exclaimed a very deep voice.

She remained silent, still reeling from the jolt. Fear made her throat go dry. She was all alone in the dark with a stranger.

But he knew her name?

"I'm sorry," he said, sounding genuinely contrite. He shifted and emerged from the shadows into the pool of dull yellow light cast by the single overhead fixture surrounded by fluttering moths.

She recognized him at once. Somesh Kori. All six feet of muscle and testosterone combined with a face that was chilling in its somberness. Despite the face, Somesh was the heartthrob of Shivraj College. A playboy. And captain of the cricket team.

"Th-that's okay," she managed to stutter after drawing a quick breath. It was a relief to discover he wasn't a robber or rapist on the prowl. "I was in a rush. I wasn't paying attention."

"But I wasn't rushing. I should have been more careful," he apologized, bending down to retrieve her bag. He handed it to her. "Did I hurt you or something?"

"Uh-uh." Her pulse was still unnaturally high.

He glanced at the bag. "Nothing breakable in it, I hope?"

"No . . . just my dance costume."

"And the delightful bells," he added, as she took the bag.

She could think of nothing to say when his fingers brushed hers, making her tremble. *Delightful bells?* Was that supposed to be a compliment, or was he mocking her? She'd seen and heard him ridicule plenty of girls.

Then he smiled at her, the slightly lopsided motion that tickled the ovaries of even the most resolute old maids on campus. He supposedly smiled very rarely, and that usually happened when his team won a match. But the smile sure did wonders for his intimidating countenance.

"Your dance was excellent, Miss Shelke," he said, his eyes raking her in one slow, easy pass. "You have such grace and precision."

She bit on her lower lip and tried to ignore the warmth rushing to her face. Any fool could see he was used to handing out flattery. "Thank you . . . Mr. Kori."

"Call me Som. All my friends call me that. It's pronounced Sohm."

She knew how his name was pronounced. "But we're not friends." He stood so close she got a whiff of his aftershave combined with cigarette smoke. With that came the forbidding thought that standing alone in the shadows with a man of his reputation was hazardous. Adjusting the bag on her shoulder, she started to move away.

"That could be remedied," he suggested, seemingly oblivious

to her fear. He fell in step with her as she hastened around the bend and toward the front of the building, where the audience was seated.

She heard raucous laughter coming from the crowd. The humorous skit that followed her recital was obviously quite entertaining. It was a comforting sound; it assured her she wasn't alone with this man.

"I'm not interested in sports, Mr. Kori," she said, putting as much starch into her voice as she could. But she wasn't very good at doing the snobbish bit.

Besides, all his friends were rich—boys with cars of their own, and girls who got chauffeured around. They wore clothes bought in big city shops, unlike her and her middle-class friends, who wore simple cotton outfits made by the local tailors. Kori and his pals went for coffee at the upscale Bombay Café, while Vinita and her friends kept to the more affordable college canteen.

"Why should that matter?" he reasoned. "I have some friends who know nothing about sports, and we're still good friends."

She looked up at him from her five-foot-two height. Despite her high heels, his face seemed far above hers. The smile was long gone, but the sparkle in his brown eyes resembled the semiprecious stone known as *rajvarki*—goldstone. He was making her uncomfortable with his steady golden gaze. "Good-bye, Mr. Kori. I have to go now."

"Som," he insisted. "Mind if I call you Vinita?"

"Okay . . . no . . . yes." She clutched at her bag to keep her hands from shaking. "You know what I mean."

He chuckled. "I know what you mean."

The sneering giant could actually chuckle? This time he *was* laughing at her. She was an idiot to get so rattled because the most popular boy on campus was asking to be her friend.

That was the puzzling part. He wanted to be her *friend*.

They had almost reached the giant *shamiana*—canopy. The light was brighter here, even though they stood on the outside. She could clearly see the clean, smart fit of his clothes, his angu-

lar face with its barely concealed expression of amused cynicism. There was strength in the jaw and the curve of his nose.
God knows those long arms and legs were capable of perform-
ing magic on the cricket *maidaan*—field.

She didn't want to be seen walking and conversing with him.
Tongues would start to wag. Definitely not good for her reputa-
tion. The girls he got mixed up with were referred to as *STs*—
Som's trollops. She didn't want to be one of *those*.

Nerves tingling, Vinita craned her neck to locate her friends
amidst the crowd of spectators. She spotted them. They had
saved her a seat, bless them. Thankfully none of them had noticed her with Kori.

The fact that he was making her hands tremble wasn't a good
thing. *You're not the type to turn into a gelatinous glob of female at the sight of a man,* she told herself. "I have to go," she
repeated.

"You really have to?" He tilted his head to one side, looking
genuinely disappointed.

She gave an emphatic nod.

"I guess I'll have to let you go, then. But it was nice talking to
you," he said with a reluctant wave, and took off.

With a perplexed frown she watched him saunter away with
the effortless grace some athletes seemed to be blessed with. She
observed him pull a cigarette and a lighter out of his pocket.
With hands cupped around his mouth to protect the flame, he lit
the cigarette and took a long drag on it. Seconds later, a plume
of smoke emerged from his mouth. Then he disappeared into
the shadows as abruptly as he'd appeared minutes earlier.

She stood on the spot for a while, puzzling over what had just
occurred. It wasn't a mirage. And yet it was all very strange.
Why was a popular playboy befriending her? Why was he lurking around the dark porch behind the building in the first place?
Where were his ever-present friends? They always moved in a
herd.

Giving her heartbeat a moment to settle, she turned around
to find her way toward her friends amidst the swarm of stu-

dents. When she plopped into the chair reserved for her, she was still wheezing. Sweat had gathered under her arms once again.

Prema Swami, her closest friend, turned to her with a frown. "Are you okay?"

"Sure. Why?"

"You look flushed . . . agitated." Prema's frown turned to narrow-eyed speculation.

"Of course I'm flushed," Vinita retorted. "I just finished a dance recital."

But Prema was right. Vinita was behaving oddly. Was she reacting to Kori like those other girls did? Som's trollops? In the next instant she dismissed it as the most ridiculous notion.

She settled back in her seat to enjoy the rest of the evening. But she couldn't help looking back once or twice, her eyes searching for a wisp of smoke somewhere beyond the canopy.

Chapter 2

V inita closed her textbook and tossed it aside to gaze outside her window. It was a typical winter morning in Palgaum—foggy, nippy, and disinclined to welcome the sun. Warmth rarely arrived until late morning at this time of year. The dew that settled over the grass and shrubs lingered until noon.

She had her red cardigan on over her *salwar-kameez*, the one her mother had knitted years ago. It looked faded and threadbare, but it was incredibly soft after innumerable washings. And it was still her favorite protection against the damp chill.

In a few minutes she'd have to stir out of her room, take a bath, eat something, and head for college. Her mother was already making breakfast for the family. The sounds of pots and pans clanging had started to emerge from the kitchen about twenty minutes ago—Mummy's not-so-subtle wake-up call to the family.

Vinita wasn't sure what her mother was preparing, but the aroma of *phodnee*—seasoning made of smoking oil with mustard and cumin seeds sputtering in it—was seeping in through the crack beneath her door. Visions of a hot breakfast with a steaming cup of tea usually made her stomach rumble. But today they didn't.

Picking up the book, she tried to make sense out of the words on the page, but a minute later put it down again. Studying was becoming hard lately. Pressing her fingers to her eyes, she wondered why she was having such difficulty focusing on her studies. This had never happened to her before.

She'd spent the last couple of weeks in a haze. She mostly kept herself sequestered in her room, sitting at her old teakwood desk, a hand-me-down from Vishal's college days. It even had his initials crudely carved in the corner: VBS.

But keeping herself glued to her desk wasn't unusual. In fact her parents expected it of her. She had preliminary exams to study for—prelims as everyone called them. She was a good student and she hoped to maintain her grades. She was looking forward to earning her bachelor's degree in two years. She had aspirations of graduating at the top of her class.

No second class would be tolerated in the Shelke family. Vishal had been a brilliant student, too. He had gone on to become a chartered accountant and had a promising job with a large financial corporation in Bombay. Academically she was expected to follow in his footsteps.

But the odd meeting with Som crept into her mind frequently, distracting her from her goal of becoming a statistician. And the fact that something that trivial could upset her steadfastness was annoying. She had no time for silly daydreams. And frankly, a drifter like Som Kori wasn't worth one single minute of her time.

His behavior was odd, too. He'd asked her to call him Som, flirted with her, and claimed he wanted to be her friend, and yet he hadn't even bothered to acknowledge her presence on campus. It was as if that chance encounter in the dark had never happened. Maybe it hadn't meant anything to a man like him. Maybe he had feigned interest in her out of politeness. Maybe she was reading too much into a casual conversation. Maybe—

She gave a frustrated groan and shifted her fingers from her eyes to her temples. All that conjecture was giving her a headache.

Several times she'd observed him lounging as usual with his gang of five by the massive wrought-iron gate of the college compound. They called themselves The Sixers—all of them athletes with little or no interest in academics. A couple of them leaned against the gate while the others sat on the brick wall nearby, like Humpty Dumpty, legs dangling.

They all wore similar clothes that looked almost like uniforms—tight, bell-bottom pants that hugged their jock buttocks, and dark-colored shirts left open at the neck and a bit beyond to showcase their manly, hair-sprinkled chests. They blew rings of cigarette smoke, and through the gray haze watched the world, especially the girls, go by.

Theirs was a life of idle indulgence. Except when they played cricket. That was the one thing they excelled at—the only thing that got them moving at lightning speed.

When did they attend classes, *if* they did? Vinita sometimes wondered. How did they manage to stay in college if they kept failing courses? Did they have any ambitions in life beyond wandering around the campus, playing cricket, and letting life pass them by?

She more or less knew the answer. They were wealthy. Their fathers donated large sums of money to the small, privately run Shivraj College. With that kind of backing, the boys could get a dummy degree certificate without ever attending a class.

College was a playground to them—until they became too old to be students, and were eventually forced to join the family business, get married, and settle down. She knew of several playboys like them, who'd taken the slow, lackadaisical route to adulthood.

Som and his pals made loud remarks when girls walked in and out of the gate each day—remarks that were often crude and hurtful if a girl was heavy or short or ugly. They teased and taunted and jeered mercilessly. Sometimes they gave an appreciative whistle or comment if a girl was pretty or passably attractive. The in-betweens were usually ignored.

And Vinita was an in-between. She had no illusions about her appearance. Her nose was tip-tilted, her chin pointed, and her eyes too wide-set to be considered pretty. Overall, it was an ordinary face. It would have been nice if she'd inherited more of her mother's features, including her attractive smile, but her father's genes had won out.

Fortunately Papa wasn't an ugly man, just plain. He was of average height, with square shoulders and a belly that had started to grow in the past few years. His hair was beginning to fall out, too, the bald spot expanding rapidly. Everything about him was average, and so Vinita was average, too: height, weight, color—all of it. On special occasions, with a touch of makeup, she bordered on pleasant. And she was middle-class, not like the rich girls who attracted certain types of boys.

Considering all that, it wasn't a surprise that Som hadn't followed up on his so-called offer of friendship. Pulling herself out of her disruptive thoughts, she sat up straight, then peeled her eyes open and picked up her textbook one more time.

She couldn't let that man interfere with her studies, her plans. Her life. She wouldn't.

Chapter 3

Waiting for a brief lull in the heavy late afternoon traffic, Vinita hastily crossed the street. College Road was lined with businesses that sold everything from saris to shoes, grains to office supplies. Vishnu Cinema Theater and the Free-Zee Ice Cream shop were snugly tucked in between a cobbler shop and a bookstore.

The theater and the ice cream parlor were the two businesses that attracted the young crowds the most.

Between the automobiles, rickshaws, bicycles, pedestrians, and stray animals, it was a wonder there weren't more traffic accidents in this neighborhood. Drivers just seemed to slither and sway in and out of one another's way by instinct, like schools of fish in the ocean.

She stopped briefly to study the giant poster planted outside the theater, advertising the movie she and her friends were planning to see the following Sunday as a post-exam celebration. Then they would go next door to have a cup of tutti-frutti ice cream and discuss the movie, critique it, moan about it, laugh over it.

Engrossed in admiring the movie's hero, the dashing man she had a secret crush on, she paid little attention to her surroundings.

The bustle of pedestrian traffic didn't bother her. People carrying loaded *pishwis*—shopping bags made of jute—pushed past her with their burdens. Brushing against one another in that casual fashion, yet ignoring everyone was the norm in the swarming streets of their town.

The odors of fresh vegetables, flowers, and herbs mingled with the stench of the semi-open sewers of the back alleys. No amount of modernization seemed to stop certain segments of the population from using the more discreet alleys as public toilets. Palgaum's laid-back residents seemed to accept it without complaint.

But Vinita noticed such things, disliked them, disdained them. Sometime in the not too distant future, she'd get out of Palgaum and its cloistered environment, just like her brother had. She had dreams of finding a career in a big city, where she could earn her own living, be independent. Two more years and she'd be out of here. She wouldn't have to put up with Papa and Mummy's conservative ideas and their constant reminders about how a good Marathi girl should behave.

If and when she decided to get married, she'd choose a man who respected her choices in life, allowed her the freedom to have a job, and treated her as an equal. She stared longingly at the hero on the poster. Now *there* was a man who loved a woman like she deserved to be loved. And he was so damn handsome, too.

She bit back a delighted grin at the thought of seeing him in all his heroic glory on the movie screen soon. Sunday couldn't come soon enough.

Behind her the rickshaws and scooters putt-putted like buzzing insects, raising clouds of red dust and exhaust. And the automobiles honked for no apparent reason. Many of the folks who could afford a car loved to show off their expensive toys by tooting their horns. That, too, was something the townsfolk took in stride.

Well, her father owned a car, too, albeit an outdated Fiat with a rusty bumper. But someday she'd have a car of her own.

In the next instant, raised voices startled her out of her fanciful thoughts. She turned her attention back to the road.

As she resumed walking down the footpath, she saw a crowd of men rushing toward her, shouting something. They were chasing two young men who seemed to be running away from them. Both were barefoot. One of them had his white shirt hanging open, exposing his skinny chest and belly.

The unexpectedness of it made her freeze in her tracks. The two men, or rather boys, sped by, nearly knocking her down. Even at that speed she could see the sweat running down their faces, smell their fear. Instinctively she huddled against the nearest store window so she wouldn't get trampled by the angry mob pursuing them.

They whooshed past her like a cresting ocean wave, men of various ages, colors, and sizes. "*Saalyana thaar maara!*" they chanted in Marathi. Kill the bastards.

Vinita's stunned eyes followed them. Who were they? What was going on?

It took her confused mind a moment to recognize another Kannada-Marathi clash. The two language-based factions, the one that spoke the Kannada language and the other that spoke Marathi, were constantly warring with each other.

As a border town located on the dividing line between two states, with two distinctly different languages and somewhat differing cultures, for several decades Palgaum had been the hotbed of cultural clashes and riots, many of them violent. Palgaum's population consisted of approximately equal numbers of individuals from both sides, with each group vying for supremacy.

Although Karnataka, the Kannada state, officially claimed Palgaum as part of its territory, the Marathi faction refused to accept the fact. They'd vowed to fight, and keep fighting to make Palgaum a part of Maharashtra, the state of the Marathi people. There was no end in sight for the bitter feud.

Vinita observed the scene, realizing there had been no warning about anything like this in the papers. If there was a planned communal march, it was usually announced ahead of time to prepare the townsfolk. And Vinita and her friends stayed home on those days. It wasn't safe for young women to be outdoors when violence could erupt at any moment. Her parents would never have allowed her to walk home alone if they'd known about this.

As she continued to watch in fascinated horror, the pursuers caught up with the two boys, and surrounded them like a swarm of killer bees, spilling into the street. They were no more than a hundred feet away from where she stood. All the traffic converging onto the intersection came to a screeching halt. It was a miracle no one was run over.

Although she couldn't see through the thick circle of enraged men, she clearly heard the sounds of violence—the dull thuds and thwacks, the crack of splintering bones. Pained moans from the victims made her cringe.

Those boys were being beaten mercilessly. Oh dear God! They'd never survive. She looked about her, eyes wide with desperation. Why didn't someone do something to help those poor chaps?

Several other pedestrians stood frozen beside her and stared, helpless to do anything. She'd seen minor skirmishes, heard irate cursing and threats tossed around, and she'd read about the thoughtless carnage resulting from these cultural clashes, but this was the first time she had witnessed a violent incident.

Gradually some of her fellow gapers came out of their trance, started to move, and advanced toward the crowd. A few brave men plunged into the fray in an attempt to stem the damage. *"Bus kara, baba."* Stop it, fellows.

A minute later, two policemen arrived on foot, pulled out their *lathis*—wooden sticks—and started to tackle the melee. Nonetheless, several seconds later the frenzied mob was still at it, and the policemen seemed powerless against what could only amount to potential slaughter.

Vinita's feet were glued to the pavement, despite her disgust. How could people casually beat someone to death like that? And all in the name of caste, language, and culture? The sheer horror of it made her stomach turn. Without warning she started shaking.

She hugged her handbag to herself, turned around and leaned her forehead against the store's sun-heated window, fiercely trying to curb the nausea and bring her racing heartbeat under control. She could not—would not—shatter to pieces in the middle of a busy street. She had to get home somehow. If she could only stop trembling.

Feeling a firm hand clamp over her shoulder, she stiffened. When she attempted to scream, what emerged was a weak squeal.

"Shh, don't panic," said a calm voice—a vaguely familiar one. "It's okay."

She pivoted on her heel and faced him. "Mr. Kori!"

"Are you all right?" he asked, the usual frown deepening with concern.

She swallowed to restrain the fear and nausea, shook her head. The crowd gathering around the scene was swelling, their voices getting louder. While she'd been trying to gain control over herself, most of the people around her had shifted to watch the action. They were certainly braver than she. "I—I . . . saw what just h-happened and I . . ." She was stuttering like a baby learning to talk.

"I understand," he said, sounding like a worried father. "I saw it, too."

His sympathy, instead of helping to alleviate her dread, made it worse. Tears started to burn her eyelids. "I'm sorry. I've never seen anything . . . like this before."

"Why should *you* be sorry?" He narrowed his eyes against the sun and turned his head to look at the mob. "It's those prejudiced *goondas* who are up to their bloody riots again."

More policemen arrived in a Jeep. They joined the others who were still trying, without success, to contain the crowd.

"Maybe now they can do something about it," Vinita croaked, trying to wipe away the hot tears dampening her cheeks.

The troop of uniformed men charged the mob with their *lathis* and the crowd finally started breaking up. The moaning from the victims had stopped a while ago. It wasn't a promising sign.

Som Kori turned his attention back to her. "I'm sorry you had to witness that." Noticing her tears, he pulled out a blue and white checked handkerchief from his pocket and handed it to her.

"Thank you, Mr. Kori," she said, accepting the kerchief. She dried her eyes and nose with as much poise as she could muster.

It was deplorable to expose her fragility in front of the strongest, most sought-after boy in college. Inside, he was probably laughing at her for being such a weakling.

"Som," he reminded her gently, examining her face. There was no sign of amusement in his expression, only concern.

"Thank you . . . Som," she repeated. How had he managed to show up when she was at her most vulnerable? And how could he look so cool and unruffled after what he'd just witnessed? She caught a flash of that hard-as-steel strength again. Was he as cold as steel deep down, too? Or was it just a façade to mask something else?

"I'm glad I happened to be only a few steps behind you," he said, dismissing her gratitude. "I saw what was happening." He scowled in the direction of the crowd. "Bastards! They're out for blood. I'm ashamed to call myself a Kannada man when I see such behavior," he spat out.

She knew what he meant. It was disgusting what her fellow Marathi folks did in the name of communalism. From what she'd gathered, at the moment they were doing a fine job of butchering those Kannada boys.

"Those young chaps could be dead," Som said, voicing her own fears.

She shuddered at his words. These kinds of violent conflicts between the factions were happening too often in Palgaum lately. And the bloodshed was escalating each year, too. Sometimes a minor disagreement turned into a battle. Nearly a dozen casualties had affected both sides within the past three years.

Along with Som she watched as several members of the offending gang were rounded up, handcuffed, and tossed into the police van like sacks of potatoes.

The sad part was, there wasn't an iota of remorse on any of their faces. Although most of them looked either angry or defiant, one or two of them sported smug smiles.

She saw one of the policemen go down on his knees to examine the fallen youths. Their clothes were filthy now, and soaked with blood. They lay facedown on the street, limp as rag dolls. The policeman gingerly turned one of them over onto his back.

The face was a mangled mass of blood and flesh. Vinita turned away in despair. The nausea returned in a rush.

"Let's hope that's the end of that," said Som, expelling a long sigh.

"It's not over yet," she cried, pressing her bag to her churning stomach. "It'll never be over as long as the clashes continue."

"You're probably right."

They stood in silence for a minute, immersed in their own thoughts. Then he finally said, "They're loading them in the Jeep. Probably driving them to a hospital."

Or the morgue, figured Vinita, swallowing her distaste. Their town didn't even have an ambulance. Patients were driven to hospitals in ordinary vehicles. Now that the moment had more or less passed, she realized the enormity of what had just happened.

"You're shaking." Som scowled again as the Jeep took off, belching puffs of exhaust. "Why don't I buy you a cup of coffee? You look like you need something to calm your nerves."

She shook her head. How could he mention coffee when two young men had just been battered to a pulp?

"I know what you're thinking," he said, reading her thoughts. "But there's not much you and I can do for those chaps. The police will take care of them." He gave a casual shrug. "The world is full of violence, Vinita. Let me help you feel a little better."

At his words she instinctively raised her hand to pat her disheveled hair back into place. There wasn't much she could do about her swollen eyes. "Thanks, but that's not necessary."

"You need to collect yourself before you go home."

That part was true, Vinita allowed. She couldn't return home looking like she did. Her mother would want to know the reason for it. Taking a few calming breaths, she willed her stomach to settle. As her mind started to function more rationally, a thought occurred. "Did you say you were close behind me?"

He nodded.

"But you don't live around here." Everyone knew the Kori family lived in a more exclusive part of town. In a mansion, no less.

"Well . . . actually I was trying to catch up with you when it all started," he said.

"Why?" All at once she became conscious of the people around them. Now that the crime scene had been cleared, a few were staring at Som and her.

"Because I wanted to talk to you in private," he confessed. He reached into his shirt pocket and pulled out a cigarette and a bright red, plastic lighter. With practiced ease he held one hand against the breeze, lit the cigarette, and pocketed the lighter.

Vinita felt something flutter inside her breast as she watched him draw the smoke deep into his lungs, then exhale very slowly, like it was the most sublime experience he'd ever had. In that instant she almost envied that cigarette he smoked with such total reverence.

"I see," she said.

"Glad you understand." The breeze disturbed his hair and he lifted a hand to tame it.

To be honest, she didn't *understand*. She understood even less the joyful little thump in her chest at watching him do something as simple as rake his fingers through his thick hair.

She and Prema usually walked together to and from college. However, this afternoon Prema had gone home early with a headache, and Vinita was alone. "What did you want to talk about?" she asked, a little out of breath because she felt an insane urge to stare at him. Stare at his sculpted body.

His charcoal gray pants were trendily tight and his black shirt hugged his torso like a second skin. His hair was a little long and the sideburns bushy—all part of the latest in campus chic, and a trend started by the latest and hottest Hindi movie idol, Amitabh Bachchan. Even the scowling, angry-hero look was the Amitabh stereotype. The quintessential cigarette was also a fashion statement.

"I never thought I'd catch you alone," Som said, tossing his unfinished cigarette on the ground and grinding it with the heel of his gleaming, pointy-toed shoes, adding to the hundreds of other butts already littering the footpath. "You're always with Miss Swami, your bodyguard."

"Prema Swami's my friend, not my bodyguard." Vinita tossed him an icy glare, in spite of the unexpected spurt of pleasure that shot through her at discovering that he had been trying to contact her after all.

Nevertheless, she started walking at a brisk pace. Her pulse was still scrambling, but at least the shaking was under control. The tears had dried up, too. By the time she reached her house, in about ten minutes, she'd be back to normal. She had to be.

He started striding beside her, as if it was the most natural thing in the world.

Folks were still staring at them. Young men and women like Som and her, walking beside each other, drew unnecessary attention. Besides, many of the shopkeepers on that street knew her parents and a few were her father's clients.

She couldn't risk being seen with Som, especially outside the college walls. At least on campus, girls and boys could socialize under the pretext of exchanging class notes and discussing homework. Besides, during the past two weeks she had managed to convince herself that Som was not a chap she should fraternize with, for all kinds of reasons. She could write an entire page of reasons.

"I didn't mean to belittle your friend," he apologized. "It's just that I always see you with her—sometimes with a whole group of friends."

"I prefer not to walk alone. I like walking with a friend."

"In that case *I'll* walk with you. And we can talk."

"About what?"

"Friends can talk about anything."

"But we're not friends." She turned briefly to face him as she repeated what she'd said the other day. "We have nothing in common. Even our mother tongues are different." At that moment, for some odd reason, she wished she had something in common with him. He was such an interesting man.

He gave her one of his rare smiles, making her already compromised sense of balance wobble dangerously. "Didn't I say we could remedy that?"

"You did?" When had he said that?

"Don't I get a little credit for making you feel better after what that wild mob did to you?"

She groaned inwardly. He had certainly kept her from passing out or falling apart by showing up at the right time and distracting her. But it looked like he was going to use that little incident to his advantage. "I'm very grateful for the emotional support and the handkerchief." She looked at the balled-up piece of fabric in her fist. "I'll return it after it's washed."

"Keep it. It's yours," he said, with a dismissive gesture—like a movie star offering a wide-eyed fan a small souvenir.

"So, what is it you wanted to discuss?" She narrowed her eyes at him. "You want me to do your homework or something . . . to return the favor?"

"Homework?" He erupted into sardonic laughter, drawing the attention of more passersby. "I don't have homework. But I'm sure you've noticed that." He looked at his wristwatch, a surprisingly plain watch with a brown leather band. "I had something else in mind. Why don't you join me for that cup of coffee?"

"I can't." Coffee with him? All by herself? Her father would have a fit if she dared to indulge in such behavior. More than her father, it was Vishal, her brother, who was protective of her to the point of strangulation.

She suspected that Vishal liked playing the role of big brother. That way he could justify his bossy attitude, and get grateful looks from their parents on top of it. It saved them the trouble of disciplining her. Besides, a brother, especially an older one, more or less played a paternal role when it came to looking out for the women in the family. It was a brother's duty to protect his sister. The good thing was, he lived in Bombay now and couldn't watch over her that closely.

In any case, she wasn't planning on telling anyone in her family about the scary episode a few minutes ago. They'd keep her locked up in the house if they found out. If they ever learned that a boy, a Kannada one at that, had touched her shoulder and held a long conversation with her in clear view of the public, they were certain to become upset.

As it was, her family barely tolerated her close friendship with Prema. They just couldn't understand why she had to pick a Kannada girl for a best friend, when there were so many Marathi girls she could befriend.

And now here was Som, talking about going out for coffee like it was an everyday occurrence. That was another thing—drinking coffee instead of the traditional tea that most Palgaum folks consumed. Sipping coffee from large, thick ceramic mugs instead of ordinary cups and saucers was the trend lately. Coffee was what Americans drank, so it was more sophisticated than the colonial custom of drinking tea. British traditions were passé, while American habits were worth emulating.

"Aw, come on," he teased. "It's only a harmless cup of coffee. Besides, I'm buying."

"It's not *that*. My parents don't like me socializing with boys," she confessed.

"Your parents don't mind you going to a café with your other friends, I'm sure."

"My other friends happen to be girls."

He shook his head. "Gender really shouldn't matter."

"It's not that simple . . . at least with people like my parents." She tossed him a challenging scowl. "I'm sure your parents are the same way."

It was no secret that his parents were orthodox Lingayats, a sect belonging to the Vaishya business caste. Just because they were rich and popular on the club scene didn't mean they didn't adhere to their conservative traditions in their home. Rumor had it that they all wore their traditional *lingams*, the sacred symbol of Lord Shiva, on a thread underneath their fancy clothes. The Koris were *zamindars*—landed gentry—with vast ancestral tracts of farmland.

Matter of fact, Vinita's information came from a reliable source. Prema's family was well acquainted with the Koris. Everything Vinita knew about Som Kori's private life came from Prema.

"Sure, they're old-fashioned, but they don't get involved in my social life," Som explained. He looked at his watch again, then raised a brow at her. "So you want to join me for a cup of coffee or not? Do I have to beg?"

Recalling the way his hard hand had pressed into her shoulder, Vinita felt her cheeks burning. She was ashamed to admit to herself it had felt good, very good—like a branding iron, but without the pain. His invitation was tempting, too. His smug yet gently mocking variety of begging was even harder to resist.

Most girls would be thrilled to receive an invitation to have coffee with Som. No boy had ever invited her before. Now here was this college idol asking her, and instead of doing happy cartwheels, she was riddled with doubts. Why? Because he was a playboy. He was a *pukka badmaash*. A thorough ruffian. He smoked and drank alcohol, too. Plus, he was a dud when it came to academics.

And that reminded her of something else. "How come you're walking today instead of driving?" He was usually behind the wheel of his car, a sleek, black-as-kohl Ambassador.

"I knew you'd probably refuse to get into a car alone with me."

"You're right." She managed to raise her eyes and meet his gaze. "Why me?" There were a dozen beautiful girls salivating over him on any given day. So why was he asking a studious girl like her, a girl who'd be rated average on her best day?

He didn't pretend to misunderstand her question. "Because you're an attractive and bright girl," he replied, shooting an arrow of desire right through her middle with those odd yet mesmerizing eyes of his. "Isn't that reason enough?"

"Most certainly," she said with a wry laugh. She knew she was bright. But attractive? She tossed him a *you're such a liar* look.

"I'm serious, Vinita," he insisted. "Why would I lie to you?" His expression was candid, his eyes wide and guileless.

Well, from a certain angle, her profile wasn't too bad, she supposed. She had a decent figure and nice hair. So maybe he wasn't lying . . . Just maybe. What was the harm in having one small cup of coffee? As long as her family didn't know about it, it wouldn't hurt them. And it wasn't like she was having some wild affair with Som or anything.

After another moment of hesitation, she stopped in her tracks. "Okay."

"Good," he said, his face relaxing.

"But I can't stay long. My mother's expecting me home soon."

"Why don't we go to Bombay Café? It's close by," he suggested.

At the next intersection, they made a right turn toward the café instead of the usual left Vinita would have made to go home.

The wizened old beggar who had made a home for himself on the footpath outside Bombay Café stuck his hand out for alms. He looked like a skeleton clad in a tattered shirt and pants. His cheeks stretched like crepe paper over his cheekbones and his beard was nearly long enough to reach his belly. Despite her feelings of deep sympathy for his condition, Vinita looked away, embarrassed at being stopped by a panhandler.

Beggars were everywhere—too many for even the most generous souls to sustain. No matter how much one gave, it was never enough. Most of them harassed citizens by falling at their feet, tugging on their clothes, and following them around until their quarry capitulated from sheer mortification and gave something. This old man wasn't all that tenacious, and yet she couldn't help turning her gaze away to avoid his hollow eyes.

But Som stopped beside the beggar. Vinita couldn't help but stop, too. She looked at Som, wondering what he planned to do.

He surprised her when he dug into his pocket, pulled out a coin, and placed it in the beggar's outstretched hand. It brought a tired but grateful smile to the old man's haggard face.

"*Ram-Ram*, Kori-saheb," the beggar murmured, pocketing the change and raising his hand to his forehead in a gesture of gratitude.

So, Som was generous in his own way. And the old man knew him by name. That, too, was a revelation. She was learning some interesting things about Som. But then, what was a single coin to a man who drove an Ambassador?

Once again she became aware of people throwing curious glances at the two of them. What would they say about a strictly raised Marathi girl like her walking with a Kannada chap—a notorious one like Som Kori? And especially in the volatile climate of their town, where extremism seemed to be mounting instead of diminishing after nearly thirty years of independence from the British?

The earlier doubts came tumbling back, but she quashed them by telling herself this was a one-time thing—a simple cup of coffee with a . . . friend.

Nonetheless the blood racing in her veins at the thought of sitting at a table with him wasn't the kind of reaction one would have to a friend. That, too, she brushed aside as first-time nerves. Once she had that first sip of delicious, frothy coffee, her pulse was sure to settle into its normal pattern.

A minute later they entered the cool café, with its black marble floors, shiny wooden tables, red upholstered chairs, and ultramodern light fixtures. The aroma of coffee and biscuits filled the air. It stood apart from all those plain, boring tea shops scattered around town.

Som whispered something to the solicitous waiter who jumped forward to greet them. It was obvious the waiter knew him well and was eager to please a favored customer. He addressed him as Som-saheb.

In seconds they were seated at a quiet, discreet booth, away from probing eyes. The booth was even curtained to ensure privacy. How accommodating was that? And exactly how many girls had sat inside that booth with Som, their skin tingling with anticipation?

Fortunately the place was almost deserted, maybe because it was late afternoon, when the sun was still beating down and most people didn't drop in for coffee and tea. In a couple of hours, however, once the offices closed and the sun went down, the crowds would pour in. For the time being, Som and she more or less had the place to themselves.

"See, this is so nice and relaxing—nothing to worry about," declared Som, leaning back in his chair, looking entirely too comfortable. Like he owned the place. Maybe his family did own the place.

Vinita was tongue-tied. She wasn't exactly shy, but this kind of socializing was different. "I must look terrible after what happened earlier," she remarked, just to break the awkward silence.

Arms folded, he leaned across the table to examine her face. "No, you look perfectly all right," he assured her.

Now that she had a rare chance to study his face up close, Vinita noticed all the imperfections. His teeth had brown nicotine stains and the lower row was crowded. His nostrils were flared, like a bull's. His eyebrows were heavy and sat low over the sockets. Maybe it was the brows and nostrils which made him look so fierce. His extraordinary gold-colored eyes were his best feature. Cat's eyes.

No, he wasn't good-looking by any standard, but the overall image, with the tall, athletic build and wide shoulders, was imposing. There was something about this man that many females found irresistible, some male element that was both primitive and wild. Despite her resistance, it was slowly reeling her in at the moment. And she didn't appreciate the loss of control.

Within minutes their coffee arrived, steaming and fragrant, with a delightful head of foam, bubbles popping. Gratefully, she picked up the spoon to add sugar to the mug. It gave her fidgety hands something to do. In the next instant the spoon flew out of her fingers and crashed to the floor with a metallic ping.

Self-conscious, she bent down to pick it up, but Som was there before her, retrieving the spoon and putting it back on the table. He offered her his spoon instead of ordering a new one. "I don't take sugar in my coffee."

"I'm sorry," she said with a rueful smile, and accepted the spoon. "I'm usually not this clumsy." Her hands were shaking uncontrollably.

"Don't give it another thought. For some reason I seem to have that effect on girls," he informed her. And he seemed dead serious, too.

She suppressed the urge to roll her eyes at the narcissistic remark. At twenty-two—or was it twenty-three?—with all the fooling around he'd done, he was an experienced flirt. So of course he had that kind of impact on girls like her—sheltered young teenagers who couldn't resist the bad-boy image and the ego as large as the Indian Ocean.

Despite all her valiant efforts at reining in her heart, she felt it slide a little.

And her pulse, instead of stabilizing after that first sip of caffeine, only crept up another degree. She was already regretting her impulsive decision to accept his invitation. But the naughtiness of it and the excitement had been too great to resist.

She looked at her surroundings once again. Was it really she, the awkward bookworm, sitting at a chic table in a small, private café with a man like Som Kori? There was a surreal quality to the scene, like an out-of-body experience. If she hadn't been so nervous, she probably would have detected the humor in it.

When she reached home sometime later, slightly dazed, her nerves still vibrating from the rush of having done something extraordinary, she was relieved to find that her mother hadn't noticed she was late. Or maybe she was under the impression Vinita had a dance lesson that afternoon.

But then Vinita learned from their maid that both the boys involved in the street incident had died from the assault. Her heart took a dive. They were merely boys, killed by a heartless crowd of zealots. And apparently the reason was trivial: the Kannada boys were caught teasing a Marathi girl in their neighborhood.

That night, as she lay in bed, she realized it had been the most bizarre day of her life. Both violence and adventure had abruptly invaded her otherwise ordinary existence. The terrifying sights and sounds of the youths being chased and then murdered would haunt her for months.

Som Kori would haunt her a lot longer.

Chapter 4

Through sleep-deprived eyes, Vinita tried her best to concentrate on her exam. Her fingers were hurting from holding the fountain pen at the correct angle for two hours. This economics exam was the hardest she'd ever encountered. All the cramming from the previous night hadn't amounted to much. Every question was turning into a minor struggle to answer.

She could only pray she'd do well enough to pass the exam—something she'd never had to do in the past. Her prayers had always been reserved for keeping her class rank at number one.

Putting the pen down for a second, she flexed her hand to get the stiffness out. She lifted her head and took a quick survey of the classroom. Everyone had their head bent over their desk. The scratch-scratch of nibs scribbling rapidly over ruled paper was the only sound in the hushed classroom. They seemed to have no problem focusing. So what was the matter with her?

"You need something, Miss Shelke?"

The brusque voice startled her. Her eyes connected with the monitor's stern ones behind the horn-rimmed glasses. It was more a reprimand than a question. Students were supposed to mind their own business and not let their gazes wander. If they needed something, they were supposed to raise their hands and ask.

"No, m—madam," she murmured, hot embarrassment flooding her face. She could sense everyone's attention on her. She'd interrupted their concentration on their precious exam.

"Then why are you wasting time?" The monitor approached Vinita's desk, the starch in her cotton sari making a crackling sound with each measured step. She was a thin, humorless woman, who made the students' bones rattle with fear. One word from her could have someone expelled from the exam, even from the college, permanently.

"Sorry, madam. My eyes were tired," Vinita mumbled. She'd never been reprimanded in class before. Tears of humiliation stung her eyes, but she fought them back.

The pigeon-faced woman glared at her, making it clear she didn't believe Vinita for one moment. Then she abruptly turned around and went back to her chair at the front of the class.

Somehow Vinita managed to keep her head down and get through the exam. Then she left the classroom and headed for the ladies' lounge, the humiliation lingering like a bitter after-taste. That was the last exam of the year. Blessed relief! And yet the familiar feeling of joyful release was absent.

Prema was waiting for her in the large, crowded lounge. Every conversation buzzing around was about exams: *Oh God, that political science exam was horrible; I think I did okay on question number three but not four; my statistics paper was so easy this time; I'm sure the Hindi quiz is going to be a killer this afternoon . . .*

"How was it?" Prema asked. She had just finished an English Lit exam herself.

"Bad," replied Vinita on a rueful note.

Prema chuckled as she lifted her stack of books off the floor. "You always say that—"

"I don't."

"—but then you end up scoring the highest marks. You're such a clever liar."

"This time I'm not lying." Vinita rubbed her temple. "I'm too tired to even think about it anymore."

Prema peered at her closely. "Your eyes are red. Getting sick or something?"

Yeah, sick at heart, Vinita thought with an inward grimace, but shook her head instead. "Didn't get any sleep last night. It's this stupid exam."

"Well, you're done for the year. We're both done for the year." Prema grinned. "No more classes and exams for eight whole weeks. Freedom!"

"Yes, freedom," Vinita echoed blandly. She followed Prema out the door and down the steps leading to the portico, the same place she'd bumped into Som that evening not long ago.

As she breathed in the hot outdoor air, she wished Prema wasn't with her. Not that she didn't love Prema dearly, but she liked walking home alone these days. It was easier to think without interruptions, to let her mind wander. And easier to meet up with Som. Besides, Prema was bouncing with excitement because the long-awaited summer holidays were finally here.

Vinita wished she could join in her friend's elation. Wouldn't that be nice and simple? Just like it used to be until recently, when the two friends let out a whoop of relief at the end of March, when final exams were over. Then they'd make elaborate plans for the months of April and May.

Back then, the summer holidays had felt like they would last forever and school was only a distant and hazy blot on the horizon. Both of them would open their arms wide and embrace the scorching sun like flowers waiting to blossom. And they'd bask in it for hours each day, ride their bikes, until their brown skin turned black, until they were ready to drop from exhaustion.

Well, those were the old days of childlike delight in the most ordinary things. Now she and Prema were nearly adults and summer had lost its brilliance. Lately, it seemed like Vinita had no interest in anything or anyone.

She lived for one thing, one person: Som.

This year, unlike the previous years, the summer holidays were going to be a major hindrance. All these weeks it had been relatively easy to steal away after classes to meet Som—an hour or two of bliss. But now, without college as an excuse, her only reason for leaving home was the occasional movie with her friends—and her dance lessons three afternoons each week.

She'd have to think of some way to work around them so she could carve out some time to see Som.

Prema interrupted her thoughts when she said, "I hope you're going straight home." Her expression was just a hair short of a warning.

Vinita avoided the censorious glare and continued to walk toward the gate. "I . . . I'm not sure."

"Vini, how many times do I have to say you're begging for trouble?"

"I won't get into trouble."

Prema stopped in her tracks and stared at Vinita, her dark eyes fairly dripping with disapproval. "That's what you said the last time I warned you. Now you're meeting that horrible chap almost every day."

"He's not horrible!" Vinita shot back, and realized too late that she'd raised her voice to the point of calling attention to herself and Prema. Students standing around were gawking with obvious interest. "Let's not talk about it here," she hissed through clenched teeth. It was bad enough that most of the campus knew about her and Som. Now they'd know her best friend condemned it, too.

"Fine, let's discuss it somewhere else." Prema started to walk faster. Vinita had to hurry to keep pace with her. Prema's thin lips were clamped shut. They practically disappeared when she was annoyed or unhappy. She had an expressive face that always indicated her mood.

As they reached the campus gates, from the corner of her eye Vinita noticed Som's friends sitting atop the wall as usual. Som wasn't with them, which meant he was probably waiting for her at the café. Her pulse did an ecstatic somersault.

The minute they were on safer ground, Prema slowed down and turned to her. "Tell me you're not going to continue this . . . affair with Som Kori . . . now that college is over for the year."

"I wish I could." Vinita shook her head. "But I can't."

"Can't or won't?" Prema demanded.

"Both . . . I guess," Vinita replied, afraid to meet her friend's punishing gaze.

"Then you're on your own. I don't want to be involved in lying to your mother anymore."

Vinita winced. "I thought you were my friend. Guess I was mistaken."

"And I thought you were brighter than the rest of us," said Prema. "Apparently I was mistaken, too."

Tears sprang to Vinita's eyes. "How can you say such mean things?"

Prema gave a frustrated groan. "Because nothing else will get through to you." She quickened her pace once again. "Som will probably be waiting for you, so I'll go on home."

"Prema, wait." But Prema was almost running, so Vinita slowed down and watched her weave her way through the pockets of pedestrians, her turquoise *salwar-kameez*-clad figure slowly dissolving into the distance.

For a moment Vinita stood still, feeling abandoned. Prema and she had been inseparable since kindergarten. Was Vinita willing to lose a precious friendship because of her unwillingness to give up Som? Was it too greedy to want to have both?

Drying her eyes, she put the handkerchief back in her purse and continued down the footpath. She hated admitting even to herself that Prema might be right. What was the matter with Vinita? Where was her common sense? Even her precious dance lessons, something she'd loved and always made time for in her busy schedule, didn't mean much anymore. What was she getting into? And yet, each time she thought of withdrawing from the madness, she couldn't. Som was intoxicating. An addiction she couldn't shake.

It was a mere eleven weeks and two days since her first cup of coffee with him, and she could do nothing but obsess about him, night and day. She was straying from the restricted path she was supposed to tread.

She'd reminded herself often of her obligations to her family and herself. Her dance guru was upset with her for arriving late for lessons several times. On a couple of occasions, Vinita had skipped lessons altogether and then lied to him that she'd been sick. She told herself her heart would break if she didn't watch out. She was walking a very fine line. And yet all that wisdom was useless in the face of the irresistible attraction Som held for her.

She was in love with him. There was no doubt left in her mind. All the pride she'd taken in being a strong girl, incapable of falling prey to an attractive body and surging hormones, had crumbled quickly. The contempt she'd once held for girls who were too weak to resist temptation was reserved for herself now.

Unfortunately, the flesh was weak, the heart weaker. The soul was apparently the weakest.

Som and she met almost every afternoon at the café. It was an unspoken agreement, and it had become a habit to take a diversion on her way home and walk past Bombay Café—after Prema had taken the turn toward her own house.

If Vinita found Som outside the café waiting for her, they'd go inside and spend some time together. If he wasn't there, she'd turn around and go home, feeling let down. He wasn't all that predictable. Besides, he had cricket matches and practice games that sometimes interrupted their routine.

She wondered if he'd be there today.

And then she saw him, seated on the top step leading into the café, wearing sunglasses that masked his eyes. One leg was folded at the knee and the other was stretched out, the creases on his pants sharp as razor blades. The bright green shirt would have looked garish on a lesser man, but on him it looked rakish. Perfect. One arm hung loosely over his knee, the ever-present cigarette dangling between two fingers.

She forgot all about her spat with Prema, and her footsteps quickened in keeping with her heartbeat.

"Hello," she said to him, trying not to show her delight.

"Hello, yourself," he replied, rising to his feet with his usual pantherlike grace. Peeling his sunglasses off, he hooked them over his shirt pocket. He held the café door open for her and followed her inside, bringing with him his unique scent.

They occupied their usual booth behind the curtain. He asked her about her last exam and she gave her an offhand answer. He wouldn't have believed her if she said she'd fared badly, anyway—just like when Prema had laughed it off. Why did people find it so hard to believe that she could do poorly on a test, perhaps even fail? In any case, things like exams were of no interest to Som. In his world, all that mattered was sports.

But in all fairness to him, he was generally charming to her, attentive, often kind, or at least he seemed to try to be all those things, for her sake. The cynical frown was there, but it wasn't that severe. He even smiled at times—and each time it warmed her heart to think maybe *she* was responsible for it.

Nonetheless, there was a part of him that remained aloof, a part he didn't share with her. He never talked about his family like she talked about hers. He never shared his dreams for his future with her. She could never get a glimpse into his heart and head. For a man with so many friends and admirers, and someone who had deliberately sought out her company, he was perplexingly private.

Whenever she brought up the subject of his siblings and parents, he gave her some flippant reply that bordered on abrupt. Questions about a future career were brushed aside with a vague reference to "eventually joining my father's business."

So she'd stopped asking him. No point in trying to chip away at a hard rock with a blunt knife, and certainly no reason to make that scowl deeper. She was happy with the simple fact that a part of him belonged to her.

Nevertheless, there was one thing he did share with total abandon: cricket—his passion, his ultimate bliss. That's when those rare smiles brightened his face—when he gave her a strike-by-strike account of some successful match or other. He seemed to come alive in those moments and pulse with the kind of energy she could almost touch and taste.

She waited till the waiter delivered their coffee, and took a sip before asking, "How was yesterday's game?"

He extinguished his cigarette in the ashtray and shrugged. "The match wasn't bad. Wasn't exactly good, either."

"What does that mean?" she asked with a lift of her brow.

The scowl turned a little darker. "I was *this* close to scoring a century," he said, holding up his thumb and forefinger to demonstrate the tiny gap. "But damn it all, just when I thought I was going to score my hundredth run, I got caught out."

"Oh no!"

"Their stupid team has only *one* good fielder." He gave a dramatic groan. "And it was my bad luck that *he* was precisely where my ball was headed."

"But I heard you scored the most impressive runs," she offered as a salve for his bruised ego. Scoring ninety-nine runs was quite amazing. The buzz in the ladies' lounge was that despite his having missed a century by a hair, he'd still left the rival team and their bowler totally frustrated. "Besides, it's only a game, Som."

"Only a game!" he hissed, his eyes wide with shocked disbelief. He reminded her of an incensed cat.

"But your team won, and that's what matters, doesn't it?" She could see she'd upset him by belittling his chief occupation. To her it was just a sport, but to him it was obviously the only thing that mattered in life.

"I suppose so, but coming *that* close and not making it . . ." He trailed off, pulling out a fresh cigarette from his pocket with one hand while the other grabbed the coffee mug. Sometimes she wondered how his body could tolerate so much caffeine and nicotine. And yet he seemed to thrive on both. She worried about his health, about his future, everything about him.

She'd have to find a way to convince him to give up smoking. It was no doubt going to be a battle.

But she liked hearing him talk about his game, watch the light glow in his uncommon eyes, and hear the unexpected laugh leap from his throat. She listened now to his voice turn gruff with pleasure as he recalled some of the highlights of the previous day's match.

Eager to please him, she had even made it her business to read about the game and learn enough so she could understand him better. When he used terms like *sixer* and *clean bowled* and *downed wickets*, she at least knew what they meant. A girl who'd more or less eschewed sports as the worthless parading of muscle and physical prowess was now taking an interest in them. It had to be love.

Was she crazy to feel this way—throw caution to the winds and think of nothing else but him? Perhaps, but it was nice to experience the heady feeling of being in love—something she'd never thought she'd feel. She'd always convinced herself it was meant for other girls, pretty and popular girls. But now *she* was one of the lucky ones to share in the experience.

She watched his hands as he lit his cigarette. Wielding a cricket bat for years had left calluses on the pads, but it lent them personality. An athlete's hands—firm hands with the resilience of steel, and yet they trembled a little when they came in contact with her skin.

It meant he cared a little. Maybe more than a little. All at once the world seemed brighter, full of possibilities.

If she had to fight a few battles to have him, she would.

Chapter 5

Six months later

The bile rose in Vinita's throat for the second time that day—bitter and scalding. Excusing herself from her friends, she hurried to the toilet. After she threw up what little was left in her stomach, she leaned against the sink, weak and shaking.

No more speculation about it. She was going to have a baby. And with it came the worst kind of fear she'd ever experienced.

She studied her reflection in the mirror. What she saw was a tired face, weighed down by stress and worry. Did the fact that she was carrying a child show in her expression? Could people look in someone's eyes and tell? She'd heard her grandmother say it was easy to spot a pregnant woman from the distinctive glow on her face. Apparently something changed in a woman's appearance to give away the secret. Only in Vinita's case, it wasn't a happy secret; it was a dirty little fact that she wished she could hide forever.

For the last several weeks she'd been going through this routine: she woke up queasy in the mornings; she hated the idea of breakfast but choked a bit of it down somehow and vomited within minutes; then she waited for the second round of nausea to hit her later in the morning. It was mid-afternoon by the time her turbulent tummy righted itself.

How had she reduced herself to this? She was the brightest girl in her class. She used to be, anyway. She was supposed to concentrate on her studies and move on to a successful career. She was also expected to save herself for a good boy, her ideal man, the one who would respect her for who she was, love her, cherish her.

She'd firmly subscribed to that viewpoint, until she'd bumped into Som Kori—literally. At the time, she'd been swept off her feet by his brand of charm, and considered their chance encounter a matter of fortuity, and that their paths were fated to intersect.

Now, as she recalled that night, she realized it was a curse. She had run into the devil himself that evening, and her simple, orderly life had started to rip apart and scatter. Even her grades were suffering. She wasn't at the top of her class anymore. Her rank had slipped to number five, much to her father's disappointment.

And things were going to get worse. Significantly worse.

At first, shocked and dismayed by the changes in her body, she'd tried to convince herself it was a mistake. It had to be! She hadn't even considered the possibility of pregnancy. She was only nineteen. She was nowhere ready to be married, let alone become a mother.

Once reality had begun to sink in, she'd prayed for her period to show up, but that had proved entirely fruitless. Whoever tried to sell the idea of the power of prayer had to be more naïve than she. Praying brought nothing.

After all the tears and prayers had dried up, she had begun to consider other alternatives. She had increased her weekly dance routine, rehearsing at home after her evening lessons were over, hoping the heavy exercise would make her womb rid itself of its contents. Then there was an old wives' tale that eating papaya caused a miscarriage. Since they conveniently had two papaya trees in their garden, she'd secretly managed to sneak some. That, too, had proved useless.

By now she'd missed two monthly cycles. She was positive she was pregnant. Night after night she lay awake. Sometimes she stepped away from her bed and paced the length of her room till she couldn't walk anymore. Sheer exhaustion and sore ankles would put her to sleep. But the next morning she would wake up tired and grumpy.

She couldn't tell Prema about her problem. It was too scandalous a secret to share with a conservative girl like Prema. Besides, she'd be sure to say *I told you so.*

Confiding in her mother was out of the question. Yet the thought of going through this nightmare alone was terrifying.

Her mother had complained that Vinita wasn't eating lately. "Is this some kind of silly diet, Vini?" she'd asked a few times. "Teenagers should not be neglecting nutrition, you know."

"I'm not on a diet," Vinita assured her.

"You have also been dancing more. Too much exercise and very little food will make you weak and sick," her mother had scolded.

"Stop worrying, Mummy. I'm okay," she'd retorted, all the while wondering how her mother would react if she discovered the real reason for her daughter's aversion to food. She would likely have an emotional breakdown. She was a very sensitive woman. Would she completely sever her ties with Vinita? Being disowned by her prudish mother was a distinct possibility.

Where her father was concerned, Vinita could more or less predict the reaction. There would be a major temper tantrum at first. Then the guilt-inducing reprimands would start. After that thorough lambasting, she'd be dragged out of town to some remote location to have an abortion. Then she'd be kept locked up in her room for a long time, away from curious eyes and wagging tongues, until the scandal faded and disappeared.

Eventually Papa would probably find some low-paid or deformed man to marry her off to, anyone who'd be desperate enough to take on a fallen woman, that is. If no man wanted her, she'd be kept hidden in the shadows forever—a foul reminder of the sins of his and Mummy's past lives coming to demand their due. Her parents would reluctantly accept it as their rotten karma.

She was even more afraid of her brother. Vishal had their grandfather Shelke's sense of haughty righteousness. It bordered on obsessive at times. Their grandfather used to be a dogmatic old man, a freedom fighter who'd fought alongside Mahatma Gandhi. Pride in family and country and loyalty to their strict Marathi traditions often went beyond common sense. Unfortunately Vishal had inherited that bombastic attitude.

Vinita had been going over her options dozens of times daily. Thoughts of swallowing some easy-to-acquire poison and ending the nightmare had crossed her mind a few times, but she was too much of a coward to follow through. And in all honesty, how could she kill the small, innocent being that was growing inside her, especially when she was so in love with its father?

That was a mystery, too. Despite knowing what kind of man Som Kori was, she'd fallen under his spell. Maybe it was the adored athlete she had discovered, and not the real man. Or perhaps it was the lure of the forbidden, the wicked thrill of going behind everyone's back, the idea of carrying around a delicious secret.

The greater excitement seemed to come from the fact that she could be naughty and get away with it. She was finally doing the things some of the more popular girls in college did.

But her stupidity lay in the fact that she'd actually believed him when he'd told her she was pretty. When she'd laughed wryly at the remark, he'd said, "But you *are* pretty. And so different from all the other girls I've known. You're refreshingly unique."

"Is that why you followed me home and asked me to have coffee with you the first time?" she'd asked, naïvely hoping for a positive answer.

His goldstone eyes had shown a brief flash of humor. "You were a delightful challenge."

"Challenge? Me?"

"Sure. You're so focused and studious. Always getting top marks. You don't allow any boys to come within ten feet of you." He'd almost smiled. "That's why your nickname is IQ."

"As in intelligence quotient?"

His smile had turned into a soft chuckle—a sound she'd heard no more than perhaps a dozen times. "That, too, but mostly it stands for . . . ice queen."

"But that's so untrue!" she'd said in indignant protest. "I'm not *that* cold."

"Hell, you don't even *know* boys exist in this world."

"Oh, I do notice them . . . at least *certain* boys," she'd allowed, gazing into his eyes.

Of course he hadn't pretended modesty or coyness. "I'm flattered." He'd reached out to tap the blunt tip of her nose. "And you—you're one of a kind."

She'd mistaken the term *one of a kind* to mean attractively unique. Like a damn fool, she'd also assumed she could change his ways. Wasn't it the universal blunder many women, even bright and intelligent ones, made when it came to falling in love with a callous rake? They actually believed they were a wayward man's savior, that they could accomplish what no other woman had.

Convinced that she was destined to be Som's soul mate, she had continued her relationship with him. It had been hard, doing it on the sly without her parents discovering it, but she'd talked Prema into lying for her. Guilt reared its head often, but the lure of being alone with Som was more compelling than the need to consider her parents' delicate sensibilities.

When she'd begged Prema to go against her conscience and lie for her too many times, Prema had told her off. But she'd begged again. And again.

Each time Prema had issued a grim warning about Som. "He's the last boy you should get mixed up with, Vini."

"He's changed a lot," Vinita had argued. "He's rather sweet once you get to know him."

"Sweet?" Prema had snorted. "You don't know the sordid details of his life like I do. In our Lingayat community, no sane girl wants to have anything to do with him, in spite of his money and influence. He's a loafer."

"No, he's not." Vinita had looked at her friend with narrow-eyed suspicion. "Wait a minute. Do I detect a little jealousy here?"

Prema had let out a loud sigh. "I give up, Vini. If you're that desperate to ruin your life, go ahead. Don't say I didn't warn you."

After that argument, Prema had pretty much left Vinita alone to dig her own grave.

However, as a loyal friend and confidant, Prema had continued to lie to Vinita's mother whenever Vinita was running late after skipping afternoon classes or dance lessons. Oh yes, now she'd sunk from lack of interest in studies to cutting classes.

She'd disappeared with Som more frequently, the secret locations gradually progressing from the semiprivate, curtained café booth to the total seclusion of a flat. They often met in secret at his friend's flat outside of town. His friend was a medical intern and was hardly ever home. For obvious reasons she took a rickshaw instead of riding in Som's car.

When he'd touched her, although hesitant at first, she'd given in when desire had replaced reason. His caresses were like a drenching yet delightful monsoon rain. He was a talented flatterer and he worked her ego like her mother kneaded the soft wheat-flour dough she used for making her thinly rolled *chapatis*.

Little did Vinita know that eighteen-going-on-nineteen was a dangerous age—teetering on the cusp of adolescence, tumbling into womanhood—when the surge of hormones could virtually destroy a girl.

Gradually Som had her believing that he was a changed man since he'd met her. Foolishly she'd thought he was serious about her, committed enough to give up his depraved ways and get the college degree that eluded him, join in his father's business and, last but not least, marry her.

Despite knowing full well that her parents would never consent to her marrying a Lingayat man, she had still begun to dream about becoming Mrs. Somesh Kori, an envied position that dozens of her contemporaries had striven for unsuccessfully. Well, *she* was different from those other girls.

Although he hadn't said as much in words, she'd had a feeling he was as much in love with her as she with him. Men were usually more wary about exposing their emotions.

That's when she'd given up her virginity to Som. If surrendering to temptation was rooted in true love on both sides, then it was neither wrong nor ugly. In fact, despite the pain and discomfort the first couple of times, the act of making love had been beautiful, more fulfilling than she'd imagined.

And he was a superb lover. She'd harbored no illusions about Som being a virgin or in any way inexperienced. He'd surely done this with many girls. But caught up in the throes of passion, she hadn't cared about his past. For that moment, he was hers. From that point forward, he would remain hers.

Alas, they were all dreams—fragile-as-glass dreams that had begun to shatter the instant she'd found out he was seeing another girl at the same time he was seeing her. Prema had mentioned it to her some weeks ago. "I know you don't want to hear this, but rumor has it that Som is involved with Sulekha."

"Sulekha Sheth?" The girl was pretty, but she was so dense she could barely spell her own name. How could Som be interested in a girl like that?

Prema had confirmed it with an emphatic nod.

The news had dismayed more than stunned Vinita. She had seen less of Som in the last several days, and whenever they'd been together he'd been preoccupied. Nevertheless, she was loath to admit that she had failed to hold his attention. She still wanted to believe he was a changed man—because of *her* good influence. He'd said so himself a couple of times.

She had also already begun to suspect she might be pregnant.

But two weeks ago, that last smidgen of hope she'd been desperately clinging to was blown away like a piece of fluff disappearing into the wind. Prema had discovered that Som was spoken for—had been for years. Since his childhood he'd been unofficially betrothed to his cousin from Bijapur, his rich maternal uncle's daughter. They were waiting for his cousin to turn eighteen, legally old enough for marriage, before announcing a formal engagement. And that was supposed to happen within the coming year.

Vinita had shaken her head at first. "How can he marry his first cousin? That's almost incest."

Prema had shrugged it off. "Happens all the time—even more frequently among rich people. It keeps the money within the family."

Recognizing the truth in Prema's words, Vinita had burst into bitter tears. Prema had comforted her the best way she could while Vinita ranted. "Why did he lie to me, Prema? Why did he pretend I was the only girl in the world for him?"

"He does this to every girl he gets involved with, Vini. He's a heartless bastard. His affairs never seem to last more than a few months. Besides, you were . . . uh . . . Never mind."

Vinita had swiped at her tears with her palm and stared at Prema. "What?"

"Nothing." Prema's lips had settled into that thin, familiar line.

"Tell me."

"I'm sorry, but this is going to . . . upset you."

"I'm upset anyway. What's a little more?"

"All right, I heard that you were part of some kind of wager."

Blowing her nose and trying to keep the pieces of her fragmented ego from scattering, Vinita had turned to her friend in confusion. "Wager? As in betting?"

"Apparently he had boasted to his friends that he could get any girl—even a serious girl like you who was focused on nothing but studies."

"You mean . . . he chose to target me because of some bizarre challenge?"

"I understand his friends dared him to seduce a scholarly girl who was wrapped up in books and would be hard to distract. They were betting money on it."

It had taken a few seconds for the truth to register. She'd been a pawn in a mindless game.

She'd turned on her heel and walked away from Prema. What little was left of her self-esteem had vanished, quiet as a puff of smoke.

Chapter 6

Som settled back in the chair to light a cigarette. He needed one after the long but satisfying day on the cricket field. It had been a tough game, but his team had triumphed in the end. Every muscle in his body ached from the workout. But his spirits were floating high, like a kite on a clear winter day.

"You look like a mogul king on his throne, puffing away at his hookah." His friend Rajendra, better known as Raju, sounded amused as he referred to the elaborate water pipe that emperors used to smoke in days gone by—at times with opium-laced tobacco. The hookah was often associated with decadent pleasures and royal depravity.

"Why not?" said Som, blowing a ring of smoke through his puckered lips and watching it travel upward, the perfect O lazily distorting into an oval before disintegrating into a shapeless wisp. He felt like a king. Sometimes.

Raju nodded wisely.

"There's nothing like a good cigarette after a challenging match . . . and a cup of coffee," Som said to Raju, who sat across the table from him in Bombay Café, sipping his own steaming brew from a mug large enough to obscure his narrow face.

Placing the mug on the table, Raju grinned at him, his perfect white teeth flashing in the light streaming in through the café's window. His teeth were his only redeeming feature. A gangly man with a bad case of acne and a worse case of low self-confidence,

Raju was a close friend and fellow cricketer. Som could ask him to do anything and Raju did it with few complaints—as long as it wasn't illegal. The chap was sometimes annoyingly principled. In some areas.

"Tell me something," said Raju. "How do you juggle two girls with such diverse personalities?"

Som lifted a shoulder and flicked the ashes from his cigarette into his empty coffee mug. "Girls are predictable."

"Really?" countered Raju with a puzzled frown. "I thought they were unpredictable."

"Not at all," Som assured him. "If you know what makes them happy, it's easy to get them to do what you want."

Admiration shone in Raju's dark eyes. "I still can't believe you got Vinita Shelke to fall for you, man."

Som raised an eyebrow. "You had doubts?" Poor Raju had lost ten rupees when he'd predicted she'd be impossible to win over.

"Some," admitted Raju, picking up his mug with both hands.

"Patience, *yaar*. Patience is what it takes," Som advised him. His four other close friends had lost ten rupees each. "I have her thinking she's beautiful and sexy."

Raju's forehead creased again for a moment. "Is she?"

Som pretended confusion. "Is she what?"

"Sexy."

He gave another casual shrug. He wasn't about to give his friend any details, if that's what Raju was fishing for. He preferred to keep the finer elements of his love life private. He had to.

His aunt from Bijapur was a shrewish woman. If she got suspicious of what Som was up to, she'd descend on Palgaum and threaten to stop her daughter from marrying him. Not that it meant all that much to Som. His cousin, Neeraja, had the countenance of a constipated horse—wiry long legs, hardly there breasts, and a face only her mother could consider attractive.

But Neeraja would come with an incredibly fat dowry, something Som's father had been salivating over for years. His father would disown him if Som did something to prevent the girl from coming into the family as the cherished daughter-in-law.

The fact that Neeraja was Som's parents' favorite niece made the situation more complicated. The only good thing was that Neeraja was a quiet, good-natured type of girl. She'd taken after her father. It could have been worse. She could have inherited her mother's bulldog personality.

"You mean you won't tell me exactly what you're doing with your two current girlfriends," pouted Raju. He looked like a little boy who'd been denied a long-anticipated treat.

Tossing his cigarette stub into the ashtray, Som shook his head. "There are some things a chap can't talk about."

Sometimes Som wondered if Raju lived out all his fantasies vicariously through him. Poor Raju—he had neither the looks nor the gumption to even approach a girl, let alone enjoy some serious action. The man was desperate for it, and had to settle for looking at dirty magazines smuggled in from some obscure shop in Bombay. There were no adult shops in Palgaum.

Raju sulked for a moment. "Not fair—especially after I lost ten rupees."

"All you need to know is that you lost the bet." But Som had to admit Vinita had proved to be a tougher challenge than he'd presumed. Since she hadn't paid attention to him after he'd whistled at her and made a few loud, complimentary remarks about her dancing talents, he'd had to come up with other ideas.

He'd been forced to engineer accidentally bumping into her after her recital, then ply her with endless cups of coffee on a nearly daily basis before she'd agreed to go somewhere more private with him. And then it was a few more weeks before she'd let him kiss her. He'd never had to work so hard to get a girl before.

After that things had become easier. Once he'd seduced her, it was like working on a clay sculpture. He could mold her in whatever shape he wanted, make her moan and beg for his body, like he wanted her to. And she was pretty good in that department, Som reflected—surprisingly good for a girl who considered a mathematics textbook more riveting than a thriller movie.

And he'd won his bet.

Vinita was the first bookworm type he had seduced, mainly because he hadn't considered girls like her worth his attention. When there were so many pretty girls who were willing and easy, why bother with someone stiff and unapproachable like Vinita? But he loved a challenge.

Nonetheless he had to admit she was a pleasant surprise. She'd even intrigued him a bit, something that almost never happened. Maybe it was because she talked about entirely different topics than other girls. She didn't seem all that obsessed with fashion and shopping. She was a refreshing change from the typical self-centered and not-too-bright girls he'd been friendly with.

"Hmm," Raju admitted grudgingly, pulling Som back into the moment. "But don't you feel guilty about breaking the heart of a sincere girl like her?"

Som caught the waiter's eye and ordered a second cup of coffee before replying, "Come on, *yaar*, who takes that sort of thing seriously? There's very little entertainment in this town, so I'm doing girls like Vinita a favor."

"How?"

"By introducing some excitement into their dull lives." Looking at it honestly, though, he was feeling twinges of guilt in recent weeks, especially when Vinita looked at him with such adoration in her eyes. But he wasn't about to admit that to Raju.

"How long are you going to keep this up?" Raju almost sounded concerned. "Aren't you supposed to get engaged to your cousin soon?"

"Yes, but my life isn't going to change all that much."

Raju's shaggy brows rose. "Don't you have to join your father's business after you get married?"

"That's not until next year. Even then, I'm not worried. Once I give my wife a few children, she'll be content." Just like his mother was content.

Besides, his father, Veerappa Kori, despite having a personable wife, had a few mistresses tucked away in various parts of town. No one had ever talked about it to Som, but he knew the women's names and where they lived. As a teenager, curious to find out where his father disappeared to on certain evenings immediately after dinner, Som had hopped on his bicycle and followed his father's car on various occasions. He'd seen and heard plenty of what went on.

Back then, he'd been dismayed to discover his highly feared and respected *appa* was cheating on his wife, the woman he proudly escorted to social functions, the woman he shared a bed with every night.

Well, the teens were a time to learn many of life's lessons, and for Som, learning about extramarital sex was one of them. At least his father couldn't punish him for something he was guilty of doing himself.

"So you'll make love to your wife at night and your latest girlfriends during the day?" demanded Raju, interrupting Som's thoughts again. Raju looked scandalized.

Som put a finger over his lips. "Shh! Not so loud." There were fellow students seated at nearby tables. "You have a twisted mind, Raju."

"No, you're the one with the twisted mind. Cheating on one's wife is beyond twisted." Raju gave him a blistering look of censure. "I plan to be faithful to my wife, no matter what she looks like."

The coffee arrived. Instead of taking umbrage at Raju's reproachful words, Som lifted his mug in a mock salute. "To my good friend, who will always be faithful to his wife." *Even if she looks like a camel,* he added silently. As he took his first scalding sip, he wondered if Raju was the luckier of the two of them. There was something to be said for living a bland, uncomplicated life. Fewer problems.

And Som had his share of problems—too many, in fact. Vinita was in love with him and she was becoming too clingy and demanding. His own pinpricks of conscience were making him uneasy. It wasn't like him to experience remorse. There was only one thing he could do. He had to stop seeing her.

So how was he going to let her down gently?

Raju continued to study him with the probing expression that Som disliked so much. It made him squirm. Despite the fact that Raju was a wealthy drifter like himself, Raju still lived by a different set of rules. He wasn't joking when he said he'd be faithful to his future wife. Raju would also turn into a seriously committed businessman once he joined his father and two older brothers in their profitable timber business.

At heart Raju was a good man. He had always been a loyal friend to Som—since they had been classmates and fellow Lingayats in a Catholic boys' school, where there were only a handful of students of their faith at the time.

Taking another thoughtful sip of the potent, bitter coffee, Som avoided Raju's incisive gaze and turned his eyes to the scene outside the window instead.

The sun was losing its luminescence, getting ready to set. The traffic was heavy—people going home from work. The nearby *masjid,* the mosque, called the faithful to their evening prayer.

He had to work out a few things, he reflected, mostly concerning Vinita. Unfortunately, she was so damn serious and committed about everything, even something like having an affair. Why couldn't she have some fun for a change?

Once again Raju interrupted Som's wandering mind when he put his empty mug down along with some money to pay for the coffee. "I have to go," Raju said, thrusting his wallet into his pocket.

Som absently lifted a hand to wave. "See you tomorrow." He watched his friend walk out the door. Then he went back to brooding.

He'd have to think of a way to tell Vinita that the thing they had together was over.

Chapter 7

The drizzle hadn't let up in five days. It was well past the monsoon season, but a rare typhoon had traveled up the coast, bringing with it relentless rain, even as far inland as Palgaum.

Vinita leaned a shoulder against the window frame of the small flat and watched it fall noiselessly, the moisture weighing down the blades of grass and the branches of the small tree in the courtyard. The window was open, so the chilly moisture traveled directly into the room with every gust of wind, making her shiver. She felt sick. Lately she felt that way most of the time.

Dead leaves and other debris floated along with the muddy water that flowed into the street and ended up in the nearby sewer drain. If this rain continued, a flood was likely.

She disliked cloudy days, and rainy ones even more. But the current weather suited her mood—gray, wet, miserable. She'd been doing a lot of weeping lately.

"What do you mean it's *our* responsibility?" Som's words jerked her out of her grim thoughts and forced her to turn away from the window. The outrage in his golden eyes could burn laser holes in anyone who dared to be close enough. The eyebrows looked menacing.

Nevertheless Vinita stood her ground and looked him in the eye, her legs shaking so badly she didn't know how long they would hold her up. "You're a big part of what's been happening all these months, Som."

His jaw tightened. "As if I need reminding."

"To you it may have been some cheap bet, but to me it was serious."

All she got in reply was silence.

This was not going well. He looked livid. But after she'd missed her third monthly cycle she'd decided that Som had to be told. She couldn't handle the crisis alone. She was facing total disaster. And time was running out.

He was in this as much as she—actually more than she, because *he* had pursued *her*. Hadn't he deliberately orchestrated their collision the night of the dance recital? Prema had told her the truth about that, too. He had asked her out, then sweet-talked her straight into his arms, and eventually into his bed. So why should she have to suffer the consequences alone? The baby was his.

He looked incredulous. "You're sure this is not a joke?"

She tossed him a blistering look. "Do I look like I'm joking? Being pregnant at nineteen is hardly a joke."

His face turned a curious shade of red, telling her the remark had struck home. Finally. He thrust his hands in his pockets and started to pace the length of the tiny sitting room of his friend's flat.

This was the place where they'd met on the sly at least once a week for the last few months. Adjoining this room was the bedroom, where the bed took up nearly the entire space.

She had considered that bed a small piece of heaven as she'd lain beside Som and listened to his gruff smoker's voice talk about his cricket team. She'd loved hearing him speak, and even come to appreciate the trademark scent of him—cigarette smoke combined with his bold aftershave. She could have picked him out in a crowd with her eyes shut, just by his smell.

He turned to her with a frown. "Couldn't you have protected yourself?"

"So it's *my* fault now? I was the inexperienced one in this relationship." She pointed a finger at him. "*You* are the experienced fellow who's had countless affairs."

"That's not true!" he growled.

She rolled her eyes. "Don't give me that, Som. You know you're the Casanova of Shivraj College. And don't even try to deny it."

"If you knew all that about me, why did you go out with me?" His nostrils flared. "I didn't exactly abduct you. So why did you go to the café with me? Why did you sleep with me, damn it?"

Clasping her hands tightly, she turned again and gazed at the falling rain, trying to keep her own temper under control. Angry outbursts were bad for the baby.

She didn't have any answer to his questions—not verbally, anyway. In her heart she knew exactly what the reasons were: she was too dazzled by his charm to see the corrupt soul that lived inside him—too foolish to decline his advances—too naïve to foresee the trouble she could land in.

She'd chosen to see only his kind side, his wryly humorous side, his altruistic side that gave alms to beggars, loans to his less fortunate friends, and generous tips to starving waiters. And she had to admit he did have all those attributes. Somewhere inside that broad chest lay a heart—but like a stagnant pond, a thick layer of slime covered up the hidden depths.

"You want to know the truth, Som?" On a defeated sigh she returned her gaze to him. "All right, then. Since I've humiliated myself to this extent, I'll go all the way and finish the job. I did it because I love you. I thought you loved me, too. I knew precisely what you were, and yet I believed you'd changed since you met me. I thought a plain girl like me had caught your attention because you were finally beginning to make the difficult transition from being an immature boy to a responsible man."

She buried her face in her hands and breathed deeply to keep the threatening tears at bay. There, she'd finally admitted to him her innermost feelings—something she'd never told anyone. Her mortification was complete.

And yet he said nothing in response.

He continued to pace silently—like a caged animal. He reminded her of the circus that had come to town when she was eight years old. Watching the wild cats pace back and forth in their cages had both fascinated and terrified her. To a free spirit like Som, maybe this did feel like being trapped in a small box with steel bars.

Finally, after what seemed like ages in that edgy, endless silence, he came to a stop in front of her. With some satisfaction she noted a look of mild regret cross his face.

"I'm sorry," he said. "It wasn't meant to go this far. But I'm willing to pay for it."

Still fighting to keep the tears away, she looked up at him. "Pay?" What the dickens was he talking about? Hope flickered briefly. Pay for their wedding . . . perhaps?

"The abortion," he murmured.

She stared at him, her speech frozen for the moment.

"I know a fellow in town who can do it discreetly. I'll pay for the procedure."

"Abortion?" She blinked.

His eyes narrowed on her. "What else?"

She shook her head. "I thought you'd . . . that we'd . . ." She had come to him with a mere speck of optimism, thinking maybe, just *maybe* there was an ounce of decency in him, enough to make him consider marriage—if not for her, then for the child they'd made together. But he was clearly too self-centered for that.

"Bloody hell!" His face registered utter disbelief. "You actually thought we were going to get married or something?"

Or something. She glanced at him with clear contempt. "Most people who get caught up in such situations . . . get married."

"In the movies, you mean?"

"In real life. A child needs . . . parents."

He closed his eyes for a second and looked up at the ceiling, as if summoning divine help. "Look, I'm trying to do my best here."

"If this is your best, what's your worst?"

His voice gentled. "I have responsibilities, Vinita. I wish I could do more, but I just can't . . . marry you."

"So you don't give a damn about our child?"

"I told you I can't do anything about it." He raked his fingers through his hair and let out a deep breath. "Why can't you take my simple suggestion? People do it all the time these days. Why do you have to be so serious about everything?"

"Because I happen to be a serious person, Som. I could ask you a similar question. How can you take something as vital as creating a life so lightly?" Taking the easy way out was probably commonplace to him. She wondered how many girls he had impregnated, and how many babies he'd helped abort by paying for it.

He made a helpless gesture with his hands wide open. "I have responsibilities," he repeated.

"Yeah, like your rich cousin from Bijapur," she tossed back, the sarcasm burning her tongue.

He went still. "What do you know about that?"

She wasn't about to give him an answer. It was clear he wasn't going to lift a finger to legitimize her child. Their child. She owed him nothing. To him the baby was a mere inconvenience to be crushed and discarded like one of his cigarette butts.

So what was she going to do?

Suddenly both panic and despair resurfaced. She had one last chance to make him see reason. She couldn't afford to be self-righteous or derisive. She hated begging, but there was little else she could do.

"Please, Som," she pleaded, softening her stance.

"I can't, Vinita."

"I won't hold you to the marriage. You can get a divorce immediately after the baby comes."

"It's not that simple."

"After the baby's born, you're free to go," she reasoned. "I'll disappear from your life forever. You'll never have to see me or your child again. I'll ask for nothing from you."

He shook his head. "You're so damn intelligent, but you have no clue how the real world works, do you?"

She remained silent. There was truth in what he said. She could do complex mathematical calculations in her mind and memorize complicated formulae, but she was a simpleton when it came to the practical world.

With that realization came the worst sense of defeat—and desperate loneliness. She was going to have to face this alone. She had used up her last chance to reason with Som. And she'd failed.

She gazed outside the window for long minutes while Som maintained his silence behind her. The damn rain just wouldn't stop. She couldn't stop shivering. The cold seemed to have invaded her bones. She longed for a single ray of sunshine. She needed the warmth, the comfort of the sun—for someone, anyone, to tell her this, too, would pass, that things would turn out all right in the end.

Finally she turned around, picked up her umbrella, and slung her handbag over her shoulder. "I guess I'd better get out of here."

"Here's some money to help you out," Som said, pulling out some large-denomination bills from his pocket and holding them out to her. When she didn't take them, he took her hand and pressed the cash into it. "I honestly wish it hadn't ended like this, Vinita. I'm sorry."

Sorry indeed. "God help you when all your sins begin to catch up with you." She placed the bills on the teapoy. "Save your money for your next lover, Mr. Kori."

Then she opened the door and walked out into the rain.

Som shifted to the window and watched Vinita unfurl her umbrella and take measured steps down the narrow walk leading toward the footpath. She was always so careful, so meticulous—with everything. Her back looked rigid and her long braid swung from side to side. Her high-heeled *chappals* made a determined *click-click* on the wet concrete.

She didn't look as though she was carrying a child. She

looked as slender as she always did. But he believed her about the pregnancy. She was too bloody honest to lie about anything.

She continued to walk away steadily, and didn't look back. Not once.

He should have known she'd never take his money. Why was he surprised? She wasn't like those other girls. She had those stupid principles, and she lived by them. How many times had she tried to convince him to change his ways, to give up smoking and excessive amounts of coffee, to apply himself to his studies instead of concentrating entirely on cricket? Even after he'd shrugged off her advice, she'd repeated it—many times.

Damn! Why hadn't he recognized that stubborn trait in her earlier? He could have saved himself a lot of trouble. And her. Come to think of it, she would have been a better match for his idealistic friend Raju than himself.

What was she going to do now? he wondered, the first rumblings of fear beginning to scratch at him. He could only hope she'd come to her senses and get that abortion. She was a sensible girl, analytical to the point of being annoying.

But what if she didn't get that abortion? What if she decided to go to his father with her accusations? That would be the end of Som. Although marrying Vinita was out of the question—his father would rather have his son dead than see him marry a Marathi girl—it would still mean facing Appa's wrath.

Besides, Som didn't love Vinita. He had to admit he had come to respect her. But love? He didn't believe in it. Silly emotions like that were reserved for women.

She'd reached the footpath now. He noticed her hailing a rickshaw and climbing in. The vehicle sputtered down the street and disappeared in seconds.

Turning around, he walked to the sofa and sat down. What was he to do?

He'd never had to face this kind of dilemma before. All the girls he'd been involved with were practical, and protected themselves one way or the other. In spite of that, two of his lovers had become pregnant.

But it had been easy enough to fix the problem. As girls from orthodox families, they had more to lose than he, so they were grateful for his help and discretion. And it had ended there. Always.

So why had it turned out so different this time? Even down to his own sentiments? He'd never felt guilty before. He pulled out a cigarette from his pocket and lit it. Inhaling the fragrant smoke was generally calming—but it provided little comfort now.

He waited till the cigarette was gone. That silly girl was going to stir up trouble. He could feel it creeping up on him, boxing him in. He rose to his feet.

Plucking the money off the table, he thrust it back into his pocket and headed for the door.

Chapter 8

Her world was quickly crumbling around her. She'd never be able to find all the pieces, let alone glue them back together. It was precisely seven weeks since Vinita had walked out of Som Kori's life.

She sat with her hands in her lap now, facing her family like a traitorous soldier at a court-martial. Remorse and fear battled inside her, and nausea threatened to drive her to the bathroom any second.

She'd brought such anguish to her family. She'd have to be reincarnated several times over to do penance for the havoc she'd wreaked on her parents and brother—all the people who'd given her so much. She was indeed a traitor.

Her brother looked as if he was ready to explode from holding all his emotions inside. Vishal was an outgoing and outspoken man, and yet he sat with his lips compressed. The poor chap had hopped on a plane as hastily as he could after he'd been given The News.

A day's growth of stubble on his dark cheeks and chin and his rumpled clothes made him look like a thug. His mustache quivered every now and then, a sure sign of suppressed emotion. His disheveled hair looked like he'd been raking his fingers through it. His normally intelligent eyes had a somewhat dazed look.

"I'm sorry," she murmured once again to no one in particular. "Sorry."

All her contrite words didn't matter. No one seemed to hear

her. Vishal and her parents remained silent as they sat in their respective seats and stared at whatever object each one had picked to focus on.

Vishal had his gaze fixed outside the partly open front door, where the noon sun was burning with blistering intensity, the heat rising in shimmering waves. The rains were finally over, bringing Vinita the warmth she'd been craving for weeks. She had stopped shivering. However, her problem had ballooned. Literally.

Traffic sped along the street as usual, reminding her that despite the dead atmosphere in their home, there was still a world out there, teeming with life.

Her father's balding head was thrown back on the sofa's headrest so he could stare at the rotating ceiling fan, as if it was the most riveting thing he'd seen in a while. Her mother sat beside him like a stone carving, her tear ducts wrung dry from hours of crying. Her swollen eyes were fastened on the family photograph hanging on the wall—as if trying to recall the moment when the sweet, domestic image of a young couple and their two small children was captured on film.

No one had slept the previous night, since Vinita had informed them about her condition right after dinner. After pondering and discarding all the alternatives she could think of: leaving home—she had no place to go; committing suicide—she was too much of a coward to attempt that; having a dangerous second-trimester abortion—her conscience wouldn't let her kill her unborn child—she'd sprung it on her mother as her last resort.

Her belly was already beginning to show in spite of her lack of appetite and the loose *kameezes* she wore and the *chunnis* she draped over them. She had been getting odd, speculative looks from her friends and fellow students in the past few weeks. Notwithstanding their silence, she knew they smelled a rat. They weren't imbeciles. They were aware of her affair with Som.

Nevertheless she'd told them a bald-faced lie—that she was simply gaining weight and needed to go on a diet. Time was running out and she had no one to turn to. Her only option was to confess her sins to her parents and accept their punishment.

Her mother had been eyeing her suspiciously for weeks, grilling her about her lack of appetite, the dark shadows around her eyes, and her midnight trips to the bathroom. Of course Mummy had suspected a serious illness. Apparently she'd even thought of stomach or ovarian cancer, but not this. Never *this*. A decent woman like Sarla Shelke wouldn't dream of it.

Her poor mother's delicate nerves had gone to pieces when Vinita had quietly informed her about her condition. "*Arré Deva!*" she'd gasped. Oh God! "What are you saying?"

Vinita had just stared at the floor. Repeating herself was unnecessary. Her mother had clearly heard every word.

After the shocked intake of breath and a moment of silence, her mother had dragged her husband into the room and made him hear it from Vinita's mouth. It appeared that her mother couldn't believe her own ears and had to have someone else corroborate the facts. "You had better hear this for yourself," Mummy had said to Vinita's father. "I can't make any sense out of it. Maybe you can."

Her father's reaction had stunned Vinita more than her mother's. When she'd braced herself for his wrath, the lectures, and the outraged order to get out of his sight and never darken his door again, she'd received a pained groan and a shake of his head.

All he'd said was, "You got involved with a Kannada boy?" She could read the rest of the question in his eyes: *If you had to disgrace the family, couldn't you at least find some decent Marathi chap who could probably marry you?*

Her father was a staunch Marathi man and had nothing but contempt for Kannada people. Although he had several of them for clients as a show of tolerance, deep down the resentment that was ingrained from the time of his grandfather and father festered. It was a chronic illness that never left the body or the mind, despite all the token lectures and slogans from the politicians.

With the battles between the two cultural blocs escalating

with every passing year, her father's sentiments had turned more bitter. But the worst affront was closer to home. Many of the skirmishes had left his accounting office in town vandalized by the Kannada side. Broken windowpanes, graffiti on the walls, and smashed roof tiles had corroded his trust in the Kannada folks.

The delinquent behavior wasn't one-sided, though. Both groups targeted one another's businesses to vent their bigoted rage and frustrations. But her parents saw only what they wanted to see.

After having expressed his sentiments about her condition, her father's shoulders had slumped, tearing at her heart. What kind of monster was she to do this to him?

Then he'd walked out of her room, picked up the phone, and called Vishal. Their murmured long-distance conversation hadn't lasted more than a minute.

Later, both her parents had settled themselves in the drawing room to wait for Vishal to arrive. He was their source of strength, their future caregiver and decision-maker. He would come to their rescue, come up with a viable solution, tell them how to handle something this incomprehensible. Without him they were helpless.

This was typical behavior on their part. The males in the house would put their heads together and handle it somehow. The women would be expected to go along. Vinita, as the daughter, would have to hang her head and wait for the verdict to be handed down.

She had seated herself in the chair across from the sofa her parents had occupied. During the night, as the three of them had waited in the gloomy semidarkness of the drawing room, it had felt like someone near and dear had died—a house of mourning.

After a while, Vinita had left her brooding parents and retired to her room to rest. But she hadn't slept—not one wink. Their silent, all-night vigil in the drawing room had wrapped itself like a shroud around her.

The need to go to them and talk it out, ask for forgiveness, had almost had her getting out of bed and approaching them a couple of times—but something had stopped her. What could she have said? All the remorse in the world couldn't obliterate the kind of burden she'd placed on them.

And now, Vishal was finally here.

It was broad daylight, and the harshness of it was blinding. What was going through her mother's mind at the moment? she wondered. That it had been a mistake giving birth to a daughter who had brought them so much grief? That she should have thanked her lucky karma for giving her one perfect son like Vishal, and then stopped having children altogether? From her frozen expression it was hard to guess what her mother might be thinking.

The four of them sat in that manner for a while, each one conscious of, and yet oblivious to the others' presence.

Then Vishal rose from his chair. "I'm going to take a bath," he announced, and headed for the bathroom.

His movements seemed to stir Vinita's parents into action—like the buzzer of an alarm clock. Her mother hastened to the kitchen to prepare lunch while her father decided to finally change out of his pajamas.

They ignored Vinita. For all the trouble she'd stirred up, she could very well have been one of those tiny house lizards clinging to the wall. And being ignored hurt more than getting scolded—more than the occasional spanking she'd received as a little girl.

She went to her room and lay down. Rest was impossible for her brain, but at least her tired body could use some help. Despite the hunger pangs, the smell of her mother's *masala bhaath*—spicy vegetable rice—and the favorite accompaniment of buttermilk *kadhi* wafting up the stairs made her get up and close her bedroom door. Even pleasant odors nauseated her lately. And *kadhi* was one of her favorite things—a soup-like dish made of chickpea flour blended with buttermilk, then cooked and seasoned with mustard, chilies, cumin, and curry leaves.

A little later there was a knock on the door. "Vini. Lunch," announced her mother.

"I'm not hungry," Vinita said, burying her face in the pillow.

"But you have to eat something."

"I can't stand eating, Mummy . . . please."

There was a long silence before she heard her mother's footsteps fade away.

As the others ate in the dining room downstairs, she heard their voices, low murmurs mixed in with the faint clunk-clunk of spoons, pots, and plates. It sounded like those three were slowly emerging from their earlier stupor, and they were discussing what to do about the elephant in their midst.

An hour later, there was another knock on her door. This time it was Vishal. "Can you come out? We need to discuss something." His tone was clipped, authoritative—not exactly brotherly.

More than likely they had come to some sort of decision, Vinita concluded. Naturally it wasn't going to be a discussion; it would be a command. Time to face the proverbial music.

She rose from the bed with a weary sigh, used the bathroom, and then headed down to the drawing room. The hollowness in her stomach made her feel light-headed, and she stopped for a moment to regain her equilibrium before facing them. At least the nausea had receded.

They were seated in the exact same spots they'd occupied earlier. Gone was the unshaved, disheveled Vishal from this morning. He looked clean and combed. His wrinkled clothes were replaced by a neat pair of gray trousers and a blue shirt. The family's fearless lion was back in form. And he was ready to spring into action.

Her father, too, was dressed and shaved. He had his arms folded across his middle, his jaw clenched tight. The controlled expression was alarming. As for her mother, she refused to meet Vinita's eyes and kept her gaze downcast. Was she that ashamed of Vinita that she couldn't even bear to look at her anymore?

Vishal waited till Vinita sat down. "I have contacted a friend of mine in Bombay," he said. "He's a doctor, and he has offered to take care of your . . . uh . . . pregnancy." He was clearly having difficulty saying the word.

Vinita absorbed her brother's remarks. So, they had already begun to arrange her life for her. And her opinion didn't matter. But then, she'd known that all along, hadn't she?

"You and I will be leaving for Bombay tomorrow," Vishal informed her.

She looked at him, her heartbeat picking up momentum. He appeared a bit too calm—in control. "What's going to happen to me in Bombay, Vishal?"

"I just told you."

"You said your doctor friend can see me through this ordeal, but what happens afterwards?"

His color drained a bit. He obviously hadn't expected her to question his decision. He'd probably assumed he and their father would find a solution and she'd bow to them—like she'd usually done in the past. But that was then. This was now. Her life had changed. She was no longer a girl. Although still a teenager, she was a woman—a woman with a problem. A small, helpless human being now depended on her.

He cleared his throat. "My friend has contacts. We'll find the child a good home."

Vinita blinked. "You mean . . . give my child away . . . adoption?"

Her shocked query met with complete silence.

She glanced at her parents for their reaction. There was total agreement in their expressions. It looked like the morning's grim silence had been replaced by this take-charge resolve.

Whenever her father was faced with a business problem, he drew up a point-by-point plan, and decided exactly how it would be executed. Now the two men were using the same methodical approach to solve her problem. For some reason the realization brought her a sliver of relief. This was more normal behavior. Last night, when her parents had sat motionless, like glass-eyed dummies in a wax museum, she'd been afraid that one or both of them were going to have a stroke or something.

Nonetheless, this reversal in behavior didn't mean she was happy about it. The first rumblings of anger started to stir inside her. How dare they push her around like a vermin-infested sack of grain!

"But . . . you never even asked me," she fumed. "You just assumed I'd agree to adoption?"

Her father jumped in then, talking to her for the first time in hours. "Your opinion has nothing to do with it. This is a matter of our family's *aabroo*—our honor. We have to do whatever is required to protect it."

Her mother nodded like a windup doll. "Papa is right. The quickest way to settle this is a discreet confinement, then find the child a decent home."

Rage slammed into Vinita like a boxer's fist. "What about *me?* Isn't it *my* body and *my* child?"

"Stop it, Vini!" Vishal threw her a scorching glare. "Don't you see we're trying to protect you from complete disaster?"

"Protect me or your precious *aabroo?*"

"Same thing!" he snapped. "A Hindu girl and her family's reputation are inseparable. We're a respectable family and we have to do everything in our power to protect ourselves."

"Damn right!" agreed her father, giving his son an approving nod.

Vinita's clasped hands tightened in her lap. *Take a calming breath,* she told herself. *Temper and nerves are not good for the baby.* "I care, too."

"And this is how you show it?" sniffed her mother.

Vinita flinched at the hurtful remark. "I've never given you any trouble before. My one and only mistake was falling in love with the wrong man."

"Yeah," chimed in Vishal. "You had an affair with a notorious *mowali,* and now you're . . ." He let the sentence trail off.

"I didn't exactly seek him out, Vishal, if that's what you're insinuating," she protested. "It just . . . happened."

"On top of everything, you're telling us it's too late to abort it."

"I was afraid to tell you earlier." She bit hard on her lip. "I knew you'd react . . . just like you're doing now."

"How else do you expect decent folks to react?" demanded

Vishal, pounding a fist on the chair's arm. "At this late stage, when an abortion is impossible, we have only one option—to get rid of it in the most humane fashion."

Her hands shook. How could Vishal use the word *abortion* so casually? He was being deliberately cruel. "The three of you have no right to get rid of anything, least of all a baby." She put an instinctive hand to her belly.

Her father's brows descended in a tight knot. "You call that rascal's seed a baby?" he asked. "Now look here, Vini, I refuse to tolerate any more nonsense from you. Just listen to me and Vishal and go pack your suitcase. You're leaving for Bombay tomorrow morning."

She stood her ground. "I'll leave for Bombay if that's what you think is best. But I plan to keep my baby. I intend to raise it myself."

"You think this is some kind of Hindi movie type of situation?" Vishal pointed a condescending finger at her. "Let me tell you, unlike the movies, Kori is not going to come riding in on a white horse and make you his bride. He's not going to wear some silly costume and dance because he's going to be a father. There is no happily ever after."

"I know that," Vinita ground out. She knew that fact better than anyone else. She knew exactly what kind of a cockroach Som Kori was.

But her mother reminded her anyway. "You know all this and still you want to hang on to his child?"

"Because I love the child, that's why. It's not the baby's fault that I made a mistake. An innocent baby can't just be given away like secondhand clothing because of its parents' foolishness. And no matter how rotten his or her father is, I care about him, too." Her voice was cracking. There was a lump the size of a tennis ball lodged in her throat.

Before she could say any more, the tears she'd been holding in began to leak out. "I can't give up the baby," she whispered. It was a product of love. At least on her part it was love.

Her attempts to explain only served to fuel her father's fury. "What kind of insane love is that? Love happens when you marry a decent young man picked by us. Until then there is no love."

Drying her eyes with the edge of her *chunni,* Vinita shook her head. "Maybe not, but I've made a mistake; I have to pay for it." If she had to raise her child alone, she'd do it. "Maybe I'll go to some women's shelter," she said, raising her chin. "That way neither you nor any of Palgaum's people have to see me or my child."

She gave them a moment to digest what she'd hurled at them and watched the incredulous looks replace the frustration and fury.

"And how do you propose to raise this illegitimate child?" her father growled.

"I have a brain, Papa. I'm capable of working—"

"With no college degree?"

She took another shaky breath. "Well . . . I'll do whatever it takes to support your grandchild."

Her mother winced. Clearly she had difficulty viewing it as her grandchild. "But you're a child yourself," she said, her voice turning hoarse. "You can't be a mother yet." She was taking this worse than the two men.

"I realize that." Vinita didn't need to be reminded of the fact. "Besides, weren't you married at eighteen and had Vishal at twenty?"

A defensive gleam flashed in her mother's eyes. "I was *married* to your father," she reminded Vinita. "Your Papa was a respectable man, chosen by my parents. He had a good job and was fully capable of supporting a wife and children."

"Damn right!" her father repeated, straightening his shoulders. Men of the Maratha caste were known for their manliness. They came from a proud race of warriors. The famous emperor-conqueror Shivaji was the Marathas' ultimate symbol of greatness.

"I know that," Vinita said to her mother.

"Then why—"

"I also know," Vinita interjected, regaining some of her composure, "it's going to be hard. But if uneducated widows and abandoned women could manage it a hundred years ago, I can do it in the twentieth century."

"That may be easier in Europe and America, where there is not much stigma attached to illegitimacy, but in our culture . . . unthinkable." Her father shook his head at her. "People do not accept such disrespectable things here."

Vinita bit back the retort that sprang to her throat. *Sex is not disrespectable—not when one's heart and soul are in it.* And wasn't it sex that had brought Vishal and her into this world? Why did Indian people behave like making love was some disease to be shunned? After all, India was probably the only country in the world that had an ancient and elaborate instruction manual on sex. And then there were those highly erotic sculptures that adorned prehistoric temples. And yet some individuals went about twisting love and sex into something grotesque and shameful.

"Why are you doing this? How do you expect us to show our faces in this town?" cried her mother. Then she buried her face in her *pallu* and started to sniffle.

"I'm sorry, Mummy," murmured Vinita. She hated seeing her mother cry. She hated the fact that her parents would become objects of ridicule in their cozy social circle.

"Vini, you're not thinking rationally," said Vishal, watching with concern as his mother shed tears of anguish. "I've known that Kori chap since I was in college. He's totally lacking in brains and morals. All he knows is how to play cricket. Even that is for a small-town college. He'll never be a professional cricketer." He wrinkled his long nose. "He has affairs with every willing girl in town, and his father has a long line of mistresses. That entire family is rotten. I'm sure you knew all this?"

"I did." She wasn't proud that she'd fallen for the devil despite knowing what he was. "But I was too weak to resist," she grudgingly admitted for the second time. What did she have to lose at this point? Every humiliating and ugly detail about her affair with Som was out in the open now.

Meanwhile her mother's sniffling continued. Her father patted her hand in his usual awkward fashion. "Shh, Sarla, why are you getting so upset? Vishal and I will deal with this."

Vishal rooted his gaze on Vinita. "It's too late to do anything about it now. We just have to look at the future." He glanced at his wristwatch. "You had better eat something and get some rest. Mummy will help you pack your things later. We have an early-morning flight tomorrow."

"Where will I be staying in Bombay?" she asked, after her mother's tears subsided.

"With me." Vishal sounded unhappy about the prospect. He obviously liked his bachelor life in his small flat. Having a sister around would be a nuisance. "After the baby comes, we'll have to decide how to proceed," he added.

"There's not much to decide." She tossed him a defiant look before rising from the chair. "I want you to know right now that I will not put my child up for adoption. I appreciate everything you're doing for me, but I promise I'll get out of your way soon after the baby is born."

"I said we'll discuss it later," repeated Vishal, holding up an index finger, making it clear the discussion was over. Then he put a hand over his mouth and stifled a yawn. "We all need to get a nap first. No one got any sleep last night."

Rising to her feet to return to her bedroom, she noticed the odd looks that passed between her parents and Vishal. They were clearly disturbed by her decision.

Nonetheless, she needed to be brave. She had to follow her conscience.

Chapter 9

Vishal, clad in white pajamas, tiptoed down the stairs and through the drawing room into the kitchen. His stomach was growling. Turning on the light, he looked around, then picked up a banana from the bunch on the table. He finished it in a minute. Discarding the peel in the wastebasket, he quietly slipped out the back door of his parents' house to catch some fresh air.

Standing on the covered veranda outside the kitchen, he gave his eyes a moment to adjust to the dark. Then he settled himself on the rectangular swing that occupied nearly a third of the veranda. The thick slab of teakwood, suspended from the ceiling by four massive iron chains, was easily large enough to seat six.

It was well past midnight, but he couldn't sleep. After tossing for a while, he'd given up and come out here to find some food and to contemplate.

Gently setting the swing in motion, he stared into the gloomy blackness. The chains were rusty and creaked a little. But its gentle, rhythmic motion was soothing, reminiscent of his growing years. The swing had been in that spot as far back as he could remember.

It was a little over a year since he'd left this house to make a living for himself in Bombay, but this was his home. It was a comfort to sleep in his old bed, in his own room.

His parents had preserved his bedroom and everything in it intact, including some of his favorite boyhood toys, and his medals and certificates won in school and college. There was almost an air of anticipation about the room—it was waiting to be occupied once again. He knew they expected him to come back to live with them, take over his father's business, get married, have a family. It was the old-fashioned way. Being an only son came with certain obligations.

Street sounds were almost nonexistent at this late hour. An occasional car passed by, but mostly it was the muffled rumble of traffic on the highway about half a mile away that he could hear. Palgaum's ubiquitous fog was out there, too—gray, stealthy, damply encircling the house like a serpent.

This was blissfully peaceful when compared with his urban flat, where the streetlights and neon store signs encroached on his nights. And the never-ending traffic outside his window, twenty-four hours a day, assailed his ears. The smell of vehicle exhaust had embedded itself in his nose and lungs.

He closed his eyes and absorbed the stillness, savored the cool air settling over his skin. The temperature was almost chilly compared with the sticky heat of Bombay.

Something stirred in the shrubbery beyond the concrete steps—probably one of the neighbors' cats. Then everything went quiet again.

The distant but shrill whistle of a train pierced the night and his moment of peace. He opened his eyes. It was the overnight express that ran the Bombay–Bangalore route. For years the whistle and the chugging of the train had been a part of their lives. Palgaum Station was just a five-minute stop for the train— a tiny dot on the map.

After his long afternoon nap following that emotional family conference, he wasn't surprised that he was up in the middle of the night, wide awake and hungry, his conflicted mind trying to come to terms with what was happening to his family.

All these years, his had been a normal, stable life, with practical Hindu values so strongly entrenched, he'd hardly noticed it. Until now.

The fragile breeze brought with it the heady scent of *mogra,* the jasmine that grew in abundance in the garden leading off the veranda.

An image of Vini as a little girl, aged eight or nine, came to mind. She used to enjoy plucking the *mogra* in the evenings, when the plump buds blossomed into waxy white flowers at dusk. She'd sit cross-legged on the veranda floor, dressed in a colorful *parkar* and *polka*—ankle-length skirt and matching blouse—with her basket of flowers and a needle and thread. She'd patiently string the flowers into two garlands—one for their mother's hair, and the other to adorn her own tightly woven plaits, infused with coconut oil and secured with ribbons.

But she was no longer an innocent little girl with oil-glossed plaits. She was a woman now. A woman in trouble. What on earth had she been thinking when she'd started an affair with that snake Kori? An intelligent, pleasant girl with her entire life ahead of her should have been wiser than that. Instead she'd been foolish and careless. Undeniably stupid.

The suppressed anger started to simmer and bubble once again. The urge to drag his sister out of bed and give her a thorough scolding was creeping up on him. In fact, that irresponsible little brat deserved a flogging. And yet, the desire to protect her was equally fervent. He had always looked out for her safety. He wasn't about to give up that role now.

Every year, his family observed the Hindu ritual of *bhau beej,* when his sister reverently waved an oil lamp before him, applied a red dot on his forehead, and wished him a long and happy life. In return he gave her a small gift, promised to protect her from evil and hardship. It was time for him to fulfill that sacred oath he'd taken so many times over the years. Vini needed him now more than ever.

Could some of this be his own fault? Had it been a mistake for him to leave his family and go to Bombay to pursue a career? But he couldn't refuse that impossible-to-turn-down job offer from a major corporation. His father had encouraged him to take it, too. Working for one of India's most reputable financial-services giants as a chartered accountant for a year or two would make him more attractive to Palgaum's elite clientele. His dream of turning his father's modest business into a major financial planning company would be more reachable if he learned everything he could from his present employer.

On the other hand, his absence had allowed his sister to go astray, directly into the path of destruction. If he'd been here, he would have discovered Vini's love affair before it could go too far. He would've strangled that worthless bastard Kori, and sent him straight to the sewer, where he belonged. Vishal would have talked some sense into Vini before she could ruin herself. If that hadn't worked, he'd have talked his parents into enrolling her in an out-of-town college, somewhere far from Palgaum.

But it was too late for any of that. Even now his fingers itched to encircle that egomaniac's neck and squeeze until the man's funny golden eyes popped out. Nonetheless, it was wishful thinking. What good would it do, anyway? Any confrontation between himself and the powerful Kori family, which had every government official and politician in their deep pockets, would end up only one way.

Besides, the Kannada-Marathi tensions were already high in this town, and any clash of that sort, however minor, could blow up into a major episode. His father could lose his loyal Kannada clients. His family could even get hurt or killed. He couldn't risk that.

At the moment, he needed to smuggle his sister out of town and keep her out of the public eye for the next few months. His parents were counting on him to accomplish that. It was going to be hard, but in that respect his being in Bombay was a blessing. He didn't know too many people there, not even his neighbors. Big-city life rarely involved friendly relationships with one's neighbors. Nobody would know Vini there.

His nice, comfortable bachelor life would be disrupted. But he'd manage somehow. It was only for a few months.

What really scared him was Vini's health. He knew nothing about caring for an expectant woman. He'd have to ask his mother about that.

As if in response to his silent reflection, the back door opened. His mother's silhouette appeared against the backdrop of the kitchen light. Her hair was an untidy halo around her head.

"Vishal?" she called softly.

"Yes."

"I heard the swing . . . guessed it was you." She spoke in whispers.

"I couldn't sleep," he said, putting both feet firmly on the floor to bring the swing to a stop.

"Me too." She sat down beside him and sniffed. "You ate a banana?"

He smiled. His mother could smell something a mile away. "Hmm."

"If you're hungry, I'll make something for you." She started to stand.

He caught her wrist and forced her to sit back down. "You don't have to feed me constantly."

She reluctantly settled back on the swing. They sat in uneasy silence for several minutes.

He inhaled deeply the humid, *mogra*-scented air. "Our Vini is going from teenager to mother," he said, gingerly introducing the subject that was uppermost in both their minds. *Unwed* mother, he corrected himself.

His mother sighed. "I haven't slept since Vini dropped the bomb on us."

"I know." Vini's crisis certainly qualified as a bomb. He was still reeling from the explosion.

"What are we going to do, Vishal?" His mother's face was turned toward him. With only a faint glimmer of light coming through the partly open kitchen door, he couldn't see much of her face, but the concern in her voice was as clear as daylight. "How can something so horrible happen to us?"

"Papa and I will take care of it," he replied, with more certainty than he felt.

"I am so relieved you are here. Your father seems more like his normal self now."

"This is very upsetting for him."

"I thought he was going to have a heart attack. Never seen him like that. I expected him to get angry, but he became very quiet after he heard the news."

"It had to be the shock," Vishal offered.

"And when he remained like that all night, I was so scared."

"I know," he repeated. He angled one foot on the cold slate floor and propelled the swing into gentle motion again. "I'll take her to Bombay . . . make sure she stays out of trouble."

"How?"

"I'll keep Kori away from her."

"That's not what I'm worried about. Kori wants nothing to do with her or the child." She touched his arm. "This doctor friend of yours. Is he reliable?"

"Very," he assured her. "His name is Ram Gupte. He and I used to be classmates in the first two years of college, but we lost touch after he went off to medical college."

"How come I never heard of him . . . or his family?"

"His father was in the army," he explained. "So they were in Palgaum for only a short while."

"So you don't know this chap all that well." She sounded dubious. "Will he keep a secret?"

"Oh yes. He's a reputable doctor affiliated with Bombay Hospital. When I explained everything to him earlier, he understood."

"But still . . ."

"He assured me he handles other cases like this—girls from respectable families getting into trouble."

She paused for a minute. "But Bombay Hospital is such a big, public hospital. Someone we know could easily see Vini there—"

"They won't," he interrupted. "Ram has his own office. He apparently treats all such . . . unusual cases there. He says his staff is very discreet."

"But I still worry about her future. If she insists on keeping the child, it will ruin her." She paused. "And us."

"I'll talk to her. She'll be staying with me for the next few months, so we'll have a chance to discuss it."

"She will not listen to you."

"She will," he said with all the conviction he could muster. "I'll convince her."

"I don't think so, Vishal."

He gave himself a second to respond. "Don't you trust me, Mummy?"

"Of course I trust you," she snapped. "But this is different. She's not herself." His mother sighed long and loud once again. "I don't know what is wrong with her. Why is she being so obstinate?"

"I don't know," he said in frustration. "Maybe it's her condition. What do I know about pregnant women?"

"Well, *I* do!" Sarla stopped the swing and rose to her feet. "It is probably best if I come to Bombay during the delivery, don't you think?"

"Absolutely! I know nothing about childbirth. She's going to need you there." *I'm going to need you.* The idea of having to see his sister through childbirth made him shudder.

"I will fly out there for a few weeks when her time comes," she said in a flat, resigned tone. "Go to bed, Vishal."

"I will, in a few minutes. You go ahead." He watched her open the door and step inside. She looked like she'd aged by a decade within the last few hours. Her petite body looked almost frail. And yet she was quite young, only in her forties. He called out to her. "Mummy."

"Hmm?" She turned around to face him.

"How are you and Papa going to explain Vini's sudden disappearance?"

"Papa thinks we should say she got a special scholarship to study at some college in Bombay."

He rolled his eyes. "Nobody is going to believe it."

She nodded. "I told him that. They'll wonder why we didn't brag about it before."

"I agree."

"I think we should say she was recently diagnosed with some kind of tumor or something and is receiving treatment in Mumbai." She paused for a beat. "At least people will understand why we kept it a secret."

Vishal stroked his mustache, considering her viewpoint. "I don't know about that, either."

"No?"

"But it sounds more believable than a scholarship, I suppose." Palgaum didn't offer many medical options, and lots of people who could afford better health care went either north to Bombay or south to Bangalore for specialized treatment. It wasn't unheard of.

"We'll have to think of something soon." She sounded exhausted, dejected.

"And we will," he said. "We will, Mummy."

She closed the door and disappeared inside the house.

Vishal sat in the stillness of the night for a long time. He wasn't sure if his mother believed him. Heck, he wasn't sure if *he* believed himself. But he'd made a promise to his parents. He'd have to find a way to keep it. It was going to be a difficult road to negotiate.

A long time later, he got to his feet and returned to bed.

He knew what he had to do.

Chapter 10

Sarla immersed herself in making breakfast—spicy omelets made with chopped onions, hot green chilies, and coriander leaves.

Cooking was like an old friend—warm, comforting, always ready to listen in silence. Whenever she was troubled about something, she liked to stand at her Burshane gas stove and cook. Besides, a good breakfast would fill her children's bellies and keep them going until their flight reached Bombay and they could get to Vishal's flat.

She gazed out on the awakening dawn through the open back door while the omelets sizzled and filled the kitchen with the aroma of eggs and onions cooking. The night's fog still hadn't lifted completely. Dew sat heavily on the bushes. The swing that she and Vishal had shared the previous night stood still on the veranda.

Vini used to love that swing. Because of its size it had been a big attraction for the neighborhood children. A half dozen of them could huddle together on it at the same time.

Years ago, Vini and her little friends had sat on it for hours, whispering, giggling. They would abandon the swing only when the sun started to go down and the mosquitoes would drive them indoors. Even now, Vini used it often, gliding gently while she studied for her exams or listened to her favorite Vividh Bharati music program on the transistor radio. On chilly winter mornings, she sat with a woolen blanket wrapped around her.

Picturing an innocent, young Vini on that swing, wiggling her tiny toes and singing Hindi movie songs along with the radio in a high-pitched voice, was enough to make Sarla sigh and turn her attention back to the stove. The tears came despite her efforts to stem the tide.

In the course of a single day, everything in Sarla's near-perfect life had gone upside down. It wasn't exactly perfect, but then whose life was? Her son was working so far away from home. Her brother and sisters and their families were scattered and she rarely saw them.

Her blood pressure, too, was a little on the high side lately, so she had been asked by the doctor to eat less salt. "How can anyone eat food without salt?" she'd asked him.

"I didn't say eliminate it. Just eat less," he'd told her gruffly. "You don't want to have a stroke or heart attack, do you?"

It was hard to curb the salt, but she was trying to use less of it in her cooking, mainly because she didn't want to die early like her father, who had died of a paralytic stroke while he was still quite young. He had had high blood pressure, too.

She hadn't been able to sleep at all the previous night, even after Vishal had assured her he'd take care of everything. Bhalchandra, or Bhal, as everyone called her husband, was finally snoring after a restless night, so to allow him his rest she'd slid out of bed as quietly as she could and headed for the kitchen.

Soon they'd all be up and bustling to get Vishal and Vini to the airport. She wiped her damp eyes with the edge of her sari. From now on she'd be alone in the house during the day. Not that it was any different in these last several years, since Bhal's business had expanded and he worked late hours in his office, six days a week, and the children were in school or college most of the day.

Since Vishal had left home for Bombay, at least her daughter had been around to talk to. Daughters were usually more attached to the parents, too.

Most evenings, while Vini studied, Sarla did her cooking or worked on her embroidery. While they waited for Bhal to come home to a family dinner, their silent companionship was pleasant.

Now, all of a sudden, Vini was leaving, too. And under such a black cloud of scandal and misfortune. Why, Lord? When things were going so well for her daughter, when she was the brightest student in her class, and had such a promising future, why had the silly girl gone in search of trouble? In some two years she would have had a degree and she could have married a nice young man and had a good marriage—and a career, too.

Even though Vini had somehow ended up committing a youthful indiscretion, why hadn't she confided in them earlier? Things could have been fixed—to some extent, anyway.

Now her chances for both a career and a marriage were reduced to nothing. Who would marry a girl with a horrible reputation? And an illegitimate child on top of that? The whole world would find out . . . sooner or later. Their town was notorious for vicious gossip.

If the ladies at the Palgaum Club, especially Vandana and Girija, discovered the truth, the news would travel faster than the rockets the Americans and Russians were shooting into space. And how was Sarla going to face her friends over the next high tea? How was she going to explain such a shameful thing to those smirking women who were jealous because Sarla's children were so intelligent and earned such high marks in class—so much higher than their sons and daughters?

And then there were the servants. They would start asking questions about Vini. Thank goodness the washerwoman didn't start work until late morning. Vini and Vishal would be long gone by then. But seeing Vini and most of her personal belongings missing, Sulu was certain to get curious. Later in the evening, the man who helped clean the house and Bhal's office would show up. He was much more withdrawn than the washerwoman, but he, too, would surely wonder where Vini was.

As soon as Bhal woke up, she'd have to take him and Vishal aside and decide what explanation they were going to offer for Vini's sudden and long absence. They had better come up with a credible one.

All this plotting and lying was giving her a headache. Oh Lord, what a lifelong burden. How was she going to survive the scandal? She could only pray that Bhal's business didn't suffer as a result of this. What if his conservative clients decided to take their business elsewhere? There was no shortage of tax preparers in Palgaum.

The omelet was turning brown on the bottom, so she quickly flipped it over and let it cook on the other side. Bhal disliked burnt food.

As the dawn sky began to lighten and turn a light shade of coral, she sliced the bread, slathered the slices with her freshly churned butter, and toasted them on the cast-iron *tava*. The tea was brewing in a stainless-steel pot.

Hearing footsteps, she turned around and saw Vini standing on the threshold. "You're up early," she said to her daughter, noticing how listless and exhausted she looked. The girl probably hadn't slept in days.

"Couldn't sleep," said Vini, stepping inside.

Now that she knew about her daughter's condition, Sarla eyed her for a moment, then looked away. A slight bump showed quite clearly through Vini's long cotton gown. Why hadn't she noticed that before today? Was she so blind that she hadn't seen something that was as clear as that sun blooming over the horizon?

She had always assumed she and her daughter were close, that there were no secrets between them. But Vini had obviously been harboring a huge secret for months. Was she afraid to confide in her own mother? She had to be, to have concealed so much. Did Vini's friends know what was going on? If yes, how much of this had already spread through college gossip?

Even if Vini had hidden the truth, wasn't a mother supposed to know every little thing about her own child? It wasn't as if there were no signs. Vini had been eating very little, studying less and slipping in her class rank, getting irritated for the most trivial reasons, rising in the middle of the night to use the bathroom, and spending several evenings a week away from home.

With so many things going on right under her nose, Sarla still hadn't guessed the obvious. And for that reason she despised herself more than her errant daughter. A mother was supposed to protect her children, prevent them from making mistakes.

She had failed in her maternal duties.

"Why don't you have some breakfast while it's still hot?" Sarla suggested. The girl needed some nutrition, now more than ever. Despite being in the family way, she'd lost weight in the last few weeks.

"I'm not hungry," she mumbled as usual. "I'll have some tea."

Sarla turned off the burner. "Now listen, Vini. You have to eat something. All this starving is not good." She pointed the spatula at her. "Look at you—thin as a bamboo."

"But I can't help it." Vinita sank into the nearest chair. "The thought of food nauseates me."

Sarla bit back a remark. Why hadn't she suspected morning sickness all these weeks when Vini had wrinkled her nose at breakfast? "Tell me what you feel like eating and I'll make it for you. Starving only makes the nausea worse. Too much acid in the stomach."

Vini rolled her eyes.

"I know what I'm talking about," Sarla said with an irritated frown. "I had the same thing when I was carrying Vishal. But eating a little dry bread usually helped."

With another eye roll, Vinita agreed. "All right, I'll have a slice of dry bread with my tea."

"No more tea for you," Sarla informed her. "You should drink milk."

"Ugh . . . I don't like milk."

"I can add a little tea to flavor a hot cup of milk."

"All right," Vinita grumbled, and slid lower into the chair. She let her eyelids drop and tilted her head back to rest it atop the backrest.

While the milk warmed in a pan, Sarla observed her daughter, the curve of her arched neck, the slight tilt at the tip of her nose. She was such a good girl, or had been . . . until now. Sarla had considered herself blessed because she had a decent husband, bright children . . . until now. God had been good to them . . . until now.

But try as she may, she couldn't withdraw herself from her own flesh and blood. Vini was still her daughter, no matter what she'd done. Sarla would have to try harder to get past the anger and disappointment and think of ways to face the bleak future. And bleak it would be, no doubt. Marriage was out of the question, so Vini's only option would be to study hard and make a good career for herself.

Using a towel to lift the heated pan, Sarla poured the milk into a cup, then stirred a little of the brewed tea and sugar into it. Putting a slice of bread on a plate, she placed both before Vini. "Try to eat a little."

Vini opened her eyes and looked up at her, holding her gaze for a long time. And for the first time Sarla saw the anguish in her daughter's eyes, churning like a storm-driven sea. Everything the girl hadn't told her seemed to be lodged there. All her secrets were in the dark orbs glistening with unshed tears—the shame, the pain, the guilt, the remorse.

Her child had made a horrible mistake. And she was suffering.

Instinctively Sarla raised her hands and cradled Vini's face in them. The cheekbones and jaws felt small and fragile. Her baby was in so much pain, and could not undo the damage she'd done to herself.

In the next instant Vini's arms wrapped themselves around her waist, her face buried in Sarla's chest. "I'm s-sorry, Mummy." The sobs that racked the girl's pitifully thin body were convulsive.

Sarla held her daughter and shed silent tears of grief, helpless to do anything beyond offering the comfort of her arms and a steady hand on the back.

Chapter 11

Bombay—1977

As one more contraction crested, Vinita couldn't hold back a groan. She'd never known such torture in her whole life.

"Take a deep breath." Her mother pressed a cold towel dipped in water to Vinita's forehead. "It will be over soon," she soothed.

"God," Vinita responded, coughing hard. She grabbed her chest till the coughing ceased. Then she collapsed deeper into the mattress as the contraction slowly subsided. Too slowly. In seconds it would come again . . . with a vengeance. This had been going on for some seven hours. She didn't know which was worse, the coughing fits or the labor pains. They seemed to coincide with each other.

The baby had not yet turned, and was breech, according to the doctor. They were waiting to see if the fetus would turn itself. Sometimes that happened spontaneously, she was told. The middle-aged nurse, Jaya, or Jaya-bai as everyone respectfully addressed her, had been rubbing her belly every now and then in the hopes that the baby would shift. But so far the child hadn't budged.

Her mother smoothed the hair away from Vinita's face. "You were a breech baby also, but somehow they massaged my stomach and coaxed you into turning."

Vinita remained silent. She had no energy left to converse

with her mother. She knew her fever was high. The coughing fits and the tightness deep inside her chest left her gasping for breath. Her eyes and throat burned. She hadn't had anything to eat or drink in several hours. Being in labor meant she couldn't have food. All she had were small sips of ice water. The hunger left her weak and shaking.

"Why are you being so stubborn?" her mother scolded. "Why didn't you take the medicine when the doctor prescribed it last week? You wouldn't have become so sick."

"It would have affected the baby." Her mother was referring to the antibiotic she'd refused. The baby's well-being came first, even if she herself was deathly ill. She had read somewhere that antibiotics taken by the mother could adversely affect her unborn child.

"If the mother becomes so sick, don't you think *that* is going to affect the baby?"

She didn't need to be reminded of that. It was something Vinita had been thinking about in the past couple of hours, when the contractions had gone from three minutes apart to two, and then one.

But no matter how acute the suffering, she was glad she had not aborted the baby. He'd been kicking with all his might for the past several weeks, reminding her that he was a human being, with all the rights he was entitled to.

She knew it was a boy. He had to be. He was an athlete's son. He'd grow up to be a cricketer one day—maybe even play on India's national team. What if he were to do that when his wretched father couldn't make it past his insignificant small-town team? Wouldn't that be something to rub in Som Kori's smug face?

Her mother blew out a frustrated sigh. "Then why don't you at least let them do a caesarean section now? You are too sick for this."

"I don't want an operation . . . Mummy," she insisted.

"You can't even breathe. You want to die giving birth or what?"

Vinita knew her mother was somewhat right. In the very last

week of pregnancy, she'd contracted something that resembled the flu. Then it had abruptly turned into pneumonia.

Another agonizing contraction started to build up and she held her breath, waiting for the pain to engulf her.

She had been waiting a long time for this—four months of living with Vishal in his flat.

All the noisy urban crowds and the traffic and pollution pressing on the outside of the tall building had not curbed the loneliness she'd felt deep in her bones. Listening to the mix of sounds outside their flat each day while Vishal was at work was like being shut inside a self-imposed prison. She hadn't stepped out of the flat other than to visit the doctor.

She had reminisced about sitting in a cramped classroom, surrounded by her classmates—something she hadn't given much thought to at the time, during her carefree days in Palgaum. College was good. Even studying for exams had appeared much more attractive than watching the world go by while her belly grew bigger and her chances for any kind of a life seemed to diminish steadily.

Such big dreams she'd had about a career, independence, a life away from her family—with just enough space to accommodate them when she chose to do so. She loved them, but didn't want them to strangle her with their conservative ways.

Several times, she'd wondered if perhaps abortion would have been the best solution. Then immediately she'd discarded the notion. She couldn't have done it. Never.

She'd thought about Prema, her parents, her other friends, and mostly about Som. Did he ever wonder what happened to her? Was he the least bit curious about whether his child was going to be aborted like he wanted, or if it lived? He hadn't even asked when her due date was. Were there other children in the world fathered by him? If so, how old were they? Had their mothers kept them or given them up for adoption?

A hacking cough hauled her back into the present moment. And the wrenching pain.

It was another half hour before the doctor showed up again. He was busy delivering other babies and treating other patients.

But Vishal hadn't lied when he'd said Dr. Ram Gupte was a kind and caring man. He was all that and more. Not once had he made her feel dirty for carrying an illegitimate child or asked her any questions about the baby's father. Ram had large brown eyes that seemed to see beyond the patient's face. He was a gifted doctor.

Ram checked her chart and shook his head. "Listen to me, Vinita," he said with infinite patience. "Your fever is too high and your breathing is extremely labored. And the baby hasn't moved. We have to do a C-section." This was the second time he'd repeated it in two hours.

"Can't we give it a few more minutes?" begged Vinita. Her skin felt like it was on fire and she felt her strength ebbing with every minute. Each breath was harder in coming.

But the thought of a major operation was even more alarming than giving birth. Surgery was so extreme. They'd cut open her abdomen and lift the baby out. She hated blood and gore. She'd heard ghastly stories of serious postoperative infections. And the baby. What if something went terribly wrong when they were administering the anesthesia?

The doctor shook his head. "The baby could suffocate and die inside, you know. It's been trying to come out for a long time, but it can't. And you don't have the strength to push." He let his words sink in. "You could die."

She pondered silently for a few seconds. Maybe she and her baby would die together. If that happened, it would serve Som Kori right. He'd have that on his conscience for the rest of his life and many lives afterwards. If he had a sense of right and wrong, that is. But her own conscience wouldn't allow her to let her baby die. She contemplated for a moment.

"Okay, then, let's do it," she murmured finally, and closed her eyes. "But I want to see Vishal first."

Jaya-bai hurried out and brought Vishal in. Her brother had been waiting outside for hours, probably pacing the length of the small waiting room all that time and driving himself insane. She hadn't given much thought to what he might be going through.

"What's the matter?" Vishal looked alarmed as he rushed to her bed. "Why aren't you allowing Ram to perform the operation?"

She braced herself for the next contraction and nearly screamed when it gripped her. As her face scrunched in agony, she managed to notice Vishal's expression. Pure panic. The poor chap was even more scared of all this than she.

A minute later, when she could think rationally, she looked at her mother and brother by turns. "Vishal, I want you to promise me something." It would be Vishal and her father who'd make the decision, so it wasn't worth including her mother in her request. Mummy would go with whatever the men decided.

"What?"

She moistened her parched lips with her tongue. "If I die—"

"You won't die!" he said, cutting her off. He turned to the doctor. "Tell her, Ram. Tell her she won't die."

The doctor adjusted his glasses. "It is major surgery. And Vinita has an infection." Perhaps seeing Vishal's terrified expression, he patted the air with both hands. "Don't . . . jump to conclusions. We perform them quite frequently—and our success rate is very high."

Vinita noticed his answer didn't exactly diminish Vishal's concerns. And it left her with little hope, too. "Vishal," she said, "I want you to take care of my baby if I die."

Her brother thrust his hands in his pant pockets and raised his face to stare at the ceiling—for a long time. Meanwhile, another contraction came and went.

She couldn't see his expression, but she knew he was hit hard by what she'd said. He'd been very gentle with her these past few months, more than she deserved. He'd made sure she was comfortable and was seeing the doctor regularly and eating well. She hadn't expected that from an old-fashioned brother who was so dead set against her decision to have her child.

It was several seconds before he lowered his gaze to her, by which time he had his stern mask in place. "I'll do my best."

"You promise?"

He nodded.

She reached out and grasped his wrist. "Make sure you keep him away from Som."

He nodded again. His eyes met Ram's and Jaya-bai's across her bed and the three of them exchanged a glance.

In the next instant, Ram and Jaya-bai were lifting her onto a gurney and wheeling her away into surgery. Too fatigued to think anymore, she sank back and let them take her wherever they pleased. Ram's clinic was small, so the ride was brief. Even through closed eyelids she could tell when the gurney came to be placed under bright lights.

She wasn't sure if it was the fever that made her hallucinate or the pinprick she felt in her arm as they hooked her up to the anesthesia that immediately started dulling the pain, but she could have sworn she saw a baby above her. It was a tiny infant, bald, naked, floating just beneath the ceiling. She saw the hazy image briefly, wanted to reach out and touch it. But her hands and arms felt like lead, impossible to lift.

Then everything went still and dark.

Chapter 12

Bombay—1982

The toddler squirmed and wailed at the top of his lungs. "Shh, *chhup, beta*," his mother said, shushing him. She managed to hold him tight against her chest despite his loud protests. If she let the little devil have his freedom, he'd be sure to run into the oncoming traffic.

Standing in the winding bus-stop queue, Vinita watched the young mother in front of her trying desperately to bring her toddler under control. The little boy looked about three years old.

He was quite adorable, despite the large quantity of scented oil his mother had slapped over his curly hair. He had a runny nose and a suspicious-looking wet stain on his shorts.

Vinita stared at the boy for a long time, until the red and white city bus arrived and picked up its passengers. As she climbed in, or rather got shoved into the bus along with the thick mass of fellow commuters, she somehow lost sight of the boy and his mother. But such was the nature of public transportation in a large metropolis.

Bombay was a harbor city that attracted the richest and the poorest of folks. It was India's equivalent of a cross between Hollywood and New York City, where movie stars and business tycoons lived in their high-rise palaces in perfect harmony alongside the shanty dwellers. No one begrudged the other their lifestyle.

In typical Indian fashion, everyone accepted their lot in life as their destiny. One's previous lives dictated what one ended up with in the present one. The rich moved around in their chauffeured imported cars while some drove their own vehicles, and the vast majority, like Vinita, used public transportation. The city had its own distinct rhythm.

Sandwiched on the narrow seat, between a large, sweaty woman and an elderly man, she craned her neck to catch one more glimpse of the boy. She heard his voice somewhere in the front of the bus, still protesting loudly about being confined. For some strange reason she had the urge to make eye contact with him, touch his smooth, coffee-colored face and watch his reaction—see if it would bring a smile to his lips.

Her son would probably have looked somewhat like that imp. If he had lived. But her baby never had the chance. The familiar tears pricked her eyes. She blinked them away. It wouldn't do to cry inside a bus filled with people.

It was her fault that her child had come into the world dead. She had refused antibiotics when the pneumonia struck, then she'd put off the surgery for hours, long after the doctor had recommended it. In her misguided effort to avoid hurting the baby, she'd done the very opposite: she'd taken away the only chance he'd had of coming out alive. She had more or less strangled him all on her own.

Waking up from the anesthesia and discovering that her baby was gone was the most devastating thing she'd ever had to face. After nearly nine months of protecting that child, she'd lost him. She'd blacked out immediately upon hearing the news. That hazy image of an infant floating near the ceiling while she was being prepped for surgery had been her son. She was convinced of that. It was her dead son's soul that was up there, saying good-bye to her.

She hadn't even had a chance to see him. Allegedly it was a miracle that she herself had survived. The severe infection combined with the trauma of surgery had nearly killed her. By the time she had woken up and become aware of her surroundings, the baby had been long dead and cremated by her family.

She'd grieved for her son for a long time. For a while she'd even sunk into a depression. But then, with Vishal's goading and her own will to survive, she'd gradually pulled herself together, and gone back to finishing up college and getting her bachelor's degree in statistics.

As Vishal reminded her occasionally, having no child was a blessing in disguise. She wasn't sure she agreed, but what could she have offered her son as a single, teenage mother? It would have been a struggle for both her and him. But she still missed her son, still grieved and prayed for his tiny soul. What would he have looked like? Every time she saw a toddler boy, she wondered about him.

Attending a college in Bombay instead of returning to Palgaum had been a wise decision, too. It had been her bossy brother's decision, but staying with him and attending a local institution had been the best balm for her battered spirit. It was far from Palgaum. And from all the ugly gossip her disappearance had spawned. And Som.

She never wanted to lay eyes on that horrible man again. She'd finally recognized that what she'd considered love was nothing but a serious case of lust mixed with hero worship. She'd been in love with the idea of being in love.

For their friends and extended family, her parents had made up some story about a malignant tumor in Vinita's abdomen. She had supposedly needed surgery and specialized treatment in a hospital in Bombay. At the moment she was allegedly in remission. But she was continuing to live in Bombay at the suggestion of her doctor—in case of a relapse.

She doubted if anyone believed that ridiculous story, but her parents were convinced it had worked. Maybe it had. But the result was that she was permanently branded as a cancer patient. On the rare occasions that she was surrounded by family, she had to put up with the pitying looks and the clucking from aunts, uncles, grandparents, and cousins. She was referred to as *bicharee* Vini. Poor Vini.

In some ways, the arrangement had worked for her, though. She had graduated at the top of her class from a large and reputable university. And now she was working as an actuary at an insurance company. She'd been promoted lately, too. She had a nice career going for herself, something she might not have had if she'd returned to Shivraj College. A year or two more and she would have enough money saved to move into her own flat. She could almost taste the tangy sweetness of that independence she'd craved for so long.

Getting off the bus at her usual stop, she took a deep breath. It had been stifling inside that bus, the air filled with the mingled odors of sweat, *attar* or perfume, cigarette smoke, and diesel fumes.

She walked carefully along the footpath to avoid the street hawkers selling their gaudy shirts, footwear, plastic knick-knacks, and kitchenware before reaching the building where she and Vishal lived. Exiting the lift on the fifth floor, she pulled out her key and approached their flat, located halfway down the long corridor.

Hearing voices coming from inside the flat, she stopped to listen. It sounded like Vishal had arrived home before her. And he had company. This was most unusual. He generally worked much later than she. She always came home to an empty flat.

Curious, she tried the doorknob, and it turned. She let herself in. And stopped short.

"Mummy!" Vinita stood still. Apparently she'd interrupted a conversation between Vishal and her mother. Vishal was in mid-sentence when she'd walked in.

Vinita hadn't seen her mother in several months. But now here she was, sitting on the maroon sofa in their small flat, holding a teacup like it was the most natural thing in the world.

Sarla's pink-and-blue print nylon sari was neatly draped over her lap and her hair looked like it had been recently combed and pulled back in its usual bun. The coat of powder on her face and the red dot on her forehead looked fresh, too. It all pointed to the fact that she'd been here a while—long enough to freshen up—and brew a pot of tea.

"What are you doing here?" Vinita asked bluntly, her gaze bouncing between her mother and Vishal.

Vishal sat in the chair across from the sofa, serenely sipping his tea. "Mummy's come for a visit, Vini."

Obviously. But why hadn't Vinita been told about it? Their mother had never before arrived here unexpectedly. In the rare event that she came to attend a family wedding or something of that nature, Vinita usually knew about the visit weeks in advance.

"It was unexpected," explained her mother. She didn't rise to hug Vinita or anything. Instead she patted the seat beside her, as if this was a daily routine for them. "Come, sit, Vini. Have some tea. I made a cup for you." There was an empty cup beside the teapot on the wooden tray sitting on the coffee table.

Despite her mother's obvious attempts at making it seem cozy and relaxed, Vinita could sense the mild undercurrent of tension in the room. This wasn't a casual visit. Her mother was here for a reason. And Vishal knew about it. He had clearly left work early and fetched their mother from the airport. He was still in his office attire—white shirt, tie, and black dress pants.

The vibrations of conspiracy were palpable between those two.

Nonetheless, Vinita discarded her sandals near the door and walked barefoot to the sofa, pretending indifference. "You didn't answer my question, Mummy," she reminded gently.

It was over five years since the day her mother had discovered Vinita's pregnancy, and yet the aloofness between the two of them lingered. Her mother had dutifully come down to Bombay and seen Vinita through childbirth. She'd waited on Vinita with unexpected tenderness during her convalescence, encouraging her to stay in bed, seeing to her every need.

But the minute Vinita had begun to recover, her mother had hastened back to Palgaum. Although the two of them had been cooped up together in the small flat for three weeks following Vinita's delivery, they'd never had any meaningful conversations. It wasn't all her mother's fault, though. Vinita had been so depressed, she'd shut everyone out of her life—especially her mother.

More recently, Vinita and Vishal had gone home to Palgaum together for Diwali, the holy festival of lights. The visit had felt wooden and uncomfortable, and she'd had very little conversation with her parents. Vishal, on the other hand, had managed to keep the conversation going, pretending everything was as it should be. He was a good talker. And a diplomat when necessary. Someday he'd make an outstanding businessman.

After all these years, well after Vinita had picked up the pieces of her life and settled into a good career, the disappointment and condescension in her mother's eyes remained to some extent. Even now, it was as if an invisible wall stood between the two of them, a wall crumbling in places, but never torn down and discarded. Both of them seemed to stumble over the fragments, not quite able to touch each other.

Her mother stared at the floor for a second before replying. "I had to come because there is a marriage proposal for you. It came up rather suddenly."

Vinita sat down on the sofa and smoothed the pleats on her sari. She needed a second to absorb the information. "I see," she said. That explained why Mummy was here. Vinita glanced at her brother. "You knew about this?"

"Only since yesterday, when the boy's family confirmed that he wanted to meet you," he admitted. "Like Mummy said, it was unexpected. Mummy was lucky she could get a seat on the plane at the last minute."

"Why isn't Papa here, then?"

"One of his major clients is being audited by the revenue fellows tomorrow," her mother offered. "Tax problems."

"Ah." She knew all about the dreaded income-tax authorities and their audits. But that didn't matter. At the moment, she wanted to know more about this bride viewing her mother had made the journey to Bombay for. "Who's the chap coming to view me this time?" She arched a cynical eyebrow. "Is he blind, lame, or an ex-convict?" Or worse, a tired old man with no job, no libido, and no teeth.

"None of those," answered Vishal, sounding annoyed.

"Then he probably has very little education and works in the

rice fields somewhere?" She couldn't help the bitterness in her
voice. Every time her family found her a match, he was considered suitable for "a girl like her." She was tired of hearing it. She
could very well be wearing a sign across her chest announcing
her "non-virgin and sullied" status.

Her relatives, who allegedly didn't know about her pregnancy and thought she was a cancer survivor, also considered
her not very marriageable material. So they, too, suggested the
most undesirable men for her—the discards. A sickly and pathetic woman like her, a *bicharee*, had to be grateful to have a
husband. Any kind of husband.

"No," answered Vishal to her caustic query. "He lives in
America. He's a mechanical engineer with a good job."

Vinita's eyes went wide for an instant. She waited, watching
her mother pour tea into the empty cup. There had to be a
catch. Educated male engineers with good careers were prized in
their society, and even more so if they lived in the U.S. When no
other information came forth, she looked at Vishal. "So what's
wrong with this fellow?"

"Nothing. He's a respectable chap, according to Kedar-
mama," he said, referring to their mother's brother, who lived in
Baroda.

Vinita nearly smiled. Respectable was a neat little term that
encompassed any number of perceived virtues, but also covered
up a lot of flaws. At least three *respectable* men had been proposed for her in the past eighteen months. All three men had
had serious handicaps. One was a recovering alcoholic; another
had a degenerative eye disorder that was slowly making him
blind; the third was a widower with a Down syndrome child
who needed a nursemaid-cum-mother.

But it was ironic that all three men had considered themselves
highly eligible. After Vinita had talked frankly to them about
her past, they'd disappeared—never to be heard from again.

Not that she cared all that much. She was glad to be rid of
those men. Besides, she was content with her single status—for
now. Unlike many women her age, she was becoming financially
self-sufficient. She didn't need a husband.

She accepted her cup of tea and took a sip. It was tepid. "So when do I get to meet this *respectable* man?"

"Soon." Vishal pointed a warning finger at her. "And don't you spoil it this time."

She blinked. "What do you mean?"

"Why do you insist on telling every eligible man you meet about your . . . episode in college?"

"I prefer to be honest." She quickly gulped the remaining tea and put her cup down. "Don't want any complications later."

"They don't need to know all that," her mother piped in. "If you keep telling them such things, nobody will marry you."

Vinita shrugged. "Then I guess I'll have to remain single."

"Stop talking such nonsense," scolded her mother. "What kind of woman wants to be a spinster all her life?"

"A woman like me?" Vinita couldn't help needling her mother. Mummy could be so annoyingly self-righteous sometimes.

"Vini!" Vishal fumed. "We're sick and tired of your defeatist attitude. You're a perfectly intelligent girl, but you insist on ruining your chances every time you're introduced to an eligible man."

"I can't help my past," Vinita said, raising both her hands in a helpless gesture. But she sometimes wondered if she did indeed do it unconsciously to punish herself for her sins. "Besides, tell me exactly which one of those three men you picked for me was eligible."

Vishal had the decency to avert his eyes. "I didn't know much about those men. They were recommended by my friends and colleagues."

"Yeah, men perfectly suited for a girl like *me*," she threw back at him.

"I'm sorry. But seriously, can't you keep your past to yourself? It's between us—family."

"Everyone in Palgaum knows about my affair and my pregn—"

"No, they don't." Her mother cut her off. The word *pregnancy* still seemed to stick in Sarla's throat. The term was not used in genteel circles. "Everybody thinks you had a serious health condition and now you're . . . cured."

"It's a lie."

Vishal slammed a big fist into the arm of his chair. "That's enough! When you meet this man tomorrow, you had better be on your best behavior. You are not to tell him anything beyond your education and your job, you hear?"

She glared at him. "Is that an order, Mr. Shelke?"

He sighed, long and loud.

"Okay, I'll try," she conceded grudgingly. So she was to meet the man tomorrow. It wasn't much advance notice. "But what if he's looking for a pretty girl?" This fellow was an engineer from America, probably full of himself and convinced that he was a great catch in the marriage market.

"Put on some makeup. Go to a beauty salon or something." Vishal waved away her feminine concerns with the typical nonchalance of a man.

As if it were that simple. A trip to the beauty salon could only do so much for an average woman. Only a miracle would make her pretty.

"And I brought a nice turquoise *bandhani* sari for you to wear when you meet him. Blue is a good color for you." Her mother was already on her feet, heading for the bedroom, probably to retrieve the sari from her suitcase. She most likely had a matching blouse and petticoat made by their tailor, too.

Vinita watched her mother's back disappear into the bedroom. Some things never changed. A bride viewing, even in Vinita's case, had to be treated with the care and respect it deserved. Protocol demanded a quality silk sari with appropriate accessories, just enough makeup for attractiveness without garishness, and proper demeanor with subdued voice and downcast eyes.

Seeing no way to escape the plan that was already in motion, Vinita sank back against the sofa cushion and folded her arms across her chest. Different day. Different man. Different attire. Same damn agenda.

As always, her parents and brother had decided what she should do. When and how, too.

Now more than ever they were desperate to get her married, or *settled* as they preferred to call it. If her baby had been born alive, there would have been no question of marriage. But since there wasn't a child to worry about, they wanted her to forget her past and get on with her life. That way they could forget it, too, and get on with their own lives.

Besides, as long as she hung like a stale garland of wilted flowers around their necks, it would be hard to find a good wife for Vishal.

A single dark deed was akin to a deadly virus. It ended up contaminating the whole family, especially the sinner's unmarried siblings and cousins. And she didn't want to ruin Vishal's life along with her own. Another thing to remember was that despite her bitter feelings toward them at times, her family meant well. They cared about her. That much she knew for sure.

Well, she'd met three men in recent months. So what was one more? "Should I assume this fellow and his parents are coming to our flat tomorrow?" she asked Vishal. It was always like that—entire families arriving to see the girl put on display. They'd all gawk at her and ask silly questions.

"No parents this time. They live in Baroda," Vishal replied. "His older sister and he are coming here tomorrow evening to have tea with us. She and her husband are local Bombayites."

Something still bothered Vinita. "You still haven't told me anything about him. What's his name?"

"Girish Patil."

"Hmm." A nice, wholesome name with a solid ring to it. Leaning forward, she fixed her eyes on Vishal. "What's the catch? And don't tell me he's *respectable*. Mummy and Papa and you don't think I'm worthy of a truly respectable man. Everyone you've brought to my attention has had some problem or other. I want to know everything about this Patil fellow."

Vishal's gaze wavered. "He's divorced."

"Aha!" That explained it. Some of it, anyway.

"He was married to an American woman. They were divorced two years ago."

The truth was slowly coming out. "Why?"

"How should I know?" Vishal gave a shrug and rose to his feet. He stacked the empty cups and teapot on the tray. "All I know is what our uncle told Mummy and Papa. Girish Patil is the nephew of Kedar-mama's insurance agent."

"Hmm," she grunted again. One of those complicated threads that ran through the fabric of their vast matrimonial network. It also meant Patil was an unknown—a man who lived halfway across the globe. He could be a wife beater . . . or an alcoholic . . . just about anything. Her eyes followed her brother to the kitchen. "Does he have children?"

"No," he replied. She heard the sound of the cups and teapot being placed in the sink.

"Thank goodness," she murmured to herself.

Other than the divorce, the man sounded like a better prospect than the others she'd met so far. Much better.

So why were her feminine instincts whispering that her mother and brother were hiding something from her?

Chapter 13

Girish Patil was not perfect. Far from it. She could clearly see now what it was her family had been keeping from her.

Fidgeting with the tassels on the edge of her *pallu,* the long end of the sari that swept over the left shoulder and draped over the back, Vinita managed to steal a few hasty peeks at the man who was here for the bride viewing.

He had a longish face, with high cheekbones. He wasn't bad looking, but he could have used a few more strands of hair along the receding hairline. He was dressed conservatively in neat gray trousers and a blue and white checked shirt. Behind his gold-rimmed glasses he had dark, intelligent eyes.

What startled her was his right hand, which he extended to Vishal for a handshake. The index and middle fingers were missing. Not entirely missing; they were short stumps.

She glanced at Vishal. He didn't seem surprised at all. So Vishal knew about it. And he'd chosen not to mention it to her. She brushed aside the brief flash of anger for the moment. She'd confront Vishal later.

Then Girish Patil pressed his hands together to wish Vinita and her mother a respectful *namaste.* Vinita returned the gesture, but her eyes remained glued to his hand. When he caught her staring, she looked away quickly, hot embarrassment rising into her face.

Things weren't going all that well, despite her family's efforts to make the occasion pleasant. Her mother had slogged away in the kitchen making *kheema samosas*—deep-fried turnovers stuffed with spicy minced meat. They had come out perfect—plump and crunchy and golden.

Vishal had brought home a variety of colorful *mithai*—sweet-meats. The usual Hindu hospitality was on full display—the ingratiating, bride-viewing kind. Laughing at the guests' jokes, attempting to impress them with the best china cups and teapot, and pressing food and drink on them were mandatory on such occasions.

Patil's sister, Mrs. Rohini Sitole, dressed in an elegant Venkatgiri sari, was trying her best to smile a lot and not ask too many questions. Her husband, Kishore Sitole, was a general surgeon, and a man of few words. He seemed disinterested in Vinita and the purpose of their visit, but appeared to be captivated by the *samosas* and tea, which of course thrilled her mother.

In spite of the camaraderie, the occasion felt forced and unnatural. Vishal and her mother were trying too hard to please.

But then, this was hardly a standard bride viewing with a never-married man coming to meet a blushing virgin. He was a divorced man and she was . . . a used item. He had two missing fingers, a fact she couldn't ignore. She was allegedly a cancer survivor, something *he* couldn't ignore.

She had to admit Girish Patil seemed like a civilized man, much more polite and well-spoken than the other chaps she'd met. He seemed at ease in their home, too. Of course, underneath that veneer a nasty personality could be lurking, but the overall image was that of a gentleman. He apologized profusely for arriving late, a mere five minutes, and later thanked her mother for serving what he called *superb* Indian tea.

Living in America for some years was probably responsible for his outward gloss.

He asked Vinita a few questions about her education and career. She answered with caution. Vishal was sitting across from her, the warning spark in his eyes as bright as a traffic light. She would have liked to talk to Patil alone and tell him the truth. She disliked deception of any kind, especially after the lesson she'd learned from hiding her affair with Som from her family.

She'd paid a steep price for lying to them. To this day, her fractured relationship with her parents showed the fault lines.

She didn't want to make that same mistake again.

As the awkward evening came to an end, she didn't quite feel the familiar sense of relief settle over her. This time she hadn't told the truth to this man. He had probably mistaken her for a nice Marathi girl from an old-fashioned family.

As the guests got ready to leave, Girish Patil did something odd—and unexpected. He motioned to Vishal to step outside into the corridor with him. "Vishal, may I please talk to you alone for a moment?" he asked.

Vishal looked flustered for an instant before he nodded. "Certainly."

The two men walked out the front door. Vinita noticed they were about the same height, except Patil looked older and stouter than Vishal.

None of the other men had asked to have a private conversation with Vishal or her parents. This time, since her father wasn't here, Vishal was taking on the role of responsible male.

While the men talked in whispers outside the door, Rohini Sitole chatted with her mother, and Kishore Sitole gazed out the window. A minute later, the two men returned. It was a very brief conversation. Vishal frowned slightly while Patil's expression remained unchanged. It was hard to tell what had transpired.

Had Patil rejected her right away? Well, what was one more rejection? It stung a little, but she was getting used to it.

Once again, her eyes remained fixed on his right hand when he said his *namastes* to them.

As soon as the door closed on their guests, Vishal turned to Vinita. "He wants to see you alone."

A spark of electricity buzzed through Vinita. How interesting! That's exactly what she wanted, too. This business of family meeting family, and everyone watching everyone else with hawks' eyes was stifling.

"What?" Her mother looked scandalized.

Vishal stroked his chin, like he was trying to make sense of it himself. "He says he'd prefer to talk to her alone. He asked for my permission to take her out to dinner tomorrow night."

"What did you tell him?" demanded Sarla.

"I said yes. He'll pick her up at seven-thirty tomorrow," Vishal replied. "He seems like a decent fellow, Mummy. I'm sure Vini will be safe."

"It's not her safety I'm concerned about."

Thanks a lot. Vinita scowled at her mother. "Then what exactly are you concerned about?"

"What will people say? A single girl going out with a stranger? Does he think this is America, asking a girl for a date?"

Vinita gave a cynical chuckle. "I'm not the average single girl." She wasn't exactly a *girl*, either. She was a little past her prime by their strict standards. "I'd like a chance to talk to him."

"Don't be silly," admonished Sarla.

Surprisingly, Vishal was the one who backed her up. "Mummy, let her go." But he issued Vinita another stern warning. "Don't say one unnecessary word. Don't ruin your one good chance, you hear?"

With great reluctance Vinita nodded. But she didn't make a verbal promise.

Later, as she looked at herself in the mirror, she wondered what the man from America had seen in her. The beauty salon had done a creditable job with her face. The makeup was just right. It had enhanced her more appealing features while downplaying the unattractive ones. Her plucked eyebrows looked shapely enough, and the sari her mother had picked out for her was an excellent choice.

It could be the man liked the way she looked. On the other hand, he could very well be getting ready to inform her that he wasn't interested. Maybe that's how they let a person down in America—quietly and privately. If that's what it was, then she had to give him credit for showing sensitivity and discretion—something the other men had lacked.

She folded the sari into a neat rectangle and put it on a

hanger along with the blouse and petticoat, and hung it in her steel *almirah* with the mirrored doors. Then she examined all her other saris hanging in a row. What should she wear for tomorrow's dinner appointment? Or should she call it a date? Although she'd had dinner in restaurants a few times with Som, those occasions hadn't been dates. They were clandestine meetings, constantly plagued by the threat of being discovered.

This was different. A sophisticated man from the U.S. was taking her to dinner—with her brother's knowledge and blessings. She had to look her best. And dignified. She had to make sure she didn't make a fool of herself, even if he was going to tell her she wasn't right for him.

What did one talk about on a date? She knew nothing about baseball, or American fashions, or anything else about the culture, other than what she'd seen in Hollywood movies and read in books.

How did one behave with a man who was used to foreign ways? She had noticed his accent and choice of words—an odd but interesting combination of Indian and American.

As she made her decision about which sari she'd wear, the image of his peculiar right hand flickered in her mind. Was it okay to ask him about it, or would it be considered offensive? And then there was his divorce. She couldn't be sure if it was proper to question him about that. As far as her knowledge went, asking about someone's age and their salary was considered impolite. But goodness knew what rules of etiquette they had about discussing divorce. And missing digits.

Nonetheless, she had a right to know about his past and present. It was always considered a man's prerogative to ask questions about a potential wife, so why couldn't a woman have the same privilege? On the other hand, he had an equal right to know about her past. It didn't matter what Vishal or her parents said. She would tell him. It was the right thing to do.

If he rejected her because of that, she'd have only herself to blame.

Chapter 14

Girish Patil arrived at precisely 7:30 p.m. And he was dressed like a college professor: crisp tan pants, white shirt, and a navy jacket. It was a wonder he wasn't perspiring in it. His scholarly expression, too, was that of an educator. The only thing out of place was the footwear—*chappals* instead of shoes. That was the only concession to his Indianness and to the sweltering Bombay weather.

Vinita had been dressed and ready for nearly fifteen minutes. She knew the salmon pink nylon sari with a dainty, white print suited her well. Worn with her pearl pendant and matching earrings, it looked dressy without being gaudy.

Accustomed to the casual "Indian Standard Time," Patil's prompt arrival was a pleasant surprise. That kind of punctuality was admirable.

Despite her earlier resistance, Vinita's mother was cordial to the man who was taking her daughter out to dinner. "Nice to see you again, Girish," she greeted him.

"Likewise, Mrs. Shelke," he said with a smile and a *namaste*. "Hope you don't mind if I whisk your daughter away for the evening?"

"That's . . . okay," Sarla replied, her wary eyes darting to Vinita and then back to him. She was probably dying to find out where he was taking her. But she dare not ask.

"Vinita and I need to talk," he explained, perhaps because he noticed her mother's hesitation. "In private."

"I understand."

Vinita quashed the urge to smile at her mother's blatant lie. Vishal hadn't returned home from work yet, so it was her mother who had to play friendly host to this man who could, by some twist of fate, end up being her son-in-law. Vinita didn't see that possibility, once she'd finished telling him about her past—but her mother had to try nevertheless. A potential *jaavayi* held a special place in a Hindu household. A son-in-law was to be honored.

"I'll bring her back by ten o'clock," he promised.

"Thank you," her mother said with a tight smile, all the while taking in every inch of his appearance. "Have a nice . . . dinner."

Stepping out of the lift, Vinita and Girish got out of the building and onto the crowded footpath.

He stopped for a beat and faced her. "You look lovely," he said, taking her by surprise.

She knew she looked her best, but lovely was pushing it. "Thanks." She searched his face for signs of hidden amusement. There were none. He appeared serious and honest. Like a professor.

They started moving again. It was awkward walking beside a strange man. She couldn't help recalling trotting beside the tall and swaggering Som. She'd felt like a dwarf next to him, always hurrying to keep pace with his long strides.

This man was a bit shorter, heavier, older. But he was close enough for her to smell his soap and aftershave, or deodorant, or whatever it was that smelled like fresh breezes and *tulsi*. Basil.

He seemed at ease with himself and the situation. After all, he had dated an American woman, courted her, then married her. He walked with deliberate slowness, obviously taking smaller steps so she could keep pace. It was considerate of him.

She wondered where they were going. Amidst the bustling crowds of pedestrians, it wasn't easy to walk side by side, so he fell a step behind her at times, then caught up again. On one occasion, he put a steadying hand beneath her elbow when her high heels stumbled over the uneven concrete blocks of the footpath.

"Is there a particular type of cuisine you like?" he asked after a minute or two of aimless strolling. "I'm trying to come up with a suitable restaurant where we can eat."

She shrugged. "I'm not fussy, Mr. Patil. Whatever you pick will be okay."

"*Mister* Patil?" he said on an amused note. "Do I look *that* old?"

"No . . . you don't . . . but you know how it is." She didn't want to offend him, but what else was she supposed to call him? He was a stranger to her.

"I know how it is," he assured her. "I was only kidding. Having lived in the U.S. for over nine years, I tend to forget certain Indian customs." His lips curved in a smile. "But please, call me Girish."

"Okay." She felt her taut shoulders loosen up a bit.

"Do you mind Chinese food? I haven't had Indian-style Chinese in years, since most Chinese restaurants in the U.S. are Americanized. I've been craving some pungent, spicy food."

"I like Chinese," she replied. "There's a good place not far from here. It's called Ming." She wondered if it was proper etiquette for the woman to suggest restaurants. Wasn't it usually the men who picked the location for a date? She had to stop thinking of this as a date.

"Excellent!" he said, putting her mind at ease. "Walking distance, or should I hail a cab?"

"Walking distance." She was glad of it, too. Sitting beside a man she hardly knew in the hot, cramped seat of a taxi wasn't something she wanted to do. With the windows down, the wind always whipped her hair into a mass of tangles and that wouldn't do at all on an occasion like this. Besides, her mother was already worried about her going out with a strange man. A taxi would feel a bit too intimate.

And the good thing was that Ming wasn't too expensive. She didn't want him to spend a lot of money on her—especially after he discovered her secret and realized she was all wrong for him.

The popular eatery was overcrowded as usual, but after a brief wait they managed to get a small table amidst the hustle and bustle of Bombay's more fashionable restaurant patrons. Eating Chinese food was the mark of a sophisticated palate.

The first thing Girish asked the waiter was whether they served wine.

The waiter looked him over briefly, as if to assess his ability to pay for an expensive alcoholic drink. He must have liked what he saw, and noted the slightly American accent. He nodded. "Yes, sir, Golconda wine."

"Golconda, huh? Is it a sweet or dry variety?"

The waiter had no clue. He scratched his head and frowned. Perhaps no one had ever asked him such a question.

"Sounds interesting, anyway," Girish said, and raised a brow at her. "Would you care to have a glass?"

She shrugged. "I've never had wine before."

"Guess what? I've never had anything called Golconda, either. Perhaps this is a chance to try our first glass of Indian wine." When she nodded, he ordered two glasses of it.

Why not try some wine, she thought, with a mild spark of excitement. She'd heard a lot about it from her colleagues, about how wonderful it tasted, but since her family didn't drink alcohol, neither did she.

While he held the menu in both hands and studied it carefully, she stole a swift glance at his hand before perusing her own menu. She'd tried hard to keep her eyes away from his hand, but it was impossible. What could have caused him to lose his fingers? Or was he born that way?

After they ordered their egg rolls, chicken soup with sweet corn, and prawns in black bean sauce, they sat back in their chairs to enjoy their wine—served in small water glasses. The restaurant obviously didn't have stem glasses. Vinita gingerly took her very first sip. It burned a little as it trickled down to her stomach. She stifled the impulse to clear her throat.

"Do you like it?" His brows were raised above the rims of his eyeglasses.

She hesitated. "Well, it . . . uh, tastes and smells a bit like cough syrup."

He let out a hearty laugh. "Cough syrup is an appropriate description. It's awfully sweet. I would've preferred something dry and mellow."

She couldn't help grinning back at him. He seemed to think her remark was funny. She didn't know what dry and mellow wine was, so she quietly took another sip. It was slowly beginning to taste better, as the sweetness coated her tongue and the alcohol warmed her throat.

"Tell me about yourself, Vinita," he said, using his right hand to dip a crisp Chinese noodle in the sweet-hot sauce served in a dainty porcelain bowl. He seemed to make efficient use of his thumb and two remaining fingers. With surprising dexterity, too.

"I'm sure you already know all about me," she said, putting the glass down and clasping her hands in her lap. Was this a good time for total disclosure? she speculated.

He crunched on his noodle and swallowed. "You mean that trivial stuff that every young lady's family tells the man she may end up marrying?"

She took another sip of wine. "Trivial stuff?" Exactly how much did he know about her?

"The usual list of things like college degree, extracurricular activities, culinary skills, et cetera, et cetera." He waved if off with his left hand. "I already know you have a great academic background and a promising career."

"You do?" she asked. "You know about my job, too?" How unfair was it that he knew everything about her and she had been told very little about him?

"Most of it," he replied. "Your brother mentioned it to my family. You're a very smart girl . . . with ambition. And an accomplished dancer?"

"Isn't every educated woman at least a little bit ambitious?" she challenged him. Hadn't he deduced that after living in an emancipated country all these years?

"I suppose so." He was silent for a moment. "I'm more interested in what you like to do besides your classical dancing."

"Like what?" What exactly was he fishing for? Was he waiting to see if she'd confess the truth about her past? Was this an integrity litmus test?

"Umm . . . let's see," he said, narrowing his eyes. "What kind of movies and books do you like? Do you enjoy sports? Do you like spicy food or mild? How about travel and the outdoors? You know . . . personal likes and dislikes."

A soft sigh of relief escaped her. "I like mystery and romance novels," she answered, after giving it careful thought. If not an honesty test, then it could be some kind of silly psychological quiz he was using on her—a bride evaluation tool. "I enjoy James Bond movies and Hindi films."

"Ah, yes, James Bond," he said with some relish. Picking up another noodle, he dipped it in sauce. "I went through the addiction phase with Ian Fleming's books. I read so many when I was a student that my mother had to hide them so I could get back to my schoolwork."

He studied her while he chewed on his noodle. "But I have to admit I never read romance." His dark eyes sparkled with amusement. "I leave that to my sister Rohini, the romantic. She's always reading the books with those sexy covers . . . a woman draped over the arm of a muscular man." He demonstrated by leaning to one side, a hand thrown across his brow and a look of mock adoration on his face.

Vinita let out a hoot of laughter at his rather apt display of a romance novel cover, then quickly clamped a hand over her mouth. She'd been shamelessly loud and forward. But he had such a quirky yet pleasant sense of humor. "You should try a good romantic mystery sometime," she suggested. "You might find it interesting."

"Romance and mystery together?" He held up his glass in a toast. "I promise to buy one this week . . . if you'll help me pick one. Let's drink to my first romance book, shall we?"

She picked up her glass and raised it, wondering if he truly meant to buy a book or if he was making fun of her. Anyway, this was her first toast. And the wine was making her bolder. "I also like spicy foods, especially cheap foods sold by vendors on Chowpatty Beach and the footpaths," she confessed.

"Me too," he said in a conspiratorial murmur. "The spicier the better."

"Can you get that in the U.S.?" she whispered on a giggle, trying to keep up with his playful banter. This kind of interaction was new to her.

He shook his head. "There aren't any Indian restaurants where I live. I buy something called hot-pepper sauce in the American supermarkets. I pour it on hamburgers, pizza, steak . . . everything."

Their egg rolls and soup arrived, interrupting him briefly. He sniffed the appetizing aromas and grinned with delight, showing a row of clean white teeth.

He was clearly a nonsmoker, decided Vinita, mentally adding one more check mark in the plus column.

"Smells fantastic," he declared. "Can you tell I'm a typical bachelor who eats all the wrong things?"

"I live with my brother and we don't cook much at home, either." She smiled. "Why do you think I like all that street food?"

He looked at her in a measured fashion. Was he sizing her up as a potential wife, an Indian woman who openly admitted she didn't cook? She felt the warm blood rush to her face under his prolonged scrutiny. She could see him mentally grading her as a failure in the column for cooking.

Probably sensing her discomfort, he pulled his soup bowl closer, blew on a spoonful of steaming liquid and tasted it. "Umm! Good choice of restaurants, Vinita. I haven't had this variety of soup in a long time." Putting his spoon down after a couple of mouthfuls, he switched topics. "Tell me, do you like sports?"

She swallowed some of her soup, giving herself a second to prepare an adequate answer. She had deliberately stayed away from cricket commentaries and anything remotely connected to sports in the past few years. "I'm not all that interested in sports."

"Not even cricket?"

Especially cricket. But she merely shook her head. And thank goodness he didn't push her for an answer. She wasn't quite ready to confess yet. But soon she'd tell him everything. Meanwhile, she wanted to savor her first wine-drinking and toasting experience, her first conversation alone with an intelligent, well-informed man, and then enjoy her delicious Chinese dinner. It was a treat for her. Vishal wasn't very fond of Chinese food, so they hardly ever ate it.

She had to admit the wine was making her feel relaxed and warm. She no longer felt tense and fidgety. In fact, she was pleasantly light-headed, like her feet were not quite on the ground.

"I love tennis myself," he said, reclaiming her attention. "I used to play regularly when I had all my fingers." He flexed his damaged hand. "Now I can't wield a racket anymore." He examined his hand briefly.

She maintained her silence and nibbled on her egg roll, pretending not to notice his hand.

Finishing up the last of his soup, he gave her a candid look. "I'm sure you're curious about my hand, Vinita."

He'd caught her staring at it the previous evening. *I'm dying of curiosity.* But she couldn't admit it. What did one say about a delicate matter like that? She cast a fleeting glance at his hand.

"You have a right to know," he said, reading her mind. "It was an accident involving a hedge trimmer a few years back. I used to work as a mechanical engineer at a manufacturing company. I lectured my staff on the safe use of industrial equipment. I helped write the company's safety manual. But you know what?" he said with a sardonic grunt. "I was too stupid to follow my own safety rules at home."

He stopped for a moment, as if to gather his thoughts. "I lost my fingers from pure carelessness," he said with a rueful sigh, and spread out his hand on the center of the table.

"I'm sorry." She winced at the thought of all that agony. The emotional trauma had likely been devastating to an otherwise healthy man.

But he clearly wanted her to see his deformity, to see that he was not ashamed of it. So she forced herself to look at the hand resting on the table. Both fingers were cut off just above the middle joint. The machine had severed them at an angle.

The unharmed fingers were thick and long, with square fingernails cut short. It probably had been a strong hand at one time—a hand that played tennis, worked with industrial equipment, trimmed hedges. She still couldn't bring herself to stare too long. Slowly she lifted her gaze to meet his across the table. "It must have been awful for you."

"It was," he admitted. "They couldn't reattach them because the nerves were badly damaged." He adjusted his eyeglasses with his good hand. "You know, one doesn't realize how important each little digit is . . . until one doesn't have it anymore."

"Did it take very long to heal?"

"Months and months. But the real healing took much longer. I spent a year in therapy to learn to reuse my hand with sufficient motor control." He folded his arms over the table. "Meanwhile I lost my job because of the accident. My employer couldn't hold my job forever."

"Oh no!"

"And my marriage went straight to hell right after that."

She couldn't help her shocked gasp. It was all beginning to make sense now: the defective hand, the stress in the marriage, the divorce. They were all connected. "Your . . . wife. What happened?" Too late Vinita realized she was prying into his personal life. Now he'd give her a failing grade for tactfulness, too. "I'm sorry. I shouldn't have asked."

"That's all right." He gave her a wry smile. "Nadine's a good woman, but I believe she had difficulty adjusting to being married to a deformed man. I can't blame her for that. And then I lost my job, and things between us just sort of . . . fell apart."

"I'm so sorry," was all Vinita could say, and kept nibbling on her egg roll to give herself something to concentrate on. She didn't know this man, and yet she felt genuine sympathy for him. To lose one's fingers and then one's job—and as if that weren't enough, to lose one's spouse, too. How much more painful could it get? And she'd thought she was the only one who'd had her heart broken. He'd had it much worse. At least she had all her fingers. "So Nadine . . . just left you?"

"Not quite," he explained. "We tried to work it out, but I was bitter and difficult to live with at the time."

"Not entirely your fault, was it?"

"Sadly, much of it was my fault," he said, unafraid to admit the truth. "We constantly bickered. I could see I was making her unhappy, so we eventually made a mutual decision to file for divorce."

"You . . . um . . . didn't have any children?" Vishal had told her there were no children, but she wanted to confirm it.

He shook his head. "Nadine was afraid children might ruin her figure and her career, so we decided to wait a few years before starting a family."

"What a shame." Maybe Vinita was being naïve, but children could hardly be categorized as figure busters.

"Nadine worked as a buyer for an upscale department store chain. Appearance and fashion were important to her career, so I understood." He paused. "Besides, just when we thought we were ready to start a family, my accident and everything else happened." He toyed with his spoon. "But . . . a child would have been nice, I suppose."

"I'm sorry," Vinita said once again. She was beginning to sound like a country bumpkin with a limited vocabulary. Not a good way to impress an educated man.

"Don't be," he advised her. "Children would have meant more complications."

"I know." She bit her tongue the moment she realized what she'd said.

But he didn't seem to notice. He smiled instead. "I do have a decent job now, in case you're wondering."

Oh yes, she had been wondering. "Where do you work?"

"In New Jersey." He finished the last of his egg roll before he spoke again. "I work for a company that makes surgical instruments."

"You like what you do?"

"Very much," he answered, with such enthusiasm that Vinita had no doubt he loved his job. "I work with a very talented group of folks. It's a good place to work."

"You're lucky, then."

"Enough about me," he said abruptly, and pushed aside his

empty blue and white ceramic soup bowl with its matching spoon. "Look, you seem like a nice girl from a well-respected family. So I honestly don't know why your family introduced you to a guy like me."

Vinita watched the waiter deliver their main course and take away the empty soup bowls and appetizer plates. She appreciated Girish Patil's honesty. He had essentially told her everything of importance in his life—his deformity, his divorce, and his present career.

"Why not a guy like you?" she asked.

He gestured to her to help herself to the prawns and vegetables coated with a thick brown sauce that smelled like garlic and ginger. "I'm not like the other Indian-American bachelors, Vinita, the young single guys who come bride hunting to India. I'm thirty-five years old, married once, and divorced." He chuckled.

She couldn't say if his snicker was from humor or bitterness or both. Amongst all the men she'd met so far, and that included Som Kori, Girish Patil came across as the most decent. He was also fun to talk to. However, she'd spent less than two hours with him so far. She'd have to hold her judgment a bit longer.

He was waiting for her reaction, so she said, "I'm not like the other young Indian women, either. I'm almost twenty-five and I...uh...I'm a cancer survivor." Oh dear. It slid off her tongue before she knew what she was saying. She had planned to tell him the truth. But that was before she'd had the wine, and much before she'd heard his life story.

His hand stopped in midair, holding a speared prawn at the end of his fork. "Is that right?" He seemed astonished.

"You didn't know?" She'd assumed he had been told about her condition.

He placed the fork back on his plate. "No."

She could tell from his expression that he was slowly beginning to comprehend why she'd been introduced to him. He kept staring at something or someone beyond her shoulder before he recovered sufficiently and resumed eating. "I'm sorry—about the cancer, I mean."

She shrugged. They were more or less even now. She hadn't been told about his fingers, either. Someone had deliberately kept them both in the dark. She knew who it was, too. "I'm cured for all practical purposes," she informed him.

"What kind of cancer, if I may ask? You don't have to answer if you don't want to."

"Abdominal," she replied. That was another question no one had asked her. But then again, none of those other men had bothered to talk to her privately. "It was a . . . malignant tumor. They removed it before it could spread. I'm in total remission."

"Glad to hear that." He seemed genuinely relieved. "I wish you a long and healthy life." He lifted his wine glass, which was now almost empty, in a salute.

It sounded like a very polite good-bye and good luck, so she merely smiled and accepted his good wishes. Vishal and her mother would be thoroughly disappointed to learn that he'd rejected her despite not knowing her shameful secret. Well, at least she was spared the embarrassment of telling him the truth. She could keep her dignity intact. Her *nice, single Marathi girl* image could remain untarnished.

So he stunned her when he finished the last of his meal and said, "This was very nice. I really enjoyed the evening."

"Thank you." It *was* indeed nice.

"Vinita, would you go out to dinner with me tomorrow night?"

She blinked. "Y-you want to go out with me again—in spite of what I told you?"

"Sure, unless of course you can't stand my company or can't accept me as I am." He narrowed his eyes at her once again. "Cancer's not something to be ashamed of, young lady."

"What about meeting other eligible girls? Didn't your sister arrange more for you?" It was standard practice for Indian men to meet several eligible girls lined up by their respective families before making their choice of a future bride—like going to a shoe store and trying out the inventory for appearance, fit, and potential wear and tear.

"I didn't come to India to seek a new wife," he explained. "I came to visit my family. They were worried about me. They hadn't seen me after my accident and divorce. So I wanted them to see that I've recovered from both, and I'm not bitter or unhappy anymore."

"I see." The situation was a little clearer to her now.

"But then my parents heard about you and suggested I meet you while I visited Rohini and Kishore in Bombay. Meeting you was a decision I made only a couple of days ago."

"You mean the proverbial killing of two birds with one stone?" At least Mummy and Vishal hadn't been lying about the bride viewing coming up at the last minute. It was a relief to know.

"Something like that," he allowed, eyeing her again with that assessing look that made her palms turn damp. "I'm beginning to think it was a good decision."

She clasped and unclasped her hands under the table. He was an unusual man. And so candid. "Okay, then."

"Okay, what?"

"I'll go out with you tomorrow night."

"Excellent. Tonight we ate what *I* like." He leaned across the table to look into her eyes. "Tomorrow we eat what *you* like. How about going to Chowpatty Beach for some spicy street food?"

"I'd like that." Excitement tugged at her brain. Another date.

"Now, would you like some dessert . . . coffee?"

She shook her head. She'd heard about coffee after a meal in America and tea in England, but she knew no one who drank caffeine after dinner. Why would anyone want to deliberately deprive themselves of sleep?

He signaled the waiter to bring their check.

Tomorrow, she reminded herself as they walked out of the restaurant a few minutes later, her feet still feeling like they weren't quite touching the footpath. The wine was still swirling in her bloodstream, making her giddy. Or was it the man who'd bought it for her? Or could it be because he wanted to take her out again?

But tomorrow she would tell him the truth. And then he'd be gone forever.

*   *   *

The next day came, and two more days after that. Girish took her out to a different place for dinner each evening. He always wore quality slacks and starched shirts. It was almost like he was courting her. For a woman who'd been used as a pawn in a mindless and egotistic game, this was a novel experience. He was a pleasant man besides being bright, and it was easy to talk to him about most any subject.

He genuinely seemed to like her company, too. He asked her educated questions about her dancing. Most men knew nothing about Bharat Natyam, but he seemed to be knowledgeable about concepts like *taal, mudra,* and *abhinaya.* Rhythm, hand movements, and facial expressions. Had he read up on such things just to impress her? If so, she was touched by the gesture. Like people who prepared themselves for a job interview, it showed diligence, and respect for the other party.

With each day she liked him a little bit more. When he took her hand in his hard, flawed one so they wouldn't lose each other in the beach crowd the third evening, she felt no more than the rough warmth and strength of it. Surprisingly the missing fingers were not an issue. She tried to imagine that hand touching her, caressing her—and she was convinced it would still feel all right. It was the man that mattered, not his hands.

She was amazed at how normal he was, despite the accident and divorce. He came across as a fighter, and he hadn't allowed his hardships to beat him down, to make him permanently bitter and resentful. His sense of dignity, integrity, and humor appeared to be untouched—a *respectable* man in every sense. But she wasn't quite convinced that she could trust him yet.

On their third date, he talked about his college years and his early student days in the United States, his old job and new job, and everything in between. He even told her more about his failed marriage to Nadine—some painful details he said he'd never revealed to anyone else.

"You have no hard feelings toward Nadine?" she asked him.

"What's the point in holding a grudge?" he replied.

"Hmm." She wondered how a person could be so forgiving.

By comparison, her own festering sentiments for Som seemed petty and vindictive.

Girish showed her photographs of his house in New Jersey. "I know it's modest, small . . . only three bedrooms," he said. "After Nadine and I split our assets, this was all I could afford to buy right away."

"Doesn't look modest at all," she assured him. She found it charming, actually, with its exterior of brick and white siding, and a variety of shrubs planted under the two front windows, which were flanked by black shutters. The house even had two floors, with the bedrooms located upstairs. It didn't look small, either. "Two bathrooms in one house is sheer luxury by Palgaum standards, and an extravagance when compared to Bombay's cramped flats."

Photos of the backyard showed some giant trees with dense foliage. "They're maples and oaks," he explained to her. "Unlike most trees in India, these turn to shades of yellow and red and orange, and they shed their leaves by late fall. They become totally bare. Then they grow the leaves back every spring."

"Is it exciting to see the change in the seasons?" she asked him.

"Yes. It's like watching a miracle unfolding—nature at its most engaging."

She tried to imagine trees covered in shades she'd never seen on leaves. She'd read all about it in books, even seen pictures in magazines of how extreme cold could cause dramatic changes in flora.

He let her gaze at the photographs for a minute. "Do you think you'd like to live in a house like that?"

She blinked at him. She wasn't sure what he was leading up to, but her pulse wobbled a bit. "I don't know," she replied with a shrug.

On the fourth night, after a simple meal of fried fish on the beach, he asked her if she'd consider marrying him. It wasn't a huge surprise; the hints had been building up little by little. It was a humble proposal, almost Victorian in its chasteness and propriety.

"I'm not a good-looking man and I'm several years your senior," he said. "But I can afford to give my future wife and children a decent living. If I'm lucky enough to have children." He took her hand and enclosed it in both of his. They were warm and they trembled a little. "Vinita, would you consider marrying me?"

There were none of the fireworks or heightened excitement that Som had ignited in her with a mere brush of fingers, but there was a quiet strength in Girish Patil she had sensed from the very beginning. He was the kind of man a woman could probably lean on and close her eyes for a long while. And when she opened them, he'd likely still be there, still holding her hand.

Every night, after Girish dropped her home, Vishal asked her if she'd managed to keep her mouth shut. When she answered yes, he'd said, "Good. Keep it that way. This is your one chance for a future."

Her mother, of course, nodded in mute agreement. In fact, Mummy was beginning to smile a lot and was even encouraging Vinita to go out with Girish. She was probably having visions of getting Vinita married quickly and packing her off to a distant foreign country, so their secret could finally be buried. Her mother could concentrate on finding Vishal the perfect wife—a delicious prospect in her maternal eyes.

However, after spending four evenings with Girish, Vinita still hadn't summoned the courage to tell him her secret. Each day, she'd promised herself she'd confess the next day. And she didn't. Was it because she had slowly begun to view America as a place to escape from her past, a place where women enjoyed much more freedom, a place where she could truly begin afresh? Or was it because she saw Girish as a really promising suitor, unlike the others?

Was she losing her courage in the presence of this honest man? He deserved just as much honesty from her, didn't he?

And yet, his forthrightness could be a clever façade. She had just met him. She had heard some grim stories about naïve young women marrying men living in a foreign country because from afar it seemed like an exciting life, only to discover their husbands were lechers, or abusive, or alcoholics. Girish could be any of those things. She couldn't let herself be taken in by his seemingly candid personality. She couldn't let herself become a victim for the second time.

Despite the doubts, she liked him, genuinely appreciated his company. The slow fire he lit in her veins when he looked at her a certain way, or teased, or said something humorous, wasn't her imagination. There was no denying a real spark existed between them.

At the moment, with his proposal hanging in the air, she looked out on the ocean for a long time. What was she to do?

He sat beside her in complete silence and let her have the time to think.

"What about Nadine?" she asked him finally, looking for signs of hidden emotion in his eyes—anything that would indicate his true nature.

"I haven't thought about Nadine in a very long time. We lost touch after the divorce." Seeing the dubious look on her face, he shook his head. "Nadine will never come into my life again. She was the one who wanted out of our marriage more than I."

"But then, I need to . . ." How in heaven's name was she going to introduce the truth to him?

"You're free to pursue a career in America. And your dancing, too," he added, misinterpreting her reasons for faltering. "There are some Indian classical dance schools in New Jersey, by the way."

When she remained silent, he let go of her hand. There was such disappointment in his expression that it squeezed her heart. "I'll understand if you decline, of course," he murmured. "You could find a much more eligible man than me. There are so many—"

"Please, Girish," she interrupted, touching his arm. "Give me one more day."

Part 2

Chapter 15

Palgaum, India—2007

Vishal Shelke swiped his face with a handkerchief. Sitting at the desk of his home office, he could feel the heat coming at him in waves from the nearby window—the humidity typical of late April in Palgaum.

He could also smell the storm brewing. The rumblings of approaching thunder were audible in the distance. That, too, was typical of the town's weather. The heat could only be dispelled by a fierce, cleansing rainstorm.

He rose to his feet and started to pace the length of the long room, wishing he could do something about the storm raging in his mind, in his life. He could smell this one churning, too. It was going to be just as violent and disturbing as the one developing in the sky. He'd tried to work on his computer, but his restless thoughts about his sister had driven him to his feet once again.

Vinita's phone call from New Jersey the other evening was most upsetting. It had been one of the hardest things he'd had to do in all his life—confess that he'd been lying to her for thirty years, lying about the fact that her son was alive. Even worse was giving her the rest of the news. That portion was downright distressing.

Wincing inwardly at the thought of his sister learning the shocking truth about her son in such a crude manner, he stopped pacing and sat in his chair once again. The crickets and mosquitoes were already setting up a racket of chirp and whine since it was turning dark outside.

Other familiar sounds drifted up from the rooms downstairs. At the moment, it was those sounds that kept his mind on an even keel. There was something therapeutic about the humdrum nature of routine.

In the kitchen, his wife Sayee was likely putting the finishing touches to their dinner. Although Anu, the maid, served their meals, Sayee preferred to cook them herself. She didn't trust anyone in that particular area of housekeeping. He could smell the mustard seeds and curry leaves being tempered in oil for the *dal*—the soupy split pea dish served over rice.

His mother was in the *dév-ghar*—the altar room—saying her evening prayers before dinner. He breathed in the scent of her *agarbattis,* the long, thin incense sticks she burned during her *pooja.* Ritualistic worship.

Ah yes, the daily sounds and smells that made up his world. And his family. What would he do without them? The house seemed a bit empty at the moment, though. He missed his twin sons, twenty-one-year-old Aneesh and Anmol. After graduating from college, they were both in Bangalore, taking a one-year certification course in some type of new software.

Neither one of his sons was likely to join his accounting business. That was disappointing. But Sayee had convinced Vishal that it was best to let the boys follow their instincts. Young men and women these days were attracted to the high-tech industry with its promise of lucrative jobs.

At least the boys were together. They were identical, always inseparable—twins in the real sense of the word. They often reminded him of what his sister had lost years ago, when she'd believed her baby boy had been born dead. She was heartbroken. Of that he was sure, although she'd put on a brave front and gone back to college.

But thank goodness Girish Patil had come along at the right time. He had proved to be a decent chap when Vinita needed a man like that in her life to make her forget Kori. Getting his sister married to Girish and sending her off to the States had brought incredible relief to Vishal and his parents. The best part was that she seemed happy in her marriage, her career, and her home.

But now some anonymous letter had brought back that old nightmare for her and the rest of the family. Who could have written it?

He heard someone come up the stairs and stop by his office door. He didn't have to look up to see who it was. He knew those footsteps well. His wife.

"Are you still worrying over the phone call?" she asked him, her round face ripe with concern.

"She's going to hate me," he said, meeting Sayee's questioning gaze. "She'll never forgive me for this."

"She's your sister. She'll get over it."

He gave her a wry smile. "You don't know Vini. She can be very intolerant at times."

"But surely she'll understand something of *this* nature?"

"Uh-uh," he said, shaking his head. His sister was a woman of contradictions—exceptionally bright but naïve in many ways, stubborn at times but compliant at others, caring and loyal but not always forgiving. He loved her, but he'd never understood her. She had secrets that she had never shared with him. Her affair with Kori and the pregnancy were examples of how close-mouthed she could be. She would always remain a puzzle.

But then, he had kept some secrets from her, hadn't he? And now they were coming back to taunt him, dark and ugly.

"Do you think I should phone her?" he said to Sayee.

Dressed in a green sari scattered with white dots, Sayee had her thick, long hair braided and pinned up into a bun. She was a plump woman, never having lost the weight after she'd given birth to the twins over two decades ago. She had a sweet, youthful face, and her eyes twinkled when she smiled. Although she was only four years younger than he, people thought the difference in their ages was greater.

She stepped forward and laid a hand on his. "Why don't you give her another day or two to calm down? Besides, it's Sunday. She'll be busy."

He nodded. Sayee and he had visited Vinita and Girish a few years back and they had observed what active lives Vinita and her family lived. "Their weekends seem to be busier than their weekdays."

"I don't know how Vinita and Girish manage to get any rest or relaxation with so much housework, and full-time jobs."

"But they seem to like the American lifestyle."

"Thank God we have servants here," Sayee murmured. She threw Vishal an encouraging glance. "Come on, let's go downstairs and watch some TV before supper."

Vishal scrubbed his face with his hands. "I have some work to do before I eat."

"I know it's not work that has you worried," she said, reading his mind. "It's Vinita. Don't make yourself sick over it. You did what you had to do."

"But I hurt her. I've lied to her for so many years."

"You were only trying to protect her."

He took the hand his wife offered him. "She won't see it that way. Should Papa and Mummy and I have told her the truth?"

She appeared to turn it over in her mind. "All of you were trying to make sure she had a chance for a future." She pressed his hand. "Besides, you were so young yourself. You were hardly qualified to think like a wise old man."

"But my parents were older, and they thought the same way I did."

"There you go. Even *they* thought it best to let her think the baby was . . . stillborn."

He could see it bothered his wife to use the word *stillborn*—just like it bothered him. Was his wife right? If he had to do it all over again, would he keep the truth from his sister? "But the problem is back, thirty years later," he said. "And it's bad. The boy is apparently dying of cancer."

He dropped Sayee's hand and tented his fingers. What exactly was Vinita going to do, now that she knew the truth? One thing he knew for sure: she was livid. She had every right to be. She had called him a liar—which he was. There was no defense for what he'd done to her.

Maybe she'd never want to speak to him again.

Just then the phone rang, startling him. He picked it up at once, instinct telling him it was Vinita. And it was.

"Vishal, I've been thinking about this," she said, getting straight to the point. "I've decided what to do."

"Is that right?" He had an idea what it might be. And his stomach plunged.

"I'm going to fly down to Palgaum as soon as I can. I want to see my son."

His guess was right. She was being her impulsive and stubborn self, as usual. "What's the point, Vini? The boy doesn't know about your existence. You'll only upset him unnecessarily."

"For heaven's sake, I'm not just coming to *meet* him," she retorted. "I want to see if there's anything I can do to help."

Vishal's grip on the phone tightened. But he chose to remain silent as his sister spoke a while longer. He gave a slow, tired sigh when he finally hung up and looked at Sayee. "She's coming to Palgaum . . . asking for trouble. Again."

Chapter 16

It was an overcast morning. The promise of a soft, soaking spring rain hung like an invisible blanket over the neighborhood. The birds were more subdued in their chirping. Even the tenacious Doris wasn't to be seen in her yard. The only things that looked delighted at the prospect of rain were Doris's newly planted seedlings. They seemed to turn their faces to the sky in anticipation.

Girish stared at Vinita across the round, glass-top breakfast table. "So you didn't trust me enough to tell me the truth?" Although it sounded like a question, it was more of an accusation. Behind the thick glasses there was bleak disappointment in his eyes. He had that wounded look one rarely saw in a man's face. His slice of toast remained untouched on his plate.

Vinita clasped her hands together in her lap and glanced away. It wasn't easy to face him when he looked like his world was crumbling around him. "I'm sorry."

He had returned from his business trip the previous evening: Friday. She'd welcomed him home, fed him a good dinner, and let him have a night's rest before spilling the truth this morning. She'd lain awake all night, debating if she should tell him at all—or if she did, how much of it she should admit.

In the end she'd decided to tell all. There was no way to confess piecemeal to something as corrosive as this. It had to be all or nothing. And it was the hardest thing she'd done in all their years together.

And now she had broken his heart—the stout, candid heart he'd offered her that day on Chowpatty Beach.

"Sorry because you hid the truth, or because it has surfaced after thirty years?" he asked. Bitterness was so uncharacteristic of him. Could one little episode from the past change a man's personality to this extent? This quickly?

She turned his question over in her mind. "Both," she admitted. "But mostly because I'm causing you so much distress."

"Why didn't you tell me this when we first met?" He raked his left hand through the limited hair left on his head. The receding hairline had crept farther back over the years. It made him look older than his age. Arya often teased him about his looks—a cross between Woody Allen and Ben Franklin, albeit a brown-skinned one.

"I wanted to. I truly did," she assured him. "But Vishal and Mummy convinced me that it was best that I didn't."

"Why?"

She switched her gaze to the scene outside the window, watching the clouds thicken as she gathered her thoughts. Once again she opted to tell the whole truth. But putting it in words was the tougher part. "I had already been rejected by three men because I'd told them the truth," she said, swallowing to moisten her throat. "On the other hand, you seemed like a promising match and . . . they didn't want me to blow my chances."

"So I was the perfect imperfect man because of my divorced status and my ugly hand with its missing fingers."

He was being deliberately cruel in his remarks, but she suppressed the need to strike back. He was justified in his cynicism. "Besides, I didn't really know you then," she said instead in her own defense.

Despite having gone out together four times, theirs was still an arranged marriage. In these types of relationships, one didn't get to know the spouse intimately for a long time. And by then it was too late to disclose closely guarded secrets, too late to betray the level of trust earned over a span of so many years, too late to break apart the bond so carefully crafted and nurtured.

Five or ten years after they'd been married, how could she

have suddenly blurted out the truth? *Honey, I have a dirty secret to tell you.* He'd already been hurt by one woman before. She didn't want that to happen to him a second time. It was a matter of protecting both him and herself from pain when she'd kept the truth buried.

But now she was hurting him worse than Nadine ever had. Nadine had never lied to him as far as Vinita knew.

He got to his feet and dumped the uneaten toast into the trash can. Then he picked up his empty teacup and plate and placed them in the sink. "But I told you everything about myself. Wasn't it fair that you did the same?"

"I should have. I realize that now, but each time we met, I didn't know how to bring up the subject. You thought I was a decent girl. You'd have lost respect for me if I had told you about my past. I thought Vishal and my mother's advice made sense." She bit her lip to stop it from quivering. "I felt guilty about it. I still do. It hasn't been easy."

"I bet," he retorted.

"Don't you think I've tortured myself all these years over the secret I've kept from you . . . and Arya?"

"And the scar on your abdomen?"

"That's . . ."

"Is that really from the cancer surgery?"

"I had to have a caesarean because of . . . complications."

His expression changed. "The cancer? Is that a lie, too?"

She met his dismayed gaze, but couldn't hold it for more than an instant.

"So it was." He peeled off his glasses and rubbed his eyes with the heels of his palms, looking worn-out despite a long, restful night. "When I worried that your cancer might come back some day and you might become seriously ill again, you never even had it." He paused, as if searching for a logical explanation. "I even prayed for your health. I didn't want to lose you to cancer."

"Really?" He'd never told her that.

"Every evening, when I said my prayers." He expelled a hollow breath. "You didn't even have the disease."

No, she never had it. And he'd worried over her, prayed for her well-being. How ironic.

He shook his head at her, like he still couldn't accept it. "Did your obstetrician know this when you were expecting Arya?"

"I told him."

"But not me."

"He would have known after my first examination anyway." Seeing his expression, she added, "I made him promise he wouldn't tell you."

"Ah, a coconspirator," Girish said in a mocking whisper.

She winced. Sarcasm was not something she'd ever observed in him. "Girish, please. How many times do I have to apologize for having had an affair when I was a hopelessly naïve teenager? I'm sorry. It was a huge mistake, the worst I've ever made. I'm sorry, okay? I'm so damn sorry!"

"This wasn't a simple love affair that broke up," he reminded her in a tart tone. "That happens to lots of young women and men. But *you* had a *son*."

"A son I thought was dead at birth."

"And he's been alive all these years. Come on, Vini, didn't you think it was a little too convenient that he was gone by the time you woke up? How could a smart woman like you take your family's word when they said he died?"

"That's just it, I wasn't a woman." She picked up her own empty cup and rose to her feet. "I was a young girl, raised in a sheltered environment."

"But even a girl would want to see her child, dead or alive. She'd demand some answers."

Feeling weak in the legs, she sank back into the kitchen chair. "I know it sounds absurd, but you have to believe me. I was suffering from severe pneumonia when I went into labor. I had a burning fever. I couldn't even breathe well, and the baby was breech. I had no strength to help deliver him, so they were forced to perform a C-section. I woke up from the anesthesia for perhaps a minute or two before I blacked out again."

"You didn't ask about your child, then?"

"Of course I did! That was my first and only question. I

wanted to keep him in spite of my family's wish to get rid of him. But I was too sick and helpless at the time. They clearly took advantage of my condition and took matters into their own hands. It was nearly three days before I was capable of having any rational thoughts." She paused because her voice was cracking with emotion. Reliving that scene always brought back the ache.

"They told me he died in the womb," she continued, despite the constriction in her throat, "that he was strangled by his umbilical cord because I waited too long to let them perform the surgery. They had to cremate him while I was nearly comatose." She recalled those hazy days. "I almost died from the trauma myself."

Now that she found herself explaining it to him, it did sound bizarre. How could a mother not know her child was alive and well? Where were her maternal instincts? The same instincts that used to wake her up at night when Arya was a baby and was sick or hurting. Even now, although Arya was an adult with a career and a place of her own, Vini could sense when her child was in trouble. How could she not sense her son's existence in her bones?

"*You* may have been a kid, but I can't believe your family lied. And then they encouraged you to lie, too," he said, turning back to the sink to rinse off his dishes and place them in the dishwasher.

"I'm having difficulty with that myself," she confessed. "They've been lying to me for thirty years."

"So have you," he said in a resigned tone.

"How many times do I have to apologize, Girish?" God, this was getting worse by the second. She'd never, ever seen him behave like he was spoiling for a fight.

He seemed to let her words sink in. "What did Vishal say when you talked to him?"

"Not much. He says he did what he thought was best for me back then."

"What about your mother? Did she have anything to say about this?"

Girish had always held her mother in high regard. Vinita could see that was gone. He'd never feel the same way about any of them.

"I didn't have a chance to speak to her." Vinita rose from her chair again. "I'm sure she'll give me the same explanation. She always went along with Papa and Vishal's decisions."

"You know what?" He stared at something on the counter for a moment. "I'm glad my parents are deceased. They would have been devastated by this."

"You mean they weren't devastated by your divorce?" she asked, tossing him a challenging lift of one eyebrow. She was just as capable of sarcasm as he.

"Of course they were. But the difference is they knew about it right from the start . . . from the time Nadine and I started having problems." He rubbed his face with his hand, like he was trying to get rid of something foul from his skin. "I don't know how I'm going to tell Rohini and Kishore."

"Then don't. I'll tell them myself." Rohini was nice enough, but she was extremely loyal to her brother. Vinita dreaded talking to her about this. Apparently Girish's divorce had given Rohini a really bad case of depression. At least in those days Rohini was young and capable of handling bad news. Now she was in her sixties and had become more rigid in her ways.

"So you've decided you want to go to Palgaum and meet this . . . young man?" There was a quiver in his voice she'd rarely heard before. He hadn't uttered her son's name yet. She had a hard time getting used to it herself, despite practicing it all these days.

"Rohit is dying of leukemia."

"How do you know it's true? All you have is a cryptic, anonymous letter."

"I spoke to Vishal. He introduced himself to Rohit's adoptive parents as his maternal uncle and—"

"Was it a pleasant little shock for them as well?" Girish almost seemed to be enjoying his role of tormentor.

She ignored his barb. "Vishal discussed the issue with them. They confirmed the information contained in the letter. My son has acute myelogenous leukemia. He's on maintenance treatment right now—but he doesn't have long to live."

"I suppose I should feel sorry for him," Girish allowed grudgingly. "But why do you have to go to Palgaum? He supposedly has adoptive parents. It's their job to take care of him."

She noticed him shift away from her as she approached the sink. Already he was putting distance between them.

"I don't know how to explain this," she said with a sigh. "I wasn't there for him when he was born. I need to be there now . . . even though he has parents." And thank God for those parents. At least her son hadn't been thrust into some cold orphanage where children were often treated like vermin.

"What exactly do you expect to do for him?"

"I've thought about nothing but this, for the last several days," she said as she rinsed her cup. "Maybe . . . I can offer my bone marrow or something. At least financial help if nothing else. His treatment must be expensive."

"Do you know what kind of treatment he's getting at the moment?"

"Vishal was very vague. I don't think he knows any details."

"The boy may have already had a bone marrow transplant."

"I doubt it. It's a very costly procedure, as far as I know."

"What about the boy's . . . real father?" Girish hesitated, as if he was having difficulty uttering the words. "Isn't he some fellow from your town?"

"He still lives there, I suppose. But he doesn't know he has a son."

"You lied to him, too?" The expression in Girish's eyes went from pained disappointment to open contempt.

Vinita knew she was fast losing her grip on the only man she'd really loved. She'd never seen him look like this, sound like this, not even during their worst marital spats. "I told him when I found out I was having a baby, but he didn't want to have anything to do with me. I begged him to marry me and then divorce me if he liked, but all he did was offer me money to have an abortion. He didn't care."

"So why *didn't* you have an abortion?"

She glared at him. "How can you say that in such a casual tone, Girish?" He had always wanted a child and Nadine wouldn't give him one. Besides, he doted on Arya. "I may have been a kid myself, but I didn't want to get rid of a baby that easily. I'm no saint, mind you. I was seriously tempted to have an abortion many times, but in the end I couldn't do it."

"An attack of conscience, I suppose?" He started to walk away, his tone tinged with both hopelessness and revulsion.

Quickly drying her hands on her robe, she reached out and put a restraining hand on his arm. "Please, Girish. Try to understand. I need to do this. It's my one chance to meet and make peace with my child." The child she'd inadvertently abandoned so long ago.

Brushing off her hand, he continued into the family room. "I don't understand any of this. I just can't." He started for the staircase. She knew he'd probably go to the study and log on to his computer. It was the one place he found peace—the only place with some semblance of order in a chaotic world.

Unable to stop him, she watched him climb the stairs. He was hurt and angry and confused, and she could do nothing to prevent it or alleviate it. He was dressed in jeans and a faded navy sweatshirt. His belly had grown a couple of sizes since their quiet, simple wedding all those years ago.

But with the two of them, it had never been about physical appearance. Although there was plenty of fire and passion, it had been more about intellect, about heart and soul. Their union was almost spiritual, for lack of a better word.

Despite her sins, God had been generous in bringing a man like Girish into her life.

As director of an engineering group at a midsize corporation, he had a demanding job, often a thankless one. But he always came home to her for serenity, for security, for companionship. He considered her his island of calm in a turbulent sea.

He wasn't the type who bought her gifts or flowers often, but he was a caring husband. He always kissed her good-bye when they both left for work. He discussed his day with her and asked about hers. He offered her suggestions when she had problems at her office. He helped her with the household chores despite his dislike for those tasks.

She'd learned from him that perfection wasn't about having all fingers and toes and a riot of hair on one's head. Perfection wasn't even concurring on everything. In Girish she had found as agreeable a husband as one could hope to find in a rather disagreeable world.

Despite the expected ups and downs, their marriage was a satisfying fusion of Indian and American traditions. But now it looked like she was going to be the iceberg that would sink the stalwart ship Girish had built for the two of them and Arya.

A thirty-year-old secret could easily break up a perfectly good marriage. She couldn't blame him if he wanted nothing to do with her anymore. God, what was she to do? She didn't want to lose him. She couldn't. She had most of her life invested in her marriage. If he'd just give it a little more thought and try to see her point of view, maybe he'd understand why she'd done what she'd done.

Of course, she had the choice of not going to India to meet her son, hoping Girish would eventually get over what he perceived as her duplicity and forgive her. But she couldn't do that, either.

Since she'd received the mystery letter and spoken to Vishal, she hadn't slept much. There were so many unanswered questions. Why had she been lied to? What did her son look like? How had he become so ill? Was it genetic—something he'd inherited from Som's side of the gene pool? Or was it from her side of the family?

The thing she feared most was the boy's death. To survive for thirty years, get a taste of life—and then die? She couldn't let it happen. The mysterious letter writer was right. Modern medicine had come a long way. Maybe there was something they had overlooked, some new therapy that could save her son.

She'd done a little reading on leukemia treatments—specifically bone marrow transplants. If she was a suitable donor, and there was a high likelihood she was, maybe there was some hope.

Her son would live—if Vinita had anything to say about it.

Out of habit she tidied up the kitchen. It was a lovely room with tall cherry cabinets, wide windows that let the sunshine slide in on bright days, glass doors that led to the deck, sleek stainless steel appliances, granite counters, and ivory tile flooring.

The house was something she and Girish had always dreamed of: a roomy four-bedroom colonial in an upscale suburb, where their only child could attend one of the best school systems in the country.

They'd sold the modest home Girish had owned when they'd married. They had moved to West Windsor after Arya had turned six and Vinita had found a job as an accountant. By then, Girish had been promoted to technical manager and later to director.

She looked around her dream kitchen, including the small altar in the corner, where her silver idols of the gods and goddesses were displayed. Perhaps God had been too generous with her in the past few years. Maybe it was time to pay her dues, her punishment for lying about having had cancer. She'd lived the lie for so many years that she'd almost come to believe it herself—that she was in permanent remission. A survivor.

Maybe the lie had now turned into truth—only in a twisted sort of way—by attacking her son.

This was retribution. Everything in life came with a price tag.

The sound of the front door being unlocked and opened jolted her out of her grim ruminations. It had to be Arya. She had called her daughter earlier and asked her to come. Good thing Arya worked and lived within twenty miles of them and could drive over often.

Vinita owed her child an explanation of what was going on. And the sooner, the better.

She put down the cleaning sponge and strode out of the kitchen to meet her. One more hurdle to cross. One more dismayed and betrayed pair of eyes staring at her. One more heart to break. She braced herself for the assault.

"Hi, guys," said Arya in a cheerful voice.

"Hi, sweetie," Vinita said, and stepped into the entry foyer.

Her daughter always brought a smile to Vinita's face. Today the girl wore tight, faded jeans and black boots with heels so high she looked nearly as tall as her father. She resembled him a great deal, but in a dainty and feminine way. Her long hair was twisted into an untidy knot at the top of her head. Her denim jacket was unbuttoned, revealing a hunter green pullover sweater. Her face showed no trace of makeup. She'd clearly left her apartment in a hurry and rushed over.

"I didn't mean to wake you so early on a Saturday," Vinita apologized.

Arya took one look at Vinita's face and closed the space between them. "Mom, what's wrong?"

Vinita caught her in a desperate hug, fighting the tears blinding her. "We have to talk, honey."

Chapter 17

Girish sat with his hands clasped, staring at the computer screen on his desk. The screensaver was a collage of family photographs taken over the years. The graphic designer on his staff who had put together the collage as a gift had made it colorful, whimsical, a work of art. Ordinarily the picture brought a smile to his face, but today it was merely a jumble of images.

How could she! How could the woman he'd loved and trusted for a quarter of a century have lived a lie—and lied to him? How could he have been foolish enough to have trusted her? He'd always prided himself on being a reasonably astute judge of character. It was one of the strengths that had served him well in his career. But it had failed him in the single facet of his life that mattered the most.

For him, it had been love at second sight with Vinita. The first time he'd met her, she had seemed a little standoffish, the flicker of rebellion in her eyes clearly telling him she was not happy about him coming to view her as a potential bride.

At the time, he'd wondered if she was against marriage entirely, or just the fact that he was a divorced man with a deformed hand. Intrigued by her attitude, he had come up with the idea of talking to her alone, finding out more about the real woman behind the aloof façade. Then when he had taken her out to dinner the next evening, he had discovered that she didn't seem to have a problem with either of his handicaps.

That's when he'd come to the conclusion that her mother and

brother had forced her into the bride viewing. He'd had no idea why they had coerced her—or why she was against meeting him.

It hadn't been easy engaging her in conversation at first. She had been cautious, obviously wary of his intentions. He had respected that, even admired her careful way of assessing him while he had assessed her in his own fashion. He was a thorough and guarded man in many ways, and understood another's need to study and probe and weigh and evaluate. They were the mark of an intelligent and analytical mind.

Eventually he had managed to thaw her out. Later that evening, and over the next couple of dates, the more he'd listened to her talk, the more he'd realized that she was indeed a bright, independent woman with a great deal of ambition and tenacity. He'd liked those characteristics in her. Bashful, modest women—the kind many of his fellow Indians considered desirable—held no appeal for him. He liked a straightforward woman with a keen mind.

He had discovered that woman in Vinita. Despite her notion that she was plain, he'd found her to be a beautiful person—both inside and out. He'd fallen in love for the second time in his life. He'd grasped the opportunity with both hands—and tried to make it last this time around.

When Vinita had candidly divulged that she was a cancer survivor, despite the surprise he had come to value her honesty.

Only now he'd found out she hadn't been honest. She had lied—about her cancer, about her past. About everything. She had hurt him in the worst way with her dishonesty. A few white lies were to be expected of everyone. People routinely lied about their age, weight, gray hairs, even on their resumes, but the kind of hoax Vinita had pulled on him didn't fall within the realm of a white lie.

What he couldn't understand was why she hadn't trusted him enough to tell him the truth when they'd been introduced. He wasn't the kind of man who would have held it against her. A mistake made in her teens would not have prevented him from falling in love with Vinita. Hell, he still loved her. And that's what chafed so much. His beloved wife was a liar—and a clever one.

Then there was his daughter—his smart, pretty, and trusting Arya. While he'd been nursing his own hurt feelings, he hadn't been thinking about his daughter's. How was Arya going to face the truth about her mother? How much more devastating would it be for a young girl who thought of Vinita as the ideal Indian wife and mother, whose morality was unquestionable?

He looked around the room—his study. Everything in it had been picked by Vinita—the desk and matching chair, the file cabinet, the thick gray carpeting, the pictures on the walls, and even the desk accessories.

The whole damn house was hers. Every inch of it bore her stamp—Vinita's favorite colors, textures, scents. He loved her so much, and so badly wanted her to have her dream house, that he'd given her complete freedom to decorate it her way. And she'd done a fine job. But now the once-pleasant study seemed to be closing in on him, stifling him.

Throwing his head back against the headrest, he shut his eyes and ordered himself to relax, think rationally. But the tightness in his chest remained. His hands were still clasped tightly.

He was already under a great deal of pressure at work. The threat of losing his job was growing with each passing week. There were rumblings about yet another downsizing. The company's stock had plunged along with the rest of the market, so his retirement fund had shrunk to less than half its former size. Many of his colleagues were just as edgy as he was.

When Vinita had questioned him a few times about his job and its stability, he had brushed it off as nothing to be concerned about. "This, too, shall pass," he'd said to her with faux confidence. He didn't want her worrying about it. Perhaps it *would* pass when the economy righted itself. But more layoffs had been mentioned in passing and Girish had been losing sleep.

And now this. Vinita couldn't have chosen a worse moment to dump this garbage on him. But he had to deal with both the grim realities. Somehow.

As long as he was surrounded by her things, he couldn't think straight. As long as he shared a bed with her, he couldn't come to terms with what had struck him with brute force only hours ago. He needed to get away from the things that constituted their life together if he was to solve this problem logically.

How was he going to handle being married to a woman he couldn't respect anymore? Could he look at her face each and every day and not remember that she'd deceived him? How could he trust anything she said or did in the future?

Then there was that man, the guy who was her son's father. Did she still have feelings for him? Was that another secret she'd kept from him? She'd visited Palgaum a few times since their marriage. She could have visited her former lover during those trips. Hell, she could have been in regular communication with him all these years.

Dear God, was there no end to the speculation about Vinita's deceit? Would he begin to question every little thing about her in the future? Could he really live that way for the rest of his life, constantly suspecting her every word and action?

He wasn't sure. What he needed was to think about it—do something to keep his sanity intact. But to do that he had to put some distance between Vinita and himself. Perhaps he could take a business trip? It would provide a legitimate reason for him to go someplace far from home. He traveled often enough on business, so it wouldn't seem strange. Within a minute, his mind was made up.

Leaning forward toward his computer, he logged on to his office calendar to check his schedule for the next couple of days. He had an important executive meeting on Tuesday morning. Once that was out of the way, he was free to travel on the pretext of checking on the company's West Coast operation. Switching over to his e-mail, he sent a brief message to his secretary, requesting her to make flight and hotel reservations for him.

He would not mention the trip to Vinita. If she could be secretive about her activities, so could he. He didn't owe her any explanations anymore, did he?

Nonetheless, the decision to keep the truth from her didn't make him feel any better.

Chapter 18

"Are you going to be all right, Mom?" Arya asked Vinita for the third time that evening as they stood in the long security-clearance line at Newark Airport.

Arya had driven Vinita to the airport and was waiting to see her off. The poor girl seemed to be obsessing over Vinita's mental condition. Arya had made it clear she wasn't exactly happy about Vinita's decision to rush to Palgaum and offer to help her hitherto unknown son.

"I'll be fine," assured Vinita. She wasn't fine, but she couldn't tell her daughter that. It was bad enough that she'd shocked and scandalized Arya with her tale of unrequited love and mistakes from the past. Telling one's child one's darkest secrets had to be one of the most humiliating and humbling experiences in the world.

But she'd survived. They'd both survived.

Arya shook her head, dubious about Vinita's pat answer. "But Dad and you have hardly talked recently." She was always highly sensitive to her parents' emotions. The most minor argument between Vinita and Girish used to have her crying when she was a child—so much so that Vinita and Girish had often waited until Arya was at school or in bed before they'd settled a difference of opinion.

Now Arya seemed so worried about the palpable tension between them that she had come to stay with them indefinitely—a self-appointed judge and mediator come to reestablish peace. She was an idealistic young lady who liked everyone around her to be happy. Vinita hoped her daughter wouldn't have to learn about reality the hard way. Happiness was only a state of mind, a fleeting and fragile condition that could be shattered in an instant. She prayed daily that Arya would always be content.

"Your dad's upset," explained Vinita in response to Arya's remark. "He has every right to be." Girish had slowly withdrawn into himself since their conversation the previous weekend. Instead of coming to terms with the bitter truth like Vinita had hoped, it seemed as though time had made the situation worse. Instead of healing the wound it had made him internalize the anguish.

Whenever she'd tried to start a conversation to clear the air, he'd been icily polite, distant. In their queen-size bed, he'd slept as far from her as he safely could. It was so contrary to their usual way of snuggling close under the covers. He hadn't touched her since that awful day.

She had watched him become quieter and quieter and, like a turtle, withdraw inside an invisible shell. And what a hard shell it was. All her knocking wasn't producing any results.

On the other hand, Arya, whom she had expected would be dismayed at hearing such staggering news about the mother who often preached morality, had been much more reasonable. Naturally she'd been agape while she had listened to Vinita. Afterwards she had asked a multitude of questions that had embarrassed Vinita. Then Arya had trudged upstairs to her room and stayed there for several hours, making Vinita wonder if she'd alienated her daughter just like she'd done Girish.

But a day later, Arya had calmed down. She had come to accept her mother's bizarre past. However, she'd gone back to her apartment briefly, packed a couple of suitcases, and moved in with them. Things between Vinita and her had settled into the old mother-daughter rhythm.

Arya had become more helpful than usual around the house, too. It could have been out of pity for her mom, or perhaps was her way of showing support. Maybe being born and raised in a tolerant and open culture like the U.S. had made Arya more accepting of character flaws, even in her own mother.

Now Arya studied Vinita carefully while the two of them moved forward a foot at a time in the snaking line of air travelers.

"But Dad's had a few days to recover from it," Arya said, countering Vinita's argument. "Why is he still sulking like a kid? I got over it." She rolled her eyes. "Even fuddy-duddy Rohini-attya got over it."

Vinita wasn't so sure about Rohini. But she didn't want Arya to know about the hurtful things her aunt had said. "It's a different kind of shock for your dad," she offered instead. "He trusted me for so many years."

"It's not like you cheated on him or anything."

"I suppose it could be called cheating, in a way."

"Not revealing a secret isn't cheating, Mom," Arya argued.

"Most Indian men are not very forgiving when it comes to something like this."

"But Dad was married before, and you didn't make a big deal about it."

"That's different."

"Oh, come on . . ." Arya made an impatient gesture with her hand.

"He was honest about it, whereas I concealed my past. I think that's what is hurting him."

Arya was quiet for a minute, seemingly mulling over Vinita's explanation. "So why didn't you tell him when you guys met the first time?" she asked finally.

I wish I had. "I was ashamed of my past, honey." Even now, just talking about it made Vinita's face feel warm with the sheer disgrace of it. "And I liked him. In those days, I wasn't a marketable commodity in the Indian marriage bazaar. I was lucky to meet your dad. He seemed like a decent guy."

"But it's not like you did anything *after* you married him. And you were only a kid when that thing happened."

"A naïve and stupid kid who fancied herself in love with a *lafanga*." Vinita cracked a wry smile at Arya's valiant attempt to defend her. On some level she suspected Arya was trying to convince herself, too. How could a young adult accept the dirty fact that her strictly raised Indian mother had a sexual fling and produced an illegitimate child? It had to be inconceivable. But Arya was trying to be supportive, and Vinita was grateful for her kindness.

They shifted ahead as the line in front of them crawled forward some more. Arya was carrying Vinita's carry-on bag on her shoulder. "But at least you got over that asshole."

Vinita shook her head. "There's a lot more to it than that. I got over that guy a long time ago, way before I met your dad. But I have a son I never knew existed. He's dying from a serious disease."

"I can't stop thinking about it," admitted Arya. "I have a half brother."

"Do you resent him?" Vinita asked. An unexpected sibling would be cause for resentment to anyone, especially an only child who'd had loving, indulgent parents.

Arya shrugged. "I don't really know how I feel about him. I don't think I've absorbed it . . . yet." She stared at the floor, like the answer to the puzzle lay in the speckled design of the floor tiles. "You think I'll ever get to meet him?" she asked, looking at Vinita.

"I doubt it. He probably hates me. I don't know of any adopted children who think fondly of mothers who give them away."

"But you didn't give him away. Vishal-mama and Ajjoba and Ajji did."

"You think Rohit understands that?"

"Maybe not." Arya's eyes clouded up again. "You're sure you want to do this, Mom, donating bone marrow and all that?"

"Uh-huh."

"You hardly know the guy."

"The *guy* is my son," Vinita reminded her gently.

"Could be dangerous for you."

"I'm quite healthy, dear. There's no danger to me. But it's risky for him." Despite what she wanted to do for him, she wasn't sure if she'd be considered a suitable donor. Hers had been an impulsive decision, without talking to her doctor or to anyone in the medical field. Overwhelmed by the discovery that she had a son, and he was dying, she had jumped into it with both feet.

"Are you nervous . . . about meeting him, I mean?" Arya asked with a curious tilt of her head.

"I'm scared stiff," Vinita confessed. She'd been praying that she could at least get there in time to see him—one glimpse of her child. If she could have more than that, she'd be beyond grateful.

As they approached the barrier beyond which only ticket holders were allowed, Arya gave her a long, tight hug. "Have a safe trip. Call me when you get there, okay?" She sniffed, trying without much success to keep her emotions under control.

"I will."

"Would you like me to come to India if . . . the bone marrow thing happens?"

"No." Vinita patted Arya's cheek. "Stay here and keep your dad company." She had to do this alone. Dragging Arya or Girish into her personal mess was the last thing she wanted. This was her problem. Hers alone.

"Mom, this is serious. How can you brush it off? I'm worried about you."

"I know, honey." Vinita ignored the lump ballooning in her throat. "I'm sorry to put you through this." She touched Arya's face again, memorizing the petal smoothness of the beloved skin. "Try not to worry too much."

"Fine," grumbled Arya. "But call me if you change your mind."

"I'd rather you take care of your dad." Vinita was more than worried about him. She'd never known Girish to stay angry at her for more than a few minutes. But then, they'd never had any serious arguments in all these years. He'd looked positively defeated these past few days. She'd managed to bring down a good man, a kind man with a temperate personality. "Make sure he takes his blood pressure medication regularly, all right?"

"Don't worry. I'll keep an eye on Dad after he comes back from his trip." Arya handed her the zippered tote bag with its airline tag attached to the shoulder strap. Then she stepped aside to let a ticket-holding passenger take her place in the line.

"Bye, honey." Vinita took the bag and fished out her ticket

and passport for the security guards. It was going to be a long flight to India. She had no idea what awaited her there.

Turning around, she sent a reassuring smile to Arya, who was still standing just outside the barricade, staring at her. She had the same expression she'd worn after Vinita had dropped her off at her first day of preschool: scared, lost, and on the verge of tears, right down to the quivering lower lip. This time Mom was going away for three long months.

Quickly reining in her own urge to weep, Vinita raised a hand and motioned to her daughter to go home. Then she lost sight of Arya as the crowd swallowed her up.

Within minutes, Vinita was placing her bags and shoes on the conveyor belt rattling through the X-ray machine. Then she collected her belongings and dragged herself down the lengthy corridor toward her assigned gate.

As she sat staring out the bank of windows at the planes landing and taking off, she wondered if all this was a mistake. What if she'd trashed the anonymous letter and gone on with her life? Would she have been any happier? Would conflict have consumed every minute of her life as she thought about a young man who was dying—and about whose son he really was?

She realized she'd never have been able to ignore the letter and live with herself. For the rest of her life she would have questioned her actions. She was curious by nature, analytical, a woman who disliked unsolved puzzles and mysteries. But she also believed in fate. And fate had decided to reveal some deep secrets at this moment, for a reason.

A half hour later, before boarding the plane, she tried one last time to reach Girish on his cell phone, but all she got was his voice mail. So she left him a message, yet again. "Girish, I'll be boarding in a few minutes. Call me back, please. I know you're upset, but please say something, dear . . . anything." She waited a beat before she added. "I love you."

If something happened to her, like a plane crash or hijacking or something, at least he'd know that she loved him. More than she'd loved any man.

Chapter 19

Vinita turned accusing eyes on her brother the instant she settled in the chair. "You remember your words to me thirty years ago, Vishal?"

"Um-hmm," he conceded.

"You promised to take care of my child if I died."

"And I kept my promise," Vishal replied testily as he stood before her, arms folded across his broad chest.

"By giving him away?" she challenged.

Vishal and Vinita were in his home office, arguing. Vishal chose to call it a discussion. Vinita's long journey to Palgaum via Delhi and Goa had taken some thirty hours. Her eyes felt gritty and she needed some rest, but she had to talk things over with her brother first.

"You didn't die," he reminded her.

"Well, pardon me," she sniffed. "Since I didn't die and neither did he, *I* should have been the one to raise him. He was mine."

Temper sparked in Vishal's eyes. They resembled her late father's so much that Vinita had to suck in a sharp breath to ignore the intimidation swirling in their dark depths. "Raised him, Vini?" His voice rose. "How? What were you going to give that boy?"

"I would have worked hard to feed and clothe him."

"Who would have taken care of him while you worked? Had you thought of that? Papa and Mummy certainly couldn't stay involved in your life once you decided to keep that child. You'd probably have ended up in some big city so you could remain anonymous."

She gnawed on her lower lip. "I—I would have managed . . . somehow."

"How, damn it?" He raked impatient fingers through his luxuriant, graying hair. "You were so bloody convinced that a nineteen-year-old could work and study and raise a child, you were totally blind to the obstacles. Did you ever stop to think that your lack of foresight would mean a miserable life for your child?"

"That's not fair—"

"Mummy and I tried to point that out," he reminded her. "But did you listen? No, you wanted to play the martyr . . . the victimized heroine in a Hindi movie."

"I was never a drama queen," she shot back, offended by his choice of metaphors.

"Yes, you were," he insisted. "You wanted to thrust that child in Kori's face and prove to him that you didn't need him— that you could survive. It was your pawn, your way of getting even with him."

"No!"

"You were determined to make him feel guilty. Of course you didn't know at the time that he doesn't have a conscience." Vishal pointed a large finger at her, a vastly familiar gesture. "Is that what you wanted for your child? Bare survival?"

"I—I'm . . ." She knew he was right. At the moment, as a sensible middle-aged woman, she could look at it a little more objectively. Maybe she had been trying to prove a point by playing the sacrificial victim. No matter what her reasons, she'd have had difficulty surviving, let alone caring for a child.

Vishal must have seen the brief spark of comprehension in her eyes. "You see why we did what we did? Instead of merely surviving, that boy was raised in a good family with good values."

"They're still strangers."

"Will you just listen to me?" His scowl turned fiercer than ever. "His parents may not be wealthy, but they're comfortable. The father worked as an engineer until he retired. The boy went to college, even got a PhD in chemistry. He's very bright. He teaches chemistry in college."

"A professor?" she asked, intrigued.

With an almost gleeful nod, Vishal confirmed it. "Would *you* have been able to educate him and make him a professor?"

Most likely not, she conceded silently. But chemistry? She with her statistics and accounting background, along with the not-too-bright Kori, had produced a son who had excelled in chemistry? How interesting. She stared at Vishal. "How do you know all this?"

He began to pace the room. Even the way he strode back and forth, with his hands clasped behind his back, was reminiscent of their father's habits. Dressed in conservative brown pants and a white shirt, the resemblance between father and son was remarkable. The only thing different was Vishal's thick hair. That he'd inherited from their mother.

"The adoptive parents are relatives of Ram's nurse," Vishal answered finally. "A childless couple."

The nurse. Jaya-bai. Something clicked in Vinita's brain. The anonymous letter writer? The *well-wisher?* It had to be that woman. Who else could it be? But that wasn't so crucial at the moment. "Where in Bombay does my son live, anyway?"

Again Vishal took his time responding. "He doesn't live in Bombay."

"Then where?"

"He was raised in Palgaum. He teaches in Palgaum."

Her eyes widened. "He lives in *this* town?"

"Yes."

"Oh my God!" All these years he'd been living here. Ever since she'd heard about him, she'd assumed he had been adopted by someone in Bombay, maybe because he was born there. Anywhere but this town. "And you never once thought to tell me."

"How could I?"

Her eyes narrowed in suspicion. "Convenient, isn't it? That Jaya *happened* to have relatives in our town? And they *happened* to be childless?" When he didn't respond, her jaw tightened. "I want the whole truth this time." Her clever brother had somehow manipulated her life and her son's. Again.

Vishal shut his eyes for an instant, as if to muster strength. "I wanted to make sure the boy went to a good family . . . had a good life."

"Very kind of you, I'm sure. But why?"

He hesitated. "Because he's your . . . uh . . . my—"

"Nephew," she interjected. "Still ashamed to say the word, Vishal?"

"Don't assume things," he warned her. "I had his best interests at heart."

"So you handpicked a family that lives here?" Something inside her tightly wound stomach eased a little, warmed even. Despite all that macho bluster and careful reference to her son as *the boy*, her brother obviously cared a little about his nephew. Why else would he go to such lengths to secure *the boy's* future?

"Not exactly. But I mentioned my concerns to Ram. He discussed it with his nurse. Her niece was childless after many years of marriage and Jaya-bai thought the niece and her husband might be able to give him a good home."

"Convenient," Vinita repeated.

"For your information, they had no plans to adopt. Jaya-bai convinced them to do it."

"Why?"

"Because he was a healthy and good-looking baby boy, something most people in our culture value very much." He sounded exasperated by her endless questioning. "And her niece couldn't have children after years of trying. It was a good match."

Vinita digested that for a minute. Her baby had been born healthy, good-looking. The sad fact was that the healthy little boy wasn't so healthy anymore. He was deathly ill. And Vishal's explanation still sounded a little too contrived.

"Why is my son receiving treatment in Palgaum when he could get better care in a big city?"

"You'll be surprised at the quality of health care in our town. Palgaum has grown big in the last decade. Some U.S.-trained doctors have set up a modern hospital that offers almost everything your American hospitals do."

That was easy enough to believe. Many foreign-trained Indian medical professionals had returned to India to start state-of-the-art medical care facilities. "Do you see Rohit at all?"

He nodded, almost grudgingly. "From a distance. I see him here and there, on his motorcycle. Of course, he doesn't know who I am—at least not my relationship to him."

Vinita considered the irony of it. Her son had been right under her nose when she'd visited Palgaum a number of times in the past. And she'd never known. She would have given anything to see him, if only from afar.

Was it possible that she could have seen him over the years, as a stranger? He could have been any one of the little boys at the ice cream shop, or the teenagers browsing through videos in the electronics store or, more recently, one of the young men riding motorbikes around town. And to think she'd never recognized him. Wasn't there supposed to be instinctive radar in every mother?

She sat in silence for a minute, looking over the room. The office boasted a modern desk and leather swivel chair, a computer, and two guest chairs, one of which Vinita was sitting in. A compact-disc player sat atop a small table in the corner.

Their old home had been expanded, with two more bedrooms and a bathroom added on, and the kitchen and drawing room upgraded. Vishal's new home office was what used to be the old master bedroom.

Vishal had taken over their father's business and made a huge success of it. He had several employees on his payroll, and a bigger, trendier office in town. Shelke & Son was renamed Shelke Financial Solutions. It was no longer just a modest accounting outfit offering income tax preparation services. It was now a financial consulting firm, with a large and wealthy clientele. As the town had gradually expanded in size and degree of sophistication, so had Vishal's business.

Vishal was living his lifelong dream. Their father would have been proud of his only son if he hadn't succumbed to that heart attack at sixty-nine.

Notwithstanding his achievements, Vishal was a first-class liar. Her temper climbed again. He'd been lying to her all along. They had all been lying to her—her brother, mother, her late father, the doctor, his nurse. God knows who else was party to the elaborate hoax.

She'd been kept in the dark by the very people she'd loved and trusted. And the fact that they'd all conspired behind her back stung like hell. She'd heard all the explanations from Vishal and the family by now, about protecting her and her marriage, but she was still enraged about their deceit.

No matter how much they loved her and wanted to shield her from the harsh repercussions of her follies, they had no right to keep the truth from her.

But now, despite all the running and hiding she'd done for twenty-five years, her past had managed to catch up with her—a past she was neither proud of nor liked to recall. All the filth she had supposedly buried deep was now unearthed. And the stench was hard to stomach.

She, the woman who'd thought there could be nothing more devastating than what had happened to her as a teenager, was now struck by a second bolt of lightning. Whoever had made up the adage about lightning never striking twice was mistaken.

"Vishal, tell me something," she said, posing a question she'd been grappling with for days. "When I ended up having to undergo a C-section, it became a convenience for you and Papa and Mummy. What would you have done if Rohit was born naturally? You couldn't very well have told me my child was dead."

Vishal's cheeks flushed and his nostrils flared—a sign of extreme discomfort. "We would still have tried to convince you to give him up for adoption."

She quirked an eyebrow at him. "And if I didn't?"

"We wouldn't be having this conversation now, would we?" he said very simply.

His calm reply only served to make her blood boil more furiously. Perhaps because he was right. And so damn sanctimonious. But she had to set aside her bitter rage over something that happened ages ago and move forward. She stared at her hands, willed them to stop shaking.

She was here for a reason. And she needed to focus on *that*.

Finally she looked up. "What does he look like?"

Vishal's eyes warmed. "Nice-looking boy. Not as tall as Kori, but looks a bit like him."

"He looks like Som?" Had he inherited that same dangerous sex appeal from his father? Was he a lady-killer and heartless philanderer like Som? She hoped not.

"I think he has your nose, but the shape of his face and eyes are like the father's." Vishal shrugged. "You'll see for yourself, since you insist on meeting him."

Good Lord, her son had those unusual golden eyes? Captivating feline eyes. Could the whole town have guessed his connection to Som? She turned her attention back to Vishal. "Did you know about his illness, or is that something you chose to hide from me as well?"

"I had no idea he was sick. I swear, Vini. He looked healthy enough."

"Hmm," she allowed with a grunt. "Do his parents know about me? That you're his uncle?"

"They do now," he said after a long pause. "The Barves and I knew of each other, but I formally introduced myself to the family for the first time after you called to tell me you were planning to do *this*." He made an impatient gesture with his hand—probably to mean her insane impulsiveness. "I was forced to tell them . . . everything."

Barve. Her son's official name was Rohit Barve. She rolled it around in her mind, tested it for sound. *Ro-hith Burr-vay.* "What did they say?"

"What do you think?" He lifted a cynical brow. "All they had been told was that the biological mother was a young, unmarried girl from a good family."

She studied her hands. "Some of it is true. The young girl from a good family part."

He came to sit in the chair beside hers. "You know how difficult it was to broach the subject to those people? After all these years, to show up at their door as their son's long-lost uncle?"

"I'm sure it was awkward."

"Try mortifying. They thought I was a lunatic. They were almost ready to throw me out of their house. Until some days ago they knew me only as Vishal Shelke, chartered accountant and businessman."

She pinched the bridge of her nose, wishing her brother hadn't had to suffer such humiliation on her account. "I'm sorry." It seemed like the word *sorry* was firmly entrenched in her vocabulary. But then she was in the habit of bringing grief to everyone around her.

He picked up a pen from his desk and twirled it absently between his fingers. "But surprisingly, they appeared somewhat relieved after the initial shock wore off."

"Relieved?" When they'd raised Rohit as their own, wouldn't they resent the real mother's appearance?

"When I told them Rohit's mother was my sister and was willing to donate bone marrow if necessary, their attitude changed. They're desperate to see him survive." He put the pen down. "But they wanted to know how I got wind of their son's illness."

"What did you tell them?"

"The truth—that you received an anonymous letter. They were completely puzzled, just like you and I."

She mulled over that for a beat. "Do they know who the father is?"

"I didn't tell."

"How come?"

"If you knew who the Barves are, you'd know why. Shashi Barve has been the leader of the Marathi movement in Palgaum for the last fifteen years or more. He resents Kannada people with a passion. On the opposite side, Som Kori is the leader of the Kannada movement."

"Som's a leader?" She shook her head. "But he hates communalism. He told me so."

"That was then, when he was a young loafer. Now he's a man with a family and a business to run. Some years ago, when Marathi vandals set fire to Kori's grain-distribution warehouse, he decided to become the leader of the Kannada faction. He and Shashi Barve hate each other. If Barve ever found out Kori is the father of his child, there'd be a mini war in Palgaum."

Vinita continued to frown. "Has the Marathi-Kannada sentiment become that volatile?"

"Much worse than it was when we were growing up. Now the Hindu Séna has joined hands with the Marathi Samithi."

"Oh no!" The Hindu Séna, literally meaning Hindu Army, was a militant group of fundamentalist Marathi men and women who stopped at nothing, including violence, to promote their culture and language. They also had some rich and influential members with ties to politicians in the highest echelons of government. The Kannada side had equally big names in their court. Neither side could be called the underdog.

No wonder it spelled unrest on a larger scale, and escalating violence in Palgaum.

"I'm glad Papa isn't here to see some of these atrocities," said Vishal, voicing Vinita's own thoughts.

"What about your office in town?" She wondered how a staunch Marathi guy like her brother got treated by the other side. "You get vandalized like Papa used to?"

He nodded. "Once in a while . . . but I've hired some Kannada employees. Plus I have a large number of wealthy Kannada clients. Between those two groups, I get spared—most of the time." He looked at her expression. "I still detest those bastards, especially Kori. But I have a business to run. I keep my personal opinions to myself. Sayee and the boys follow the same rule."

"Good for you." Smart man, thought Vinita, with a mental nod. She always knew her brother would make a good businessman. She didn't know he was this diplomatic, though. If other businessmen in town would do the same thing and keep their personal ideals and business lives separate, Palgaum would be a much better place.

"So you definitely want to do this?" he asked, reverting to the topic at hand. "You really want to dig up all that rotten history and let the stink spread?"

"I have no other choice, Vishal."

"We're dealing with two influential and vindictive men with political power. This is likely to pitch them against each other."

She turned that over in her mind for a second. "But no one has to know who Rohit's father is. I won't tell anyone."

"The truth has a way of coming out—whether we want it to or not."

"I have to do it," she said, ignoring his warning note. "I'll understand if you want to stay out of it. I can stay at a hotel, do this discreetly on my own . . . make sure your name is protected."

"Stay out of it? How, when I'm in it up to my neck?" he demanded. "There's no question that you will stay here. This is your home." He dismissed any further debate with a stern scowl. "But what if your son is hostile?"

"I'm willing to risk it. Someone took the trouble to write me an anonymous letter for a reason."

Vishal stroked his mustache in his typical pensive gesture. "I think I know who might have written that. I even called Ram with my suspicions. He agrees with me."

With raised brows she waited for him to continue.

"I bet it's that nurse, Jaya-bai. She has to know about the boy's condition."

"That was my guess as soon as you told me who the Barves were." She'd deal with Jaya-bai later—if she needed to. Right now the important thing was that the truth was finally out in the open.

"You still want to meet your son?"

She nodded. "It's a bit scary," she confessed.

"Then think about it some more before we take the next step. Maybe you'll change your mind." He sounded hopeful.

"Not likely." She hadn't come this far only to turn tail and run back home to New Jersey.

He looked at the clock on his desk. "You must be exhausted from jet lag. Why don't you get some rest before dinner?" He plucked the cordless phone from his desk and handed it to her. "You should call Girish and tell him you arrived here safely."

"Thanks," she said, accepting the phone, loath to tell her brother that Girish couldn't care less about her safe arrival. What she was suffering was beyond exhaustion. She'd been functioning purely on adrenaline for several days. The widening rift between Girish and her had added to the stress.

He hadn't even said good-bye to her when he'd taken off on his business trip a few days after she'd sprung the news on him.

He'd packed up his suitcase, left for work in the morning, then gone directly to the airport from his office.

It wasn't unusual for him to do that, being a busy man with a job that involved frequent travel, but what was different was that he hadn't called from the airport like he always did before boarding a flight. And he hadn't called after arriving at his destination, either.

She had a feeling he'd deliberately chosen to be out of town on the day she was flying to India. Maybe it wasn't even a business trip. It could be his way of punishing her. Or he could have gone off to lick his wounds, to come to terms with what she'd done to him.

"I'll rest a little," she said to Vishal, rising to her feet. She walked out of the office with the phone in hand and through the passageway toward the guest room. Sitting down on the edge of the bed, she wondered how she was going to handle her problem with Girish. He had seemed distant while they were home in the U.S., but now, with her in India, he seemed even more uncommunicative.

When she dialed Arya's cell phone, Arya picked up within two rings. Vinita informed her that she'd arrived in Palgaum, assured her again that she was going to be okay. "Any news from Dad yet?" she asked, hoping there'd be some sort of message from him. Girish's continued silence was troubling.

"Yeah. He sent me a one-line text message. But he didn't give me his address. Can't he at least tell us where in California he is?"

"Did you ask him?" Vinita wondered if he was really in California or somewhere else.

"Uh-huh. I texted him twice."

Vinita drew a long, slow breath. "Important thing is he's all right. I bet he'll eventually call you. He can't bear to not talk to you for too long."

"Okay, but if he doesn't call by tomorrow, I'm going to be really mad. I'm ready to yell at him."

"Give him a couple of days, babe. Let him cool off."

Arya agreed reluctantly and ended the call. Vinita left another voice-mail message for Girish. This time it was on his office phone. He couldn't ignore that, could he? Where was he? His secretary, who was usually very friendly whenever Vinita called, had given a vague answer when Vinita had spoken to her a couple of days ago, politely implying that Girish had sworn her to secrecy.

It was as if he'd made a deliberate effort to disappear from Vinita's life.

Earlier, before her conversation with Vishal, she'd unpacked her bags and handed out the small gifts she had brought for everyone in the family. Following that, she'd had an awkward conversation over a cup of tea with her mother and sister-in-law. Sayee had brought out some of her most delicious homemade snacks to go with the tea, but Vinita had barely touched them. Food was the last thing on her mind.

Her mother's eyes, now weakened by macular degeneration, had looked at her with both gloom and wariness. It was so unlike the other visits Girish, Arya, and she had made in the past, when Mummy had welcomed them with warm smiles and plied them with their favorite foods. Arya had been spoiled and pampered as the only granddaughter. Girish and Vinita had been treated like visiting royalty.

During this visit, however, the message in her mother's eyes was clear: *Why are you here to stir up trouble again? Haven't you done enough damage already?*

Vinita lay down on the wide bed. This was her old room—awash with bittersweet memories. It had been repainted and the furniture was different. Her report cards, certificates and prizes earned in school and college, and her dog-eared autograph book with hundreds of signatures collected from classmates and friends, sat in two cardboard boxes stored under the bed. If all of her childhood and adolescence could fit into two small boxes, they hadn't added up to much.

But then, some memories weren't worth saving.

Compared with the old days, the present sounds outside the small window were a din, with the increased traffic, both auto and pedestrian. Palgaum had evolved from town to city by government definition—which meant a huge swell in population. Now there were new movie theaters, schools, colleges, shops, restaurants, and hotels.

Her friend Prema was married and settled near Bangalore for the past twenty-seven years. According to Vinita's mother, Prema and her husband had three children, all boys. She could almost picture Prema's face with its thin mouth, reprimanding the boys over some misbehavior or other.

Under ordinary circumstances, she and Prema would have still been friends. But they hadn't been in touch since the day Vinita had boarded that plane and gone off to Bombay to have her baby. She would have liked to visit Prema, exchange news about their respective lives—see if Prema still liked to gossip, still liked fiery hot food and sweet-as-sin sugarcane juice. It would be wonderful to meet Prema's husband and children, too.

But she couldn't contact Prema at the moment. Maybe never.

Staring at the ceiling fan, Vinita recalled something. While she'd been lying on the operating table all those years ago, just before succumbing to the anesthesia, she had seen a ghostlike image of a baby floating near the ceiling. She'd convinced herself it was her dead child. Now that she knew her son was alive, she wondered if it had been her drugged mind playing tricks on her.

She turned onto her side and tried to take a nap. But she was too wound up to relax. Tomorrow she'd most likely meet her son. It was ironic that he had been not only right under her nose all these years, but his real father and adoptive father were bitter enemies. And both lived in the same town. What a bizarre coincidence. But then . . . it wasn't really. Vishal, in partnership with her previous obstetrician and his resourceful nurse, had more or less orchestrated it.

On the heels of that thought came another one. Was her brother right? Would her desire to save her son mean more problems for everyone? It was likely to stir the incendiary Marathi-Kannada monster for sure.

What if her actions caused serious damage to the town? Was it worth that kind of violence?

Chapter 20

Vinita cast a glimpse outside her bedroom window as she got dressed. It was very early in the morning. The first sounds of traffic were building up. The sun was not quite visible yet. But it was there, in the eastern sky. Soon it would burn through the early-morning fog, warming the air, brightening the landscape.

Going down the stairs a little later, she sniffed the pungent air, infused with the aroma of onions, chilies, and curry leaves sizzling in oil. She heard the kitchen radio delivering the news. Sayee was obviously up earlier than anyone else and already busy in the kitchen. But she had help. Anu, the girl who helped her, apparently came in at dawn, too. Breakfast was likely to be elaborate and delicious.

Seeking out her mother, Vinita headed past the kitchen toward the *dév ghar*, the altar room. Sure enough, she found her mother sitting on a *chatayee*, a straw mat, rolling the cotton wicks she burned each day in the oil lamps on the altar.

Mummy's hair had grayed a lot more since Vinita's last visit, but it was plentiful. Her mother still had good posture, upright and proud. She was every bit the Maratha woman, steeped in her warrior roots. Her skin, despite the expected wrinkles, showed no age spots.

"Vini!" Her mother looked startled at seeing her standing on the threshold. "I didn't expect you to be up this early." The greeting was cordial enough, but there was no smile to accompany it.

"Am I disturbing you?" Vini hesitated to step into her mother's sacred prayer chamber, although she'd spent many hours in this very room while growing up.

"Not at all. Come, sit down," Sarla invited her, patting the place next to her on the mat. "I'm only making some wicks."

"Let me help." Vini came to sit beside her.

Sarla studied Vinita closely as she settled on the mat. "I don't need help, you know. We can just talk."

Despite her mother's words, Vinita broke off a small wad of cotton from the fluffy white ball and started rolling it between her palms.

An awkward silence stretched between them as they both steadily worked the wicks. It was not easy to guess what was going on in Mummy's mind, but her tight expression signified disapproval.

Sarla was the first one to speak. "Tell me, how is little Arya? We didn't talk much about her."

"She's doing well." Vinita smiled. "She's not so little anymore. Wants to go for a master's soon."

"Getting another degree is a way of postponing marriage, I suppose." Sarla chuckled. The amused snicker was unexpected and rare. "So, how is Girish?"

There was a slight pause. Vinita's smile vanished. "He's fine."

Her mother threw her a sharp look. "Girish is angry, isn't he," she said, not so much a question as a statement.

Vinita went still. "A little," she admitted.

"Why, Vini?"

"Why what?"

"Why did you not leave the matter alone? Girish and you were happy. You have a nice life, a comfortable house—and Arya."

Vinita's lip quivered. "I also have a son. The son you and Papa and Vishal kept from me."

"We had to do it for *you*."

"You did it for yourselves—that inflated sentiment you call *aabroo*."

"But we—"

"You were ashamed to have a daughter who was tainted by scandal," interrupted Vinita, "so you did everything to smooth it over." Like putting a bandage on an ugly wound and pretending it wasn't there. "You set out to make yourselves respectable again."

"Maybe," conceded her mother. "But it was something we had to do so you could have some kind of future. And Vishal, too."

"Vishal would have done okay."

"Who would have given their daughter in marriage to your brother if word had spread that his sister had disgraced herself, and on top of that kept her illegitimate child?" Mummy stared hard at Vinita before picking up another cotton ball. "Did you want your brother to suffer?"

"Of course not."

"You can't deny it has been a good life for you since you married Girish. Why are you deliberately trying to ruin it? I'm sure your husband is very unhappy about this."

"Mummy, please." Vinita tossed the half-rolled wick on the mat. "If you must know, Girish isn't just unhappy, he's devastated."

"I knew it," her mother said. "What about Arya? That poor child must be in shock."

"She's handling it quite well, actually. She's been very supportive."

"Hmmph." Mummy frowned. "Does Girish know the *entire* truth?" she asked.

Vinita nodded. Tears were beginning to burn her eyes.

"Years ago, you were too young and inexperienced to make intelligent decisions. But now you're a responsible woman and the mother of a marriageable girl. Who will marry your daughter if they discover this?"

"Arya will be fine," Vinita said, defending herself. "The kind of young men Arya meets in the U.S. are different. Their attitudes have changed."

"Then why haven't *you* changed? You're still acting childish and selfish." Mummy made a clucking sound with her tongue. "Don't you ever think of anyone except yourself?"

Tears began to roll down Vinita's cheeks. She chose not to answer Mummy's question.

"After successfully deflecting your scandal years ago, we managed to recover. Now Vishal is a happily married man. His business is thriving. The Shelkes are respected in this community. But now we are surely headed for ruin," Mummy lamented. "A second time."

Vini blew her nose with a handkerchief. "I *am* trying to think of someone else: my son. I want to give him a chance to live. Is that selfish on my part?"

"But he is not the only person in your life," her mother reminded her. "There are others—many others whose lives could be ruined."

"If I were truly selfish, I would've tossed that anonymous letter and pretended it never existed. Later, after I'd discovered my son was alive, I still could have ignored the fact and gone on with my life with Girish and Arya."

"But you didn't."

"I couldn't. If my son dies, do you think I . . ." She pinned her mother with a cutting look. "You think *you* could live with that? He's your grandson."

Mummy shifted her gaze. "He could still die. I hear transplants are not always successful."

"But would you let him die without at least trying to help?"

"I don't know, Vini. I don't know."

"But you must have at least given it some thought," Vinita demanded.

"I have given it a lot of thought, more than I have to any other problem in many years. I don't see any good coming out of this. I think your stubbornness is going to cause trouble."

"It's too late to go back. Vishal is driving me this morning to meet Rohit."

"The rest of your family means nothing to you, then?" her mother asked in a tight voice.

Vinita sat still and silent for a second, then rose to her feet and strode out of the room.

Powering down his computer, Girish folded his arms over his desk and lowered his head over them. He was home now, back from his trip to California. He'd returned only after he was sure that Vini had arrived in Palgaum. He wasn't ready to face her. Not yet.

All the soul-searching he'd done for days in his hotel room hadn't helped much. He was still miserable, still undecided about his feelings regarding Vini's shocking disclosure, still wondering if he could ever forget it.

He'd just finished reading her latest e-mail. She'd been sending him lots of e-mail. While he was on the West Coast, she'd left him voice-mail messages, both on his office phone and his cell. When he'd failed to respond, she'd started sending e-mail, apologizing for her deceit, telling him about her plans to leave for India to see her son.

Later she'd written about her arrival in Palgaum, told him that she was bracing herself to meet her son for the first time, and that she missed Girish. That she loved him.

Damn it, why was Vini tormenting him with her long messages? Why didn't she leave him alone to wallow in his unhappiness? Did she really have to tell him every tiny detail of what was going on in Palgaum?

Nevertheless, he couldn't help but read every one of her messages, over and over again. It was almost an obsession—so much so that on the one day she had failed to send him a message, he had missed it, wondered if she'd given up on him. He'd gone into his e-mail account and searched for the familiar address. Finding no address, he'd felt let down.

Why couldn't he just hate her for lying to him for so long, for letting him think she was a cancer survivor, and making him fall in love with her? But he couldn't detest her, even if he tried. She was the woman who had brought order to his aimless bachelor life, and warmth to his cold, empty shell of a house. She'd given him a purpose in life, a home, a precious child.

After he'd recovered from his divorce from Nadine, he'd set out to find a wife in order to have a more stable lifestyle, a companion. In fact, he'd been a little afraid to commit his heart completely. He'd been hurt once. He couldn't handle it a second time. However, Vini had slowly become his focal point, his better half, and he'd fallen in love with her, much more deeply than he'd done with Nadine.

Lifting his head from the desk, he sat back in his chair. The chilly spring rain had stopped. The house was quiet, except for the sounds of the heating system kicking in every now and then. Arya was visiting with her friends tonight. She needed some time away from him. She'd moved back into the house even before Vini had left. Then she'd stayed on, supposedly to keep him company while her mother was in India.

He was grateful for his daughter's cheerful presence, but she nagged him constantly, needled him into talking about Vini. She'd lambasted him for not calling sooner while he was away in California. "I was concerned about you, Dad. All I got from you during the first three days was a cryptic text message."

"I'm a grown man, Arya," he'd lashed out, annoyed at himself for making his daughter suffer because he was disappointed in his wife. Nevertheless he'd tossed back a defensive frown at Arya. "I don't need to check in with you each and every day."

"Yeah, but Mom and I were worried. What if something happened to you while you were on a so-called *business* trip?" she'd shot back, her eyes ablaze with indignation.

They'd argued about it, then managed to call a truce after a day or so. He could never stay angry with his daughter for too long. But Arya continued to badger him at least once a day about calling her mother, writing to her. Arya could be as stubborn and aggravating as a gnat sometimes. "Don't you miss Mom?" she queried often.

Of course he missed his wife. He didn't want to . . . but Lord knew he did. The past few days had been some of the loneliest of his life. He'd tried to come to terms with the truth, but it was difficult. He still couldn't understand why Vini had felt the need to hide something so significant from him. She'd said she was afraid of his reaction.

Was she really that intimidated by him? He'd never been harsh with her. He'd always given her all the freedom she'd needed or wanted, always supported her in everything she'd done. He would have understood about the indiscretion in her past—*if* she'd told him at the beginning of their relationship.

So why had she never allowed him into her private world? She'd never trusted him.

Her latest e-mail said she was going to meet her son for the first time. It was early morning in Palgaum now. Vini was probably up and raring to go, dressed in something neat and subdued—suitable for meeting her grown son.

Naturally Girish was curious about the boy. But he quickly banished the thought from his mind. He didn't want to waste a single thought on his . . . stepson. Vini could have all the pleasure of meeting her unknown son all by herself.

Convincing himself that Vini's illegitimate child was of no interest to him, Girish stood, shut off the desk light, and made his way toward the master bedroom. The photograph of Vini and him on their brief honeymoon in Goa stared back at him.

He'd been looking at the photo a lot lately. Her face had looked so fresh in that picture, so innocent, so damn honest. He never would have guessed that his bride had been keeping secrets from him.

After brushing his teeth and changing into pajamas, he slipped into bed. The mattress was cold, but he settled himself into a comfortable position and tried to get some sleep. Tried to pretend he didn't miss Vini's warm body nestled against his.

Chapter 21

Vishal parked his car along the narrow street, shut off the ignition, and turned to Vinita. "Last chance to change your mind."

"No way." Vinita held his gaze. Her brother looked well-groomed and distinguished in his office attire. His hair was combed back from his forehead and he wore a pleasant aftershave. Her brother had always been a sharp dresser. This morning he was going to drop her back home after this visit with the Barves, and then drive directly to his office.

"Let's go, then," he said in a resigned tone, opened the driver side door, and climbed out.

Vinita stepped out from the passenger side. Despite the town's progress, this street hadn't changed much in thirty years. The potholes were visible on its tarred surface and the reddish dust native to these parts clung to the edges.

The culverts on either side of the street that used to drain the rainwater and some amount of sewage were now covered with concrete slabs. And what a relief that was.

She lifted her gaze to study the Barves' house. Her son's house. It was a single-story structure with an old-style roof of terra-cotta tiles. The whitewashed front and the teakwood door and windows looked clean and cared for. Two small shrubs flanked the concrete steps leading up to the front door. A shade tree cast a heavy shadow on one side of the house. It was a typical middle-class bungalow in suburban Palgaum.

Her hands trembled a little at the thought of meeting Rohit.

Before Vishal or she could knock, the door was opened by a slight, balding man, who looked to be in his seventies or thereabouts. He was dressed in brown trousers and a cream bush shirt. He stared at Vinita for a moment, his small eyes behind the glasses appraising her thoroughly, from head to toe. The look was perhaps no more than one second more than was considered polite when a man looked at a woman, but it was a piercing glance nonetheless. The blood rushed to her face.

"*Namaste,*" he said finally, joining his hands in greeting. "I'm Shashi Barve. Please come in." He held the door wide open.

Returning the *namaste,* she and Vishal crossed the threshold into the drawing room. "My sister, Vinita Patil," said Vishal, introducing her to Barve.

It was a cool, sparsely decorated room with whitewashed walls and a gray slate floor. A simple black vinyl couch was backed against one wall, a sturdy coffee table separating it from two chairs placed against the opposite wall. Blue and white print cushions and matching curtains on the window provided the only splashes of color. But it all looked scrupulously clean.

What captured Vinita's eye were the photographs monopolizing two of the walls. Mr. Barve was everywhere: flanked by politicians, shaking hands with dignitaries, accepting an award, wearing a garland of red and white roses and smiling broadly, leading what looked like a rally, holding a picket sign.

In person he looked harmless enough—smaller than the men surrounding him. But every one of the pictures was a clear indication of his serious involvement in politics.

Vishal was right. Barve appeared to be a fanatical activist. Something about the intensity of the sentiment behind the photos and the sharp, dark eyes that continued to assess her made her uneasy. This was the man who had raised Rohit. Had he instilled the same radical spirit in his son?

She glanced again at Shashi Barve, taking in more details as he motioned to them to sit down. He had a narrow gray mustache. Not exactly the larger-than-life, charismatic community leader she'd pictured. He looked anything but inspiring.

Her wandering thoughts were interrupted by the entrance of a woman: obviously Mrs. Barve. She was slim, slightly taller than her husband—a bit unusual in their culture. Maybe Barve wasn't the typical macho Indian man who had issues about marrying a woman taller than he. But then he was a hero in his own right.

Dressed in a soft, powder blue sari that made her face seem ashen, the woman looked like her son's illness had taken its toll on her. She was probably in her late sixties, but looked older. The large red *bindi,* the dot on her forehead, stood in deep contrast to the paleness of her skin. Her mostly gray hair was pulled back in a neat braid that reached her waist. A simple woman—living in a simple house.

"My wife, Meenal," said Barve, and motioned once again for them to sit.

More *namastes* followed before they all settled down, Vishal sitting beside Vinita on the sofa, and the Barves occupying the chairs.

Vinita compared herself to the other woman's austere getup. Her own shoulder-length hair, the touch of lipstick, and the green, pear-shaped *bindi* with a gold outline to match her green sari and matching blouse suddenly seemed fussy and out of place. She tried to put it out of her mind and smiled at the woman—Rohit's mother.

Barve wasted no time coming to the point. "Mrs. Patil, I am told you are willing to help Rohit?" he asked, looking directly at Vinita.

"Yes, sir," murmured Vinita, her hands in a tight clasp. Somehow *sir* seemed like the right way to address him. He looked old enough to be her father. "I'm hoping I'm a suitable donor."

She could feel Meenal Barve's eyes boring into her. A mother being protective of her son was something Vinita could understand. But she wasn't sure if the watchful eyes were judging her for her more fashionable ways, her past indiscretions, or assessing her value as a potential savior.

"As you probably know, my wife and I were both tested and declared incompatible," Barve said.

Vinita nodded. "Vishal mentioned it to me."

An uncomfortable silence followed, making Vinita shift in her seat. "Can I . . . may I meet Rohit . . . if he's here?" she asked finally, unable to stand one more second of the tension in the room.

"No," replied Meenal Barve.

Vinita's head snapped up. "Oh?" Had she come all this way just to have Rohit's adoptive mother toss her out even before she could utter her son's name? Anger sparked. What did they take her for—a robot to be harvested for bone marrow and then sent home? Without ever being given a chance to see or meet her son?

"He is in the hospital," the woman explained. "He has a bronchial infection."

Vinita's temper skidded to a halt. She took a slow breath. "When did the infection occur?" She wondered how serious his condition was. Was she too late in coming to his aid?

"He was admitted yesterday."

"Will I be allowed to see him?"

Both the Barves nodded in unison, albeit reluctantly. Barve looked at his wristwatch. "A bit early. Visiting hours start at nine o'clock." He glanced at his wife. "Why don't you prepare some tea, Meenal?"

Vinita was getting reading to say *no thanks* to the tea, but refrained. Her stomach might be in knots, but she needed these people on her side. Refusing refreshment in an Indian home was considered rude, and she couldn't afford to antagonize them. She observed Meenal Barve stand up and walk away to comply with her husband's request.

Her brother and Mr. Barve managed to keep up a polite conversation while the tea was being made. Eventually Vishal asked about Rohit's health problems. Vinita remained mostly quiet, absorbing the facts.

"Rohit's sickness was a complete shock," explained Mr. Barve.

"Any idea what may have caused it?" Vishal queried cautiously.

Barve shook his head. "Could be anything—his chemistry experiments, the water in Palgaum, the electric power plant. Maybe it is genetic, like his juvenile diabetes."

"Rohit has diabetes?" Vinita asked, her stomach plunging. Her poor son.

"Since he was a young boy."

Could it be genetic? Vinita wondered. Was there a predisposition to blood cancer as well as diabetes in her ancestry? But no one in her immediate family had leukemia or diabetes. Could it be Som Kori's genes, then?

"Exactly when was the leukemia diagnosed?" asked Vishal, voicing one of her own questions.

"Two years ago, when Rohit started to get a low fever almost every night. Then his leg started to become painful. Only after that did he go to the doctor." He explained to Vinita and Vishal some of the tests and treatments that had been tried so far. "They have tried different types of chemotherapy. They have even tried experimental medicines that have not yet been approved."

"Really? Then how did you manage to acquire the drugs?" Vinita asked.

"The black market, of course," he said, without batting an eyelash. "They didn't work, anyway. Nothing did."

"I'm sorry to hear that."

"In fact, his diabetes got worse every time he was treated with chemo."

Vinita wondered how much they'd paid for the medication. The very term *black market* implied prohibitive prices.

Several minutes later, Mrs. Barve appeared with a tray of four scalding cups of potent-looking tea, dark brown and thick. "Rohit never told us he was not feeling well," she said, joining in the conversation. "It was when his fever came daily and his pain became unbearable that we found out." She put the tray down. "He told us only last year about the leukemia, when we forced him to talk." Her eyes had begun to glisten with tears.

Vinita was tempted to reach across the table and touch the woman's hand, offer some comfort. But she accepted a cup of tea instead. Mothers often blamed themselves for their children's illnesses. She knew it firsthand. Arya rarely told Girish and her about such things because they'd worry and fuss over her. But how could the Barves not have seen the obvious signs? "Didn't you guess anything was wrong?"

Mrs. Barve shook her head. "Not in the beginning. He has his own flat—quarters provided by the college. We don't see him daily. Maybe once a week. Mostly Sundays." She handed Vishal a cup. "Sometimes not even that."

"He has his friends' circle, his own interests," added Barve. "Staying with parents means lack of freedom for the younger generation."

"I understand." Vinita was familiar with that, too. Arya had moved out of their house to go to college at eighteen and never really moved back with them. Besides, the Barves were even older than her and Girish. They must have been approaching middle age when they'd adopted Rohit. The generation gap was so much wider.

"Rohit can be very independent and stubborn sometimes."

It sounded familiar. Now *that* trait was definitely genetic. Wasn't that what her family said about her? What she herself said about Arya? "What kind of treatment are they giving him right now?" she asked, wondering how much these people were willing to share with her. So far they'd been quite forthcoming.

"Everything possible has already been done," replied Barve, sipping from his cup. "The only thing left is a transplant."

They talked a little while longer, until the strong, sweet tea was gone and the clock read nine o'clock. Then they all climbed into Vishal's car because the Barves didn't own one, and drove to the hospital. Vinita and Meenal Barve sat side by side in the backseat, the awkwardness still lingering despite the earlier icebreaker.

When they arrived at the hospital, Palgaum Medical Center, Vinita stared in awe. The brick building with its spacious parking lot and clearly marked signs was quite impressive. While she was growing up, there were a number of small private clinics that could hold no more than a dozen beds, but proudly called themselves hospitals.

This could match any medium-sized American or European hospital. Even as she admired the modern facility, the tension was mounting inside her. The urge to confess to Vishal and the Barves that she'd made a mistake and needed to go home was creeping up on her, but she quickly suppressed it. She wasn't a coward.

They walked through the double glass doors and Barve ushered them into a reception area with a high ceiling and marble-tile floor. He stopped at the front desk and whispered something to the receptionist, then led them down a long corridor. The man had a quick stride, and Vinita hurried to keep up.

Her heartbeat climbed a notch higher. She was about to meet her son. She adjusted her shoulder bag and wiped her perspiring hands on a handkerchief. The tea she'd forced herself to drink was beginning to churn in her stomach. Or maybe it was the butterflies, flying in tight circles.

Stopping at one of the many open doors, Barve entered, motioning to the rest of them to follow him. She glanced at Vishal. He seemed calm. He gave her elbow a brief, reassuring squeeze and propelled her forward.

Ignoring the dry feeling in her mouth, she stepped inside, head held high. She was not going to let the moment make a nervous wreck out of her.

The room was small, with cream walls and one window. Dark green curtains were pulled aside to let the sun in. The bed sat in the center, monopolizing most of the space. An intravenous pole stood next to a night table on one side of the bed, and a wooden chair sat on the other. A single light fixture and fan hung from the ceiling.

After the quick survey of the room, her eyes fixed themselves on the man reclined against a pillow—her reason for coming here. He had set aside the magazine he was reading and was looking directly at them.

Her heart did a quick flip and settled back into her chest with a thump.

She stared at him—drinking in every detail. If she could, she would have cupped his face in her hands and studied his eyes, run her thumbs over the planes, the sharp cheekbones, the length of his nose, the contours of his square jaw, and even counted his eyelashes. But it was out of the question. And gawking wasn't polite, so she quickly looked away.

For a moment it was like seeing a young Som Kori all over again. It appeared that Vishal had deliberately downplayed the resemblance. The likeness to Som was quite remarkable. The arresting gold-brown eyes, the low-slung eyebrows that looked like a perpetual frown, the full lower lip, the angry movie-hero look: all Kori traits. His dark hair was short and spiky. His cheeks and chin bore a shadow of stubble.

But the tip-tilted nose that hinted at arrogance—that was hers. She suppressed the urge to chuckle. Of all her features, he'd inherited *that* one? But he was a handsome boy nonetheless. At least in that, Vishal was right.

Since Rohit was covered with a sheet below the waist, it was hard to judge precisely how tall he was. He had on a green hospital gown with short sleeves, so his shoulders and arms were visible. They were wide. His hands were large. She was glad he wasn't small boned like her.

The name Rohit meant the color red. It suited him. It was an auspicious color.

They went through another round of introductions.

Rohit didn't bother greeting either Vishal or her when they both said hello and smiled. There was no reciprocating friendliness in the eyes that measured her first, then Vishal—very briefly. He'd obviously been told to expect them. He didn't seem particularly irritated or displeased—just disinterested. She and Vishal could very well have been the bedpan or the slippers tucked under his bed.

On the other hand, his gaze warmed noticeably when it descended on his parents.

Mrs. Barve moved to his side and put a hand on his shoulder. "How are you feeling, *beta*?" she asked. Maybe it was her way of easing the tension in the room.

"About the same," he replied, smiling faintly at his mother.

"They are trying a new antibiotic?"

"Uh-huh," he replied. The lopsided smile, too, was slightly reminiscent of Som, giving Vinita her first mild pinprick of envy for Meenal Barve. The emotion surprised her. She didn't know this young man; she didn't even know of his existence until recently.

"Then perhaps that will help, Rohit." His father beamed, clearly trying to boost Rohit's spirits.

"We'll see." Rohit didn't sound optimistic. His voice was nothing like Som Kori's. In fact, it was a lot like Vinita's late father's and a bit like Vishal's. Strange how certain characteristics trickled down through the generations. There was so much Shelke in him.

And thank God for that voice. If he'd inherited Som's voice, half of Palgaum would have guessed Rohit's parentage.

"Did the doctor say anything about the transplant?" Mrs. Barve smoothed his cover sheet.

"No," Rohit said sharply, like he didn't want to pursue it further.

"But he knows Mrs. Patil is here for that purpose only," pressed Barve.

"I didn't want to discuss it with him," Rohit said.

"Why?" his mother demanded.

Rohit glanced at Vinita and Vishal, once again his eyes registering very little emotion. "Because I'm on the list of bone marrow recipients. It could be a long wait. Why discuss it now?"

Barve looked at Vinita for an instant before returning his attention to Rohit. "But this is your . . . birth mother."

"I heard."

"She has come here from the United States to find out if she is a suitable donor, and—"

"Heard that, too," Rohit interrupted.

"She is willing to give you her bone marrow immediately. No waiting, you see."

"I'd prefer to wait."

"But there may be no need to wait," Vishal interjected, taking the words out of Vinita's mouth.

Rohit turned toward her for a second. "You wasted your time coming here, Mrs. Patil."

"Please don't say that," Vinita murmured.

"Why don't you just go back to the United States?"

Vinita paused for a beat. "I . . . can't."

"Why not?" A muscle flexed in his jaw.

"I'd like to at least try to help."

"Really?" He lifted one dark eyebrow that was so much like Som's it made Vinita swallow hard.

Thankfully Vishal jumped in to defend her. "Look, Rohit, my sister and I understand how you feel, but you have to look at it rationally."

Rohit waved them away with one hand. "No, thank you."

"No other donor will be as good a match as your biological mother," Vishal persisted.

"Not interested," retorted Rohit.

"But, Rohit—" protested his father, clearly beginning to get annoyed.

"I don't want to hear more, Papa."

"You *will* hear!" Mr. Barve's voice sounded like a whip cracking.

Vinita stared at the older man. The fearless political leader was emerging from behind the seemingly harmless image. Rohit must have recognized the change, too, because his hard expression eased a bit. Was he used to such sternness from his father?

"Mr. Shelke is right," continued Barve, his tone softening. "You need a donor, Rohit. You need one immediately—not next year, not two years from now."

Rohit was silent for a moment or two while the four people standing around him stared at him in anticipation. When he spoke, it was in a quiet, reasonable fashion. "I have a perfectly good mother. I don't need another. I don't want her bone marrow . . . or anything else."

Vinita opened her mouth to speak, but the words seemed to stick in her throat. She turned around and headed for the door, choking on a sob.

Chapter 22

Vinita stumbled out of the room and down the corridor, blinded by tears. She nearly collided with a nurse coming from the opposite direction, wheeling a trolley. But she managed to dodge both the nurse and the trolley in the nick of time.

Rohit's words weren't all that unexpected. Nor were they vicious. She'd known her son would be unfriendly. How could he not, when he believed she'd rid herself of him like garbage right after he was born?

She thought she'd come prepared for his hostility. But it was his quiet logic that hurt: *I don't need another.* Its sheer simplicity made it sound heartless. Maybe hatred would have been less cutting than the passionless statement.

"Vini."

It was Vishal calling her, but she ignored him and continued striding forward.

"Vini, wait." He caught up with her in the next instant and guided her into what looked like a waiting room, with chairs lined up against three of the walls. "Sit down," he ordered, pushing her into one of the chairs.

He waited until her sniffling subsided. "What did you expect? Warm and friendly?"

"Unfriendly I can handle," she said, blowing her nose.

He stared at her with raised brows.

"All right, maybe I can't. But he was being deliberately cruel. You heard him."

Vishal started to say something, but they were interrupted by the Barves' entrance.

"I am sorry about Rohit's behavior," said Mrs. Barve, looking contrite. "He is not himself."

"He is usually a very polite and well-behaved boy," added Mr. Barve. He motioned to his wife to sit down and then plopped into the chair next to Vishal.

Vinita sniffed. *He's not a boy. He's a college professor.* But she couldn't say it aloud.

"He's sick . . . under a lot of tension, Barve-saheb," Vishal offered. "It's understandable."

Vinita knew her brother was right. The boy was ill and couldn't be expected to behave rationally.

"Yes, yes," agreed Mrs. Barve, clearly relieved and willing to grasp at any excuse. "All those medicines have side effects, also."

How true. Vinita gave herself a mental kick. What was wrong with her? Like Vishal had pointed out, she couldn't have expected anything but resentment on Rohit's part. Under the circumstances, the young man had shown remarkable restraint. He'd never raised his voice or shown anger or open hostility. He'd calmly told her to stay out of his life.

Maybe she had taken umbrage unnecessarily. But she was under a load of stress as well.

"I'm sorry, Mrs. Barve," she said. "It was silly of me to get upset."

Mrs. Barve nodded, her face looking more haggard than before.

Vinita realized all this had to be even more nerve-racking for Mrs. Barve. The woman had been suffering through this for quite some time.

"My wife and I will talk to him," offered Mr. Barve. "Make him understand."

"He is a very stubborn boy," added Mrs. Barve. "But he is not unreasonable."

Vishal looked across at them. "Do you think it would help if I talked to him?"

Both the Barves shook their heads.

"It is best that we do this on our own," said Mr. Barve. "He is a bit shocked right now, but I think he will listen to us when he feels better."

Vinita stared at the wall across the room, and the brass plaque engraved with the names of several generous donors to the hospital. A couple of the names were familiar—old names she'd known all her life—wealthy philanthropists. But her interest in them was fleeting. All her thoughts were centered on her son.

Had her trip to Palgaum been for nothing? Had she jeopardized her relationship with Girish and her marriage for nothing? Like a madwoman she'd rushed to get on the earliest plane so she could help her dying son. Her one thought had been to rectify her past mistakes. Now it seemed he was so hostile that he wanted nothing from her, even if he knew he'd die.

She remained silent for a long while before turning to the others. "I'm the one who should talk to him."

Mrs. Barve's eyes widened. "But—"

"I need to talk to him privately," Vinita said, cutting her off. "There are some things he has a right to know. Perhaps I can make him understand the circumstances under which he was . . . born and adopted."

She noticed Vishal's face hardening. She was offering to drag the sordid details of her past out into the open. It was his worst nightmare. Anything that cast a shadow on the Shelke family's reputation and integrity was a catastrophe for him. It was even more damaging for her aging mother. But there was no other way.

Vinita sent her brother a mute look of apology. But his expression remained frosty.

The Barves exchanged anxious looks. A long, awkward moment followed. The only sounds were from the two other people in the waiting room, speaking in whispers.

"Okay," said Mr. Barve finally, his stance clearly telling Vinita that this was surrender on his part. "Maybe you can try to convince him."

"Please don't upset him too much," pleaded Meenal. "He is very sick and he gets emotional easily."

Vinita sighed. "I can only promise to try."

"But you have to be very careful, you see."

"I don't know him or his personality. What I'll tell him would not be easy for anyone to understand, let alone Rohit." She saw Meenal Barve's mouth open to protest, and her husband grabbed her arm to stop her. "Thank you," she murmured to both of them. "I'll do the best I can."

Vishal got to his feet, his dark eyes looking like cool, polished marbles. "Vini, what the hell do you think you're doing?"

"What I need to do."

"One simple remark from him earlier got you upset . . ."

Vinita started moving toward the doorway. "That was an instant reaction. It won't happen again."

"Like hell it won't!" He fell in step with her. "If you're going to upset that boy and tell him every dirty secret, then I'm going with you."

"No." She stopped in her tracks and glared at her brother. "Haven't you done enough damage by keeping my son away from me?"

His brow descended in an enraged scowl. "How does common sense and taking care of one's family translate into damage?"

"Damn it, Vishal!" She heaved a sigh. "I didn't mean it that way, and you know it."

"What else does it mean?"

She ordered her taut shoulders to loosen a little. "Look, I need to talk to Rohit by myself. It's not something a man would understand." A tension headache had begun to set in. "Just leave me alone with my son for a while." She glanced up at him and held his gaze for a beat. "Please?"

He shut his eyes briefly, a habit of his when he was trying to rein in his temper—a habit Vinita knew well. When he opened his eyes, the ice had thawed around the edges. "Suit yourself." But he held up an index finger. "Don't say I didn't warn you."

He looked just like their late father. Vinita shivered a little.

Nonetheless she nodded her agreement and turned around to go back down the same corridor she'd walked twice in the past half hour. This time she proceeded slowly, using the time to think, to plan what she was going to say to her son—assuming he allowed her in his room. He could very well order her out and she'd have no choice but to leave. And then what?

The door to his room was open. She straightened her back and tucked her hair behind her ears before approaching it. She was going to deal with her mulish son one way or the other. She could be just as headstrong as he.

She heard voices coming from the room and hesitated for a moment. She and Vishal and the Barves had barely been out of there a few minutes and Rohit already had other visitors? It was a female voice that conversed in hushed tones with Rohit's baritone. Did he have a girlfriend? She mulled it over. Entirely possible. And why not? He was an attractive young man—hopefully with a healthy and happy future.

Her speculation ended when a plump, middle-aged nurse came out of his room. She eyed Vinita with interest for a second and went on her way. So much for the girlfriend theory.

Hands clenched into fists, Vinita stood on the threshold of Rohit's room. He was still propped up with pillows, reading the same magazine he'd been reading earlier. He seemed relaxed, very different from the uptight young man she'd met a little while ago.

He must have sensed her presence, because he lowered the magazine and looked up. Immediately his expression turned to stone. "You're still here?"

"I want to talk to you." She battled the urge to turn and run.

"I don't want to talk to you." His mouth compressed into a tight line.

She took a firm step forward. "What you *want* isn't important," she informed him, despite the nervous perspiration gathering under her arms. "What you *need* is."

He slapped the magazine down onto his lap. "Who are you to decide what I need?"

"I'm your mother, whether you like it or not."

"Is that right?" One thick eyebrow rose in contempt.

"Neither you nor I can change that."

"Doesn't mean you have a right to come barging into my life."

She drew a calming breath, reminded herself not to lose her temper. "Perhaps not. But you owe it to yourself to grab whatever help you can get."

"I have all the help I need. You can go back to your comfortable life in the U.S."

Despite the lecture she'd given herself, anger shot through her like a speeding arrow. But she quickly sheathed it. "I came here for a reason, and I don't plan to go back until I'm finished. Or at least given it my best."

"You have given it your best." He folded his arms across his chest. "Now go back."

"No." Vinita crossed her own arms to emulate his stance, then locked her gaze with his. Two could play this game. "You want to live, don't you?"

"Of course I want to live. But I'll do it on my—"

"Then stop being a brat. You're a college professor. Start behaving like one."

"What if I don't?" he tossed back.

"I'll return," she replied. "I'll keep coming back till you get it through your thick head that I'm not your enemy."

"What else would one call a mother who dumps her bastard and takes off to make a cozy life for herself?"

The boy certainly knew how to go for the jugular, but she refused to back down. "An ignorant bitch . . . perhaps . . . but not an enemy."

Vinita bit into her lower lip to stop the trembling. She hardly ever used vulgar language. But it gave her satisfaction to see the look in her son's eyes go from mutiny to astonishment. "Shocked you, huh?"

His arms unfolded and fell to his sides on the bed. "I don't feel very well. Please go."

She noticed the droopy look to his eyelids and mouth. Although the rage continued to spark in his eyes, he did look feverish and exhausted. Guilt enveloped her instantly. Regardless, she wasn't ready to give up on him yet. At least she'd managed to engage him in a conversation of sorts. That was something.

"I'll go for now. But I'll be back later," she said. "You can be sure of that."

He slid lower into the bed and lay flat on his back. "Is that a threat?"

"No, it's a promise."

Chapter 23

She woke up with a lethargic feeling and a headache for the second morning in a row. Today the pain in her skull was significantly worse—pounding like a hammer around the crown. Vinita dismissed it as the result of a restless night punctuated by bad dreams. For some reason, during this trip, jet lag was still bothering her after several days of being in India.

As she reluctantly slid out of bed and stood up, an unexpected wave of dizziness made her sway and slump back onto the bed. It passed in seconds, but a violent shiver ran through her, giving her goose bumps. She blinked a couple of times to clear the peculiar sensation.

Maybe it was frustration and tension that were causing her to feel fatigued. She was tired of waiting for Rohit to recover and get discharged from the hospital, tired of waiting for her blood tests to be done, tired of waiting to hear from her irate husband.

She hoped Rohit could go home today. His infection had supposedly cleared up. About time, too, since he'd been there for several days.

Her blood test for HLA typing was scheduled for later that morning. It would determine if she was a compatible donor for her son. As his mother, it was more or less certain she would pass the test, and she was impatient to get that over with. The sooner she could donate her bone marrow to Rohit and see him on the road to recovery, the better she'd feel.

Minutes later, as she bathed, her shivers intensified. Was she coming down with the flu? If so, the timing was rotten. The blood test would have to be postponed. But she couldn't afford to wait. She'd already used up several days of the maximum twelve weeks of family leave she had been granted by her employer. She couldn't stay in Palgaum indefinitely. She *had* to stay healthy. Quickly she toweled herself dry and put on some clothes.

When she appeared for breakfast a while later, Sayee eyed her with a frown. "Are you all right?"

"Sure." Vinita put on her sunniest smile.

"Your eyes are red. You look tired."

"Lack of sleep." She mulled it over for a bit. "I think it's also those tests I've been going through." As a potential marrow donor she'd been tested for everything from stress to hypertension and asthma, from heart disease to lung and liver function during the past week. She'd been forced to talk briefly to a psychiatrist as well.

She'd readily agreed to each and every one of those tests. And she'd passed every one.

"You may be right." Sayee put a scalding cup of tea in front of her. "What you need is a good breakfast. Anu is rolling fresh *chapatis*. I made fresh garlic chutney to go with it."

"Sounds delicious." Vinita took a sip of the rich tea and closed her eyes. "This tastes wonderful. Hot *chapatis* and tea brewed with loose tea leaves are a luxury for me."

"Relax and enjoy, then." Sayee busied herself getting plates. "Mummy should be done with her *pooja* in a few minutes."

The thought of having to sit across from her mother and face her silent condemnation was hardly pleasant. Vinita braced herself for it.

Thankfully, before Mummy could appear at the table, Vinita finished her breakfast and escaped to the sanctuary of her room. The feverish feeling had worsened while she was eating, so she lay down and covered herself with a blanket, then fell into a deep sleep.

Later that morning, Vinita watched the rich, cherry red blood trickle from her vein into the glass tube. The sight of her own blood rarely bothered her. It was other people's blood that made her light-headed. When Arya was a child and had to have several stitches in her head after she'd fallen off her bicycle, Vinita had become so dizzy from looking at the copious amounts of blood oozing out of Arya's scalp that she had nearly passed out.

"That's the last of it, Mrs. Patil," said the lab technician as he gently drew the needle out of Vinita's arm and pressed a wad of cotton on the punctured skin.

"When will I know if . . . I'm a match?" Vinita asked the technician.

He was a somber young man with eyeglasses and a goatee. Quiet, fast, and efficient, he had square, steady hands that seemed to be built for his occupation. He tossed the cotton ball into a trash can and put a small adhesive bandage on her arm before answering her question. "The results should be back within a day or two. The doctor will talk to you about it."

"All right." She observed him while he carefully sealed and labeled the tubes of blood. It had to be a hard job—taking samples of blood, urine, mucous, saliva, and God knows what else from people all day, every day. Inaccuracy could literally be a matter of life and death.

Thanking the man, she stepped out of the lab. It was a relief to walk away from that sterile room with its rows of tubes, bottles, syringes, and charts. It reminded her of what lay ahead.

What if, after all this effort, she still lost Rohit? It was hard to imagine, now that she'd seen him in the flesh, talked to him. Transplants were dangerous, unpredictable procedures. Rohit could die sooner than anticipated. The uneasy thought made her shiver. The headache from the morning was still with her.

Standing in the hallway for a minute, she ordered herself to ignore the chills and put a stop to the pessimism. This was only the beginning. She needed to be strong for the rest of the difficult journey. Maybe giving blood was making her a little shaky. Another long nap in the afternoon would fix that.

She started walking toward the staircase and took the single flight of steps down to the lobby, her legs feeling a little weak. What was the matter with her?

Sayee, who had driven her to the hospital and had been sitting in the waiting room, gave her an anxious look. "Did everything go okay?"

"Yes." Vinita mustered up a smile for Sayee's sake. Her sister-in-law generally had a ready grin and a warm sense of humor. Vinita didn't want to ruin her sunny mood.

"You still look tired—in spite of your long nap this morning," Sayee observed, rising from one of a dozen or so wooden chairs in the waiting room. "Let's go home and make sure you eat a good lunch." Sayee's answer to any problem was eating a hearty meal.

"I'm not hungry," said Vinita.

"After you give blood, you should drink and eat something immediately," Sayee scolded gently. "Otherwise you'll feel weak."

"I don't want to go home yet."

"You want to go shopping, then?" There was no mistaking the eager note in Sayee's voice. Next to feeding people she loved shopping.

Vinita shook her head. "Why don't you go on home, Sayee? I want to visit Rohit before he's released from the hospital."

Sayee's smile vanished. "I heard the boy was very nasty to you the other day."

"Can't blame him. He's been stuck in a sickroom for several days. He's impatient and frustrated." Vinita was surprised at her need to jump to her son's defense.

"Of course I feel sorry for the poor boy," Sayee allowed. "But Vishal and Mummy will be upset if I leave you alone with him."

"Vishal and Mummy get upset over the most trivial things."

"They care about you, Vini."

"I realize that. I'll explain to them later. You go on home and I'll take a rickshaw after I'm done here."

Sayee hesitated. "If you're sure . . ."

"Positive." Vinita nudged her toward the exit. "I'd like to get to know my son."

"Rohit doesn't know that you have already taken the compatibility tests, does he?"

"No. But I intend to tell him." She gave it a moment's thought as she and Sayee walked out of the waiting room. "There have been enough secrets around here."

"It's not Vishal's fault that he kept Rohit a secret. He was only trying to protect you. So was Mummy."

Vinita couldn't help smiling. Sayee was such a loyal wife and daughter-in-law. "It doesn't make it easier to forgive, though."

Sayee pushed open the doors leading out into the blinding noon sunlight. "If you can't find a rickshaw, then call me, okay?"

"I will." Vinita stepped outside with her and squinted against the glare of the sun. The tropical heat felt marvelous on her chilled skin, like an electric blanket wrapped around her. "Thanks for driving me here and waiting for me."

"Don't be silly." Sayee dug the car keys out of her bag and turned toward the parking lot.

"Don't delay lunch for my sake. Go ahead and eat without me." Vinita watched Sayee get behind the wheel of the car and put on her driving glasses. She was lucky to have a sister-in-law who was so protective and caring. Despite the upheaval Vinita was causing in their lives, Sayee was handling it with her characteristic cheerfulness.

Sayee waved at her and drove away.

Vinita stood there for several minutes, trying to soak up every bit of sun. An unexpected sense of loneliness crept over her. The building behind her seemed more cheerless than it had earlier that day, a place where people often went in and never came out, a grim reminder that life was fragile and could crumble any second.

Right from the time she'd read that anonymous letter, she'd been alone in this mess. Matter of fact, she'd been alone going all the way back to her teenage years, when she'd first bumped into Som Kori. More than three decades later, she was still paying the price for surrendering to the lure of the forbidden.

Turning around, she found her way to the wing where Rohit's room was located. The chills returned immediately and she started shivering again. It had to be the air-conditioning, she told herself. She'd always been a lover of warm weather.

Just outside Rohit's door, she waited, listened for voices. If he had visitors, or maybe a nurse attending to him, she didn't want to interrupt.

Hearing no voices and seeing the door open, she did what she'd done the other day: she stood on the threshold and gazed at him. This morning he wasn't in bed. He was dressed in street clothes and sitting in the only available chair, which was pulled close to the window. A black canvas bag sat on the floor next to him. It looked like he was being released. It was a relief to know he was finally well enough to go home.

He was staring pensively at something outside the window. He didn't notice her presence. Taking advantage of the opportunity, she studied him, absorbing all the details she hadn't had a chance to until now.

It was amazing how this deep need to know every little thing about her son had come upon her the moment she'd discovered his existence. In fact, in an attempt to absorb the odd wonder of it, she'd silently chanted *I have a son* over and over again. It was still difficult to comprehend that this young man was her child—the baby that had kicked her with all his might for weeks while growing in her womb. She'd always known her baby was a boy.

Despite his fierce Kori looks, she could see the resemblance to his cousins, Vishal's twin boys—mostly around the jaw and hairline. It was satisfying to note that he had some Shelke in him. But she found no likeness to Arya—because Arya had taken after Girish's side of the family. She hoped her children at least shared some mental and emotional characteristics.

Dressed in jeans and a white T-shirt, Rohit's hair was neatly brushed. He sat with one foot resting over the other knee. He wore casual *chappals* on his large feet. He was quite tall for a boy whose mother was petite. The foot resting on the floor was tapping a quick, rhythmic beat.

Impatience, she concluded, looking at that restless foot. Vishal often did that, too. Rohit seemed to be deep in thought, with his elbow braced on the arm of the chair and his cheek resting on his fist. What was he thinking about? Pleasant thoughts? Or were they about his chances of survival? About his real mother, who had suddenly popped into his life and was now causing such turmoil?

And what was it *she* felt for this boy? She couldn't quite call it love. She didn't know him enough to love him in the true sense. And yet, the sudden rush of emotion she'd experienced just now, when she'd laid eyes on him, had to mean something.

When she'd had her fill of observing him in silence, she knocked on the door.

Startled, he turned his face to the door. Then he hissed out an unmistakable sigh.

She stepped inside the room despite the openly hostile reception. She might as well have been a poisonous insect that had flown in unannounced. "I made a promise that I'd be back."

"Hmph," he grunted. "I don't remember asking you to come." A spark of angry defiance lit up his golden eyes, giving them a feline appearance.

"No, but I happened to be at the hospital," she replied, managing to sound nonchalant. "I came to get myself tested as your potential donor."

He didn't respond, but she saw the slightest twitch in his jaw. Her words had registered on some level. The boy was probably all bark and no bite. She'd take her chances with him. He could push her away all he wanted, but she knew how to shove back with equal strength.

"May I please sit down?" she asked, pointing to the bed that was already made. There was no other place to sit.

He shrugged, clearly indicating he didn't care whether she sat down or hung upside down from the ceiling.

Without waiting for his reply, she sat on the edge of the bed and placed her handbag beside her. She badly needed to sit. She gave herself a moment to think of something suitable to say. "Looks like you're being released today?"

"Hmm." He returned his gaze to the scene outside the window, turning his back to her. Rude behavior—but justifiable in his case. Every time he behaved like a bear, she had to remind herself that he was unwell. Cancer wasn't some simple illness like the flu. It ruined a person physically, mentally, and emotionally. He was entitled to a little boorishness.

"Is your . . . are your parents coming to fetch you?" She looked at her wristwatch. It was past noon. She probably had very little time alone with him if they were expected soon.

"Hmm."

She sighed. But if he thought his monosyllabic answers and body language were going to send her running, he was mistaken.

"Look, I know you hate me," she said in a matter-of-fact tone. "But will you at least let me explain something?"

He shrugged again.

"So you're not interested, but I'm going to explain anyway. I would have told you the other day, but you as good as tossed me out of here."

He remained silent, so she continued. "Rohit, I didn't know I had a son until a few weeks ago. I had no idea you existed."

The last thing she expected was laughter, but he exploded into it, a harsh, barking sound that startled her. "Good story."

"It's the truth," she insisted. "Didn't your parents tell you anything about your birth? How you came to be adopted by them?"

She got no answer. It seemed like they hadn't told him much. So she'd tell him the facts—from the beginning. She'd set him straight. "You were delivered by caesarean under general anesthesia. When I woke up several hours after the surgery, they told me my child was born dead."

"They?" That's when he turned around to look at Vinita. "Who are *they?*" His expression still held traces of the earlier mockery. But he wasn't laughing. Plus, he was talking. They were having an actual conversation, which was more than she'd hoped for.

"My family and the doctor . . . and the nurse," she answered. "I understand she's your great-aunt?" *Anonymous.*

"You believed them?" His eyebrows were raised high.

She glanced upward at the ceiling, recalling the scene from long ago—the familiar sense of loss, the emptiness that had slowly sunk in when she was told her baby was born dead. The memory still brought a certain amount of hollowness.

"I know it sounds incredible, but I was suffering from pneumonia," she explained. "I had a raging fever. You were a breech baby and I was too sick to breathe normally, let alone give birth, so the doctor suggested a C-section. But I refused to have it until the very end, thinking it would harm the baby. I was convinced that the baby would flip over on its own and be born the normal way."

That seemed to gain his attention. He shifted in his chair so he faced her. "And it didn't?"

"No." She swiped her knuckles across her eyes to dispel the tears that insisted on escaping. She didn't want to cry before her son—show him how weak and vulnerable she was where he was concerned. "They told me the baby died—deprived of oxygen because I waited too long to let them perform the surgery."

He appeared genuinely intrigued now. His tawny eyes were narrowed on her. Som used to look at her like that at times—in quiet speculation. "Didn't you ask for proof?"

"Believe me, the first thing I asked was to see my child. You can ask your great-aunt about this. She was there."

"Hmm."

That annoying grunt was all he gave. Vinita wondered if he'd ever been told that his aunt had been instrumental in his adoption. Exactly how much did he know?

"I was told my baby had died hours earlier, and they had to dispose of the body, do what they had to do—as quickly as possible." She paused for a beat. "For me the burden of guilt was overwhelming. My stubbornness had killed my baby." That was the part she'd never forgiven her family for, more than anything else. She'd carried the burning guilt all these years, when there hadn't been any need for it.

His eyes were wide with dismay. He obviously didn't know this part. "What about a funeral for him?"

"A funeral?" It was her turn to give a wry laugh. "I accepted that he was probably cremated very quietly in the dead of night. The whole thing was a big secret, you see. My pregnancy, the childbirth . . . everything. The minute I confessed to my family that I was having a baby, I was quietly packed off to Bombay and kept behind closed doors in my brother's flat."

"You didn't protest?"

"I was a helpless teenager. I had no place to go and no money, so I had to let my parents and brother take care of me. Besides, I was having the baby against their wishes. They wanted me to have an abortion to save them and myself the shame and humiliation of an illegitimate pregnancy. I disobeyed them on that count, so the least I could do was cooperate with them in other matters."

Rohit leaned forward, his arms braced on his thighs. "I'm surprised they allowed you the luxury of disobedience."

Her mouth tilted at the corners despite the tears that continued to fill her eyes. "If killing me were a viable option, I think my father would have resorted to it. Under the circumstances, they had to do what was best for the family's reputation. An unwed mother was viewed as a disaster three decades ago."

He nodded, probably understanding for the first time what her predicament must have cost her. "It's still a disaster in our culture." He glanced at her. "Did they manage to keep the secret?"

She hesitated. "I think so. The doctor was a friend of Vishal's and his clinic was in a quiet suburb of Bombay. And then the baby was supposedly born dead. It was hushed up very quickly."

He steepled his long, lean fingers and studied Vinita, his expression bland. "And you got on with your life, while your bastard son became someone else's responsibility."

The boy didn't mince words. The term bastard was precise, if nothing else. "If I had the merest suspicion that my son was alive, he would have been *my* responsibility. I wanted him . . . Wanted you."

"You were going to raise your child alone?" There was aloofness in his tone, like he was speaking about a stranger.

"The child was *you*, Rohit. I would have worked at a nursery school or even as a domestic servant to support you. But I would have raised you on my own." She gave him a moment to think about what she'd told him. "I'd never have given you up."

He stared at her. "But I *was* given up."

"Yes—by my family, not by me." When was he going to get it through his supposedly smart brain that she had been as much in the dark about his adoption as he was? "Not by me," she repeated. "But I'm glad you were raised by good, honest people like the Barves." She raised a brow at him. "They are good parents?"

"The best." The same look that had relieved the harshness of his expression the last time settled over his face. He seemed to be genuinely fond of the Barves. "I consider myself lucky when I see some of the misery."

"You mean other adopted children?"

"I mean the children in orphanages. They're practically starved . . . and they suffer from every kind of disease, malnutrition, neglect."

"My family would never give away a child to some orphanage." She wasn't sure of that fact, but she was duty bound to defend her own.

"You said they were strict—"

"But not heartless," she cut in. "Vishal apparently did some research on your parents when your aunt recommended them. He thought they would give you a good home."

"And they did."

"I'm glad."

"And you just pretended like nothing happened."

She shook her head. "I never forgot my experience or my child. Yes, I went back to college, got myself a job. What other choice did I have?" She paused for a beat. "I even got married, which was a miracle, considering how I'd been ruined as a young woman. But I never stopped thinking about my son."

"Your husband didn't mind your past?" Some of Rohit's earlier aloofness had vanished.

She wondered how much she should reveal, then decided to err on the side of honesty. "He didn't know about my past."

"You deceived him?" His expression bordered on contempt.

"For a reason. You see, I kept telling the truth to every potential groom who was introduced to me . . . and every one of them turned me down."

"Can you blame them?"

"No," she admitted. "Men can do whatever they please in our society and still get on with their lives, but a woman makes a single mistake and she pays for it forever."

Rohit nodded his agreement and Vinita glanced at him in surprise. What, no defending his own sex?

"Eventually, when a man living in the U.S. came to our house to meet me as a potential bride, Vishal ordered me to keep my mouth shut," she continued. "For some reason I couldn't tell this man the truth. I wanted to, but I couldn't. Something held me back. Anyway, Vishal's command worked."

"Does this goddamned Vishal dictate everything to you?" retorted Rohit, his nostrils flaring.

"Don't swear!" she reprimanded. "Vishal's my older brother. He's your uncle, and you wouldn't be where you are today if it weren't for him." She realized at once that she'd instinctively sprung to her brother's defense. Vishal wasn't exactly in her good graces, either, but he'd likely done whatever he'd done out of a sense of duty. And she wouldn't allow anyone to malign her brother.

"Hmph," was all she got from Rohit. He definitely needed a few lessons in propriety.

Nonetheless, she decided to overlook his churlishness and proceed with her story. Her watch told her she was probably running out of time. His parents could arrive at any moment and whisk him away.

"Girish, my husband, was divorced, but he was a decent man," she said. "When he proposed to me, I accepted."

"I see." Rohit was staring at the floor now.

"I'm glad I did. He's been a good husband and good father."

Rohit raised his gaze back to her. "Tell me something. How did you find out about me—that I was alive—and that I had leukemia?"

She wasn't sure if she should mention the anonymous letter. It could be from his great-aunt, and if that was true, then the entire family could turn against the old woman. She had to be quite old by now. "Somehow I managed to discover your existence," she said.

"How?" he demanded. "Who told you? Your brother?"

"No."

"Then who?"

"I got a . . . letter from some unknown person." She ignored the chill crawling over her skin and making her shudder again.

"Is that the truth?" he demanded.

"Why would I lie to you? My family certainly wasn't going to tell me. Some stranger wrote me a letter and told me my son was alive, but he had leukemia and I could perhaps help by donating my bone marrow." When he looked like he wanted her to continue, she added, "I didn't believe it at first. It was a shock, but then I called Vishal, and he finally admitted the truth." She paused. "But he didn't know you were seriously ill until I asked about it."

Rohit stared at his hands, as if the answer lay in them somewhere. "I wonder who it could be—your anonymous communicator."

Vinita decided to keep her suspicions to herself. "I can't think of anyone. It's a big mystery." She gave him a second to get his mind back on track. "But you know what? I'm glad someone decided to spill the truth at last. I would've gone through my entire life not knowing I had a son."

Suddenly he changed the subject. "You have children?"

Vinita smiled. "One daughter. She's twenty-three years old."

"Does she look like you?"

"Not much. She's prettier than I am. And she's a sweet, bright girl."

For the first time since she'd met him, a hint of interest flitted across his hard face. "I have a half sister?"

"Yes. And she knows about you."

"She probably hates me, I bet." He seemed to enjoy the idea that a stranger hated him. This young man had an odd temperament for sure.

"Not at all. Arya's an affectionate girl. She wants to meet you someday, if possible."

"She doesn't mind? I mean . . . about me?"

"You don't know my daughter. She's a generous soul." Vinita's smile returned. "She has a short fuse, and she can be extremely stubborn, but she's got a big heart all the same."

He grew quiet for a long time and went back to staring at his hands. Vinita wondered if her time was up. Maybe she was dismissed. She had to be grateful for the time she'd been lucky enough to have with him. She cleared her throat to nudge him out of his introspection.

He finally looked up. There was an odd expression on his face. "Who's my father?"

Her stomach clenched. She knew the question was bound to come up sooner or later. But she didn't want to face it. She shook her head. "That's not important. He's someone I banished from my mind years ago."

"Why didn't you marry him?"

"Don't you think I tried? I would've liked to give my son his rightful place in society. The boy . . . man who was your father, offered to pay for an abortion. He thought it was all a joke—a simple mistake that could be easily rectified."

"How did you get involved with a man like that?" Rohit asked, his lips curling in contempt.

"It's a long story. Like I said, I was a gullible teenager with a sound brain but very plain looks. The first boy who claimed to find me attractive was . . . whom I got involved with."

"What exactly happened?"

"Like a bad movie, my life went straight into the gutter the minute I met him."

"You must have met him in college?"

She didn't answer that. Rohit's line of questioning was getting dangerously close to some things best left alone. "So, how are you feeling today?" she asked instead. "Are you still on antibiotics?"

"I'm fine. That's why I'm finally going home." He gave her a pointed look. "Please don't change the subject. I want to know who my father is."

"It doesn't matter, Rohit. He . . . he wasn't a very nice man. You're lucky not to have known him."

"I'll decide that for myself."

"Mr. Barve appears to be a good father. Don't go looking for trouble."

Rohit's jaw tensed, telling her his temper was stirring. He raised a finger at her. "Listen, Mrs. Patil, you're the one who came in here offering to help me. You're the one who insisted on telling me the details of how and why I was born. You're the one who is sitting here now, trying to dissuade me from learning the truth about my real father. You can't have it both ways. You need to tell it all."

Vinita slid off the bed and stood up, fighting the sensation that the room was spinning a bit. "I'm looking out for you and your parents, Rohit. Try to understand that. It could lead to a lot of problems."

God, what had she done? Why had she felt the need to tell her son the repugnant details of her past? If she'd just donated the bone marrow and then disappeared from his life, she'd have been all right. They'd all have been. But this silly urge to get through to her son, get to know him a little and make him accept her, had led to other things.

He stood, too. For the first time she could see how tall he really was. He probably stood about five foot ten or so. Notwithstanding the nervous knots in her stomach, a warm beam of light seemed to melt and loosen some of those knots. Despite the ravages of leukemia, he was a handsome boy. And he was smart—like herself and her brother. If Rohit had brains, they couldn't possibly have come through the Kori genes.

With what sounded like a threat, he looked down at her. "You think I can't find out a simple fact like who you had an affair with? I teach at Shivraj College. You probably attended the same college."

"Don't do this, Rohit," she pleaded. But even before she'd

said it, she knew it was futile. There was that unfortunate proclivity for obstinacy in her side of the family. He'd go after the facts like a bloodhound and hunt them down.

"I can easily find out who my father is." His jaw was working and the eyes had a stubborn look about them, proving her hunch.

She rubbed her forehead. *What to do?* "Please, Rohit, stop asking me. A lot of people could get hurt." Once again, Vishal's and her mother's dire predictions came to mind.

"I want to know who my father is," he affirmed.

Footsteps were coming down the corridor. She hoped she'd be saved by them. "Someone's coming," she said, tilting her head in the direction of the door.

"Mrs. Patil, *who* is my father?" he repeated, ignoring her remark.

The footsteps were closer now.

"You win, Rohit. But don't say I didn't warn you. If you must know, your father is Somesh Kori."

Vinita heard a gasp and turned to look toward the door. Meenal Barve stood frozen on the threshold, her eyes wide, her hand pressed against her mouth.

Mr. Barve was a step behind her, his expression hard as diamonds.

Vinita turned her attention to Rohit. Her son's golden eyes had turned dark with emotion. Was it shock? Disgust? Fury? It was impossible to tell.

Chapter 24

The odors of his mother's cooking met Rohit the instant he unlocked the front door and stepped into the drawing room of his parents' home. Fish curry. She was making his favorite—fiery red gravy with pomfret.

His mother was trying hard to draw him out, to cheer him up. But neither his appetite nor his spirits showed signs of perking up.

Just another day in the life of a cancer victim.

Kicking off his black leather *chappals,* he shut the door behind him and leaned back against it. He was exhausted. Teaching just two classes, followed by the short motorcycle ride, had worn him out. The antibiotic prescribed for his latest infection must have been powerful. He had stopped taking it, but the weariness persisted.

Pocketing his keys, he went to the sofa and stretched out on it. It was a relief to feel the firm, cool vinyl underneath his weakening body, which eased the deep ache inside his bones. He rarely spoke about it to his parents, or even his doctors.

What was the use of complaining, anyway? All they'd do is pump more medicines into him, fuss over him, and force him to eat. He was sick of medicines, sick of food, and even more sick of attention.

News about his illness had spread very quickly through the community. Not at all surprising in this gossip-hungry town. His fellow professors looked at him with uncharacteristic pity lately, offering unexpected gestures of kindness. The unfriendly ones were stopping to have a word with him. Even the stingy ones were offering to buy him a cup of tea—as if leukemia somehow made a man penniless on top of destroying his health.

His students, even the ones who used to play practical jokes on him, had begun to treat him with more respect. Who needed pity disguised as respect? Why couldn't everyone treat him like they had in the past? He was sick of being handled like an injured butterfly.

He shut his eyes and threw an arm over them. The only sounds in the house were the scraping of spoons against pots in the kitchen, and his mother's radio. The daily news was on, the monotonous voice of the reader annoyingly soothing, cultivated, and trained not to irritate the listeners. And yet its very refinement grated on Rohit's nerves.

But none of that was the reason for his present state of mind. It was something else. Ever since that woman, his biological mother, had informed him that his real father was Somesh Kori, Rohit had had difficulty focusing on anything—even his work. If there was one thing that usually took his mind off his illness, it was his job. But the shock of learning about his real identity was destroying his mind—and to some extent, his body.

He'd always known he was adopted. His parents had made no secret of it. But no one had known he was a Kori—no one other than the Shelke family.

Why hadn't he made the connection before? His unusual eyes should have been an indication. There was only one man—one conceited man—that Rohit knew, who had those very same eyes: Som Kori. Of all the men in the entire world, that one had to be his father.

Something else struck him in that instant. The two Kori girls, who were his students, were his . . . half sisters. Good Lord, one of them even had eyes like his. Why hadn't he paid attention to that before? It was so clear now, the resemblance.

"You're home early, Rohit." His mother's voice interrupted his thoughts as she emerged from the kitchen, wiping her hands on a towel. "How are you feeling?"

"I'm all right," Rohit replied testily, reluctant to tell her he had cancelled his last class because he'd felt too weak to stand before a group of students for nearly an hour and deliver a lecture. She'd end up asking more questions and he wasn't sure he had the answers.

"Would you like some tea?" she queried.

Rohit shook his head. Tea wasn't likely to remedy his problem. "I think I'll rest a little." His parents had insisted that he move back in with them for a while, so they could keep an eye on him. He didn't like the idea of giving up his privacy, but he was too exhausted these days to do anything for himself, so it was convenient to stay with them.

His mother quickly strode over to his side and put a hand on his forehead. "You don't have a fever, I hope?"

"No fever. I'm just . . . tired." She worried too much. He looked at her face. He'd been looking at her a lot lately—staring at her at times, like studying a stranger with an objective eye. This was the woman who had reared him as her own. She was thirty-nine years old when she and his father had adopted him. Shashi Barve was forty-three then.

She wasn't a pretty woman, but her face had kindness and tolerance embedded in every line and spot. There was a certain quiet dignity in her that commanded respect. From the servant who came in each day to do the household work to their friends and acquaintances, Meenal Barve was looked upon with fond regard.

He couldn't remember a single day when she'd raised her hand or her voice to him—not even when he'd disobeyed her or his father, or landed in trouble. And he had got himself into lots of mischief as a little boy, and later as a teenager.

She'd discovered that he was secretly smoking cigarettes for a while, that he had been cutting classes while in college and nearly failed in two courses, that he was betting money on card games and losing badly. But she had quietly treated him with a firm hand, and she had never broken her promise not to mention his indiscretions to his father.

To this day, Papa didn't know about those incidents. It was

their secret—his and his mother's. He smiled at her. "I'm okay . . . really."

"Why don't you try to sleep until Papa comes home from his meeting?" She tucked a pillow under his head.

He stiffened. "What meeting?"

"Political, of course," she replied. "They are planning something big. Your father will not tell me, but I know."

"Hmph," Rohit groaned, his eyes going to the photos lining the drawing-room walls. Papa's proud legacy.

His father's political activities were the reason for most arguments in their home. It hadn't been as bad when his father had initially become involved with the Marathi Samithi because of his deep love for the Marathi language and culture, and his belief that Palgaum rightfully belonged in the Marathi-speaking state of Maharashtra. Rohit had even admired his father's passion, his capacity for selfless service to the cause.

Eventually, after retiring from his job, Shashi Barve had taken on the role of chairman of the organization. His anti-Kannada sentiments had become more acrid, then turned into a personal battle. Slowly he'd become consumed by his need to destroy the Kannada people of the world.

But Papa had backed off a little after Rohit's illness had been diagnosed. That was the only good thing that had come from the leukemia.

"You know what that means," said Meenal, interrupting his musings again. "He is going to be moody."

Rohit shifted from his back to his side so he could face his mother. "I thought he had withdrawn a little from the Samithi since my sickness."

"Yes, for a short time, because he wanted to spend more time with you. But now that you have returned to work and you are waiting for a donor, he has gone back to it." She was silent for a beat. "I'm worried about something, Rohit."

"What?"

"Since Mrs. Patil told us about . . . you know. . ."

"Som Kori," Rohit prompted. Both his parents seemed to have difficulty saying that name.

She nodded. "Your father has become more . . ."

"Vindictive? Hostile?"

"Both." She sighed and turned to go back to the kitchen. "Get some rest until dinner."

His eyes were beginning to shut even before she was gone from the room. It was almost as if the energy was draining from his body in droplets, slowly depleting him of life. In actuality, it was. He was tired of living this way.

The woman who claimed to be his birth mother was now offering him her bone marrow. Although the offer was tempting, he didn't want anything from her. Besides, the cost of a bone marrow transplant was prohibitive. His own meager savings would never cover the price, and he certainly wouldn't allow his parents to deplete theirs. After all that, what was the guarantee that he'd live? A minor infection could kill him when his immune system was reduced to nothing.

But the fact remained that the woman had traveled all the way from the U.S. to help him.

He wasn't as enraged at her now as he was the day he'd met her. When she'd explained how he'd ended up being adopted, he had reluctantly accepted that he had been better off as the Barves' son than the illegitimate son of a teenager. He wouldn't have had a life. He wouldn't have acquired a good education, or taken on a respectable profession.

The Barves weren't wealthy and Rohit would never become rich as a college professor, but he liked his job. He was respected in Palgaum as a man who had earned a PhD at an early age, and instead of going into private industry he had decided to take up a less lucrative but more honorable occupation. He was happy. At least he used to be happy—until leukemia had abruptly invaded his life.

What was he to do now? Accept that woman's offer? Reject it because he was too proud to accept charity from a woman who was his mother but not really his mother, and eventually die? What if she wasn't even a compatible donor? She'd go back to where she belonged and he could go back to facing a death warrant.

But, as his mother, the chances of her being compatible were nearly perfect.

An hour later, Rohit woke up from his nap and found himself in near-total darkness. His mother must have deliberately kept the lights off in the room so he could sleep.

The temperature was noticeably cooler than when he'd fallen asleep. He sat up and stretched. The aroma of fish curry was stronger now, so it was dinnertime or thereabouts. He wondered if his father had come home from his meeting yet.

Rising to his feet, Rohit swayed a little and grabbed the arm of the sofa. He resented the weak feeling. He used to be a star cricketer in his college days—despite his diabetes. Now he was reduced to this pathetic weakling. It wasn't fair.

Shaking off the self-pity, he turned on the lights and padded toward the bathroom. He needed to take his insulin injection before sitting down to dinner. The tile floor of the drawing room felt cool on his bare soles and woke him up some more. As he headed down the short passageway, he heard his parents' voices coming from the direction of their bedroom.

His father was home. Rohit would have ignored their voices if it hadn't sounded like a heated argument.

He halted in his tracks. They spoke in low tones behind the closed door. But it was still a quarrel.

His mother sounded distressed. "Just because we know that man is Rohit's father, you can't just—"

"I didn't do anything!" His father was angry, defensive.

"Then why is this happening *now* . . . within a few days of finding out about Kori?"

"Coincidence. Some of our Marathi young men are hot-headed."

"Why do you instigate such things?" she demanded.

"Inspiring people to take pride in their heritage is not instigating," retorted his father.

"We have so many things to worry about and you are out inspiring people? Rohit is sick again. There is the transplant, and

Vinita Patil . . ." His mother's voice trailed off, the frustration clearly evident.

Having heard enough, Rohit quietly proceeded to the bathroom. This was one of the main reasons he'd moved away from home and into his own flat. As his father had grown older, he had become more bigoted. Besides the photographs, the house was filled with pickets, banners, cuttings from newspapers and magazines, people coming over for impromptu meetings. Everywhere Rohit turned, he was bombarded by politics.

His father had progressively gone from an ordinary engineer to a political hero. Rohit was terrified of his father's philosophy. It was a virulent form of cancer in itself, not unlike Hitler's view of Semites, albeit on a small scale.

To top it all off, Rohit's parents' arguments had escalated. There was so much unnecessary strife. His own illness and the ensuing tension were making the situation worse.

As an educator, Rohit had very little interest in politics. While he was still a young and idealistic college student some years ago, he had marched in a few Marathi rallies. But that had become stale after a while. Now that he was older, wiser, and he taught an equal number of students from both the Marathi and Kannada communities, his focus had shifted. Politics was something he'd left behind a while back.

He wished his father would do the same and enjoy what was left of his retirement.

Minutes later, when he emerged from the bathroom, everything was quiet. His parents' disagreement had come to its natural conclusion: his mother had likely shaken her head in resignation and his father had marched out of the bedroom, belligerent and unwilling to give up his beloved cause.

He heard the sounds of his mother setting the table for dinner—the clang of stainless steel *thalis,* spoons, water tumblers. A variety of fiery hot pickles and chutneys would sit in the center of the table. What used to make his hungry stomach rumble with anticipation now managed to nauseate him. He rubbed a hand over his roiling belly.

His father was seated on the sofa, watching the evening news on television.

Shashi turned his head when he heard Rohit's footsteps, studying his son for a second. "How are you feeling?" he asked. There was no lingering anger or resentment from his earlier argument with his wife.

"Better. I slept a little," replied Rohit, and sat down in one of the chairs.

"Took your insulin?"

"Yes." He kept his eyes on the TV. He didn't want his father to guess he'd overheard some of the conversation behind the bedroom door.

The local Palgaum news segment came on, instantly capturing Rohit's attention. Plastered across the screen were the graffiti-covered wall and broken windows of Som Kori's office. The bold black-and-white sign was hanging crooked. KORI ENTERPRISES. So this was what his mother was accusing his father of instigating.

He glanced across at his father, who sat in stoical silence. The expression on his lined face was benign, that of a retired man who lived a quiet, uncomplicated life.

It was hard to tell with certainty if the old man was responsible for this latest round of violence.

Chapter 25

Vinita gaped at the doctor. "What?" He'd just dropped a bombshell by informing her that she couldn't donate her bone marrow to Rohit. And the reason sounded preposterous. What in God's name was he talking about?

"That's right, Mrs. Patil," he repeated. "You have malaria." Dr. Panchal was a heavy man with a balding pate and small, round eyes. He shifted in his chair, making it groan. He seemed so businesslike, so distant—almost robotic in his movements.

"Malaria?" she whispered, her heart taking a dive. "But . . . but how?"

"Malaria is endemic in these parts," he calmly reminded her. "You have the symptoms, don't you?"

"I guess so." She racked her brain for a logical answer to the puzzle. Granted, there were mosquitoes all over India. Palgaum had more than its share of the pesky insects as well. She had bites all over her body to prove it.

"Most permanent residents develop immunity to the carrier mosquito," the doctor explained. "But you've been living in a different country for many years."

"Is it fatal?" Had she come all the way to Palgaum only to die?

He shook his head. "You have the vivax variety and not the dangerous falciparum. It is easily treatable." He managed to crack a wry smile. "Didn't you talk to your physician about antimalarial drugs before you left the U.S.?"

"No . . . I didn't." The thought hadn't even crossed Vinita's mind. She had never gotten immunized for her past visits to India, either. She hadn't imagined a disease like malaria would ever attack her. How stupid was that?

She hated the thought of being so sick. No wonder she'd been suffering from chills, headaches, and fever the last couple of days. She'd denied it, fought it with aspirin, but nothing had helped. Now she knew why, hard as it was to comprehend.

She and Vishal were seated across from the doctor's desk in his overcrowded office. It was obvious he was a very busy hematologist-oncologist. Back when she and Vishal were growing up, there were no specialties called hematology or oncology, let alone a specialist in both in their town. Apparently now there were loads of people suffering from all sorts of cancer.

"But what about after she recovers?" Vishal countered, sounding as incredulous as Vinita. "She can become a donor in a week or two, right?"

The doctor shook his melon-shaped head. "Even after she makes a complete recovery, assuming she does, she'll have to wait more than a year to be tested again as a donor."

"Oh no!" Vinita's eyes opened wide when a thought struck her. "Is it contagious? Could I have given it to Rohit when I visited him?" She'd been in denial that she was ill when she'd visited him. The need to see Rohit and make him accept her had been uppermost, to the point of obliterating common sense.

"No. It's not contagious," the doctor replied.

"Thank God!" Nonetheless, all her hopes about saving her son vanished in that instant. She'd had such dreams—that he'd become healthy again—that they'd stay in touch after she returned to the U.S. Perhaps he could visit her in the future, meet Arya . . . maybe even meet Girish.

There was so much catching up to do. She wanted to know everything about Rohit. She wanted him to go back to his job, get married, have a family.

It had been a pleasant dream. Now, as the doctor explained the facts, her spirits sagged. Her fever was rising, too. She could feel it. It seemed to climb in the late afternoons and peak in the evenings. The nightly chills were the worst. She'd managed to hide them from her family as much as she could, but Sayee and her mother had been questioning her about her listlessness and lack of appetite.

Vinita glanced at her brother. He was frowning, probably having the same thoughts she was. She'd undertaken a long, expensive trip to offer herself as a donor, taken uncompensated leave, and she'd paid for the donor tests from her own pocket. But now she was being told all of it was for naught.

She gave herself a minute to mull over the doctor's words. "You're sure it's not just some ordinary virus?"

Dr. Panchal got up from his chair, making it clear he wasn't amused by her question. The meeting was over. He was a busy man, with a roomful of patients waiting their turn outside the door. "Positive, Mrs. Patil. You'll need to get treatment immediately." He pinned her with a bland look. "Our lab here is as efficient as any in the U.S."

"I know it is. It's just that . . . Never mind." Vinita reluctantly stood up. "So what do we do now?"

"We can hope that someone new joins the donor registry and turns out to be a match," was the doctor's matter-of-fact reply. He walked toward the closed door and grasped the doorknob, Vishal following on his heels.

"Rohit may have to wait forever," murmured Vinita.

"We can only hope for the best," was the doctor's brisk reply.

"Thank you for your time, Dr. Panchal," said Vishal, nudging Vinita toward the exit. "You've been most helpful."

The doctor nodded in acknowledgment and held the door open for Vinita and Vishal to pass. "If we hear anything from the registry, my office will contact you immediately."

He had to be kidding, reflected Vinita. What registry? There was practically no registry to speak of. This was the end of the road, then. It seemed so pointless now, all this frenzied activity, excitement, submitting herself to so many tests.

She staggered out of the office and followed Vishal to his car. He immediately turned to her with a cutting rebuke. "Damn it, Vini, why didn't you tell me you were so sick?"

"I didn't think it was anything serious, Vishal," she replied in her defense. She settled into the passenger seat and waited till her brother slid behind the wheel. "Besides, Panchal could be wrong, couldn't he?" Deep down, she knew he was right.

"Panchal is the best around. He was trained in the States—some prestigious teaching hospital in Boston, I believe."

"Maybe he's right," she mumbled, winding the *pallu* of her sari around her shoulders to ward off the chill.

"How could you not know you're sick?" He studied her closely for a moment. "Look at you. The car feels so damn hot, and you seem to be cold."

"That's because I'm angry and frustrated. I never expected—"

"Stop being a fool. Malaria can be fatal." He put a hand to her forehead, his frown deepening. "You're burning up."

"I'm sorry." He was right. She was feeling pretty awful.

"I'm taking you to Dr. Desai right now," announced Vishal, making the decision arbitrarily—as usual.

But she didn't bother to argue. He was right. She was very ill and needed help.

They drove to the doctor's office in silence.

Chapter 26

The next three days were hell. Vinita spent them in bed, alternating between chills and hot sweats, depending on whether her fever was rising or falling. She'd never experienced such high fever in her entire life.

Sayee fussed over her like a mother hen, clucking and insisting on bringing her meals to the bedroom on a tray.

Not that Vinita was eating or drinking much of anything. The constant nausea and vomiting, side effects of the prescription drug called chloroquine, made her turn away from the sight and smell of food. She'd been surviving mostly on soft drinks. Frequent trips to the bathroom left her weak and hurrying back to bed.

The only good thing about her illness was that her mother came to sit beside her bed often, to offer her solace. "At least try to drink something, Vini. You need your strength. You're getting too thin," she often said, holding a glass or spoon to Vinita's mouth.

For once Mummy's face didn't register displeasure. She was full of sympathy, reminding Vinita of that other occasion when her mother had been the embodiment of maternal kindness—when Vinita had given birth to Rohit.

Mummy had been so uncommonly tender back then. She was being that once again. And Vinita was grateful for the reprieve.

By day number four, Vinita's fever began to recede. With a sense of relief she sat up in bed and swallowed some soup and bread that afternoon, much to Sayee and Mummy's relief. Poor Sayee had been convinced Vinita was going to die from the dreaded malaria.

The chloroquine pills had to be used up within the first three days, and she was now on something called primaquine, a single pill a day, which was to continue for two weeks—to prevent a relapse. This particular drug was a little less harsh in its side effects. But the weakness lingered.

It was more than a week later that Vinita actually felt well enough to step outside the house for some fresh air.

With misery wrapped around her like a shroud and a vast amount of time to brood while she'd been confined to her bed, she'd missed both Girish and Arya fiercely. Naturally Arya had been calling each and every day to check on her after she'd found out how ill Vinita was. It had been Vinita's ten minutes of comfort each morning. She could picture Arya sitting in the recliner and talking into the phone, twirling a lock of hair around her finger, or eating fat-free tofu ice cream right out of the container. The picture was so vivid, Vinita had nearly wept with the need to hug her daughter.

But Girish never called. Not once.

"Has Girish rung you yet?" Vishal inquired nearly every evening, when he came to check on her after he'd returned from work.

"He's on a business trip," was Vinita's stock answer.

Vishal had merely shaken his head in disbelief and walked away, obviously drawing his own conclusions.

Mummy, on the other hand, had been more candid the minute she'd realized Vinita was out of danger and on the mend. She had immediately switched back to her old ways. "See, you should have left the matter of Rohit Barve alone. At least you and Girish would have been happy together."

"I know what you told me, Mummy," Vinita had murmured. "It wouldn't have made a difference in my decision." It had been easy enough to ignore her mother, since Vinita's mind was focused on other, more urgent matters. Rohit was at the top of the list.

One afternoon, as she lay on the drawing-room couch and watched TV, a thought flashed in her mind. She sat up and shut off the TV. Why hadn't it come to her before?

Climbing into a rickshaw, Vinita gave the driver the address. Settling back in the bright orange vinyl seat, she wiped the perspiration off her face with a handkerchief.

She'd walked some distance to the rickshaw stand and was feeling breathless. She was still recovering from the malaria. She'd also lied to her mother and Sayee, saying that she was going out for a walk and some badly needed fresh air.

As the rickshaw zigzagged in and out of the heavy traffic, she nearly lost the tea and biscuits she'd consumed earlier. The pace at which her driver was snaking through the streets was terrifying. She clutched at her purse, afraid it would fly out the door. In wide-eyed anxiety she watched the throngs of people and vehicles surrounding the rickshaw, hoping he wouldn't hurt someone or cause a major accident. But she had to admit he had amazingly quick reflexes. All the rickshaw drivers in this town did.

She blew out a sigh of relief when they emerged from the city traffic and into the more quiet suburban area where she was headed. When the rickshaw deposited her in front of the large house that was her destination, her heart was still racing. But she knew it wasn't all from the wild ride. There were other reasons for her breathlessness and clammy hands.

Walking up the long driveway that led to the house, she stood facing it for a moment. It triggered memories that hadn't come to mind in years. While she was growing up, she'd considered this a grand old mansion, with its elegant gardens, flowering *gulmohar* and *champak* trees, and innumerable windows.

She and her family had rarely ventured into this part of town—only when they had been invited to a party somewhere in the neighborhood. But every time she'd passed by this distinctive house, she'd stared at it in awe, visualizing the grandeur of the rooms inside, and the kind of people who lived there. Her imagination had conjured up some impressive images.

Whenever she'd voiced her thoughts, her mother had snorted in contempt. "Those people own a big, posh house, but they have no morals."

Despite her mother's words, Vinita had carried an inflated image of the house in her mind. But now there were lots of rich folks in Palgaum, with much grander homes. When compared to those, this one looked a little worn around the edges. The paint had faded, the garden looked overgrown, and the concrete driveway had cracks in it. The bushes needed pruning.

It was strange how one's perception changed with maturity. Of course, now she also knew someone who lived in the house rather well. Too well.

As she climbed the flagstone steps leading up to the front door, she began to wonder about her decision to come here, especially without discussing it with Vishal or her mother. Surely they'd have stopped her from going, or lectured her sternly at the very least.

It wasn't an impulsive decision. She'd thought about it, long and hard. Turning back was tempting, but quitting at this point would be cowardly. And she was no coward.

She pressed the doorbell with one trembling finger. Seconds later the massive wooden door opened with a groan. A young man with a well-greased head of hair and an equally oily face appeared. He wore faded black shorts and a black T-shirt. He held the door partly open and gave her a bored look.

Assuming he was one of the many servants, she asked, "Is Kori-saheb at home?"

The man frowned. "You mean Kori-bayi?"

"No, Kori-saheb," she corrected simply. Clearly the man was confused as to why a strange woman had come visiting his master and not the lady of the house. But Vinita stood her ground. "Is he at home? I'm Mrs. Patil."

The man scrutinized her a bit longer. She must have passed inspection, because he opened the door wider and allowed her inside. She had dressed very carefully for the occasion—a sky blue chiffon sari and matching accessories. She wore makeup and a blue and silver *bindi* on her forehead, too.

If she was going to face Som Kori after all these years, she wanted to look her best. It wasn't to impress him. She couldn't care less about his opinion. Careful grooming was her armor against what she could be facing.

"Please sit down, madam," the servant said to her with surprising politeness, ushering her through a short corridor into what appeared to be the drawing room. "I will tell Kori-saheb." He disappeared in the next instant, still wearing a baffled expression.

The only sound in the drawing room came from an ancient grandfather clock ticking in one corner of the room. She smelled food cooking—the familiar scents of cumin and garlic. Somewhere in the back, the evening meal was being prepared in the Kori kitchen.

The room she was in was square and large. In the light coming through one of the many windows, the furniture looked like well-rubbed, antique teakwood—two comfortable-looking sofas and four chairs, upholstered in maroon damask. A matching teapoy sat on a Kashmiri area rug with a *chinar* leaf pattern. Round end tables and brass lamps completed the ensemble. Nothing was as impressive as she'd imagined in her younger days.

A landscape painting of a waterfall monopolized the wall above one sofa. She recognized it as Gokak Falls—a picturesque place she'd visited during high school class trips. Two sepia portraits of Kori ancestors hung above the second sofa. She figured they were Som's grandparents and moved closer to study them.

The man in the photograph wore a turban, a heavy white mustache curled upward at the edges, and a forbidding expression. But then, pictures from the old days never had smiling people. It just wasn't done for some reason. Looking happy and carefree was considered frivolous, perhaps.

The woman had a thin, pinched face that told its own story—discontent and a hint of melancholy despite the proud, oversized *bindi* on her forehead, the symbol of a married woman. Her husband, assuming it was her husband in the other picture, had probably been cheating on her, too. Promiscuity seemed to be the Kori trademark, Vinita reflected with a sneer.

Something about the woman's face was familiar. She had Som's light eyes and low-slung eyebrows. It was hard to tell the exact color of her eyes, but Vinita was sure they were golden brown.

She turned around from staring at the photographs. The room had the solid, seasoned look and feel of old money.

As she moved about the room to give her tense legs something to do, she wondered if Som had any children. All she knew was that he'd married his cousin, as expected. Vinita had never discussed Som with her family during her past visits to Palgaum. Kori was more or less a taboo subject in their home.

The sound of approaching footsteps had her hands instinctively curling into fists. *Stop it,* she told herself. *He has no hold over you anymore. He's just another man, an ordinary man.* She faced the doorway and braced herself to face her old lover. Would that familiar jolt of electricity strike her like it used to back then? Would her heartbeat rise and start throbbing painfully if he smiled at her?

A second later, Som Kori swept in. Somewhat startled, despite being ready to face him, she held her breath for a beat. She felt none of those wild, emotional highs she'd experienced in her youth.

What she did feel, though, was blistering anger—for what he'd done to her. The bastard had ruined her life and gone on to live his own with such careless disregard for hers. On the other hand, it was a relief to note that he had no other effect on her anymore. Even the quick flash of resentment subsided in the next instant. Her fists loosened up.

He looked nothing like the old Som. He'd put on a load of weight. The wide shoulders and arms looked thick and fleshy. A distinct belly spilled over the waistband of the expensive black pants. She suppressed the urge to grin. *This* was what she'd thought would make her pulse jump?

What a change from the swaggering, lean athlete-hero she'd known in her youth. This was clearly a fifty-something man who'd given up all physical exercise and indulged in food and drink. His now salt-and-pepper hair had receded, too.

"Mrs. Patil?" He stepped forward with his hands joined in a wary *namaste*, and those fierce brows drawn in a knot. He clearly had no idea who she was.

"Yes." She didn't bother returning his *namaste*. "Mrs. Vinita Shelke-Patil."

His eyes went wide for an instant. "Vinita . . . Shelke?"

"I've changed a lot since college," she explained, feeling the familiar sting of knowing she, too, had aged beyond recognition. At least she was still slim, unlike him, she considered with childish glee.

"Not all that much," he said, tilting his head, examining her closely. But then, he'd lied to her before about her looks. Why should she believe anything he said now?

Her hair, too, had thinned, and was colored to cover the stray grays. Crow's-feet fanned out from the outer corners of her eyes. A sprinkling of age spots had bloomed on her cheeks.

Uncomfortable under his intense gaze, she smiled a little. "We've all aged over the years, haven't we?"

"I know *I* have," he said, patting his bulging middle. At least he wasn't under the egotistic illusions he used to harbor in his college days. "So, what brings you to my house today?"

"A personal matter."

His face froze visibly. *Déjà vu.* All the suppressed memories of her begging him to marry her came back in a rush. She'd wept back then, humiliated herself, before picking herself up and sailing out of his life.

Unfortunately, despite her resolution never to set eyes on him again, she was here to beg one more time. Fate was an odd thing. Events returned full circle sometimes, leaving one helpless and struggling against the tide. This time around, she'd certainly resisted the urge to reach out to him.

In the end, she'd succumbed to the very same need as the last time: survival. Her son's survival.

"Please . . . sit down," he said. "Be comfortable."

"Thank you." She sank into the nearest chair, glad to sit

down and allow her legs a chance to relax. He was still putting on the gentlemanly façade, still turning on the gruff charm. But she knew how to look beyond it. Underneath it all, she was sure he was the same old Kori.

He sat on the nearby sofa, somewhat stiffly. "I hear you have settled in the U.S."

"Yes. I've been living there since I got married." She didn't tell him exactly when she'd married. He probably knew that through the grapevine. And where was his wife? Vinita had expected to see her, was curious to see her. She'd come prepared to face the woman who'd married her former lover. She'd even rehearsed what she'd say to her.

She almost felt sorry for the poor woman who'd ended up with a man like Som Kori for a husband, a slithering snake no woman would ever be able to tame. Simple marital fidelity was an alien concept to him. He was probably wired that way at birth.

For the first few months after marrying Girish, Vinita had wondered what her life would have been like if Som had honored her tearful plea and made her Mrs. Kori. Would she have been able to overlook Som's transgressions? Would she have forgiven him? Detested him? Ended up divorcing him?

Later, after she'd come to care deeply for Girish, she'd realized that she'd have been miserable married to a man lacking in basic morality. She'd been lucky to have escaped that particular fate. Her pity for Som's wife went up another notch.

"I see." Som steepled his long fingers, with their nicotine-stained fingernails. His hands still looked the same, except for a few wrinkles over the knuckles and a heavy diamond ring on the middle finger of the left hand. "Where in the U.S.?"

Vinita shifted. "New Jersey."

"Quite a few people from Palgaum seem to have emigrated to New Jersey." After an awkward silence, he spoke again. "I'm glad you got married and settled down."

I bet you are. And believe me, I'm very glad myself. Of course, at the moment, she didn't know if she had a marriage anymore. Girish had still not communicated with her.

"Any children?" Kori asked. Then he was suddenly seized by a dry, hacking cough. He put a fist to his mouth and coughed into it. His skin turned a dark coffee color with the effort and he began to wheeze when it finally subsided.

Emphysema . . . or some other smoker's ailment, Vinita concluded. He was so typical of his breed—an affluent businessman who indulged in every available vice and didn't give a damn about the consequences. The very things that gave him pleasure would likely kill him.

"One daughter," she replied, after waiting for him to recover from the coughing spell. "She's grown and working now."

He seemed to ponder that for a bit. "I'm married, too."

"I know. You married your cousin."

He nodded. "My wife and I have three daughters," he supplied, clearing his throat with a guttural sound. The wheezing didn't improve.

"Good for you." She suppressed the urge to giggle. In fact, she nearly wanted to roll with mirth. Three daughters? How ironic was that, in a society obsessed with sons? The Kori family was probably devastated that their only son had produced girls and no boys to carry on the family name and business. And wasn't it even more bizarre that he actually *did* have a son? A bright and handsome young man who would have made Som proud.

"Would you like some tea or a soft drink?" Kori asked, reluctantly playing the polite host.

"No thanks. I'm not here for a social visit."

His frown returned. "I gathered that." He cast an uneasy glance at the giant clock. "Why are you here, Vinita?"

She stared at the area rug. Where should she start? "Remember many years ago, when we . . . when I told you I was . . . having a baby?" she asked, lifting her gaze to him.

His frown deepened, but his silence was enough to tell her he remembered it.

"I didn't abort the child like you wanted me to."

It took him a while to respond. "What exactly did you do?"

"I gave birth to a boy."

His intake of breath was sharp, almost a hiss. He rubbed his temple with his fingers, like he had a headache coming on. He was clearly trying to come to terms with the truth. No doubt it was a shock. "Where?" he finally asked.

She swallowed to moisten her throat. "Bombay."

"Hmm." He continued to rub his temple.

"But he was adopted . . . by a family in Palgaum."

His eyes dilated. "Here?"

She nodded. "He's a chemistry professor at our old college." That part still caused her to wonder. There were no chemists in her family. No one had remotely liked the subject. Were there any in Som's family? Where had Rohit inherited his interest and liking for it?

"Then he probably teaches my two older daughters. They attend Shivraj." Kori's nostrils flared—a sign of stress. His eyes traveled to the door for a brief moment. "What's his name?"

"Rohit Barve. *Doctor* Rohit Barve."

It took about two seconds for the name to register. Vinita noted the exact moment of comprehension from the way he blinked rapidly. "You mean . . . Shashi Barve's son?" He threw another quick sidelong glance at the door before returning to Vinita.

"Yes." She let him digest that, and watched a variety of expressions chase each other across his face. The years were catching up with him in a hurry. He was probably cursing the day he'd made that insane bet with his friends and started an affair with her.

Sometimes small, youthful indiscretions had a way of coming back as adult catastrophes.

He reached for a pack of cigarettes sitting on the table beside him, plucked one, and lit it with a red plastic lighter. He still smoked the same brand—still used those disposable lighters. The hand holding the cigarette shook visibly, like an old man's.

Hadn't he learned yet that smoking causes cancer? He probably already had the disease, from the way he was coughing and wheezing. But with his arrogant attitude, he was probably in denial, content in his imaginary invincibility.

"Why are you telling me this now, after thirty years?" he demanded.

"So you do remember the exact number of years." She smiled at him. "I thought you'd have forgotten by now. Surely there were plenty of other girlfriends since me?"

She almost enjoyed watching him flinch. She wasn't vindictive by nature and she didn't like making others suffer, but for some perverse reason she found satisfaction in seeing him shaken. That's when she realized she'd never forgiven him—not in the true spiritual sense.

He didn't respond to her question, but placed the burning cigarette in an ashtray and clasped his hands. He threw yet another quick, anxious look at the door. Was he expecting someone, or was he afraid someone was eavesdropping? His wife? His children? The servants?

"Rohit is very ill," she informed him.

He shifted and crossed his legs, stirring the air. She caught the familiar whiff of cigarette smoke mixed with his cologne. He wore the same fragrance from long ago, too. It was like being transported to her college days again, the nerve-wracking days of meeting him on the sly, the discovery that she was carrying his child. His rejection.

"What's wrong with him?" he asked.

"Acute leukemia."

"Hmm." He picked up the half-smoked cigarette, again with an unsteady hand. Vinita couldn't be sure if it was her news that set his hand trembling or just some physical or neurological problem.

"He also has juvenile diabetes." She paused for effect and held his gaze. "Are you a diabetic, Som? Do you have type one diabetes?"

His eyes narrowed. "Why do you ask?"

"Is that why you never took sugar in your coffee? And rarely ate sweets?"

He hesitated. "Yes."

"I gathered he'd inherited that from you, or someone in your family. There's no history of diabetes in mine."

"You were always good at that—deduction, logic. Every damn thing involved your bloody logic." He seemed angry for some reason.

She dismissed it with a shake of her head. "But that's not the issue now. The leukemia is. All forms of treatment have been tried."

"And?"

"Nothing has worked so far."

"Why should it mean anything to me?" His sneer was reminiscent of his expression when she'd told him she was pregnant with his child. He was probably seeing the parallels, too.

"His last resort is a bone marrow transplant."

He went silent for a long time, puffing hard on his cigarette, like he was desperate to suck every last bit of nicotine out of it. "So you want me to donate *my* bone marrow to this boy?" His temper was simmering, as far as Vinita could guess.

"I wouldn't ask if it wasn't an urgent need." She fidgeted with the clasp on her bag. "I flew here from the U.S. to donate *my* marrow, but unfortunately I came down with malaria. That prevents me from being a donor for now."

His eyes were flashing sparks of gold now. They still had the same hard brilliance. "So you thought you'd come to me."

"You're his father."

"I can't do it, Vinita." He finally dropped the tiny stub into the ashtray and raked his fingers through his hair.

"Why not?"

"I have to think of my wife and children. My eldest daughter is to be married soon. Her fiancé comes from a prominent local family."

Well, at least he wasn't denying he was Rohit's father. "No one has to know, Som," she suggested. "You could quietly get tested as an anonymous donor. It's painless."

"It's not the pain, damn it! It's the gossip in this town that will ruin me." He pointed an irate finger at her. "And why should I do any favors for the boy's father?"

"Shashi Barve."

"Barve is a bloody bastard. He and his *chamchaas* set fire to my grain warehouse once. Just the other day they vandalized my office . . . ruined the building."

"But this is not for Barve senior. This is for the son. *Our* son."

"I said I can't do it."

She shot to her feet and glared at him. "Can't or won't?"

He rose from his seat, too, then went over to the window to gaze outside, with his back to her. Maybe he didn't want her to see his expression anymore.

"I guess I'm being as stupid and naïve as I was in my teenage years."

"You don't understand, Vinita. Back then the circumstances were difficult enough. Now they're worse. I have a family."

"Just think about it, Som. You've been blessed with three daughters and no sons. Rohit is the only son you have." She paused. "At least I think he's the only son. There could be others, I suppose," she couldn't help adding.

"What are you implying?" He turned around to face her, livid.

"I'm not implying." She'd never said anything so bold and impertinent in her life, but she was in a rare mood now—itching to lash out. "I'm saying very bluntly that there could be any number of Kori children around this town . . . and other towns."

"That's enough!" he growled.

"Let's face it, Som. This is Palgaum; everyone knows everyone else's business. People talk."

"Don't I know that?"

"Do you honestly think your secret mistresses are a secret?" She inclined her head toward his ancestor's portrait. Now that she was on a roll, she couldn't stop herself. "Not just you, but your father and grandfather were notorious for their transgressions."

"How dare you come into my house and insult me!" His breathing sounded extremely labored and his nostrils twitched. "Please leave. Now!"

Something registered. She'd been rude. Worse than rude. Insulting. Her heart was beating furiously. What was wrong with her? Did she have the right to seek him out and hurl insults at him, no matter how much of a heel he was? It took only one second to answer her own question. If it meant shaking some sense into him for Rohit's sake, she was justified in using any means available. She was *that* desperate.

"I'm sorry," she said grudgingly.

"Just go, Vinita."

She picked up her handbag and faced him squarely. "I wonder why I even imagined that you'd lift a finger to help your son. You were always a shallow, self-centered man. But you know what? Someday your sins will come back to torment you."

Without waiting for his response, she stepped outside the drawing room and into the corridor, taking a sharp breath to calm her fevered nerves. The scene was almost an exact replication of the one from her past. The only difference was that this time he wasn't offering her cash to get rid of their child. The Soms of the world never changed.

She stood there for a moment, feeling an odd prickle. Someone was watching her. Instinctively turning her head, she saw a tall, thin woman standing a short distance away, staring at her with dark, unblinking eyes. Her gaunt face seemed carved out of wood. She stood so still, she could have been a department store dummy. Dressed in a butter yellow sari and heavy gold jewelry, she looked about Vinita's age. Vinita at once guessed who she was. Som Kori's cousin-wife.

Something about the woman was eerie, her expression hollow yet tinged with sadness. Had she overheard the conversation in the drawing room? Vinita couldn't be sure. It didn't really matter, though. Som's wife probably knew all about his concubines as well as his sleazy past. What was one more scandal?

Turning on her heel, Vinita grasped the doorknob and managed to open the massive front door. She stepped out into the evening light, sensing the woman's eyes boring into her back until she shut the door behind her. She needed to rid herself of the nasty vibes inside that grim house, filled with God knows what kinds of secrets.

All her childhood fantasies of a magical lifestyle within those four walls had vanished with a single visit. Suddenly her open, sunny home in New Jersey seemed a million miles away, and a wave of homesickness swept over her.

She wanted to be dressed in one of her comfortable old sweatshirts and fuzzy socks, sitting in the recliner beside the fireplace, reading a romance novel and sipping *masala chai,* while Girish watched a ball game on TV. The picture was so vivid, it hurt. She willed it out of her mind and started to move.

The orange-red brilliance of the setting sun was a welcome sight. It was a relief to breathe the fresh, clean air, thick with the scent of the pink and white roses growing on both sides of the stoop.

Striding down the driveway, she reached the street and looked around. It would be difficult to find a rickshaw in this out-of-the-way residential neighborhood. She might as well walk the mile or so into town and look for one there. Besides, a brisk walk would do her good—help to banish those assorted emotions of rage, loathing, and homesickness.

And the loneliness. Just like the last time, she was on her own once again, trying to find her way in the dark, hopeless morass. She longed for Girish. She so badly wanted to feel his arms around her. She had become so used to that hand with its missing digits. She'd come to love the unique strength of it, the warmth of it.

Right about now she was willing to settle for hearing his voice over the phone. *Come on, Girish, at least drop me a line by e-mail.* Vinita had been using Vishal's computer to check on her e-mail.

But that wasn't likely to happen. Maybe he was even planning to file for divorce by now. He'd done it once before. He could do it again.

Som watched Vinita through the window, until she disappeared from his line of vision. His hands were still shaking with rage, and the damn cough felt like a fire burning in his chest.

How dare she come to his door and talk down to him! He didn't have to take that from anyone. Anyone.

It took another second or two before his coughing subsided and his breathing became more even.

But damn it, why did she have to be right? She hadn't changed over the years—still just as proud and stubborn, just as self-righteous, and so bloody full of idealistic bullshit.

Why the hell hadn't she aborted the child? Didn't the woman have any common sense? But she had always been one of those highly intelligent types who belonged in a lab or classroom, not the real world. He reached for another cigarette.

However, despite his irritation, he grudgingly admitted to himself that she was a woman of courage and tenacity. Against all odds she had borne the child he had rejected. She'd never again asked for his help. It took guts to stand up to one's family and all of society and have a child out of wedlock.

Back then, he had concluded he'd never met a girl like her. To this day, he still hadn't come across another woman like her. That's what was hard to understand—his reluctant admiration for her. She wasn't beautiful or charming, or even fun to be with. And yet, what was it about her that made her stand out in his mind?

The irony of the situation wasn't lost on him. He had a son—a grown son. Som had always wanted a boy who would be an athlete in his youth, then take over the business someday, live in this big house, and carry on the family name and tradition. Every time Neeraja had become pregnant, his parents' as well as his own hopes had soared, only to find out it was a girl.

After the third time, they had decided they didn't want to take another chance. That was the end of it. His mother had passed away some years ago. With no grandson bearing the Kori name, she'd died a disappointed woman. His father was too old and senile to care anymore.

Now that Som had discovered he actually had a son, it turned out the boy had been adopted by his worst enemy, Barve. Of all people, why did it have to be *that* man? Was this Som's karma, a twisted form of punishment for his sins? Maybe Vinita was right about his sins coming back to torment him.

And his son was a college professor, an intellectual. Wry laughter rose in his throat, but what sputtered out was another coughing fit. Who would have thought he'd produce a son who would grow up to earn a PhD? The boy's brains had clearly been inherited from Vinita—bright, serious, studious-as-hell Vinita—and her stuffy chartered accountant brother.

Som was the first one to admit that he himself had been a bad student. His daughters weren't stellar students, either. His youngest, however, was a talented singer. But all three were good girls, well mannered and elegant, groomed for good marriages. Neeraja was responsible for that.

He knew who Rohit Barve was, too, mostly because the boy used to be a good cricket player as a student. Som always kept one eye on the college cricket team, the one thing he truly cared about. He had never dreamt that Shivraj College's young cricket star from ten years ago was his son.

Why had it never occurred to Som that the boy could have been adopted? Barve and his wife were easily in their seventies, while their son was a very young man. It was a logical conclusion that Rohit Barve couldn't be their real son. And yet Som had never been interested enough to pay attention to such details. He'd admired the boy's talent for the sport and that's all it was.

For a moment he wondered what it would have been like to see the boy grow up—excel at Som's own game. If encouraged a bit more, the boy could have become a professional cricketer.

The boy had probably given up the sport to pursue his doctorate—just like Som had given up his sports dreams to get married and join his father's business. Some dreams were not meant to be fulfilled.

Som turned away from the window and stopped short.

Neeraja stood in the doorway, quietly observing him. From the look on her face, he couldn't tell if she'd overheard the conversation between him and Vinita. Neeraja rarely allowed him inside her mind.

Living with his wife was like living with a ghost. She was there, and yet it seemed only her long-limbed body was present. Where was the rest of her—her heart, her soul? Why was she always so remote, like an observer and not a participant?

He was sure she knew all about his activities outside the home—personal, business, and political. But she never once questioned him about them. Always the compliant wife, she was a gracious hostess to guests and visitors, a devoted mother to their children, and an excellent homemaker. The household and its large staff functioned very efficiently under her supervision.

Although his father was now a burden because of his deteriorating physical and mental health, Neeraja was patient with him. Sometimes Som wished his wife would speak up, talk to him like other wives did to their husbands. He wished she'd argue with him, nag him, fight for her rights, even chastise him for his vices. But she never did.

He didn't know if he was fortunate or unfortunate in having Neeraja for a wife. Had she molded herself into the perfect wife for a reason? Or was she made that way?

He looked at her now, standing before him in her elegantly draped sari. He wondered if she'd question him about the strange woman who'd come to visit him. But she didn't.

"Your tea is ready," she said instead, and strode away.

Chapter 27

"I might be coming home sooner than anticipated, honey," Vinita said to her daughter, her spirits sagging more than ever. Arya had called to check on her, like she usually did every day.

It was heartwarming to know there was at least one person who supported Vinita wholeheartedly in her mission to save Rohit. And waited anxiously for her to come home.

Cradling the cordless phone between her shoulder and ear, Vinita shut the door to the guest room and plopped on the bed. She liked to converse with her daughter in private. It afforded her a few precious minutes with Arya. Mainly it was a way to gather news about Girish. She hungered to find out what was happening with Girish, and Arya was her only connection to him.

"Really?" Arya's voice became excited. "When?"

"I'm not sure, but since they informed me I can't be a donor, I figured there's no point in my hanging around here. How long can I wait for another donor to surface?"

"Mom, don't be so depressed," advised Arya, sensing Vinita's mood. "It's not your fault that you got sick."

"I know, but it's so frustrating. I was hoping . . . you know." It was hard to explain. No one would understand her sense of hopelessness. Only a mother—a mother who was forced to stand by with her hands tied and watch her child die—could relate to her sentiments.

"Are you sure you're completely recovered?" asked Arya. "Is it okay for you to travel?"

"Yes," said Vinita, suddenly feeling very tired. She hadn't slept well since that visit to Som Kori two days ago. She hadn't told anyone about her visit to Som, either. If Vishal and Mummy ever found out, they'd lambaste her for not only humiliating herself but the whole Shelke family. All that drivel about family honor and reputation would start all over again.

But how could Som be so inhuman? Hadn't age done anything to soften him up? Most people learned lessons from living, but he was just as cold and heartless as he was in his youth. And his wife, assuming that wooden-faced woman was his wife, had looked at Vinita with such expressionless eyes. What were her feelings about what she might have overheard in the drawing room?

"Before you change your travel date, you had better check with the doctor, Mom," suggested Arya, drawing Vinita's attention back to their conversation.

Vinita couldn't help smiling. "I did that, and I've been told it's safe to travel."

"Good."

"I just wish I'd been more careful with my own health."

"I'm sorry, Mom. I know you had your heart set on this." There was a long pause. "I have a suggestion."

"What?"

"Do you think *I* would be able to get tested as a donor?"

"No! That's out of the question."

"Why not? It's only logical that he and I have the same DNA, right?"

"Logical, yes, but impractical, honey." Vinita felt a rush of emotion grip her. It took her a beat to recover. It was beyond generous for Arya to offer her own bone marrow for a boy she'd never met, never even known about until a few weeks ago. "I won't allow you to do it, dear. It's very kind of you, but it's much too generous. Besides, he's a very stubborn and proud young man. He's likely to balk at the idea."

"But I want to help, Mom."

"I know you do, babe. But it's not practical."

"I could be the ideal donor."

"I won't hear of it, Arya. Just forget it."

"All right, whatever," Arya grumbled. "If you can't do anything more for him, then at least come home. I . . . we miss you."

The anguish in Arya's voice was genuine. Her daughter was worried about her, and clearly missed her. Vinita waited for Arya to say something about Girish, but she didn't. "How's Dad?" she asked finally.

"He's okay, I guess. He's in the study, working . . . or something." Arya hesitated. "You want me to give him the phone?"

Vinita gave it a moment's thought. "Don't bother. The last time you asked him to get on the phone, he suddenly had to go to the bathroom, remember?"

Arya's sigh was loud enough to be heard. "Yeah. I won't bother him." She went on to tell Vinita about a conference that was coming up, and her weekend activities.

"I'll let you know when I'm returning," said Vinita. "I have to check with the airline and see what's available. I'll have to pay quite a bit extra to get the date changed, I suppose."

"That's okay. Just come home," Arya repeated. "I think . . . I think Dad needs you here."

Instant alarm set in. "Is something wrong with him?"

"He's okay. Don't panic."

"His blood pressure?" Vinita had been obsessing over his blood pressure since the minute she'd told him about Rohit. She had a suspicion that his numbers had climbed that day and never returned to normal. He could be headed for a stroke. And she'd be the one responsible for it.

"He's fine," Arya assured her. "It's just that he looks so lost without you. I wish he'd give up his silly grudge and talk to you."

"I wish he would, too, Arya. But we can't force him. He has to come to terms with this in his own way. Take care of him for me, okay?"

"Okay. And, Mom, don't overdo it. Rest and get well."

"I will."

"Don't forget I'll come to the airport to get you. Just let me know when. Give my love to everyone."

"Okay. Thanks, baby."

Long after she hung up the phone, Vinita lay on her bed with her eyes closed. Nothing was going right. In fact, everything was going wrong. Her son was dying. Her brother and mother were sore at her for stirring up trouble all over again. Sayee's usual cheerfulness was beginning to wane. Arya sounded depressed. She herself was still slightly weak from her illness.

But by far the worst casualty was her marriage.

With every passing day, the chances of Girish forgiving her were diminishing. She'd been in Palgaum over a month now, and still he hadn't made an effort to communicate with her. She'd stopped leaving him voice-mail messages. What was the point? She could almost feel the void every time she thought about the possibility of divorce. What was she going to do if Girish decided to leave her? Life as she knew it would come to an end.

She'd survive somehow. There was no doubt in her mind that she was a survivor by nature. She had a career and she could be financially independent. She wouldn't be able to afford the lifestyle she had enjoyed for the past two decades, but she could manage to live on her salary alone. Nonetheless those were material things. Her life, her real life, would be empty without the man she loved.

There was a knock on the door. Startled from her reverie, she said, "Come in."

The door opened and her mother stuck her head in, looking hesitant. "I didn't hear you talking anymore, so I assumed your conversation was over."

"You're right."

"Are you feeling okay?"

"Yes. I was merely resting a little after talking to Arya."

A smile thawed Sarla's somber face. "How is Arya?" She stood on the threshold but didn't cross it.

"She's doing well. She sends you her love."

The smile widened, lighting up her mother's face. "She is a good girl. Very intelligent and bold. But it is time she thought about getting married."

"I'll tell her you said that," said Vinita, chuckling, wishing her mother would smile more often. It transformed her face—made her look younger, prettier.

But the smile vanished just as abruptly as it had appeared. A troubled look replaced it, making Vinita sit up. Something was wrong. Come to think of it, Sarla rarely came into her room since Vinita had recovered from the malaria, unlike Sayee and Vishal, who stopped by often.

"Come in, Mummy," she invited, patting the space beside her on the bed. "Sit down."

Sarla shook her head. "I just came to tell you something."

"What?" Her pulse jumped. It had to be news of Rohit. Unpleasant news, judging from her mother's demeanor.

"Shashi Barve was in an accident. I heard it on the radio."

Vinita stood up. "What happened?"

"He was walking to the bazaar when he got hit by a car, they said. He's in the hospital."

"Is he . . . He's not badly hurt, is he?" She didn't even want to consider the word *dead*.

"The report said he has a broken arm and some other injuries."

"How sad."

"You know what else they said?"

"What?" Vinita had an odd feeling about this. Something in her mother's expression was a bit too familiar.

"They said it may not be an accident. Someone tried to kill him."

Vinita's hands instinctively went up to cradle her face. "Oh my God!" A hit-and-run. Or maybe it wasn't. No sense panicking over a radio report. "How do they know it wasn't an accident?"

"There were many witnesses. They said people saw the car going at high speed over the footpath, directly at Barve. If Barve had not moved in time he would be dead."

"Did anyone get details on the car and driver?" She was clutching at straws, hoping the witnesses were wrong, that someone wasn't out to kill Barve.

Sarla shrugged. "The report did not mention that."

Vinita stared at the floor. Just when she'd thought things couldn't get any worse, they had managed to turn nasty. They were quickly spinning out of control. And they could escalate even further. Deep in her gut she had an ominous feeling that this was only the beginning of something big.

"Does it not seem a little strange?" asked her mother, as if reading Vinita's mind. "All of a sudden Kori's office is damaged and Barve is almost killed? Where is all this leading?"

Her mother had a valid point. A name popped up in Vinita's mind, followed by mounting alarm. Som! It was too soon after her visit to Som for this to be a coincidence. Could he have engineered this? Could he be a killer besides being a callous heel?

"Maybe I should go to the hospital and see Mr. Barve?" She wasn't sure if she'd be welcome. She had come to know the Barves in the past few weeks, and in some ways they had become family now. Her heart went out to Meenal Barve. The poor woman had to be suffering. First her son, now her husband. How was she holding up under the strain? Vinita would have liked to offer some comfort, but how? She looked at her mother for her reaction.

With a troubled sigh, Sarla took a step back. "Like I always say, some things are best left alone." With that said, she turned around and walked away.

Vinita listened to her mother's soft footsteps going down the stairs.

Dear heaven, what had she done?

Chapter 28

The instant Vishal walked in the front door, Vinita rushed forward to meet him. She'd been anxiously waiting for him to come home, ever since her mother had mentioned Barve's mishap. Vishal was running very late this evening and she'd wondered if something awful had happened to him as well.

Sayee had been throwing anxious looks at the clock for the past hour, and Sayee rarely fretted about anything. Now she stood beside Vinita, looking relieved that her husband was home. "I'll get dinner ready," she said, and hurried off toward the kitchen.

"Did you hear about Barve?" Vinita asked Vishal. She had a feeling Sayee had deliberately left Vishal and her alone.

He gave Vinita a measured look before nodding.

She noticed the lines of fatigue around his eyes and mouth. It wasn't just his usual tired face after a long day of work. This was a worn-down look. She was responsible for his condition in addition to everything else.

"I'm sorry, Vishal," she said, knowing full well that an apology didn't even begin to address the guilt weighing on her conscience. "I know I'm responsible for Barve's condition."

He took off his shoes and socks at the door and nudged them into a corner of the entry foyer, where everyone left their footwear. He went into the drawing room, Vinita close on his heels.

"You don't know that for sure, Vini," he said quietly, turning on the television.

"But I feel like all this is happening because of me."

"He's not all that badly injured. It's just a fracture and some bruises," he said, sitting down on the sofa.

'How do you know that?"

"I went to the hospital after I heard the news on the radio."

"Why?"

"He is the father of my nephew, isn't he?"

"Hmm." Vinita stared at Vishal for a second. He'd never openly referred to Rohit as his nephew. "Did you get to see Shashi Barve?"

"No. Half the Marathi Samithi were there—Barve's friends and followers. It was a mob scene, angry people crowding the hospital."

She groaned inwardly. This was worse than she'd imagined. A pack of enraged men was nothing short of chilling. She recalled the gruesome scene from her college days, the day she'd witnessed the two young men bludgeoned to death—the day Som had put into motion his grand plan to seduce her. She suppressed the mild shiver that shot through her.

"So how did you find out about the extent of his injuries?" she asked.

"I asked someone in the crowd."

"What are all those men planning to do?"

"I don't know. They were milling around, incensed about what's happened to their leader." He inclined his head toward the TV set. "Maybe there is something on the news."

The foul feeling in Vinita's gut persisted—the premonition that something was about to happen. It was like a ticking bomb that one could hear, but couldn't locate or determine when it was set to explode.

A minute later the news came on, capturing her attention and Vishal's. After some major national headlines, the news moved on to local events. And Barve. A young male reporter standing outside the hospital gave a detailed account of the episode.

The police were apparently convinced that Barve's accident was indeed attempted homicide. They were looking for a late-model black Maruti automobile. They even had the license plate number.

The camera swept over the crowd gathered outside the hospital's main entrance, while the reporter's clipped voice continued to issue his commentary. Her eyes combed the throngs of people for two familiar faces: Meenal Barve and Rohit. There was no sign of them. They were probably sequestered in Barve's hospital room.

"This probably means the Samithi will retaliate, right?" she asked her brother when the segment ended.

"Of course. Each party wants to outdo the other," he said, shutting off the TV and rising to his feet. "Come on, let's go eat."

"I'm glad Aneesh and Anmol are away from here." The boys' absence was a godsend. But they'd surely find out about any riots that made national news. She could only pray her nephews wouldn't find out about the rest—not yet. In time, they'd have to be told about her secret. It wasn't fair to keep them in the dark.

Her nephews were so young they might find it hard to comprehend any of this—their middle-aged aunt's past sins coming back to affect their lives in such an abrupt and violent way. She didn't want them to be touched by violence.

"Me too," said Vishal. "They're safer in Bangalore."

At the dinner table, Vinita kept her gaze down most of the time and ate in silence, while her mother, Vishal, and Sayee discussed Barve's attempted killing. All the while, she could feel her mother's eyes on her.

Unable to sleep most of the night, Vinita got up early. She had to do something, or half the town could be destroyed by violence. And for what? Just so two obstinate and egotistical men could prove to the world which one of them had more power? But this time *she* had a role in their ridiculous testosterone-fueled war. Therefore it was up to her to do something about it.

After a bath and some breakfast, she felt a little calmer. On the pretext of going out for some window-shopping, she strode down to the end of the street. There she hailed a rickshaw and had the driver take her to the hospital.

It seemed like the hospital was becoming a second home. She'd expected that, since she'd come to Palgaum with the sole purpose of helping her dying son, but she hadn't thought she'd be visiting the boy's adoptive father as well.

She wasn't sure if Barve was still there or had been released. But the previous evening's news report had mentioned something about him staying in the hospital overnight for observation.

There was no crowd outside the hospital today—only a handful of people going in and out. Everything seemed normal. At the front desk, she found out that Barve was still in his room. She was asked to sign her name in a register, then given his room number and a visitor's pass. This was not routine procedure. It appeared that the police were taking extra precautions to protect Barve. For Vinita there was some relief in knowing that.

As she approached Barve's room, she heard men's voices, loud and clear as the sound floated outside into the corridor. He clearly had visitors. Barve's was the only voice she recognized.

She hesitated, debating whether she should go home and return later. But later could be too late. He could be released to go home. She had to do this now. Coming to a standstill, she eavesdropped for a few moments.

The rage was obvious in the men's words. *Do they think we are that stupid? If they consider us docile* bakras, *lambs, they are very much mistaken. As soon as you return home, Shashi-dada, we will assemble again and discuss this matter.*

Fear snaked up her spine. They were planning to retaliate for Barve's so-called accident. *Assemble again and discuss.* Most likely discuss how to continue the cycle of violence, she concluded. They talked some more before she heard them bidding Barve good-bye.

Not wanting to be caught snooping, she quickly tiptoed to a safer distance down the corridor. When the men eventually came out, she would start walking toward Barve's room once again, pretending she was just another visitor for some other patient in the same wing.

A minute later, the men spilled out into the hallway—five of them, perhaps in their forties and fifties, considerably younger than Barve. No wonder they'd addressed Barve respectfully as Shashi-dada. They were so busy talking amongst themselves they barely noticed her.

She stood at the door to Barve's room. He was lying on his back, his eyes shut, one arm resting over his chest. The other arm was enclosed in a cast. There was an adhesive bandage over his left cheek. A dark circle had formed around one eye, making him look like a tired pirate, past his prime.

He looked vulnerable like this, so unlike the commanding man in the photographs hanging in his home, so different from the fearless leader of an organization that committed the most atrocious crimes in the name of heritage.

With some relief she noted that neither Meenal nor Rohit was there. Barve was alone. His eyes remained closed. He was probably exhausted from having visitors. She hesitated for a moment before knocking softly on the door.

His eyes flew open. He stared at her with raised brows, clearly surprised to see her. "Vinita-bayi!"

She joined her hands in a *namaste* and approached his bed. "Sorry to disturb you, Shashi-saheb." They had gradually progressed to using first names, albeit with a respectful suffix. She called his wife Meenal-tayi—older sister.

He studied her with wary eyes. She didn't know what to make of it. Did he suspect her role in this latest development? If so, he probably wanted her gone. She'd brought him enough trouble.

"I wanted to see you . . . briefly," she said.

He nodded and pointed to the chair beside his bed, motioning to her to sit down. "Meenal has gone home to bring some fresh clothes for me," he explained. "She will be back before they release me."

"I see." She sat in the chair, wondering how long it would be before Meenal showed up.

He looked uncomfortable, probably because women who weren't immediate family didn't usually visit a male patient alone. But her circumstances were hardly normal.

She moistened her lips. "I'm sorry about what happened."

He shrugged, then winced, as if that slight movement was excruciating. "Being a leader of a sociopolitical organization has its dangers," he murmured.

"Are you in a lot of pain?" she asked.

He took a deep breath but didn't say a word, clearly loath to admit weakness.

He turned his gaze on her. "Why did you want to see me?"

"This attempt on your life has made your members and friends very angry, I suppose?"

"Killing is something to be angry about, is it not?"

She nodded. "I saw the TV report last evening. It seems your organization is looking to launch some sort of counterattack."

He frowned. "Why do you think that?"

"A clear-cut assassination attempt on a popular community leader and an angry group of his supporters coming together can mean only one thing, Shashi-saheb."

"It is not that simple."

She studied the drawn look on his face, wishing it *were* that simple. "Can't you stop the violence if you choose to?"

"Being a leader is not being a father." He smiled. It was an unexpected gesture that made him appear benign. "Even a father cannot control his children these days. You can see Rohit rarely listens to my advice."

"But you're a charismatic leader. You're highly respected. You have to do something to stop this from escalating."

"Some things have their own momentum . . . like a raging river during the monsoon season. No one can stop it."

"Building a dam can," she prompted.

"Ah, but a dam takes money and years of hard work. As you can see, I am an ordinary man. I am no dam, Vinita-bayi."

Exasperated by his indifference, she raised her voice. "Let's just forget the metaphors for now. Can't you see what this will do to this town? Killing each other is not the answer to anything. Why can't you men just get along?" They were acting like brats.

His eyes narrowed on her slowly . . . suspiciously. "Why are you so concerned about all this?" he demanded.

Vinita lowered her gaze. "Rohit needs you now, as a father and supporter. If you're involved in political activities, you can't give your son your undivided attention."

"Is that all it is, your concern for Rohit?"

"Of course it is. What else would it be?"

"Somesh Kori was . . . *is* Rohit's father. Your sympathies are naturally with the Kannada people, I presume?"

"My sympathies are with Rohit," she snapped. "He's my only concern."

"We appreciate that," he said with reluctance. "But we were told you cannot be a donor."

"I'm sorry. It was most unfortunate that I contracted malaria."

"Not your fault, but naturally we are disappointed." His sigh was loud and long. "It will be impossible to find another donor."

"Never say impossible, Shashi-saheb. There's no reason to give up hope . . . yet." She couldn't tell him that she'd approached Som. That wretched man would probably never come forward to save his son, of course. But her stubborn heart still had a fragment of hope left—mainly because Rohit was his only son. Surely there had to be a heart beating in Som's chest. "Meanwhile, wouldn't it make sense to put an end to the violence?" she reminded Barve.

"It is not easy to explain." He shifted, wincing again. "But surely you must understand community spirit and dedication to a cause."

She chewed on it for a moment. "I was never into community spirit at any time in my life. After having lived in the U.S. for so many years, I'm even less interested in that sort of allegiance to any organized movement. My dedication is reserved for my family and friends, and for my career."

Barve's eyes widened. "But you're a Marathi woman married to a Marathi man. How can you not have pride in your roots?"

"I do have pride!" she tossed back. "But I don't condone shedding blood to sustain it. Other communities, religions, and nationalities have an equal right to be proud and to coexist alongside us."

"Don't you understand this is not merely for pride?" He now had on his patient father-leader expression, making Vinita realize why his followers found him so irresistible. "We are fighting to make Palgaum a part of the state of Maharashtra. Karnataka State took over this small town several decades ago and made it their own. In the process they have ruined its prestige and rich culture. It is up to people like us to return Palgaum to its rightful place and restore its old glory."

"And wasting precious human lives is how one goes about restoring glory?" Her voice quivered with contempt. "There's neither pride nor dignity in needless violence. And I don't particularly care which state Palgaum belongs to, as long as it's peaceful and prosperous. As far as I can see, my small town has turned into a thriving city. Nothing's wrong with it, if you ask me."

He shook his head sadly. "You are obviously influenced by American ideas." He said it as if she were suffering from some hopeless disease and deserved to be pitied.

"Nothing wrong with that, either," she retorted. "It's about time all Palgaumites—Marathi, Kannada, and the rest—stopped fighting like spoiled children and learned to get along."

"I agree," said a familiar voice, interrupting them. Meenal Barve stepped into the room, neatly groomed in a white and purple print sari, carrying a large plastic tote bag. Her gaze switched between her husband and Vinita. She greeted Vinita with a slight smile.

Vinita smiled back. "I hope you don't mind that I came to visit Shashi-saheb."

Meenal shook her head. "I'm just surprised, that is all."

"I needed to discuss something important with him," Vinita explained.

"About Rohit?" Meenal set her purse and bag on the floor and sat on the edge of her husband's bed.

"Mostly about Rohit." Vinita noticed the bleakness in Meenal's expression the instant Rohit's name came up. Now that Vinita had been dismissed as a possible donor, their last hope had been squashed, and Meenal appeared to be the one most affected by the news. "I'm sorry I couldn't help him. I had . . . we had all hoped . . ."

"I know. I know," said Meenal, sounding exhausted. "Are you planning to go back to the States, then?"

"Soon." Vinita rose from her chair. "I have to check into available flights." Leaving Rohit behind was going to be hard. The son she'd met only weeks ago had grown on her, become precious. Knowing she'd failed in her attempts to keep him alive was frustrating.

And yet, she *had* to accept it.

"I'd better leave now," she said. "I'm sure Shashi-saheb is anxious to go home." She moved toward the door. She turned to Barve. "I hope you recover quickly, sir." There was so much more she wanted to say to him, make him understand why it was important to stop the rioting and carnage. But she'd have to leave that to his conscience.

He nodded his good-bye.

Meenal stood up and followed her. "I'll walk you to the main door."

"No need for that . . . really." Vinita was out the door. "I know you have to help Shashi-saheb get dressed."

"There is no rush." Meenal started walking beside her down the corridor. "I have to talk to you about something," she whispered.

"I had a feeling you did," Vinita said. "I'm sorry this happened to Shashi-saheb because of me."

"It is not your fault."

"If I hadn't told Rohit about Som Kori, it would never have happened."

"This sort of thing happens around here frequently, without much reason." She looked at Vinita. "What exactly did you say to my husband?"

They'd reached the lobby now, but they still spoke in whispers because there were other people in the area. Vinita tossed Meenal a frank look. "I told him to put a stop to the violence. There's been enough bloodshed in this town."

"Very true."

"Rohit's life shouldn't be the cause for more heartache."

"What did my husband say?"

"Not much. He said these things have their own momentum . . . or something like that. He didn't offer to do anything to stop it."

"I didn't think he would." Meenal wrapped her arms around herself and rocked on her heels, like she was cold. The earlier distress was back in her face. "He is *khaddoos,* a stubborn old fool."

Vinita's jaw fell. Despite her own conclusion that Barve was a stubborn old fool, she'd never thought Meenal Barve was capable of calling her husband that. As far as she could see, Meenal was a *pativrata*—a dedicated wife. "Really?"

"Don't you think I have tried to persuade him to give up his nonsensical politics? Do you know how many attempts have been made on his life? But does he ever learn from them?"

Vinita frowned. "You mean this isn't the first time?"

With a shake of her head, Meenal let her arms fall to her sides in defeat. "At least three other times he has almost been killed. Even Rohit has tried to make him understand that this sentiment called Marathi pride is not worth dying for."

"Rohit doesn't approve of it, either?"

"Not at all. He dislikes violence. But my husband will not give it up. As long as Som Kori is the head of the Kannada faction, he will continue to fight him."

"You mean it's a personal thing rather than communal?"

"It is a long story." Meenal looked around at the folks

crowding the waiting room. She inclined her head toward the parking lot. "Let us talk outside."

"I am not sure I should be telling you this," Meenal said when they were at a safe distance from prying eyes and ears.

"I understand. You don't have to tell me anything you don't want to."

Staring at the ground, Meenal seemed to deliberate for a moment before making up her mind. "You have to promise not to tell this to anyone."

"Like I said, you don't have to—"

Meenal held up a hand to stop Vinita. "I think you should know this."

"Why?"

"Because only *you* will understand it."

"I will?" Vinita's brow puckered. It all sounded so mysterious.

"My sister-in-law, my husband's older sister, was a young girl in college when she became involved with Kori's uncle. They were classmates."

Vinita's mouth fell open a second time. "Another case of Marathi girl falls for Kannada boy?" A Kori boy, as coincidence would have it.

It was a day of unpleasant surprises. And the Koris seemed to feature in them. Was there no end to the Kori depravity? Had every man in that family somehow managed to ruin some innocent girl or other? No wonder Meenal thought Vinita would be the one person to understand.

Meenal nodded. "Apparently my father-in-law found out about the affair and demanded that Kori marry his daughter."

"Your father-in-law must have been a broad-minded man to be willing to accept a Lingayat son-in-law."

"He had no choice, since the girl's reputation was ruined. Kori refused to marry her, and my father-in-law and he got into a serious fight."

Vinita wondered if Barve's sister had also become pregnant like herself. But she dare not ask. It was too personal.

"So what happened then?" Vinita asked instead.

"Nothing. My sister-in-law eventually married someone else. She has passed on now, but her life was happy . . . comfortable. She had children and grandchildren. She died a contented woman."

"Thank God for that. So she did what I did—got on with her life." Vinita had plenty to be grateful for. But she could still see the lingering resentment toward Som in her brother's and mother's eyes. She could imagine why Barve hated the Koris with a vengeance. "I can see why the hostility is still there."

"I do, too, but it frightens me, Vinita," said Meenal. "Some day they will succeed in killing him." She drew a long breath. "Or maybe the Marathi Samithi will end up killing Kori."

"It could go either way."

"Or, even though neither of them is a violent man, they could both end up dead. And for what? Some silly episode from the past, or an equally insane reason called pride in one's heritage?"

"I wish I had the answer," replied Vinita. A sense of relief passed through her. It wasn't all her fault that the communal tensions were heating up. It was still her mistake to a great extent, but she needn't take the full blame for it.

She put a hand on the older woman's arm. "Go back inside, Meenal-tayi. You have to take Shashi-saheb home. He needs to rest."

Meenal squeezed the hand that rested on her arm. "Thank you for coming forward to help Rohit and us. We will never forget your generosity. I'm grateful to my aunt."

"Your aunt?" Vinita straightened. "You mean Jaya-bai?"

"She is the one who informed you about Rohit."

Vinita chewed on this new bit of information. "You know this for sure? The letter was anonymous."

"I questioned my aunt about it. She admitted that she wrote the letter." A smile crossed Meenal's face. "I think she feels responsible for Rohit and his welfare because she arranged for the adoption. She is very fond of him."

"Of course," said Vinita. The aunt's proprietary interest in Rohit made complete sense. At least the mystery was solved, although she'd always suspected it was Jaya-bai. "I wish I could have been a donor." She thought for a moment. "If you do find a donor, you will inform me, won't you? And the offer to pay for it still stands."

"But we can't take money from you, especially if you are not the donor. It is too much."

"Please," said Vinita, slowly withdrawing her hand. "It's the least I can do."

"We'll think about it." Meenal hesitated for a moment, then gave Vinita what amounted to an awkward hug. "Have a safe journey back to America." Her eyes were glazed with tears.

Vinita held her in a hug for an instant. Sometime during the past few weeks, an invisible bond had formed between the two women, a bond shared by two mothers who had been unexpectedly thrown together. "I'll pray for Rohit," she said, her voice turning hoarse. "Maybe there is the perfect donor somewhere out there."

"Maybe there is," repeated Meenal, obviously trying to muster a smile, but without success. She stood there till Vinita said a reluctant *namaste* and hurried toward the rickshaw stand outside the hospital campus.

As she climbed into a rickshaw, Vinita turned her head to look back. Meenal was standing in the same spot. If fate really decided to be cruel to Meenal, she could end up losing her son and her husband in the near future.

Fate. Vinita was beginning to detest the word.

Chapter 29

A day and a half later, the Kannada man who had tried to kill Shashi Barve was arrested. But the news reports claimed the man refused to divulge who had hired him. Within hours after the arrest, riots broke out in town, leading to so much vandalism and violence that the police had to impose a curfew, shutting down nearly the whole town and allowing only essential services to continue.

Suddenly the town seemed dead, like the movie version of the aftermath of a war or pandemic. She missed the hum of traffic, the voices of street vendors peddling their wares, the children yelling at each other across the street. It was almost like the town was in mourning. She couldn't stand the abnormal quiet.

Besides, her plans to catch a flight to the U.S. had to be postponed.

Four long and frustrating days later, things returned to some degree of normality, but not before there were two deaths, one on either side of the warring groups, and dozens of injured men. Som Kori and Shashi Barve were still alive.

Vinita heaved a sigh of relief when the shops finally started to open for business, and the traffic returned to its noisy, polluting routine. There was comfort in knowing her town was alive, and it would gradually shift into its natural rhythm.

In the midst of it all, Arya called in a panic one night. "Mom, are you okay? We heard on the Indian cable news about the stuff going on in Palgaum."

"I'm fine, dear," Vinita said.

"Why didn't you call and tell us?"

"What would be the point? The entire town is affected by the riots. Vishal's office is closed, but he's working like a fiend from home. And we're all doing fine. At least for now."

"Thank God." Arya demanded to know exactly what was happening. Vinita gave her a brief account, without divulging that some of it could have been her own fault. She still felt guilty about the part she might have played in all this havoc. Arya didn't need that kind of aggravation on top of what she was already going through.

"So there's water and food at least, right?" asked Arya.

"There's plenty of both," assured Vinita.

A moment passed before Arya added, "Mom, you'd better get on the first plane available and come home."

"I'm trying."

Arya seemed to hesitate for a second. "Dad's worried about you as well."

"He is?" Vinita was too stunned to say any more.

"Yeah. He was worried when you were sick, too. He asked me if I'd talked to you since we heard about the riots in Palgaum."

"That's a switch for him. I was under the impression he was maybe . . . considering divorce." Vinita gnawed on her lip. She didn't know if Arya's words were significant enough for her to get excited. It could be a temporary thing—a sense of duty and obligation. Once he knew she was all right he'd likely go back to ignoring her.

"Divorce?" Arya went quiet. "Where'd you get that insane idea?" she asked finally.

"The way he's been behaving says a lot, don't you think?"

"No, Mom, he's really concerned," repeated Arya. "He asked me a couple of times to check on you. I think he's finally coming around."

"If he's beginning to thaw a little, maybe you should apply some shock treatment and tell him I died of malaria."

"Mom! It's not funny," scolded Arya.

"I wasn't trying to be funny. Your dad needs to wake up. He can't keep sulking forever. Things aren't going to change because he can't bear to face reality."

"I agree, but telling him you died isn't the way to do it."

They talked for another minute and ended the call. Vinita refused to allow herself to get excited about what Arya had just said. Maybe Girish was a bit troubled, but it didn't mean anything. If he was really worried, he'd have called—at least sent her an e-mail. He hadn't bothered with her even when he knew she was seriously ill.

She'd been desperately checking her e-mails. All she'd been getting was upbeat messages from close friends and colleagues. No, she couldn't let her hopes rise, only to have them crushed later.

Why was a sensible, practical man like Girish behaving this way? He'd been through two personal traumas in his life and he'd come through them with no visible emotional scars. So why had he become so bitter and unforgiving this time around?

She couldn't wait to return to New Jersey. Now that her business here was concluded, despite her complete failure at helping Rohit, she hungered for her home, her job, her friends. It was time for her to pack her bags and return home.

Mainly she missed Arya. And Girish. She longed for him with an intensity that surprised her. She'd always missed him when he was away from home, but this time her emotions were loaded with fear and desperation. She was dying to see him, and yet she dreaded facing him just as much.

Would she be returning home to her husband, or soon-to-be ex-husband?

Chapter 30

Girish shifted uncomfortably in his chair and tried to nibble on a slice of pizza. Arya was frowning at him across the kitchen table, condemnation written all over her face.

The pizza had turned to cold leather. Since Vini's departure for India, Arya and he had mostly been surviving on takeout food—pizza, Chinese, Thai, sushi. Neither he nor his daughter had any talent for cooking. The house was a mess, too. No one had cleaned it since Vini had left.

"How long are you going to torture yourself and Mom?" demanded Arya, pushing her empty plate aside and folding her arms.

His daughter had a direct way of facing an issue—a trait Girish had always admired and encouraged. But at the moment that very characteristic was making him squirm.

"Thanks for buying the pizza," he said. He didn't have the heart to tell her it was one of the worst he'd had—undercooked crust and overseasoned sauce. It was some kind of organic and environmentally friendly whole wheat product that fit into Arya's latest fad.

"Don't try to change the subject, Dad. I know the pizza's awful—and I don't give a damn about it."

"Who said anyone is being tortured?"

"You're not eating much, you're up at all times of the night, and either pacing or working on your computer since you returned from your so-called business trip."

"How do you—"

"You think I'm blind and deaf? I know everything that's going on, Dad," she interrupted curtly. "I know you miss her like hell. I know you were worried sick when you heard she came down with malaria. You've never looked this lonely before."

"Of course I miss her," Girish admitted with great reluctance. "We've been married a long time."

"Twenty-four years, eleven months, and two days." She wore a smug look.

"I'm capable of doing the math," he snapped.

"And yet you're behaving like an ass."

"How dare you talk to your father like that!" Girish dropped the pizza on his plate and pinned her with his sternest glare.

Arya didn't flinch, and held his gaze without a smidgen of alarm. She'd never been the kind of child who feared authority. "What else would you call a man who loves his wife and misses her, and yet pretends he has no feelings left for her?"

"I didn't say I don't love her." Arya was way too meddlesome and perceptive for her own good.

"Then why don't you tell her that?" She let him ruminate on that for a second. "Poor Mom is miserable."

"Serves her right for lying to me . . . to us . . . all these years."

"Don't you think *I* was hurt and confused when I found out the truth? But I got over it. If you look at it rationally, she was only a kid when she made that mistake. Vishal-mama and everyone else forced her to lie, and she did."

"But she was a grown woman when I met her. She could have made up her own mind and told me the truth."

"But telling the truth could've had you running. She couldn't risk that. I think she liked you too much to lose you. Shouldn't that count for something, the fact that she fell in love with you and didn't want to lose the chance to marry you?"

Girish picked up the half-eaten pizza once again and took a bite. He hadn't really thought of Vinita's actions in that light. He knew she loved him. Deeply. But had she developed strong feelings for him right after they'd met, just like he had for her?

She hadn't said anything about it to him. But then, neither had he. Expressing love had come after they'd been married a few months, after the awkwardness had passed and they'd reached a certain level of comfort.

"You honestly think that was her reason for hiding the truth?" he asked after a pensive bite or two.

"Of course it was. She went against her own conscience and hid the truth for a reason."

Girish mulled it over for a couple of seconds. "She told you that?"

Arya nodded. "She said she was lucky to meet a man like you when she didn't deserve to. Apparently she didn't want to lose the one decent man who'd finally come into her life."

"She didn't tell me that." He was discovering a few things about his wife. And himself.

"Maybe not, but she's proved it to you all these years. Isn't that enough?"

Girish rose to his feet and dumped the rest of his pizza in the trash. He wasn't hungry anymore. "I need some time to think about it, Arya. I really don't know what to make of all this."

Arya got up from the table and put her plate in the sink. "Dad, you've had plenty of time to brood. How long are you going to punish Mom for a mistake she made so long ago?"

He rinsed both their plates and placed them in the dishwasher. "You think it's that easy to forgive someone?"

Arya stood with both hands planted on her slender hips. "If you ask me, it's you who needs forgiving. You've been behaving like an ass instead of supporting Mom when she needs you the most."

"You don't understand what—"

"Dad"—she cut him off again—"no more excuses. Mom's been very ill. She's depressed because she can't donate her bone marrow and her son is dying. She's devastated because she thinks you hate her so much you're going to file for divorce."

Girish turned from the sink and scowled at Arya. "What gave her *that* idea?"

"You did."

"Me?" How and when the hell had divorce come into the picture?

"You haven't answered her voice mails or e-mails. What else is she supposed to think?"

"But I . . . didn't say anything about divorce."

"Not in words, but certainly in the way you've been treating her. I'm surprised she still feels the same way about you when you've been so horrible to her."

"I haven't said *one* word to her, Arya."

"Exactly my point." Arya put away the leftover pizza in the refrigerator.

Girish contemplated for a while. Had he been punishing Vini for her deceit? If it could be considered deceit. Was it time for him to stop acting like a wronged child? His wife was clearly going through a difficult time. Very difficult.

Arya wiped the table with a damp paper towel and threw him a sidelong glance. "If I were you, I'd start thinking about how to make it up to her."

"And I suppose you have some brilliant ideas on how I should go about it, too?"

"Your twenty-fifth anniversary's coming up," she said, discarding the paper towel. "I'm sure you can think of something." She swept out of the room, her expression smugger than ever.

Girish listened to the steady hum of the refrigerator and sighed. His daughter was a brat. She had a damn big mouth, too. But she was right about one thing. He was an ass.

Chapter 31

"W—what did you say?" Vinita dropped the blouse she was packing in her suitcase to stare at Sayee. Her sister-in-law had just walked into Vinita's bedroom and made a startling announcement.

"They found a donor for Rohit," Sayee repeated, beaming, clasping her hands with obvious glee.

Vinita stood still. It couldn't be true, could it? She wondered if she was beginning to imagine things—a mother's heart dreaming of the impossible. She'd prayed for a miracle, but she'd learned that miracles rarely, if ever, happened.

Too overwhelmed to reply, she pushed aside the pile of clothes lying beside her suitcase and sat down on the bed. "So soon?" she finally asked.

Sayee nodded and beamed at Vinita.

"You're not joking, right?"

Sayee's smile vanished, like the sun slipping behind a cloud. "Would I joke about something like this?"

"No . . . no, you wouldn't." Vinita put a trembling hand to her throat. "Who told you?"

"Uh . . . Dr. Panchal rang Vishal at his office."

Vinita frowned. "I wonder why the doctor called Vishal and not me."

"He thought you had already left for the U.S."

"Of course." She plucked the cordless phone from the bedside table. "I'm going to call Vishal and get the details."

"Vishal just left his office to meet a client."

Vinita put the phone back. "Do they know who it is? The donor, I mean."

Sayee shook her head, disturbing the tendrils of hair that had come loose from her braid. "You know they don't give out that kind of information. It's against their rules."

"Who follows rules in this country?" Vinita rolled her eyes. "The last time anyone followed rules was when I was about two years old."

"This is different. Medical ethics, you see."

"I suppose so." Vinita absently folded the blouse once again and tucked it into the suitcase. "But I'm still puzzled. We had no donors until an hour ago. Now all of a sudden we have a mystery volunteer." She gave it some thought. "What if this person is not a match?"

"But this particular donor does match. Apparently they did the tests and everything."

Vinita tossed a pair of underwear into the suitcase. After a week of problems, she'd finally managed to get a seat on a plane from Goa to Delhi, and then from there to Newark. Now it looked like she'd have to stay here a while longer—once again postpone her return home.

Talk about wretched timing. No surprise there. Everything in her life lately was turning upside down. "I'd just finished getting my tickets changed," she said to Sayee.

Sayee picked up a *salwar* and folded it, placed in on the bed, then reached for another one. "You don't have to alter your plans, Vini. Vishal and I are here for Rohit."

"No, I *have* to be here if Rohit undergoes a transplant."

"But you have been away from home and Girish for so long."

She threw Vinita a look that spoke volumes. Sayee was worried about her. Everyone in the family was. They knew Vinita hadn't spoken to Girish since she'd arrived in Palgaum. Although she hadn't said a word about it to anyone, they were fully aware. Every time Girish's name came up, they looked at her with anticipation, then dropped the subject.

Sayee pushed aside the heap of clothes and sat down beside Vinita. "Girish is all right, I hope?"

Vinita shook her head. Girish was not all right. He'd never be all right. Tears of self-pity welled up unexpectedly. Before she could say a word, they began to roll down her cheeks.

"Oh, Vini, I am so sorry." Sayee gathered her in her chubby arms.

"I d—don't know what to do," Vinita admitted on a sob.

"Shh, everything will be okay. I know it will."

Instead of Sayee's soothing words making the situation better, they only served to worsen Vinita's sobbing. She'd held it in for weeks—the shock of discovering she had a son; the difficult decision to take leave from her job and make the long journey to Palgaum to save him, followed by her unexpected and severe illness; the frustration of finding out she couldn't help him— and the fear of losing Girish. The haunting fear of losing Girish.

Now it was all spewing out like froth from a shaken soda can, and she couldn't stop it. Despite telling herself not to let her hopes soar, she'd seen a tiny spark of hope when Arya had mentioned that Girish had been worried about her during her illness and the Palgaum shutdown. But once she'd recovered, the tensions had ebbed, and the town's routine had been restored, Arya had never mentioned Girish's concerns again. He'd obviously gone back to indifference, or loathing, or whatever it was.

Sayee handed a handkerchief to her. "There, you'll feel better if you cry a little."

"I'm sorry," Vinita mumbled.

Sayee rubbed Vinita's back. "It has been a very difficult time for you."

"It's silly to cry when there's finally some good news, isn't it?"

"Sometimes good news can do that . . . especially if it comes so unexpectedly," soothed Sayee. "You're entitled to a few tears."

Pulling away from Sayee, Vinita tried to work up a smile. "How come you're so wise? You're younger than I am."

Sayee smiled back. "Natural wisdom."

Vinita couldn't help laughing. "I wish I'd been born with a bit of that."

Getting to her feet, Sayee offered Vinita a hand. "Come on, enough of this depressing talk. We should be celebrating. Let's make something special for dinner today, shall we?"

Taking the offered hand, Vinita stood up. "Like what?"

"How about your favorite dessert, *bahsundee?* It's Vishal's favorite, too."

"It's one thing I can't refuse." Vinita loved *bahsundee*—milk boiled till it was reduced to a thick, rich pudding and garnished with pistachios and almonds.

Sayee led the way out. "Let's go make it, then."

"Do you know when they're going to do the procedure?"

"No, but Vishal will find out before he comes home this evening. He promised to stop by Dr. Panchal's office."

As she followed her sister-in-law out of the room, Vinita wondered about the mystery donor. It was all very strange.

That night, Vinita sat at her brother's computer and sent Girish an e-mail, like she did every other night. It had become almost a ritual, sharing her experiences with him, like she used to in person every evening back home, while they ate dinner together. If she couldn't talk to him in person, e-mail was the next best thing.

She doubted whether he read any of her messages. But she wrote to him anyway, felt a little better for doing it. It was her only connection to him.

> *Hi, dear,*
> *Guess what? A bone marrow donor has been found for Rohit. I realize you don't want to hear any of this, nor do you care, but you're still the only person I share all my news with. There was a time, not too long ago, when you would have rejoiced in something that gave me joy, but now I can only hope for it. I'm not sure when the transplant will take place, but I'm sure it will be soon.*

I wish you'd find it in your heart to forgive me
once and for all. For the hundredth time, I admit
I was wrong to keep secrets from you, but I don't
think I deserve lifelong punishment for it, either.
I miss you. Take care of yourself.
Love,
Vini

Rohit sat in Dr. Panchal's office with his hands folded in his lap, feeling a bit light-headed—probably a side effect of his latest medication.

His mother sat on one side of him and his father on the other, pathetically protective as always, sadly naïve in their belief that together they would somehow protect him from doom. They looked as overwrought as he felt. His mother looked fragile, brittle enough to break. His father's arm was still in a cast, but his face was almost back to normal, except for a scar on his cheek, where the stitches were healing. Nonetheless he sat upright, the proud, relentless lion who would fight till the end.

Since they'd been informed by Dr. Panchal the previous day that an anonymous marrow donor had come forward, neither he nor his parents had been able to sleep. The news had left them exhilarated yet anxious. They had stayed up late into the night, talking about the unexpected development.

His mother's buoyant expression had nearly brought tears to his eyes—something that didn't happen often. She'd clearly been dreaming of seeing him healthy again, perhaps even capable of giving her a couple of grandchildren in the future—before it was too late. Having been childless herself and forced to resort to adoption, her dearest wish was to see him have a family of his own.

It was a nice dream to have, no doubt. And yet he didn't dare to entertain such fantasies.

Until a day ago, he had been staring certain death in the face. Without a transplant, he could probably carry on for another year or two. The latest treatments had kept him functioning on some level for the past two years, and they could probably do it a while longer.

He'd been prepared to face a bleak future, where every time he faltered they would likely pump him with steroids, antibiotics, and some newfangled drugs. They would give him a few more months' extension on his contract with God. But despite the medical intervention, there would be no guarantees.

Now, all of a sudden, he had a chance to live. Or maybe not. His body could reject the transplant. Or the donor could back out at the last minute. Or he could end up with a fatal infection. The possibilities for failure were too many to count. He had done a fair amount of research on his condition. And yet he'd felt a quick surge of hope the moment the doctor had rung him.

One significant detail had plagued Rohit all night: Who *was* this donor? The person had apparently been tested and was found to be compatible, which meant he or she had come forward to help some days ago. When he and his parents had asked questions, they had been told that the individual preferred to remain anonymous.

Why had this person come forward so suddenly? Why now?

The doctor spoke to Rohit directly, disrupting his thoughts. "Rohit, we have to do a series of tests before we consider you fully ready for a transplant."

"But all the tests were done some time ago," Rohit's father remarked. He had on his most irritated frown. "Why do them again? Waste of time and money, is it not?"

Panchal heaved a long-suffering sigh. "Mr. Barve, those tests were done months ago, and for different reasons. Rohit has had some infections since then. Now we have to make sure that he is in good condition to accept the transplant. It is a complicated procedure and we need to be very careful. When—"

"All right," Rohit interrupted, holding up a hand. He had heard enough arguing. His father loved a good fight, and the doctor was a thorough man who clearly left nothing to chance. "Whatever you have to do, just do it, Doctor. I'm ready. Do it tomorrow if you can." He was profoundly tired. He wanted this to be over.

No doubt it was going to be too damned costly to get a transplant, but he was willing to go through with it. His parents were ready to borrow money if they needed to. In the end, he could still die and they would be in debt for the rest of their lives. But they would never let him back out if his decision was based on lack of money.

Besides, his real mother was insisting on paying for most of it. He didn't know if he should accept it, even though she could obviously afford it. It was charity. And yet it was tempting. He wanted to live.

"Tomorrow? It's not that simple, Rohit," retorted the doctor. "It will be at least another week before we can do a complete round of tests to check on your heart, kidneys, and liver. We'll need to do a brain scan, dental screening, a spinal tap, and then we need to give you radiation and chemotherapy to prepare your body to accept the transplanted marrow . . ."

Rohit closed his eyes for a moment, shut out the doctor's endless list. He should have known it wasn't simple. Nothing in his life was simple. Right from the day he was born—in fact, right from the moment he was conceived—things had been complicated for him. He was a bastard child, borne in shame under a bleak karmic cloud. And he was a diabetic.

His stomach clenched at the thought of more chemotherapy. He could almost feel it now—the familiar attacks of nausea, the blinding headaches, the hyperactive bowels, the weakness in his limbs so intense that he could have sworn his legs were made of rubber, and his hair falling out in clumps—every blasted symptom.

And yet . . . if he cared to look deep inside himself . . . he wanted to live. Maybe there was a very remote chance that he would survive and recover, and perhaps scrape up the courage to dream of a normal life.

"Besides, don't forget you're diabetic. We have to take that into consideration every step of the way," rambled the doctor. "Treatment has to begin days before the actual transplant."

Opening his eyes, he nodded at Dr. Panchal. "Okay. Whatever you say, I'll do it."

The doctor's bland face cracked a rare half smile. "We'll get you started on the tests right away."

Chapter 32

Rohit flipped the switch to turn on the overhead fluorescent lights in the laboratory and blinked. Bright light bothered his eyes lately. He wondered if it was a natural result of his condition or yet another side effect of the drugs he'd been subjected to.

But he loved the clinical, sterile comfort of the lab. It was like coming home when he stepped into the long, narrow room that served as Shivraj College's chemistry lab. The smell of it, the feel of it, and the stark look of it—they were all so familiar.

Most people tried to get away from their place of work when they needed rest and relaxation. But Rohit often came to his lab to relax, where scarred wooden tables and tall stools ate up most of the space. Row upon row of jars, pipettes, test tubes, and beakers stood at attention, like soldiers ready for battle. They sparkled in the harsh light. He insisted on neatness in his lab and his students complied with his command. Most of the time.

He smelled the pungent odor of bleach in the air. Someone had probably left a jar of chlorine open, despite his rule of extreme caution in working around unsafe substances. He located the offending jar and tightened the lid. Careless kids.

There had been a time, not long ago, when he'd have lost his temper at such carelessness when handling chemicals, even harmless ones. But today he merely shook his head. The thought of imminent death was humbling enough to make an emotion like anger at a student seem trivial.

He inhaled deeply, let the mingled odors of the chemicals sink into his weakened lungs. This was his world. Ever since he was a young boy in school, he'd loved chemistry for some reason, perhaps because his father was a chemical engineer. The idea of combining different substances to form odd and interesting mixtures that could produce anything from a flu remedy to a bomb had fascinated him.

Cricket and chemistry—the two Cs had consumed his high school and college days, and thankfully his parents had encouraged both.

He could memorize so many chemical formulae and retain them that his teachers used to be astonished. He'd even given up cricket to pursue that doctoral degree. He had never regretted his decision.

Nevertheless, lately he'd been speculating about it, wondering if his obsession with chemistry could have something to do with his leukemia. It was entirely possible that working with potent chemicals for many years could have led to cancer.

He hadn't discussed his suspicions with his doctor or his parents. It was something he had pondered in private. He didn't want his parents to try to convince him to give up his career and take up something else. He could never be anything other than a chemistry teacher.

Even if his suspicions held weight, it was too late to do anything about it. He had chosen his occupation despite knowing the hazards associated with it. He prayed his students knew the risks, too.

He ambled over to the far end of the room and sat down on one of the stools, then opened a chemistry textbook someone had left behind. The book looked almost new. He flipped through the pages. There were no handwritten notes or scribbles anywhere. It was nice to come across a neat student for a change. They were young, often thoughtless, sometimes sloppy, but this one was not.

Turning to the cover page, he looked for a name. Perhaps he could find the owner and have it returned to them. Textbooks, especially the thick, hardcover science books, were prohibitively expensive and few students could afford them. Many of them ended up buying used books from the previous year's students.

Finding no name to identify the owner, he started turning the pages once again. Then he found it. Not exactly what he was looking for, but something else—much more interesting.

It was a crudely written note on a piece of ruled paper. There was no name, but it was obviously meant for Rohit. *Cancer will kill you soon, you Marathi bastard! Ha-Ha!*

His stomach jumped in response, causing a sudden spurt of nausea. He'd faced his share of practical jokes. What professor at Shivraj hadn't? Students loved to torture their teachers with itchy powder sprinkled over their chairs, wads of chewing gum stuck where their shoes would rest, mobile phones pilfered, and missing pens and notebooks.

But this didn't feel like a practical joke. The message was packed with malice, despite the humor inserted at the end. He could sense it in his bones.

Did he have students who hated him that much, enough to delight in the fact that he had a life-threatening illness? He tried to visualize as many faces and personalities as he could, at least the Kannada ones. But there were so many—too many to remember them all.

Any one of them could have done this. It could have been more than one—an entire group of hate-mongers. It could be a coworker, even a fellow Marathi, hoping the blame would automatically be laid at the feet of the Kannada faction.

Maybe it was best to turn over the book and the note to the police. He carefully closed the book without touching the note. He'd read enough crime fiction and seen plenty of movies to know one wasn't supposed to touch anything that might become potential evidence. But in the next instant he realized this was no crime, and there was no threat involved. It was just a statement of the cruel truth.

Someone was trying to remind him his end was near. As if he needed reminding. He didn't want any more damned reminders.

If that silly note was meant to scare him, the sender had failed. What was there to fear anymore? He was standing on the brink of a precipice, looking into a black, yawning chasm. He could get pushed off the edge in a heartbeat, with or without the transplant.

He looked around, studying every piece of steel, glass, plastic, ceramic, and wood. He'd worked so damn hard to be able to work in a lab like this, teach in a small, privately funded college, and make a difference in the lives of at least a few students. He wasn't a greedy sort. He hadn't asked for too much in life. Suddenly his modest dreams were crumbling faster than termite-infested wood.

Somewhere, halfway across the world, he even had a half sister, a young woman whose existence he'd only recently discovered. A girl he'd probably never get to meet. At first he had hated the idea of having to face his real mother, and the thought of having a sibling, a new cluster of cousins, uncles, and aunts.

Suddenly all those strangers, most of them faceless, were becoming very real—the people who were his kin. He'd been thinking about them a lot lately. The strangest part was discovering that the Shelke twins, whom he'd taught in the recent past, were his cousins. On the paternal side, there were the Kori sisters—his half sisters. Both were his students at the moment—both quiet, rather shy.

And the Kori girls and the Shelke boys didn't know of their odd connection to each other. At least he didn't think they did.

The whole tangled web was mind-boggling yet endlessly fascinating. Some weeks ago, he had thought himself an orphan, an only child, adopted. Now Palgaum was exploding with relatives—his real family.

What would have happened if he'd grown up in their midst, surrounded by Shelkes and Koris? He dismissed the notion. The staunch Marathi Shelkes would never have mixed with the unbending Kannada Koris. It would have been one long, never-ending feud.

He wondered if any one of them had suffered from leukemia. Was it hereditary? If so, which side could it have come from?

Setting aside his thoughts about family for a moment, he ran his palm across the book's cover. He knew almost every page of this primer on the principles of analytical chemistry. How long would he be able to turn those familiar pages, face a classroom full of eager faces, and introduce them to the magical world of chemistry, a subject that touched every little thing in their lives, including their own bodies? Not long at this rate.

This could even be his last glimpse of his precious lab.

Some of the more expensive equipment in this room was here because he had convinced the board members it was a necessity if they wanted their students to learn and compete with other colleges. He had spent long hours canvassing each tight-fisted member. His efforts had paid off to some extent. The lab was now cleaner, brighter, and better equipped. If nothing else, he had made a small difference to Shivraj College's chemistry department. It would be his legacy after he was gone.

His left hand shook as it lay splayed on the book. His body convulsed. *It's only a side effect of those drugs,* he told himself. The damn shivers set in very easily these days. It was nothing to worry about.

It wasn't until his right hand started to throb that he realized he was pummeling the table with everything he had. Pounding, pounding till the knuckles were skinned and bleeding. An empty test tube had overturned and fallen down, the shards scattered over the tile floor.

Blood streaked the table. He was clearly losing his mind along with his body. *Why, God? Why me?* His chest started to heave without warning and hot tears started to roll down his face.

He was crying. Oh, for God's sake! How much more pathetic could he get? He quickly pulled out a handkerchief from his pants pocket and dabbed his eyes, then his injured hand. Good thing he was alone. His doctor would have scolded him for hurting himself. Between the drugs and the diabetes, even minor injuries were dangerous in his condition.

What the hell was the matter with him? He never cried, and almost never surrendered to fits of rage. Grown men weren't supposed to cry. For any reason. And they weren't supposed to beat their hands to a pulp, either. It had to be those blasted drugs, messing with his brain and body—whatever was left of them.

The nausea rose higher now, and the bile shot up into his throat. He raced to the sink at the far end of the lab in the nick of time—and vomited. Damn disease! Rinsing his mouth and his bloodied hand at the tap, he wiped both with his none-too-clean handkerchief and headed back toward the door.

He had plans to meet some friends for dinner later. It was a party at a married friend's home. The couple was celebrating their second anniversary, and the impending arrival of their first child, due in three months. Except for one, all his close friends were either married or engaged.

Feeling a stab of pain in his hand, he winced. He'd have to run to his flat and put some first-aid cream and adhesive bandages over the abrasions and pull himself together. It wouldn't do to let his friends see him like this. They had stopped asking him when he planned to get married—not even in jest. In the usual Indian tradition, they used to nag him mercilessly about acquiring a wife. Now they gave him pitying looks and made awkward inquiries about his health.

But they meant well, so he didn't mind their concerned curiosity. As a matter of fact, he was looking forward to this evening. Not the food—the thought of food made him sick—but the company. It could even be his last party.

Tomorrow he was being admitted to the hospital for pre-transplant treatment. It was likely to be the longest few days of his life. At the end of that period, God knows what lay in store—staying in the hospital till death came knocking, or going home, feeling better. Staying alive.

He didn't want to think that far ahead. Lately he had begun to plan his life in terms of one day at a time. One precious day.

Enough self-pity, he ordered, and straightened his sagging shoulders.

Before leaving the lab, he swept the broken test tube shards off the floor and discarded them. He took one final look around the lab, trying to commit its last detail to memory. Even if he survived the transplant, it could be nearly a year before he could return to work. A year seemed like a lifetime at this point.

He put the book back where he'd found it. Despite the nasty note enclosed, he sent its owner a mental message: *Hope you pass your chemistry exam, my friend. Professor Ramchandra is not as liberal in his grading as I am.*

Shutting off the lights, he closed and locked the door to the lab and walked down the steps to the covered portico, where he had parked his motorcycle.

Outside, a thunderstorm was just beginning to spit out the first plump drops of rain. Standing there for a minute, he observed the storm unleash its fury. A jagged streak of lightning tore the sky, illuminating the landscape for a split second. Winds whipped through the row of tall, slender eucalyptus trees planted alongside the building, making their boughs sway madly.

It was a beautiful sight. Strange, but he'd never thought of a rainstorm as a thing of beauty before.

The late-summer storm that was passing would drive away the sticky heat and allow for some good sleeping weather at night. Not that he would sleep all that much.

He waited for the earsplitting boom of thunder to pass before stepping beyond the portico. Lifting his face, he let the delightful moisture slide over his face, settle on his tongue, soak through his shirt. He hadn't done anything like this in years, either.

It could be his last rainstorm.

Her pulse pounded in her ears. Vinita read the message one more time . . . to make sure she hadn't completely lost her mind. Stress could make one's brain do strange things. But the message was clear—rather brief and cool, but it was certainly an improvement over Girish's total indifference.

> *Vini,*
> *I'm sure you'll be surprised to hear from me. But I honestly needed some time to myself. I've been doing a lot of thinking since you told me about your past. A few things are becoming clearer, now that the shock of discovery has worn off. I'm sorry to hear that you had malaria and that things haven't been going well with Rohit and your plan to donate marrow.*

*But I'm glad someone has come forward to
help. I won't keep you long. I'm sure you're
spending most of your time at the hospital. I hope
Rohit comes through this ordeal successfully. I
also hope you're feeling better.*
  Girish

She sat back in the chair and took several deep breaths to let
the raging emotions subside. Took him long enough to respond.
No word for weeks, and then all of a sudden this?

Surprised, he'd said. He had to be kidding, she fumed. *Try
stunned, my dear, judgmental, pigheaded husband.* There was
no remorse in his note, no words like *worried,* or *concerned,* or
love, or even the usual affectionate closing.

She wanted to lash out at him, scream at him for putting her
through such anguish for weeks. But where would anger and re-
venge leave her? They'd both just end up at an impasse again.
Did she want that?

What had brought on this sudden change in attitude? she
wondered. Arya was probably nagging him to pieces, but he
could be equally mulish in many ways. He'd been thinking, he
said. He was a careful, contemplative kind of man. But thinking
for this many damn weeks?

Calm down, she ordered herself. *At least he's communicating
now.* She wasn't sure she wanted to respond to his message right
now—when she was angry on the one hand, but grudgingly relieved on the other.

One wrong word from her and he'd probably clam up all
over again. Best to leave it alone, for now, she supposed. She'd
respond when she was calmer, more rational. What she needed
was a good night's sleep—time to do her own *thinking.*

Maybe tomorrow she'd see his message in a different light.
Perhaps come to accept it as his way of calling a truce. If she
was willing to look at it from a certain perspective, she might
even feel gratitude.

She'd chew on it some more first.

Chapter 33

It smelled of antiseptic cleansers, the way hospitals were supposed to smell. And yet, to Vinita, slouched in a chair in the oncology wing's waiting room, toying with the clasp on her handbag, it was a grim reminder that her son was to undergo a life-changing procedure the next day.

Since she'd arrived in Palgaum, it seemed like she'd been in this hospital practically every other day. She had come to know every square foot of it by now, and all the odors and sounds associated with it. Even some hospital staff were beginning to recognize her. Some of them greeted her with a smile.

Besides, it wasn't every day that they came across a juicy story like hers and Rohit's. The gossip mill was alive and well in Palgaum, despite its having grown from a small town to a mid-size city in the quarter century she'd been gone. Most everyone in town probably knew her saga by now—the estranged mother from America who had suddenly discovered she had a son, and had flown halfway across the world to save him.

Looking at it from that perspective, it sounded like a movie plot. The whole thing had been bizarre right from the start—all the way back to the time Rohit was conceived.

More than a week had gone by since she'd been informed about the mystery donor. She still had no clue about the person's identity. She'd been making a mental list of possibilities. After considering, then discarding, the individuals on that very short list, she had settled on Som.

It had to be Som. Maybe her plea to him had made an impact after all. Or was it the Indian male ego, the one that fed itself on the fact that he'd fathered a male child? Had that spurred him to come forward and save his only son? No matter what his reasons, for once in his reprehensible life he had decided to do the right thing. Just for that she was willing to overlook every rotten thing he'd done.

If Som helped save Rohit's life, she was willing to forgive him anything.

She was interrupted in her reverie by Meenal. "Shashi and I are going home now," she announced. "If you want to spend some time with Rohit, please go ahead."

Startled, Vinita looked at Meenal. The woman looked more exhausted than ever. Wet bands of perspiration darkened her blouse around the armpits. She'd been at the hospital nearly all day. Her hair was flattened on one side, like she'd been resting her head against the back of a chair.

"You don't mind?" Vinita asked.

"Rohit is alone now. He might appreciate some company before he goes to sleep."

Mr. Barve nodded his agreement. His injuries appeared to be healing. The black eye had all but vanished and the scar on his cheek was a thin brown line. But his arm was still in a cast.

"Thank you." It was so generous of the Barves that Vinita didn't know what else she could say. She'd arrived at the hospital an hour ago and parked herself in the waiting room, hoping to find out how Rohit was doing on the eve of his transplant. The poor boy was likely going through hell with what they called conditioning—intensive chemotherapy and radiation to kill any remaining cancer cells and prepare his body to receive the new marrow and help it grow.

Her last visit with him was five days ago. He'd been looking somber that day, more or less resigned to the poking and prodding, the IV pole a permanent fixture beside his bed. But she'd also sensed a spark of buoyancy in him. Like everyone else around him, his feelings had seemed mixed—optimism tempered by a sensible dose of caution.

By calling the Barves every day, Vinita had managed to get a daily status report on Rohit. Each day, she had detected the anxiety mounting in Meenal's voice. Each day, Vinita had tried her best to boost the older woman's spirits. Each day, her own disquiet had climbed one more notch. But amidst the tension and unease, she and Meenal had become friends.

The impending transplant and the knowledge that their son just might have a chance to live had served as the glue to bring the two women even closer together than before. No other friend or family member would have understood what they shared.

Today Vinita couldn't stay away from the hospital. She had felt compelled to be in the same building as Rohit, as near as she could get to him. But her plan had been to chat with the Barves in the waiting room, wish them luck, and then leave. Vishal had promised to pick her up whenever she was ready to go home. She hadn't actually expected to see Rohit. That was a privilege reserved for his parents.

She was merely hoping for crumbs—one last chance to get firsthand information before the procedure. Although the transplant itself was supposedly as simple as a blood transfusion, the fear of losing him afterwards was real. The need to see him as much as she could was turning into an obsession.

After wishing the Barves good night, she sprang to her feet and quickly made her way to the area where she had to scrub her hands and arms with a special germicidal soap.

A nurse thrust a clean towel into her hands. "No touching the patient," she reminded Vinita.

"Thanks." Vinita knew the routine from her last visit. She dried her hands and rubbed the alcohol-based liquid purifier on her hands and arms. All the while the nurse watched her like a prison warden, making sure she obeyed the hospital's stringent rules about safeguarding patients.

She padded over to the closed foyer that led to Rohit's room. The door was shut to keep the germs out and maintain the specially created positive-pressure environment, so she knocked and waited a second before entering.

This room was larger than the last one he'd been in. It had no windows, for obvious reasons. It was sterile, air-conditioned with special filters, and painted a stark white. The next day, after the procedure—assuming it went as planned—he'd be moved to an even more sanitary room than this one, monitored closely by assigned staff only. He'd be kept in a veritable bubble for a few days.

"Hello, Rohit," she said. He was lying on his back, staring at the ceiling, seemingly deep in thought. A shuddery breath flew out of her the instant she noticed how drawn his face looked. He'd lost weight in the space of five days.

It took him a second to shift his focus to her. "Hello." He looked grim. The spark from the previous visit was missing.

"How are you feeling?" She closed the door behind her. She stood a little distance from his bed, afraid she might contaminate him if she got any closer. Her eyes raked him, though, wondering how he could have deteriorated so rapidly. His expressive golden eyes had receded deeper into their sockets.

She quelled the urge to move closer and touch him, to smooth a hand over his beard-roughened face, to experience the feel of his skin, like she sometimes did with Arya. Until this moment she'd had no idea how quickly the maternal instinct could kick in, even toward a child who'd been a complete stranger until recently.

"Other than an ulcerated mouth, hair loss, diarrhea, vomiting, and a blasted headache, I'm okay," was his sardonic reply to her question. His voice was weak.

"I'm sorry. It was a silly question to ask. You must be miserable."

"All part of being a leukemia patient," he said with a snort. "I've become an expert at it."

"I hope you don't mind my visiting you this late. Your parents were kind enough to let me spend some time alone with you," she explained.

"I don't mind."

Three simple words, yet they tugged at the deepest recesses of her heart. Her son had come a long way since she and Vishal had visited him the very first time. "I promise I won't stay too long."

He glanced at the IV pole. "I have all the time in the world. I'm not going anywhere, as you can see."

"But you need your rest."

He gave a wry smile. "I'll be resting for a long time after tomorrow."

"Have they explained the procedure to you in detail?"

"In excruciating detail," he said, rolling his eyes. "Briefly, the infusion of marrow will be done through my central venous line." He pointed to his chest.

She couldn't see the tube because he was wearing a hospital gown and a sheet covered him up to his neck. But she nodded. "I read about it on the Internet last night."

"After that they'll keep me in a sterile room and watch me closely to see if engraftment begins and starts to produce new blood cells."

She nodded again. Signs of engraftment, if any, were apparently seen about two to four weeks after the procedure.

"Are you stuck here all that time, or can you go home in a week or two?" She had hoped he'd be out of danger within a few days and she could fly back home, knowing he was on the mend.

"That depends on how my body reacts to the transplant— rejection, infection . . . who knows," he murmured with a shrug. He seemed resigned to his fate. "Like I said, I'll be resting a long time."

"But the important thing is to keep thinking healthy," she said, working up a sunny smile for him, despite the shiver that ran through her at his ominous words, *resting a long time.* "You'll be on your feet and back at work before you know it."

He snorted again. "Yeah, sure."

She wondered if the doctor had said something to him to make his spirits sink so low. Or was it the effect of the powerful treatment he'd been undergoing these past few days?

"Who do you think is my donor?" he asked, jolting her despite knowing he'd probably be speculating about his potential savior, just as she and the rest of the family were.

"No idea, but I've considered some possibilities." Noticing his blanket hanging off one side of the foot of the bed, she shifted and adjusted it, making sure not to touch his foot. It gave her something to do while she pondered his question.

"Who did you come up with?" he asked when she said nothing.

"You may not want to hear this."

"Try me."

"I think it is Som Kori."

He frowned, the descending eyebrows looking so much like Som's that she nearly smiled. "He doesn't even know who I am."

"He does . . . now."

"How?" The glazed look in his eyes instantly turned to a hard sparkle.

For a brief moment she wondered if she should have pretended to have no idea who the donor was and left it at that. The last time she'd mentioned the Kori name, Rohit and his parents had nearly had a seizure. But Rohit had a right to know. Besides, if it *was* Som, by tomorrow he would probably be discovered through the hospital grapevine. What difference would a few hours make?

"I told him," she confessed.

"Why?"

"Because he's your father and perhaps the most perfect match in the world for you. That's all that matters."

Rohit shut his eyes tight, like he was trying hard to keep his emotions under control. She prayed her bombshell hadn't done something awful to his blood pressure or heartbeat or some other vital function. She had no idea how it would affect a person with a weak immune system.

"I'm sorry," she murmured. "I realize you detest the man and he's your father's arch enemy and all that, but I just couldn't stand by and let you slip away." She paused for breath. "Som *had* to be told." She wondered what she could say to offer comfort, while Rohit struggled to come to terms with what she'd just told him. "I couldn't let you die, Rohit."

It was a long minute before he opened his eyes. He was clearly still grappling with the shocking truth. "That's okay," he said at last. "I don't hate the man as much as my father does."

She stared at him, puzzled. "But the other day, when I mentioned—"

"I don't have any reason to," he said, cutting her off. "I have no interest in politics. I honestly don't care which state Palgaum belongs to."

"I thought you believed in your father's cause."

"What he wants is impractical. He's fighting a silly battle where there are no winners, only losers."

Vinita continued to stare at him. "I'm glad you're not involved in any of the violence." It was a relief to know Rohit didn't harbor the biases of his real father or his adoptive one. In that respect he'd taken after her. She actively disliked politics, most especially the corrosive, destructive kind that bred distrust and hatred.

"His daughters have been my students," he said. "They're nice girls." He gave a raspy chuckle. "Of course, I didn't know they were my half sisters."

She beamed at him. "I'm so relieved you're not angry about Som."

He scrubbed his face with one hand. "Anger is such a wasted emotion when you don't know whether you'll be alive next week or not."

"Puts it all in perspective, doesn't it?"

"You know about that?" He gave her a strange look.

"Oh yes. I nearly died while giving birth to you. That's when I realized anger was a silly emotion. I know you don't believe this, but at that moment, all that mattered was my unborn child. I made Vishal promise that he would look out for you if I died. All I wanted was the best for *you.*"

Unfortunately, after she'd survived childbirth she'd gone back to her old stubborn ways—anger, belligerence, and all those other negative emotions. But she didn't tell him that.

"I believe you now," he said, closing his eyes again, looking weaker than he had minutes before. Every passing second seemed to drain his energy. "My parents *are* the best . . . if you overlook my father's fanaticism."

"I know. I've come to know them rather well these past few weeks, especially your mother." It was odd how Vinita's initial resentment toward Meenal had evaporated so quickly. Matter of fact, she felt immense gratitude for Meenal's devotion to Rohit. More and more, Vinita had begun to recognize the wisdom in her family's decision to give Rohit up for adoption. Of course, she was loath to admit it to them. She couldn't take their smug *we told you so* looks.

"Tell me about your daughter," Rohit said in the next breath, pulling her out of her thoughts.

It was an unforeseen request. He'd never asked about Arya in all these weeks. Was it only idle curiosity, or the fear that he could die soon and never have a chance to find out about her?

"Your half sister is a bright, attractive young lady." She wondered how Arya was managing, especially with Girish acting like an obstinate old goat. But if anyone could straighten him out, it was Arya. She suffered neither fools nor people who wallowed in self-pity or held grudges. But so far, even she had not been able to make a dent in the wall Girish had constructed around himself.

"What does she do?"

"She works in the research division of a pharmaceutical company."

"Is she a pharmacist?" His eyes lit up briefly. He was probably wondering if she liked chemistry like he did.

"No, she's a bioengineer. She graduated from Johns Hopkins last year, a prestigious university in the U.S., noted for its bioengineering department." Vinita couldn't help showing off. Her baby was so damn smart. Both her kids were smart. In fact, she'd given birth to two bright *and* personable children. How had she managed that?

The corners of his mouth lifted in a genuine smile. Vinita detected no bitterness. "She's very clever, then," he said simply.

"Her work involves research in combining drugs and prostheses in stroke and accident victims with partial paralysis. Of course, with only a bachelor's degree, it's mostly routine work that she does for the senior scientists."

"It still sounds interesting," he said after mulling it over. "I envy her." He was quiet for another second. "Is she planning to study further?"

"Yes. She starts on her master's degree this fall. Maybe even a PhD like you in the future. Who knows?"

"Who knows?" he repeated, sounding like a tired old man.

"Would you like to see a picture of her?" She lifted a brow at him, eager for a positive response. She so badly wanted both her children to get to know each other.

"Sure, why not?"

Vinita rummaged through her handbag and realized she didn't have the pictures. "Sorry," she sighed. "Guess I forgot to put them back in my bag after I showed them to my family."

"That's all right," he said with a dismissive wave. "Some other day, perhaps." He coughed, a brassy sound that came from deep inside his chest. "If I'm still alive after tomorrow, that is."

Vinita's heart constricted. "Of course you'll be alive! You'll even get to meet your sister sometime soon," she said, hoping to put some much-needed optimism into this gloomy conversation. She couldn't let him lose heart. Not now.

"Maybe." He was beginning to fade. "If fate will allow." Again a fatalistic remark.

"Everything will be okay, Rohit. I'm praying for your recovery. I know your mother is doing all kinds of special *poojas* at the temple, too."

"I know. She hasn't stopped praying for the past two years." His eyelids were drooping.

"I want you to know something. Arya had offered to fly down to Palgaum and be a donor."

His eyes flew open, the astonishment clear. "Very generous of her. I'm just a stranger."

"No longer. She's a very caring girl. She wants to help you if she can."

He gave her one of his rare smiles. "Tell her thanks."

"I will," she promised, her throat beginning to close up. Once again she quashed the need to reach over and touch him. A hug would have been nice. She'd never touched her son. Ever.

There was a knock on the door before it opened. A nurse appeared. "Visiting hours are over, madam," she informed Vinita, tapping her wristwatch as she approached Rohit's bed.

"I had better leave," Vinita murmured, and shifted reluctantly toward the door. "Good night, Rohit."

He didn't respond. The nurse had already started to shove a thermometer into his mouth. Vinita shut the door and stood in the foyer for a second.

Let my son live, God, she prayed as she started to open the second door leading into the hallway. *Please don't punish him for my sins.*

Chapter 34

The house was eerily quiet as Vinita emerged from the bath-room and got dressed. Dawn was barely breaking, so there was not much traffic yet. The only sounds outside came from the crows foraging for food. Urbanization had spurred a growth in their population.

The air was a little cool after last night's thunderstorm had brought a short but heavy downpour, and she shivered as she gathered the pleats on her sari and tucked them in at her waist. She prayed it wasn't a relapse of malaria. She never wanted to go through that nightmare again.

She heard a familiar car engine start up and drive away. Vishal's car. The poor man worked such insane hours. But she supposed he had to. It was his nature to work hard, just like their father used to. All this success didn't come without a lot of dogged work.

She hoped Vishal didn't work himself into the ground at an early age, too, like Papa had. She made a mental note to have a talk with her workaholic brother. Better yet, she would talk to Sayee. Someone had to make sure Vishal slowed down a little, now that he was in his fifties. Surely he had enough money saved by now and didn't need to slave as much. Hopefully at least one of his twins would soon take over some part of Vishal's business.

But no matter how busy he was, Vinita knew for sure that he would stop by the hospital later to check on Rohit's progress, and on her. He was worried about her. Despite Vishal's attempts at remaining aloof, she had managed to catch a glance past his façade.

By the time she went downstairs, her mother and Sayee were already on their second cup of tea. The kitchen smelled of *upama*—a spicy cream-of-wheat dish seasoned with roasted mustard, cumin, chili peppers, and curry leaves.

Both women looked fresh and neat—bathed and dressed for the day ahead. They seemed a little tense, though, both sitting at the table in complete silence. It was unusual for Sayee to be subdued. She was usually glowing with good cheer, even as early as this.

Vinita speculated whether Sayee and her mother could have had an argument. It rarely happened, since Sayee was such an accommodating sort and got along with everyone. But she was human, and Mummy could be a difficult woman to live with.

Rohit's transplant was obviously making everyone edgy. Vinita felt the familiar prick of guilt. She was the cause of all the tension and discord her family was suffering.

"I heard Vishal leaving early," she remarked, hoping to inject a little conversation into the glum stillness.

"Hmm," murmured Sayee absently, offering no explanation. Vinita didn't belabor the subject. Clearly Sayee was in no mood to talk.

Her mother, on the other hand, gave Vinita an assessing look before pouring a cup of tea for her. "Did you get any sleep?"

"A little," Vinita lied. She hadn't slept at all. How could she, when her son was about to go through a rare medical procedure? She hadn't come all the way from the U.S. to sleep or rest. She had come for Rohit. And his life lay in the balance. The threat of rejection or fungal, bacterial, and viral infections was too great to be ignored.

Every time that possibility stabbed at her, she felt her heart slide a little lower. Was the transplant even worth considering? It was too late to speculate now. Rohit would be going through the procedure within three or four hours. Praying was all she could do now.

"Have some *upama*," said Sayee, stirring from her stupor. "I'll heat some for you."

"No *upama*, please," said Vinita. The thought of eating was making her queasy. "I'll just have a slice of toast. Don't get up," she said to Sayee, motioning to her to sit back down. "I'll help myself." She went to the toaster and inserted a slice of bread into it.

She looked around the kitchen while the bread browned. Along with the rest of the house, the old kitchen, too, had been remodeled, with new cabinets, appliances, and flooring, but the sturdy old dining table and chairs remained. A lasting relic from her childhood.

Hadn't she sat at this very table once, a teenager on the brink of disaster? She clearly remembered that morning, when she had walked in and found her mother making omelets. Mummy had offered a fresh omelet and toast to Vinita, and the sight of them had made Vinita's stomach turn over, like the *upama* was doing now.

But this time Vinita's reason for nausea was different. Well, not so different. It still had to do with her illegitimate son. And his survival.

As she retrieved the toast and put it in on a plate, she sensed her mother's eyes on her. "I'm going to the hospital as soon as I finish eating," Vinita said, before Mummy could start grilling her. "And I plan to stay there as long as it's necessary."

"I'll go with you," offered Sayee.

"No, I need to do this alone." Vinita returned to the table and spread a bit of butter on her toast. "I appreciate it, but I just . . . have to do this on my own. I'll walk up to the corner and take a rickshaw."

"All right." Sayee threw a glance at her mother-in-law, making Vinita wonder why the two women were so jumpy.

"I'll call to let you know how things go," Vinita offered.

Finishing her breakfast, Sayee rose from her chair and gathered up her empty plate and her mother-in-law's. "But at least come home for lunch," she said to Vinita.

"I'll try, but don't wait for me. I can easily find something there." She mulled it over for a moment. "Maybe I'll go to Vishal's office and see if I can talk him into joining me for lunch somewhere in town."

The plates in Sayee's hands rattled and fell to the floor with a crash. "Oh no!" She sank to the floor to pick them up, her hands trembling. "So stupid of me."

Vinita sprang up from her chair to help her. "It's okay. They're stainless steel. Nothing's broken." She picked up the plates and stacked them in the sink while Sayee grabbed a wet rag to clean the floor.

"I'm usually not this clumsy," explained Sayee. Her voice quivered.

"Are you all right?" Vinita asked, contemplating whether Sayee was coming down with something. Malaria instantly sprang to mind. But she'd been assured it wasn't contagious.

"I'm all right." Sayee rinsed out the rag and hung it on one of the steel bars over the window to dry. "I think it is just early menopause or something."

Vinita patted her on the shoulder. "I doubt that. You may be coming down with a virus. Take it easy for a change. Let Anu handle the cooking." She gave up trying to finish her toast and tossed the leftover piece out the window to the crows glowering at her. They swooped down on it in a frenzy of flapping wings and greedy caws.

Sayee began to clear the table. "Mummy and I are worried about you and Rohit."

"No need to worry about me. Save your prayers for Rohit." Vinita glanced at her mother, who was still sitting at the table, wearing a pensive look. It was hard to say what she could be thinking.

Vinita picked up her handbag and said once again to the two women, "I'll call you from the hospital." She checked to make sure she had enough cash in her wallet, then stepped out the back door.

Hazy sunshine was struggling to penetrate the last remaining wisps of fog as she strode down the street. As soon as the sun turned on its full glare, the temperature would go from cool to warm, and eventually hot.

She took a slight detour toward the Shiva Temple on her way to the rickshaw stand. The need to visit the temple and pray for Rohit had been nagging her since the previous night. Now her feet automatically took her there.

Vinita noticed that the temple was already dotted with early worshippers. It was a holy icon in their town, a spotlessly clean building surrounded by lush gardens and lawns maintained by the local military base. She should have felt optimistic, with masses of fragrant roses in bloom and the grass still sparkling like a carpet of emeralds in the morning light. And yet optimism was not what she felt. It was more like a pulsing ache in her chest.

Armed military guards were posted around the periphery of the compound at all times, which in a way was comforting rather than intimidating. Because of their presence the temple was a safe place, any time of day or night.

The sweet, woodsy scent of *agarbattis*—incense sticks—met her nostrils the minute she discarded her *chappals* outside the building, climbed the dozen or so steps, and entered the temple. Inside the sanctum, it was cool and damp and dimly lit.

Two tall, brass oil lamps were burning before the idol of Lord Shiva. The idol itself wasn't very large, but it had an electrifying presence, as if the Lord's watchful, unblinking eyes missed nothing. As always, He was decked in fresh garlands of jasmine, roses, marigolds, and *marva,* a fragrant herb. His forehead was covered with holy ashes, a vermillion dot at the center.

Vinita stood for a moment and drew a breath, let the hallowed peace sink in and soothe her troubled spirit.

Over thirty years ago, when she'd discovered she was pregnant, she had stood on this threshold, begging God to help her, give her strength. Today she was here again, pleading with him to save the child she'd carried in her womb back then.

Stepping closer, she picked up a flower from the basket left there by the priest and laid it at the base of the Lord's idol.

Pulling out a hundred-rupee bill from her wallet, she pressed it into the slot of the wooden donation box—her humble contribution to the temple.

She went down on her knees, shut her eyes, and joined her hands. Ignoring the tears dampening her cheeks, she prayed. If nothing else, at least she gathered blessings for Rohit. If God had to take away her son, despite all the expert medical help he was receiving, the boy would at least go to his Maker with a clean soul.

He's so young, she pleaded. *Let him see more of life, get married, have a family. And bless the person who has come forward as a donor—whoever it is.* She hesitated a moment. She didn't want to be too greedy, but she added another plea anyway. *Please make Girish forgive me. Don't take him away, too. I couldn't stand it if I lost him.*

It was customary to sit down for a minute or two in the temple after praying, so she got to her feet, stepped out of the inner sanctum, and found a place to sit in a darkened corner beside a pillar.

Folding her feet under her, she sat on the cool granite floor. She rested her head against the pillar. It was so peaceful here. She could have sat there for a long time if it weren't for the fact that she had to get to the hospital soon. But she couldn't get Girish out of her mind for some reason, perhaps because she and Girish had visited this temple a number of times during their visits to Palgaum. Her husband had liked this temple, admired its gardens and serenity.

Stress, she concluded. It was the stress of recent weeks that was making her miss him so intensely. On a day like this, when she was scared and unsure of the future, she needed him more than ever. But he wasn't going to offer her comfort. She had to be strong, she told herself. She could do it on her own—keep the faith, mainly for Rohit.

Curiousity about the donor crowded her mind once again. Why the secrecy? Something about the timing bothered her, too. But the rules of anonymity had to be respected. The person must have reasons for remaining nameless.

If it was indeed Som, he was probably doing it without the knowledge of his family. She understood his motives. He couldn't afford a scandal. Maybe she'd never know who the Good Samaritan was. All she could do was send a telepathic blessing to the mysterious individual.

She rose to her feet and slung her handbag over her shoulder. Just as she started to move she stopped short. She noticed Sayee climbing the steps and striding into the temple. She looked distressed, as if the burden of the world lay on her shoulders. If she had seemed oddly agitated a little while ago, she looked worse now. Something was very wrong.

Out of curiosity, Vinita stood concealed behind the pillar and watched her sister-in-law go directly to the holy chamber and pray. She could almost sense Sayee's angst. Vinita emerged from behind the pillar and approached her.

When Sayee turned around and discovered Vinita, her eyes went wide with astonishment. It took her an instant to recover. "Why aren't you at the hospital, Vini?"

"Are you all right?" Vinita asked, ignoring the question.

Sayee hesitated, then let her gaze drop. When she looked up there was something resembling fear in her eyes. "I don't know," she murmured.

Vinita shifted and took Sayee's hand. "Something is wrong, isn't it?"

"I—I'm really worried about Rohit."

"Of course you are. And it's very generous of you to have such fond feelings for my son." Vinita tugged on Sayee's hand and led her out of the temple. Together they walked down the steps. "Come on, I'll walk you home before I hail a rickshaw."

Sayee thrust her feet into her *chappals*. "I'm not going home. I'm going to the hospital."

"I don't need a babysitter," Vinita assured her, putting on her sandals.

"I know, but . . . it's not just that. I *have* to be at the hospital."

Vinita frowned at Sayee. Her behavior was getting odder by the second. "Okay, if you insist. In that case, we'll take your car,

I suppose?" They started down the winding concrete path that led out of the compound and toward the road.

"No, we need to take a rickshaw."

Vinita felt the first real prickle of unease. "Why?"

"Because . . ." Abruptly Sayee stopped and faced her. "I have something to confess."

Vinita felt the familiar goose bumps on her arms. "What?"

A fine gleam of perspiration had formed on Sayee's upper lip. "It's . . . um . . . about the bone marrow donor."

Suddenly it all began to make sense. "You know who it is?"

"Yes." Sayee swiped at the perspiration with the back of her hand.

"Why didn't you say something before now?"

"I . . . um . . . I was sworn to secrecy." Guilt was written all over Sayee's round face—the classic look of a child caught lying.

"Then why are you telling me now?" Vinita's eyes narrowed in suspicion.

"I think you have a right to know."

"So why didn't you tell me sooner?"

"It wasn't my decision to make." Sayee bit her lip and held it in for a beat. "I wasn't supposed to tell you until after the transfusion."

"But you're breaking your oath now?"

"Because . . . it's different now, you see. You are sure to find out this morning."

"All right." They both resumed walking. "But I think I already know. It's Som, isn't it?"

"Som Kori?" asked Sayee, coming to a dead stop once again. "Whatever gave you that idea?" Her expression was almost comical in its disbelief. "Why would you think *that* man would come forward to save his son?"

Equally puzzled, Vinita frowned at the ground. "Because . . . well . . . it made sense." Lately she'd been so convinced the mystery donor was Som that she hadn't bothered to look at any other possibilities. Realistically there were none. Unless . . . oh God! Her heart missed a beat. "Is it Arya? Has that crazy girl secretly arrived in Palgaum?"

Sayee shook her head. "It's not Arya."

"Thank goodness." Vinita's wobbling heartbeat settled a little. "Then who is it?"

"It's Vishal."

Vinita's hand flew to her mouth. "Oh . . . my!"

Chapter 35

Nearly an hour after Sayee had given away Vishal's secret, Vinita was still staggering from the shock. Her brother. Of all the people in the world, the donor had to be her brother. With all the speculating she'd been doing, why hadn't she thought of *him*?

Was it because she'd never dreamt her brother would go to such extreme lengths to help Rohit and ensure her happiness? Was it because she'd never really had total faith in Vishal? Was it because she'd wanted to protect him and the family from more scandal?

After a moment of introspection she knew the answer was yes to all of the above.

She stood waiting for Sayee outside the hospital doors now, her hands clenching and unclenching, oblivious to the people going in and out of the building. Loath to sit in the waiting room, where she felt stifled, she'd preferred to wait outdoors. The sun was out. She needed its light, its heat, its promise of life. She needed to think.

She and Sayee had arrived at the hospital a few minutes ago and learned that Vishal was being readied for the marrow to be harvested from his hip. They were told there was just enough time for Sayee to see him briefly before he was transferred to surgery.

At the moment, Vinita didn't know whether to cry or let out

an angry shriek. But she wasn't the type to do either of those in public. So she stood in place and rocked gently on her heels.

How could Vishal have been tested as a donor and deemed suitable, then offer to give his marrow without her knowledge? When had he done all that? Why hadn't he said a word to her? Why hadn't either Sayee or her mother said anything? They had all carried the secret around for days. No wonder Sayee had been distracted.

Come to think of it, Sayee had been a little evasive in the last couple of days. Her mother had been quiet, too—but that wasn't so unusual. Silent disapproval was something her mother did well. Besides, Vinita had been too consumed by her worries over Rohit and Girish to pay attention to anyone else.

But how much blinder could she have been? Vishal had looked tense and worn-out lately. She had naturally assumed it was work related, especially after the riots had affected his office routine. All those evenings when he'd said he was working late, he had probably been going through the required donor tests.

What troubled her more was that she hadn't had the time to talk to Vishal before he'd gone into surgery, ask him all those questions she was dying to ask, thank him for his generosity. Vishal's actions were beyond generous—another one of the reasons she'd never thought to ask him to be a donor. She could not ask for yet another favor. She would not. She bit back the tears. Her brother was making her weep again.

When she'd heard his car driving away very early that morning, why hadn't she guessed that he wasn't headed for work but to the hospital? Much later, when Sayee had said she needed to ride in a rickshaw and not drive to the hospital in her own car, even then Vinita had not guessed the truth—that Vishal's car was parked in the hospital's parking lot and Sayee had to drive it back home.

Vinita sent up a silent prayer for her brother.

"They're doing it now," said Sayee's voice beside her, startling her.

Vinita gave her a bristling glance. "Why didn't he say something to me, Sayee?"

"He wanted to keep it a secret for some reason." Sayee didn't look pleased with his decision, either.

"I still can't understand why."

"I advised him to tell you, but he said he didn't want to get your hopes up unnecessarily."

"So damn protective!" Vinita clenched her teeth at her brother's obsession with secrets. But damn it all, he was in surgery right now, giving lifeblood to her son. Her son—the boy she'd thought Vishal didn't care about.

And to think she had condemned her brother for being a brute, for wrenching her son away from her right after birth, faking the infant's death, lying to her, and then not bothering with the child's welfare. All this time, Vishal *had* cared—more than cared—about her, about Rohit. She was also just beginning to discover that Vishal *had* been keeping tabs on Rohit, albeit from a distance. Being in the same town, he had to have been able to watch Rohit's progress.

In fact, Vishal had secretly and cleverly engineered Rohit's entire future, all the way from Vinita's shocking pregnancy up until now. She returned her attention to Sayee, who looked small and miserable. "I shouldn't have taken out my frustration on you," she apologized.

"We're all under strain." Sayee's capacity for tolerance was amazing.

"Did they say how long? The procedure?"

"I'm not sure, but the doctor assured me it is short—and safe for the donor."

"But you're naturally worried." The very nature of general anesthesia was dangerous. It was the closest a healthy person could come to induced death. The thought scared Vinita. Nevertheless she said to Sayee, "He'll be all right. Vishal is a strong man."

Sayee nodded. "Then they'll move on to Rohit. They immediately start the transplant—as soon as they get the amount of marrow they need."

Vinita drew a heavy breath and squeezed Sayee's shoulder. "Come on, let's go find ourselves a place to sit down and maybe have a cup of tea," she suggested. "It's going to be a long wait."

They walked across the street to the small tea shop that was doing a brisk business, despite its dingy looks. It was a while before a table became available. It had streaks running across it and smelled like it had been wiped with a moldy rag. The slate floor felt sticky, probably from spilled tea and coffee. But it was the best they could do under the circumstances.

They both ordered tea. "Make sure the cups are clean," Vinita said to the tall, leggy young man who took their order. His jet black hair was combed into a stiff, glossy puff. He reminded her of the boys she'd gone to college with. Sadly, he also brought to mind Som, back in those days when he used to dress like a movie star.

"Yes, madam," said the waiter, grinning, making it clear he found her request highly amusing. It probably was in this greasy little café. "Our cups are always clean," he assured her.

"I bet," Vinita murmured under her breath, waving away a persistent fly hovering over the suspicious streaks on their table. "Bad idea, coming to this place," she said to Sayee the moment the waiter's back was turned. "We could catch a stomach virus or something." She pulled a wry face. "I don't want to get sick again."

"Don't worry. I have had tea here once or twice."

"Why here?" Vinita looked at the crowd of patrons and wondered why they were all here.

"It is the only place this close to the hospital. If you can overlook the basic lack of hygiene, their tea is quite good."

Well, that explained why so many people were lined up at this particular *chai* shop. Vinita actually smiled, despite the dreariness. "Maybe it's precisely the lack of hygiene that makes it taste so good. When I was in college, my friends and I used to love eating at the canteen, filthy as it was. But their *batata vadas* were delicious," she reminisced, wondering if they still served those spicy mashed-potato balls, coated with chickpea batter and deep fried to a crisp.

The thought of the canteen brought on a gush of unexpected nostalgia. And thoughts of Prema. The urge to get in touch with Prema nipped at her. It would be wonderful to see her friend again, exchange news that hadn't been exchanged in more than three decades. She wondered what Prema looked like now. Maybe she could find out her phone number or something . . . that is, if Prema's parents still lived in Palgaum.

And if she was lucky enough to find Prema, she'd tell her friend the truth about the past and why she'd vanished without any explanation. She felt she owed it to the one true girlfriend she'd ever had in her whole life. Prema had warned her, scolded her, even mothered her in a way, and yet Vinita had ignored her wise friend's advice, and had used her for her own selfish purposes.

It was thirty years too late for it, but she owed Prema an apology.

Vinita wrenched her mind back to the present and looked across at Sayee, who was trying her best to put on a brave face. Poor thing was as tense as she was. So much was at stake here. Two men they loved were lying in that hospital, one striving to save another's life and the other determined to stay alive.

The grinning waiter brought their *chai*, interrupting Vinita's musings. The cups were tiny and barely held half a dozen sips. But the tea looked delicious—fragrant and steamy, brimming with rich milk.

Vinita took a cautious sip and decided Sayee was right. It was excellent tea, even if it was rather sweet. Sayee was sipping hers quietly, her eyes trained on the hospital building visible through the wide-open door. She'd been glancing that way off and on.

Reaching across the table, Vinita patted Sayee's hand. "Vishal's going to be all right."

"I hope so. And Rohit, too," replied Sayee, reluctantly bringing her gaze back to Vinita. "I have been praying for both of them." There was so much love and concern in those dark eyes that it nearly broke Vinita's heart. Vishal was a lucky man to have a wife like her. Sayee not only tolerated his overbearing nature, she adored him. And she was so patient with Mummy, despite the older woman's difficult ways.

"Can I ask you something?" She raised her brows at Sayee.

"Sure." Sayee finished her tea and set the cup down in its saucer.

"How long have you known about my . . . past?"

"Vishal told me before we got married."

"And you still agreed to marry him, despite his having a sister who had disgraced herself?"

"You didn't disgrace yourself, Vini. You made an innocent mistake." Sayee shook her head. "Besides, what does that have to do with my marrying Vishal? He and your parents looked like respectable people, so I said yes to the match."

"As simple as that, huh?" Vinita smiled at Sayee's remarks. It was such a different marriage proposal from her own. Hers had been fraught with deceit and complications.

Sayee flashed a wide smile. "And Vishal is so handsome."

Vinita chuckled. "That, too. But still . . ."

"I honestly didn't care about your past," Sayee affirmed. "Vishal explained to me how young you were and that Som Kori was a *mowali* who took advantage of you."

"It was still a stupid mistake for a sensible girl to make—a mistake I'm still paying for." Vinita drained the rest of her tea and stared at the flecks of foam clinging to the rim. "A mistake all of us are paying for, including you." She caught the waiter's eye and motioned to him for their check.

"Don't be silly," said Sayee, rising from the table. "We're family."

"You're very kind, Sayee," said Vinita, opening her handbag and pulling out some bills. She handed the money to their busy waiter, telling him to keep the change.

He blinked, then grinned at the clearly unanticipated tip. "Thank you, madam."

"Kindness goes both ways, you know," Sayee said, continuing their conversation without missing a beat.

They stepped out of the hot restaurant and crossed the street once again, hurrying back to the hospital. "You've been a blessing to our family," Vinita said.

They found Shashi and Meenal Barve seated in the waiting room, looking just as jumpy as the two of them. Vinita and Sayee greeted them with *namastes* and sat down in chairs nearby.

The four of them tried to chat, the kind of stilted conversation that families have while waiting to hear about the fate of a loved one. There were no other people in the room. Unlike the crowded visitors' area of the main hospital, the oncology wing was generally quiet.

Vinita had come to the conclusion that the reason for it was probably the prohibitive cost of certain types of cancer treatment. Despite its availability, not many patients could afford bone marrow and organ transplants in a town like Palgaum.

"We are very grateful to Vishal-saheb for donating," said Meenal Barve, glancing first at Vinita and then at Sayee. Gratitude was written all over her homely face.

So, the Barves had discovered the identity of the mystery donor, too, Vinita realized. Once again she bit back the surge of emotion the words brought on. Donating. It sounded straightforward enough, and yet it held all sorts of possibilities. *Life*, mainly. "I'm glad it's going on schedule," she said simply.

"We are indebted to your brother, Vinita-bayi," said Mr. Barve, echoing his wife's remark. "But until this morning we had no idea the donor was your brother. It was a complete shock."

"To me, too," she said with a dry smile.

The Barves stared at her. "He didn't tell you?"

Vinita shook her head. "He didn't want to raise my hopes, in case he got rejected . . . or something went wrong."

"I see." Mr. Barve stroked his chin.

Meenal turned to Sayee. "He did not tell *you*, either?"

"He did, but he asked me not to tell." Sayee inclined her head toward Vinita. "Vini just explained why." She shrugged. "Even now . . . who knows what will happen?"

"But we are thankful, anyway," insisted Meenal, her eyes bright with unshed tears. "It is very generous of Vishal-saheb. And Vinita is paying for the treatment. We can never repay that," she said hoarsely. She dabbed her eyes with a handkerchief as the tears gathered.

Vinita brushed it off with a wave. "Rohit is my son, too." It felt good to say it aloud. *My son.* Finally.

They gradually subsided into silence, settling in for the long wait. A little while later, Vinita's mother arrived in a rickshaw to join them. She had waited until Anu and the maid had finished their chores, then locked the house and arrived there as quickly as she could.

Vinita wondered when Mummy had been told the truth about Vishal.

Now her mother sat in stony silence, her eyes glued to the doorway that led to the surgical area, where her son lay on an operating table. Vinita wasn't all that sure if she worried about Rohit. Mummy had yet to acknowledge him as her grandson.

It was nearly noon before a nurse came to inform them that Vishal had recovered from the anesthesia and that he was asking to see his wife. Sayee hurried to his side.

The visit was brief. Sayee came out less than ten minutes later, smiling a little, looking more optimistic than she had earlier in the day. "Vishal is feeling okay," she announced to the four expectant faces staring at her. "The doctor says he can go home this evening."

Vinita blew out a silent breath of relief.

"Did they say anything about Rohit?" demanded Mr. Barve, raising a taut face to Sayee.

"I asked . . . but they didn't give me any information." Sayee gnawed on her lip. "Maybe they want to discuss it with you first?"

Meenal glanced at her husband. "They told us they had to process the marrow before administering it to Rohit, did they not?"

But Barve rose from his chair anyway, and marched up to the

reception desk. Vinita could hear him demanding to know what was going on with his son.

Sayee put a hand on Vinita's arm. "Vishal wants to see you after Mummy has a chance to see him."

Sarla shot to her feet and was off in the next second. Vinita watched her rushing down the corridor. In a way she felt sorry for her mother. The poor woman had to have known the truth, and been suffering for so many days, knowing what Vishal was about to do. But she'd been good about keeping his secret safe. She had to be applauded for that, if nothing else.

Vinita was anxious to see Vishal, too. There was so much she had to say to him. There were no words to express the depth of her gratitude, but she needed to say something nonetheless.

Hearing the main door to the wing being thrust open with urgency, she turned to see two young men barreling in, panic written on their faces. Immediately her spine went rigid.

She glanced at Sayee and Meenal to gauge their reaction. Meenal's eyes were narrow slits as she watched the men's gazes search the area for a second, locate Shashi Barve at the reception desk, and make a beeline toward him.

Vinita wondered what they wanted with Barve. In the next instant she recognized it—political alarm bells going off. She turned to Sayee. "This doesn't look good," she whispered. She hoped she was wrong.

Sayee was too busy gawking at the men to respond.

The men and Barve talked for a minute before the two men rushed outside again. Barve slowly made his way back to them. "Bad news," he announced to the women, looking like he'd just been struck over the head with a heavy object.

"What?" his wife demanded.

He sank into his chair. "Som Kori died a little while ago."

Chapter 36

Silence blanketed the group for one second before Meenal clamped a hand over her wide-open mouth. "*Arré Deva!*" Oh God!

"Died?" Vinita murmured. Som couldn't possibly have died. She'd seen him only days ago, full of life, bursting with typical Kori confidence and egotism.

"Hit by a lorry," Barve replied.

So he'd been killed by a truck. Vinita's gut clenched tighter. How gruesome.

Meenal's lips were trembling. "This was in retaliation for you being hit by a car?"

Barve shrugged. "I don't know. All they said was that he died instantly in an accident when his car was struck by a loaded lorry."

A sick feeling began to settle inside Vinita's stomach. It wasn't an accident. The timing was too convenient. It was happening again, the same thing that had occurred when her actions had nearly gotten Shashi Barve killed. This time she had really gone and done it—got a man murdered.

Despite her bitter feelings about Som, what she felt now was deep remorse. She didn't believe in wishing death on anyone, no matter how grievous their crimes. Som didn't deserve to die. She wanted him to suffer for his actions, atone for them, but not like this, and most certainly not because of *her* actions.

This was only the beginning. This time the riots in town would be so much worse than last time. The respected leader of the Kannada faction was dead. There would be serious consequences. How many casualties, how much damage to the economy, and for how long? She shuddered at the possibilities.

Sayee's words jolted her out of her terrifying thoughts. "Vini, I'm so sorry."

"Me too." Vinita shut her eyes to dispel the image of Som Kori's mangled body lying in a puddle of blood. "He has a wife and three young daughters."

She thought of Girish and Arya, and her throat felt like something large and prickly was wedged inside it. What if it were Girish who'd been killed in a similar manner? It was unthinkable. That poor woman she'd seen the other day—Som's wife. What must she be going through? Had she even been told about Som yet? And their daughters? They were mere children. Som had mentioned something about the oldest being engaged to be married.

Vinita's mother returned just then and stopped short when she noticed their expressions. "What happened?"

It was Sayee who replied, "Som Kori was killed in a car accident."

Instantly Sarla's gaze fixed itself on Vinita. She didn't utter a word, but the silent message was hard to miss.

Vinita turned away from her mother's accusing eyes. This time Mummy would never forgive her. The entire town of Palgaum would never forgive her.

"Aren't you supposed to see Vishal?" Sayee reminded Vinita gently.

"Oh yes . . . of course." Vinita shook herself out of her trance and dragged her feet toward the recovery room. Minutes ago she'd been anxious to see her brother, but now she was reluctant to face him. He'd have to be told about Som's death. Vishal would naturally blame her for the mess. And he had every right to.

She wasn't quite prepared to see her brother looking disheveled and confined to a bed. Big, strong Vishal wasn't supposed to look weak. And yet here he was, looking vulnerable as he lay on a cot in the recovery room with his eyes shut. Nonetheless he looked peaceful, resting for a change.

Her heart squeezed painfully as a sudden rush of affection for Vishal seized her. He'd always been her stalwart pillar of support, her protector. Most of her life she'd been too blind to recognize it. And she'd had the audacity to call herself smart.

"Vishal," she called to him, approaching the cot.

He opened his eyes and blinked a couple of times, as though the light was too bright. "Vini," he murmured.

"How are you feeling?"

"Groggy, but otherwise okay." He sounded raspy, like he had sawdust in his throat.

Putting on a brave front for his little sister, she reflected. "Are you in pain?"

"Not at the moment, but they tell me I'll have some soreness in my hip and back for a few days."

She gazed at him for a long time before asking, "Why, Vishal?"

"Why what?" He frowned.

"Why did you decide to donate your marrow to Rohit?"

He closed his eyes. "It was the only solution."

"You didn't have to, and yet you did," she said gently. "I can't even *begin* to thank you for what you did for my son," she said.

"It was the simplest and most practical answer to the problem." He opened his eyes. "I'm his uncle, and likely to be a decent match." He gave her a moment to ponder. "You're a bright woman. Why didn't *you* think of it?"

"I didn't want to." She hesitated. "I just couldn't bring myself to ask you. I had already forced you to do too much for me . . . despite your feelings about the family's loss of face."

"Huh?" He appeared confused.

"Becoming a donor would mean the whole town would discover Rohit's heritage. Imagine the scandal. Mummy would hate me even more for it." She'd already faced enough of her mother's contempt and wrath.

"Mummy doesn't hate you," he retorted.

"Regardless, it was too huge a favor to ask, after all you and Sayee have done for me. I couldn't ruin what little was left of your reputation."

He gave her a cool look. "But this was a matter of saving Rohit's life."

"Very logical." What a good pretender, she thought, a spark of anger mixing in with her other highly charged emotions. Why couldn't he let his heart show for one single moment? Was it so hard to admit he was human?

Her tears were close to the surface and would start to flow any moment. "Damn it, Vishal!" She lashed out at him, annoyance winning the first round amidst her warring sentiments. "Why do you have to be so manly all the time? Why can't you just admit you love Rohit and that you've always loved him?"

Vishal merely pressed his lips together.

"Is it so hard for you to admit you're human, that you have softer feelings? Papa was of a different generation."

"What's Papa got to do with it?" he growled.

"Everything. You try so hard to be just like him. But men of your generation are allowed to show emotion. It's acceptable for grown men to be sentimental. Even our American presidents these days hug people and shed tears in public."

He gave her a bland look. "In India, men don't go around hugging and talking about love."

She reached down and patted his hand. "That's okay. You don't have to say a word. Your actions gave you away." She smiled through her tears. "It'll be our secret. And I'll always be in your debt."

"Don't patronize me, Vini," he hurled back. "You owe me nothing. All this crying and thanking is unnecessary. I happened to be here, healthy and ready to donate. Not much to it."

"Whatever you say, Vishal," she said in an indulgent tone. But the tears were coming fast and furious now. Her flimsy cotton square of a handkerchief was getting soaked.

"Now stop sniveling and tell me how Rohit is doing. No one is telling me anything," he fumed.

"Shashi-saheb was inquiring about Rohit, but before he could get any information . . ." She wasn't sure if this was the right time to tell him about the latest tragedy.

Vishal's brows snapped together. "Did something go wrong with the transfusion?"

"It's too early to know anything yet." She shifted her feet. "Something else happened while Shashi-saheb was at the nurse's desk asking questions."

"What?" Vishal demanded, sounding like his usual arrogant self.

"There's been an incident," she said after a moment of wavering. Vishal would find out sooner or later. "Som Kori was . . . killed in an accident today."

Vishal became still for a long moment. "I'm not surprised," he said finally.

She frowned at him. "Really?"

"You don't know the volatility of the politics in this town. It's like a tinderbox, waiting to ignite. I didn't think Shashi Barve's attack was going to go unpunished."

"You don't believe it's an accident?"

"Accident?" he scoffed. "You're an intelligent woman, Vini. Figure it out."

"I did. And you're right." She tossed him a resigned look. "Go ahead, tell me I'm to blame for this. I'll feel a lot better if you say it aloud, unlike Mummy's subtle accusations."

He rubbed at his temple, like he was fighting a headache. "It's not your fault."

"How could it not be my fault? Since the day I set foot in this town, I've caused nothing but problems—for you, for your wife and kids, for Mummy. Since I was eighteen years old I've been a menace to the Shelke family. Now I've caused Som's death and become a hazard to the Kori family." She bit down hard on her trembling lip. "Hell, I'm single-handedly ruining an entire town."

He stunned her with a mocking laugh. "Don't overestimate your influence, Vini. The way things stood between Kori and

Barve, they were both asking for trouble. They have been at each other's throats for years."

"But my revealing to Barve that Som was Rohit's biological father was what led to this," she insisted. "It could affect you. Your office in town could be torn to pieces."

"Your revelation may have hastened the process a bit, but not by much," he assured her. "Don't worry; I have insurance for my office. Every businessman in Palgaum has to have adequate protection in this environment."

Sayee walked in just then and interrupted them with some news. "They just told us that the transfusion went without any complications. Rohit is okay for now."

"Thank God!" The relief in learning that at least something was going right was incredible. Vinita started weeping in earnest.

Sayee put an arm around her waist and pulled her close. "He will be all right, Vini."

"I—I hope so," Vinita cried. "Especially after Vishal went through all this." *And Som died.* There wasn't another thing she could take at the moment. Every one of her nerves was in tiny shreds.

With whispered words Sayee soothed her until the tears subsided. "Come on, I'll drive you and Mummy home. I'll come back later and pick up Vishal after he is officially discharged."

"All right." She turned to Vishal. "Thank you . . . for everything."

He shooed her away. "Go home and rest. They won't let you see Rohit, anyway. He'll be in isolation for several days."

With some reluctance Vinita let Sayee nudge her toward the door. "I'll see you at home, then." She waved at Vishal.

A little later, after saying good-bye to Shashi and Meenal Barve, who appeared to be in a more positive mood, Vinita climbed into the car with her mother and Sayee. She sat in the front passenger seat while Mummy sat in the back, where Vinita couldn't see her expression. She didn't want to face her mother at the moment if she could help it.

At the house, Sayee made chutney and tomato sandwiches and ginger-flavored tea for all of them, then insisted that Vinita and her mother rest a little before Vishal came home. "No one got any sleep last night, so you two should take a nap."

"What about you?" asked Vinita. "You ought to be exhausted, too."

Shaking her head, Sayee picked up several tote bags set aside for grocery shopping. "I'd better go and get some provisions before the stores shut down completely. God knows what the mob will do to the shops in town."

"Oh dear, I hadn't thought of that." Vinita glanced at the bags. "Why don't I go with you? You'll have too much to carry."

"No need, the shop has *hamaals*—porters—to load the car," Sayee assured Vinita.

"You're sure?" Vinita felt guilty about Sayee doing all this work alone while she was being urged to take a nap.

"Yes. Now get some sleep." Sayee was already halfway out the door. She appeared to have regained her cheerful energy. Seeing Vishal recovering from his ordeal, and hearing Rohit was holding his own were probably what had put the pep back into her. "Don't worry about anything. I'll pick up Vishal later and drive him home."

Turning around, Vinita found her mother gazing at her. "I know what you're thinking," Vinita said to her. "If the town is falling apart and Vishal is in pain, it's entirely my fault." She sank into the nearest chair. "You're right. I have no defense against that."

"I didn't say that," murmured her mother.

"But your expression says it all. Since the day I arrived here, you've been accusing me with your eyes." Vinita shrugged. "All I can say is, I'm very, very sorry."

Her mother shook her head. "Being sorry is not going to heal the wounds of an entire town damaged by riots, and it's not going to take away the stain on our family's honor." She paused. "But I'm beginning to understand why you did what you did. I hope Rohit recovers soon."

"You don't hate Rohit, then?" Vinita rose to her feet, stunned.

"I could never hate my grandchild," Mummy said quietly. Then she left the room and headed for the stairs. A minute later Vinita heard her mother's bedroom door shut.

Exhausted, Vinita went up to her own room. Changing into a comfortable caftan, she lay down on her bed. Sleep wouldn't come. Her mother had a way of pushing the right buttons to trigger remorse, resentment, and wretchedness, all at the same time. At least she had admitted she didn't abhor Rohit. Vinita had to be content with that for now. Expecting her mother to love him was asking for a miracle.

And she couldn't stop thinking about Som. It was impossible to think of him as gone forever. What a needless tragedy. She sent up a prayer for his scarred soul.

Sayee and Mummy were right. Riots were probably brewing in town right now. It was almost like the townsfolk were holding their breath, waiting for something to happen. Vinita could feel the tremors, too—the approaching storm.

Finally, after nearly an hour of tossing, she fell asleep. She had no idea how long she slept, and how deeply. She had a dream—a most disturbing one. Girish was at its center. He was accusing her of ruining his life, informing her that their marriage was over.

Arya stood in the background, looking so small and hurt and alone, it broke Vinita's heart.

Her eyes flew open. It was dark in the room. Disoriented, she couldn't tell where she was. Then the familiar feel of the bed made her realize she was still in Palgaum. But her heart was galloping. Divorce. The dream had been about divorce. Abandonment. Devastation. Her subconscious was probably trying to tell her to brace herself.

She was lying on her side, her face turned toward the window. It was dark outside as well, except for the streetlight directly across from the house. All at once the day's events came back in a rush. And her own problems receded. There was so much else to worry about. Had Sayee returned from her shopping? Had she driven Vishal home yet? What was Rohit's present condition? Had the rioting begun? How could she have slept through all of that?

She glanced at the bedside clock—8:17 p.m. She'd slept for nearly five hours.

Why was the house so quiet? she wondered. This was supper time normally. No one had come to wake her, either.

She turned around and tried to rise from the bed. That's when she saw him. More like sensed him. And froze. There was a man sitting in a chair beside her bed. She nearly choked on the scream that sprang from her throat.

"Shh, it's only me, Vini," said a familiar voice.

"Girish!" It couldn't be. She tried to focus on the figure in the semidarkness, but couldn't see very clearly. She blinked hard, but that didn't help. He was still there. Good Lord, it wasn't just a dream, but a nightmare in which she was imagining things. She was going insane.

Closing her eyes, she lay back again. "It's only a dream," she murmured in an effort to calm herself and rationalize the hallucination. The trauma of the day had done something to her brain. "He can't be here," she whispered. "I *must* be dreaming."

"No, I'm really here," said Girish's voice, contradicting her.

She sat up again, convinced she had lost her mind. "Don't do this, Girish. Please, just go away. Leave me alone. I've had enough nightmares."

"That's the problem. I've left you alone far too long," he said in his soft, accented tone.

She frowned at him. There was something surreal about this scene. She was having an imaginary conversation with her husband. "What do you mean?" she asked. What the heck, she might as well continue this dream, or whatever it was—and see where it would go.

In reply he stood and came to sit beside her. She felt the air stir around her, heard the rustle of his clothes. She gingerly touched his arm. He felt solid. Felt real. "Girish?" she repeated.

"It's me, Vini. You're not dreaming anymore. But you were a while ago. You were mumbling in your sleep." He took her hand in his, the one with the missing fingers. And she knew then that he was really there, in the flesh. The hand felt amazingly warm and firm. And so dearly familiar, it brought a lump to her throat.

"What are you doing here?" She peered at him in the semi-darkness. Now that she was wide awake, she could see his profile in the jaundiced glow coming from the light outside. The sharp nose, the outline of his eyeglasses, the angle of his jaw—they were unmistakable.

"I got here a couple of hours ago." He squeezed her hand.

"Why?" she asked, still grappling with the shock.

"Didn't you get my e-mail? I sent you one just before I left home in Jersey."

"I haven't checked my e-mail in a while." She'd had too much on her mind. Arya hadn't called in a couple of days, either.

"I've come to take you home," he said simply, as if he'd seen her yesterday and not weeks ago.

"You want me to come home after what's happened?" she asked. "I thought you were filing for divorce."

He gave a wry chuckle. "I'd never divorce you, Vini. I love you."

Fury kicked in at his casual admission of love. "Then why the hell were you behaving like a sulking brat all these weeks? I begged you to call me or e-mail me and you ignored every damn attempt I made."

"I was an idiot, okay? Too blind to realize it wasn't entirely your fault that you didn't tell me the truth."

She withdrew her hand and stared at him suspiciously. "What brought this on all of a sudden?" Something didn't add up.

"It wasn't sudden. I was beginning to see things a bit more clearly when I heard you were very sick, and again when the riots broke out the last time. That's when I really started to worry about you, what could happen if . . . if I lost you. I knew I had to come and take you back home."

"But you didn't. You didn't even bother to answer my e-mails," she accused, spoiling for a fight. He had no right to torture her for weeks and then behave like it was nothing.

"I'm very sorry. Like Arya said to me, I'm a complete ass, I'm stubborn and set in my ways, and I'm a fool."

"She said that to you?" Vinita nearly smiled to herself despite the resentment churning inside her. It sounded just like Arya.

"And a lot worse. You know Arya doesn't mince words. Between her and your sister-in-law, they made me see how stupid and blind I've been."

"Sayee? What does she have to do with this?"

"She called me last week . . . told me you were miserable."

Vinita buried her face in her hands and let out an aggrieved huff. "You were forced into coming."

He put an arm around her shoulder, a bit diffidently, perhaps because he knew she was fuming, and he feared rejection. "No, Vini. I was getting ready to come on my own. I just had a couple of things to wind up at work before I could leave. The company's going through a downsizing and it's been very tense at the office." He let her absorb that. "That was another thing that was preying on my mind these past couple of months."

"Why didn't you tell me how things stood at work?"

"I didn't want to worry you."

"Is *your* job safe?" Her anger vanished in an instant at this bit of news. It wasn't completely unexpected, with the state of the U.S. economy in a shambles, but he hadn't let on about his situation. He'd been going through a rough time, too, while she was gone.

"Safe for now," he said.

"Thank God." She let him hold her, albeit a bit reluctantly. It was awkward after all these weeks of distance between them. But it was comforting nonetheless.

"Am I . . . forgiven?" he asked with great caution.

She turned the question over in her mind. She'd never known him to falter. He was a confident man for the most part. "I don't have a choice," she replied after a while, "since you seem to have forgiven my mistakes."

"You did nothing wrong, Vini. It was I who was a fool. Took me long enough to realize that. I'm glad Sayee called and Arya nagged."

"How is Arya, by the way?"

"Still living at our house and lecturing me to death. She said she wanted to keep an eye on me while you were gone."

A chuckle escaped Vinita's mouth. "Good for her." Her baby girl had done a fine job of watching over her dad and beating him over the head till he'd finally come to his senses. She'd have to thank Arya privately one of these days.

"Did Sayee fill you in on what's going on?" she asked.

He nodded. "By the way, your brother's home and resting. He and I had a long talk."

"About what?" She relaxed a little and inhaled Girish's familiar scent. He was wearing something soft and it smelled like the fabric softener from back home. He hated doing laundry, so Arya was apparently doing the laundry—her least favorite chore. Another astonishing occurrence.

He pulled Vinita closer. "Vishal explained everything to me about what happened to you thirty years ago. He also told me the man who got you in trouble died in a car crash today."

"I think he was murdered. He was deep into hate politics."

Girish rubbed her back with a familiar, gentle motion. "Do you still have feelings for him?"

"Lord, no!" she snapped. "Any feelings I had were gone by the time I was out of my teens."

"I'm sorry I was nasty to you," Girish admitted. "I was a little jealous of that guy."

"You could have told me. I would've assured you that all I felt for that man was contempt. And now he's dead." She looked up at him. "Don't you think I was jealous of Nadine at first?"

"Were you . . . really?" He seemed astounded at her remark.

"I'm only human, Girish. Nadine was your wife. But after a few years I got over it."

He made a sound of frustration. "So I've been obsessing over nothing for weeks."

"You have, but it's not all your fault," she assured him.

They sat in silence for a long time, holding each other, deep in their own thoughts.

"What happens now?" she finally asked.

"I was thinking maybe we could stay for a week or two, until your son is out of danger."

"Palgaum is bracing itself for more riots. We could be stuck here for a while."

"The trouble's already begun. I took a taxi from the airport and the driver had to take some crazy, circuitous route to get me here. He said there's violence in town—a curfew in some areas."

"So you'll stay with me for a bit?"

"As long as you want me to."

"There's an old friend I want to contact. I owe her an apology—something left over from thirty years ago."

He looked at her quizzically, perhaps wondering how many more painful secrets she still kept tucked inside her. "Would you like me to go with you?" he asked instead, stunning her once again.

"Prema lives in Bangalore, so I just might have to settle for a phone call—if I can manage to track her down, that is." Vinita wasn't sure it was possible, but she would certainly try. "Would you like to meet Rohit one of these days?" she asked him cautiously. "If he makes it."

"I'd like that."

Girish's reply settled in her belly like a warm cup of tea on a cold morning. "I think you'll like him. He's a bright young chemistry professor, and he used to be a star cricketer in college." She could hear the pride in her own voice. She desperately wanted to believe that the son who'd come into her life so unexpectedly would live a long and productive life.

"I hope he makes it, Vini," Girish said, as if he'd read her mind. "I wish him well."

Vinita slid off the bed and turned on the light. Seeing Girish's